Dear Readers,

I'm excited about the first of its kind—a collection of my stories—that were written for several anthologies I participated in with other authors and include a Madaris story.

Over the years I've received e-mails and letters from readers asking for a particular story that was no longer in print or hard to find. I appreciate St. Martin's Press for seeing the need to put together such a collection for my readers.

In this book you have five of my stories taken from *The Best Man, Welcome to Leo's, Let's Get It On, An All Night Man,* and *Mr. Satisfaction.* The title of this book speaks for itself—*Some Like It Hot*—and for those who enjoy sizzle and steam, between these pages are stories that are hot as well as romantic. And I hope you will also find them unforgettable.

Happy Reading,

BRENDA JACKSON

Brenda Jackson

some like it hot

 ST. MARTIN'S GRIFFIN
NEW YORK

SOME LIKE IT HOT.

"Main Agenda" copyright © 2000 by Brenda Streater Jackson.
"Strictly Business" copyright © 2003 by Brenda Streater Jackson.
"Irresistible Attraction" copyright © 2004 by Brenda Streater Jackson.
"The Hunter" copyright © 2005 by Brenda Streater Jackson.
"Extreme Satisfaction" © 2006 by Brenda Streater Jackson.

www.stmartins.com

Library of Congress Cataloging-in-Publication Data

Jackson, Brenda (Brenda Streater)
    Some like it hot / Brenda Jackson.—1st ed.
        p. cm.
    ISBN-13: 978-0-312-57046-0
    ISBN-10: 0-312-57046-5
    1. African Americans—Fiction. 2. Erotic stories, American. I. Title.
    PS3560.A21165S66 2009
    813'.54—dc22

                                                        2009006905

First Edition: May 2009

10 9 8 7 6 5 4 3 2 1

To my sister, Robin Hawk Ware.
This one is for you.

CONTENTS

ACKNOWLEDGMENTS

To my readers who missed my earlier novellas with St. Martin's Press, this very special Brenda Jackson Collector Series, *Some Like It Hot*, is for you.

To my husband, Gerald Jackson, Sr., with all my love.

some like it hot

main agenda

We can make our plans, but the final outcome is in God's hands.

—PROVERBS 16:1 (THE LIVING BIBLE)

ONE

Lincoln Corbain sat at the bar of Leo's sizing up the crowd of people there. Since moving to D.C. over a month ago, he had discovered the upscale establishment was one with a very impressive clientele that ranged from politicians, musicians, and foreign dignitaries to college professors, bankers, and, like him, attorneys.

Compared to many of the supper clubs he had patronized in other major cities, this one had a certain homey warmth with its round rosewood tables that held small Tiffany-style lamps and colored oil candles. But at the same time it maintained a high degree of classiness with its double mahogany doors with brass fixtures, narrow floor-to-ceiling stained-glass windows, and intricately patterned parquet floor area specially designed for dancing. Even the bar stool he was sitting on was tall and padded with a contoured back that provided comfort to one's body while it coaxed you to relax and get in the groove.

Most of the people here tonight were, as he was fast becoming, regulars who usually rounded out certain evenings by dropping by to enjoy the good food, live entertainment, and an atmosphere that allowed you to unwind with someone or, if you preferred, by yourself, the latter of which he had decided to do tonight.

"So are you all settled in now?" the bartender named Flint asked Linc as he took away Linc's empty glass and placed another mixed drink in front of him. During the day Flint St. Johns worked as an agent for the IRS. He claimed the reason he moonlighted as a bartender one or two nights a week was because the extra money was too good to pass up and he enjoyed meeting people. He was also a close friend of Noah Hardcastle, one of the owners. Noah shared that ownership position with his younger identical twin brothers, Tyrell and Tyrone, and Ayanna Hardcastle, their female cousin.

Since the night Linc had first visited Leo's he'd decided that another thing he liked about this place was the open friendliness of the four owners. They usually made themselves visible each night and occasionally mingled with their customers.

"Yeah, I'm pretty much settled in," Linc replied, lifting the glass to his lips to take a sip of his drink. Whatever comment he intended to add was forgotten when he noticed the couple who walked in. He frowned, thinking that even in the dim lighting the woman looked familiar. His gaze sharpened as it flowed over her entire body from head to toe. When the memory hit him of where he knew her from, he drew in a deep breath seconds before his entire body went completely still.

Raven.

Linc forced himself to draw in another deep breath as he recalled exactly how long it had been since he had seen her. It had been well over four years since they had met during Black Colleges Week in Daytona Beach. At twenty-seven he had been in his last year of law school at Southern University, and at twenty-two she had been a senior at Florida A&M University majoring in journalism. And with the memory of their meeting came the memories of the red-hot nights of passion they'd shared within days after they had met.

He suddenly had poignant flashbacks of her body under his, wet and wild as she moaned out his name over and over again. Blood rushed to Linc's midsection when he remembered how she had felt in his arms and the immense pleasure he had gotten from having her there. And he had made doubly sure each time they made love that every intimate part of her body had felt cherished. He had been her first lover, an issue she had refused to talk about after he had realized that surprising fact.

Linc averted his gaze from her to the man by her side. Was he her husband, lover, friend, or associate? He released a deep sigh, realizing he didn't have a right to know the man's relationship to Raven, nor did he have a right to feel the heated jealousy that suddenly ripped through his gut.

His gaze returned to her. He liked the way she wore her hair now, chin-length and cut into a trendy and sassy style. The last time he had seen her she'd been sporting braids, a head full of them. They had met on the beach during a week when college students were known to have a wild and rip-roaring good time. They had both decided that after years of enduring countless nights of burning the midnight oil studying for exams, and with graduation only a few months away, they deserved to have fun and experience a week of momentary madness.

And they had.

At the end of that week, they had had no excuses or regrets for what they'd shared. Their time together had been too special for either. Nor had they made any promises to keep in touch. They had both walked away accepting that week for exactly what it was—a spring-break fling.

But that hadn't stopped him from thinking about her often since then, or realizing that any woman he had been intimate with since Raven had failed miserably in comparison. Nor had it stopped him from traveling to Tallahassee, Florida, the weekend after his graduation to look her up, only to discover she had left town already.

Linc sighed as his gaze continued to take in all of her. She was more beautiful than he remembered, and there was a certain degree of sophistication about her. It was probably the outfit she was wearing, he decided. The light blue dress flattered her body, as the silky material clung to her curves and showed off her gorgeous long legs. Her attire during their week together in Daytona Beach had ranged from skimpy tops and shorts and alluring bikini swimwear to nothing at all.

He had preferred her in nothing at all and had seen her body completely nude most of the time. During those times there had not been anything sophisticated about her. She became a sensuous and passionate diva whenever their bodies mated.

"Drink too strong?"

Linc glanced up at Flint and saw the man looking at him quizzically. "No, the drink's fine." When he glanced back in the direction of where the couple had been standing seconds ago, he saw a hostess leading them to a table on the other side of the room. Linc's irritation grew and he frowned into his drink before taking another sip.

"You sure the drink's OK?"

Linc lifted his head and noticed the look of concentration on Flint's face. "Yeah, I thought I may have recognized someone," he said, once again glancing across the room.

Following the direction of Linc's gaze, Flint studied the couple being escorted to a table. "Which one do you think you know? Raven or the man she's with?"

Linc lifted a surprised brow. "You know Raven?"

Flint lifted a brow of his own. "Maybe," he answered smoothly as a hint of a smile played at the corners of his mouth. "Do *you* know her?"

Linc stared at the bartender narrowly. He felt like he was being cross-examined and didn't relish the feel of that one bit. He also couldn't help but wonder what Flint's relationship was to Raven, since the man had suddenly gone from friendly and talkative to tight-lipped inquisitive—a real IRS man.

Linc shrugged. He would never divulge to anyone the extent of his past relationship with Raven. What they had shared that week in Daytona was private and personal. "I met Raven while in Florida one year during college spring break," he finally said, hoping that bit of information would appease Flint's curiosity, because that was all the information he was giving out. "How do you know her?"

Flint went about dusting off the counter, and for a minute Linc thought he would not respond to his question. Finally Flint answered, "Raven is a friend of the Hardcastle twins."

Linc nodded. After a few silent moments he asked, "What about the man she's with?"

"I don't recall ever seeing him in here before."

"I wonder if they're an item," Linc said, glancing up at Flint, wondering if the man knew more than he was actually saying.

Flint stared at him a moment before leaning over the bar and saying, "If you really want to know that, why don't you just walk over there and ask her?"

Linc couldn't help noticing the challenge that flickered in Flint's dark eyes. He returned his stare. "I won't go that far, but I don't see anything wrong with saying hello to an old friend, do you?"

The smile at the corners of Flint's lips widened. "Not if that's what you want to do."

"What the hell, why not? Like I said, there's nothing wrong with saying hello to an old friend," Linc said as he slid off the stool. What he and Raven had shared four years ago was in the past but not forgotten... at least not on his part. He doubted that he would ever forget their time together. It had been too passionate, too mind-blowing, and too unforgettable.

As he crossed the room toward the couple, who did not notice him approaching, he knew it was not his intent to put Raven on the spot. Nor was it his intent to place her in an uncomfortable situation with the man she may be currently involved with, but there was no way he could leave the club without saying something to her.

And if the man she was with had a problem with it that was just too bad.

"This is a nice place, Raven. Is there any particular reason you brought me here?"

Raven Anderson looked up from studying her menu to meet

John Augustan's gaze and couldn't help but smile. His eyes penetrated her as if they could see into her very soul and read her inner thoughts. And she knew they probably could. He hadn't built his publishing company into the huge success that it was by not being able to read people. After working for him for nearly a year, there was no doubt in her mind that he read her loud and clear. But to save time, she decided to cut to the chase.

"I have this wonderful idea for a story that I want to do for the magazine about the revived popularity of supper clubs."

John Augustan lifted a dark brow, looked down at the menu he held in his hand for a minute, then back up at her. Raven knew that in that brief moment he had pondered her idea. The question of the hour was whether or not he was interested enough to go for it. *The Black Pearl* was an informative magazine that dealt with real issues as well as entertainment news. A little less than two years old, the magazine had garnered a worldwide readership, and John was very selective about the articles that went into it. That was one of the reasons Raven enjoyed working as a reporter for his magazine. It had real class.

She was fully aware that John knew her time with his company was limited. She was a woman on the move, namely, to the top of her profession. But she was realistic enough to know that, in her chosen career, in order to get where she wanted to go, she needed to know all facets of journalism. Her constant goal was to be the best at whatever form of reporting she was involved with. Journalism was her life and she was good at it. Her dream was to one day become a Pulitzer Prize winner. Her mother had had that same dream before she'd let a man rob her of it. Raven was determined not to make the same mistake. Nothing would ever deter her from the one thing she wanted most in life.

John closed his menu. Raven could tell from the look in his eyes that he was interested. "Supper clubs like this one?"

"Yes. I think Leo's would be the perfect place to spotlight. It's the epitome of what a supper club is."

Raven stopped talking when the waiter came to take their order. It was only after the man left that she continued. "For a moment let your mind focus on at least one healthy meal a day, along with a dose of community, and what you'll come up with is Leo's."

"A dose of community?"

Raven smiled. "Yes. A place where several friends or acquaintances meet to share a meal periodically at a very classy nightspot."

"Sounds like a nightclub," John said, taking a sip of the drink he had ordered.

"No, it's something totally different. Even the clientele is different. It's more diverse. A nightclub would appeal to a lot younger age group. Supper clubs normally draw people between the ages of twenty-five and seventy. They're more of a social and dining club for professionals who want to mingle with other professionals."

Raven glanced around before adding, "Elaborate decor, high standards, extremely good food, and live music. It's a place where new friendships are established and important business contacts are made."

"You're also painting a picture of a very intimate atmosphere where romantic relationships can be formed," John casually added, smiling.

"Yes, for some I suppose," Raven said quietly. In truth, there was nothing casual about what John had added. He of all people knew she didn't have a social life that included romance. He also knew that she preferred it that way. Serious involvements had a way of distracting people from their main agenda in life.

It was no secret to those who knew the three Anderson sisters, Falcon, Robin, and Raven, that they shared more than the names of birds. They were also of the same mind that making it to the top of their chosen professions was everything, and things like love and romance were way down low on the totem pole. John had found that out the hard way when he had fallen in love with Falcon Anderson last year.

Although the subject of her oldest sister was something Raven and John always avoided, she couldn't help wondering if he still felt the same way he did when he'd asked Falcon to marry him and move with him to D.C. Falcon had turned him down, choosing her career as a stockbroker in New York over a lifetime with him. Raven had understood her sister's decision. Although John was an extremely handsome man at thirty-five and would be a great catch for any woman, their mother had drummed into her three daughters' heads very early in life not to let any man come between them and their dreams. Their father had convinced Willow Bellamy that she hadn't needed to pursue her dream of becoming a news reporter, so she had dropped out of college and had gotten married instead. Then a couple of years later, he had convinced her that it wasn't important for her to work outside the home because he would always be there to take care of all her needs. But that was before he'd run off with his secretary, leaving his wife and three daughters, all under the age of five, fending for themselves.

"Well, John, what do you think of the idea?" Raven asked, not wanting to think about the hard times her mother and sisters had endured after her father's abandonment.

"Let me think about it. I'm sure you have a proposal ready for me to take a look at."

"Yes," she said, smiling. "It will be on your desk first thing in the morning. I just wanted to bring you here tonight so you can get a feel of the place."

"I'm impressed. How will the owners handle you doing an article on their establishment?"

Raven's face lit up. "They don't have a problem with it. I know two of the owners, Tyrone and Tyrell Hardcastle, personally. They're identical twins. Tyrell dated Robin some years back when the two of them attended the Culinary Institute of America."

"Who's Leo?"

"Their father, who's a retired army captain. They named the place after him."

John nodded. "And you're sure they don't have a problem with you hanging around and using this place as the basis of your research?"

"No, in fact I've already cleared it with them. They know I will do a good job with the article. They also know that I—"

Raven stopped talking when she noticed John's gaze shifting from her to an object over her shoulder. She was just about to turn around in her seat to see what had captured his attention when she heard the sound of the rich and painfully sexy voice.

"Hello, Raven."

Raven drew in a quick breath. There was no need for her to turn around. It had been over four years, but she would know *that* voice anywhere. She still heard it from time to time even while she slept. Memories of that voice whispering seductive, inviting, and passionate words in her ears while his body stroked hers into a feverish pitch consumed her and made her feel all hot inside.

She forced herself to blink when Linc moved into her line of vision and stood next to their table. Her mouth opened to form a word of greeting, but nothing came out. She was too shocked, seeing him after all these years when wanting to see him again had once been an ache she couldn't soothe. What they had shared that week had been too special to walk away from, but they had done so anyway.

"Linc," she finally found her voice to say, in a whispered breath. "What are you doing here?"

Raven watched his lips curve into a sensuous smile and felt robbed of her breath yet again. His smile had been the reason she had wanted to get to know him up close and personal when they had first met. If there was such a thing as actually drooling over a man, then she'd drooled profusely the moment Lincoln Corbain had smiled at her that day on the beach in Daytona. He was such a good-looking man, with his towering height well over six feet, broad and muscular shoulders, medium-brown skin, and clean-shaven head. She had never considered a shaven head on a man sexy until she met Linc.

"I moved here last month to take a job with Brown, Gilmore, and Summers as one of their attorneys. And you?" Linc asked.

"I moved here a year ago and began working for Augustan Publishers."

John Augustan took the opportunity to clear his throat, reminding Raven of his presence.

"I'm sorry, John; I'm just so surprised to see Linc. We haven't seen each other in over four years."

John's lips curved into a smile. "I understand."

Raven glanced quickly at John, thinking that perhaps somehow he really did understand. "John, I'd like you to meet Lincoln Corbain. Linc, this is John Augustan, my boss and good friend."

John stood and offered Linc his hand. "It's nice to meet you. Would you like to join us?"

"No, I was about to leave. I just wanted to come by and say hello to Raven. We haven't seen each other since college."

John nodded, smiling, as he sat back down. "The two of you attended the same college?"

"No," Linc replied, shifting his gaze from John's face back to Raven's. Heat touched her body just as though his gaze had touched her intimately. "We met during spring break one year in Daytona Beach." He flashed Raven another smile. "And for some stupid reason, over the years we didn't stay in touch."

Raven released a low sigh. The reason they had decided not to stay in touch had not been a stupid one. They both had had goals in life that did not include a serious relationship with anyone. His dream had been to one day enter politics. Apparently they were both still hacking away at fulfilling their dreams.

"It was good seeing you again, Linc." She reached out and offered her hand to him.

Linc was silent for a moment, thoughtful as he took her hand and held it a little longer than necessary before letting it go. His gaze roamed over her face before settling on her mouth.

Raven couldn't help but remember the steamy, passionate kisses they'd shared and wondered if he was remembering those kisses as well. The contact of his hand when it had held hers, and her heart racing were causing extreme sensual heat to settle in the lower part of her body. There had been this hot, blazing chemistry between them from the very first. It was the kind of chemistry that had continuously burned between them that week they had been together. Even after four years he could still effortlessly ignite her flame.

"It was good seeing you again, too, Raven," Linc finally said. Nodding to John, he turned and walked away.

Raven didn't know whether she felt relief or disappointment that he had done so.

TWO

"Raven? Are you OK?"

Raven nodded, refusing to look at John for fear he would know that she was not OK. She had almost forgotten to breathe when Linc looked at her that one last time before walking off. She momentarily closed her eyes and drew in a deep breath.

She reopened them, thinking, *Incredible. Lincoln Corbain is still simply incredible. It should be against the law for any man to have this much of an effect on a woman.*

"You sure you're OK?"

John's question reminded Raven of his presence. "Yes, I'm fine," she replied. Her words were strained, unconvincing.

"Do you want to tell me about him?"

Raven looked up. John was smiling. "Come on. You can tell me. There was a time you and I were close to becoming a family."

Raven couldn't help but return John's smile. She knew he was trying to get her to loosen up some. He'd evidently realized that seeing Linc had her all tied up in knots.

"Linc could have become to me what you became to Falcon," Raven said bluntly.

Surprise widened John's eyes at her comment. He leaned back in his chair as his eyes met hers intently. "Which was?"

Raven's gaze was steady as she returned his stare. "The first man who made her think seriously about putting her heart before her career."

John was quiet for a while, almost too quiet. Then he asked, "And to you, Falcon, and Robin that's a bad thing, isn't it?"

Although Raven knew he was trying to make light of the question, his voice was tinged with anger, hurt, and pain. He stared at her, sipped his drink, waiting on her response. She knew he had loved Falcon deeply and probably still did. She also knew that Falcon had fallen in love with him and still loved him, although she had turned down his marriage proposal.

"Yes, it's a bad thing for us, and you know why we feel that way," she said, finally answering him. "I'm sure Falcon explained everything when she said no to your proposal."

John shook his head, not wanting to relive the memory of the night his heart had gotten ripped apart. Falcon, as well as her two sisters, staunchly believed that falling in love meant becoming dependent on that person. They believed getting serious with someone meant losing your identity and tossing aside your dreams. And nothing he had said could convince Falcon otherwise. Their mother had instilled it deep within their brains to always pursue their dreams and never become dependent on a man.

"I know you don't understand, John," Raven said, knowing the two of them had gone from being employer and employee to friends. "You don't know how hard it was on Mama and on us. You don't know the things we girls went without while growing up and the numerous jobs Mama worked to make ends meet. And all because she'd become dependent on a man and believed that he would take care of her. Mama tossed aside her dreams for my father and then he left her high and dry."

"Every man isn't like your old man, Raven."

"No," she said. "But I have no desire to fish out the ones that are and toss them back. When I do become involved in a serious relationship it will be only after I've fulfilled every dream I've ever had or ever thought about having. No man is going to rob me of my dreams."

John took a deep breath and sighed. "And you think I would have done that to Falcon?"

Raven stared at him for a long time before replying. "It really doesn't matter what I think, John. Evidently Falcon felt that you could have."

He shook his head. "The three of your minds work alike. You know what they say about birds of a feather flocking together."

An inkling of a smile played at the corners of Raven's lips, but she didn't comment on his teasing her about the sisters' names.

"So what about Lincoln Corbain, Raven?"

Raven stared into John's eyes. "What about him?"

"Do you see him as a threat to your dreams?"

Raven nodded. "He could be if I allow him to be."

"But you won't?"

"No, I won't. You know what my goals are, John. I don't have time for a serious involvement at this stage in my life."

John smiled. "Then I'd have to say the man you just introduced me to may be your biggest challenge. He seems to be the type of guy who goes after what he wants with all intentions of getting it. And from the looks of things here tonight, he definitely wants you."

As soon as she got home Raven undressed and went into the bathroom to take her shower. Moments later she turned off the shower and toweled dry. Reentering her bedroom, she began smoothing lotion over every part of her body, loving the scent of it as it was absorbed into her skin. After that was done, she slipped into her nightgown. As she placed the bottle of lotion back on her dresser, her gaze was drawn to the framed photographs sitting there.

The first one was a picture of her mother that had been taken a year before her death. Willow Anderson had worked two jobs to send her three daughters to college and had died of cancer a couple of months after Raven, the youngest, had completed her studies. Her mother's struggles and determination to provide for her daughters without her ex-husband's help had earned her her daughters' undying love, inspiration, and respect. Willow had never asked David Anderson for anything; whether that decision had stemmed from pride or embarrassment Raven never knew. The only thing she did know was that her and her sisters' dreams had become their mother's main agenda. She had been determined to see to it that her daughters reached whatever level of success they aimed for. She never wanted them to find themselves in the position she had found herself in because of love.

Raven's gaze moved to the next picture. It was one of her and her sisters taken together last Christmas with Santa. Raven smiled. Of course it had been Robin who had insisted on sitting on Santa's lap. Raven shook her head at the memory. Robin and Falcon were more than just sisters to her. They were also her very best friends. Falcon was the oldest by two years and Robin next oldest by one. While growing up they had been one another's playmates and confidantes. In a way they still were. Although they now lived in different cities, they made it a point to get together at least three or four times a year.

Deciding to read before going to bed, Raven walked over to the bookcase and pulled out a mystery novel. Going into her living room, she got comfortable by stretching out on her sofa. Then it happened. Memories she had been holding at bay began to race through her mind. She thought about the Florida sun, the Atlantic Ocean, the sands of Daytona Beach, and the ultra-fine body of Linc Corbain in a pair of sexy swimming trunks while he played volleyball with some of his frat brothers. After the game was over he had walked over to her, introduced himself, and invited her to take a stroll with him along the boardwalk.

They had spent the next two days getting to know each other. He had told her that he was from Memphis, Tennessee, and came from a family of attorneys. His parents as well as his siblings were practicing lawyers. She in turn had shared with him that her single mom in South Carolina had raised her and her two sisters.

After those first two days that she and Linc had spent together, she had spent the rest of the week with him in his room at the Hilton Dayton Beach Hotel. She had given him her virginity and he had given her a week of treasured memories.

Since the last time she had seen him, Linc's features had matured and were even more handsome. He had looked so good tonight dressed in a pair of casual slacks and a sports jacket. She hadn't noticed a ring on his finger, which probably meant he was still single.

She scowled to herself, disgusted that her thoughts would even go there. It should not have mattered to her if he was single or married.

But it *did* matter and she was not in the mood to try to convince herself otherwise. From the moment she had first laid eyes on Linc four years ago, everything about him had mattered. But she had been realistic enough to know that although their time together had been special, that week had meant the same thing for them that it had meant to the other thousands of students who had escaped to Daytona Beach. They were there to enjoy their break from school and to have a good time. No one had come to Daytona looking for any serious entanglements or lasting involvements. Nothing about that week was to be taken seriously. Her mind had understood that, although at times her heart had tried not to. It was only after she'd returned to school and gotten refocused that she remembered that no matter what, the career she wanted would always come first in her life.

She dated occasionally, but she had not yet met a man whom she allowed herself to get serious about. When a man became too demanding of her time, she'd had no qualms about cutting him loose and asking him to move on.

Leaning back against the sofa, she closed her eyes as she remembered other things about Linc tonight. His lips were fuller. Her gaze had been glued to them all the while he had been talking. Those lips had taught her how to kiss—really kiss. She could still, even now, recall every earth-shattering moment of their first kiss.

She had also noticed that his shoulders beneath his jacket seemed wider, stronger. She remembered holding tight on to those shoulders while he carried her piggyback across a stretch of beach to keep sand from getting into her sandals. Then there was the memory of the feel of her hands clutching those shoulders while he'd been on top of her, making love to her; sensuously stroking his body inside her, taking her over the edge of mindless passion and fulfillment; imprinting himself in her mind and a part of her heart forever. During that week she had spent with Linc, she had experienced the wonders she'd only heard were possible.

For months following their time together, her body had throbbed endlessly for his, craving the pleasures he had given her, remembering the sensations of sharing herself with him. To combat those feelings she had thrown herself full force into her first job after college as a reporter for a newspaper in Boston. But still, it had taken her awhile to get over the hunger for his touch.

Raven opened her eyes, no longer wanting to dwell on those thoughts. She didn't want her body to long for his touch like that again. And there was no way she could get involved with Linc again without the possibility of that happening. A hot and heavy involvement with him would be too easy to get into and would be hard as nails to get out of.

He would become to her like John had become to Falcon. A man she wanted but could not have; a man she could fall in love with; a man who could make her rethink her position on not putting her heart before her career. He was not one she could easily cut loose and ask to move on.

And those were things she could never risk happening.

Linc walked out onto the balcony off his bedroom and breathed a deep frustrated breath. His jaw tightened as the memory of Raven and John Augustan consumed his mind.

She had introduced him as her boss and her friend. They seemed comfortable with each other, and Linc couldn't help wondering if perhaps something was going on between them, although the man didn't seem the least bit territorial.

Why are you trippin', man? an inner voice asked Linc. *You don't have any claims on her. It's been over four years and you didn't have any claims on her even back then, so chill. She can mess around with anyone she wants to. After all, she's not yours.*

Linc shook his head, refusing to accept what his mind was telling him. She was his. She was his in a way he had never considered before. During that week in Daytona he had made her his in the most elemental way, and in every sense. Somehow more than their bodies had gotten connected. He'd known it then but had walked away, not realizing its significance until he'd seen her again tonight.

From the moment he and Raven had met, he had known there was something different about her. When she had walked around on the beach, she seemed unaware that most of the guys she passed by stared at her with open mouths. She'd been the first woman he had met that week in Daytona who had not been totally absorbed in the knowledge of her appeal and allurement. That noticeable quality had stood her apart from all the other sistahs on the beach that day. It was obvious that she felt confident about herself and hadn't felt the need to prove anything to anyone by putting herself on display or by doing anything to draw deliberate attention to herself. That was what he had admired most about her and what had caught his interest. There had been something so open, unselfish, and unpretentious about her. She had embraced life to the fullest, and that week, while around her, so had he.

Walking back into his bedroom, Linc paced the floor a few times before making a couple of decisions. One, he was determined to find out exactly what the real deal was between Raven and Augustan. And two, no matter what that situation was, he intended to make his interest known. He had long ago accepted that that week in Daytona had meant a lot to him.

After seeing her again, there was no doubt in his mind that something was still there between them, something unfinished. The Lincoln Corbain she had seen tonight was more matured in his thinking, a lot surer about the things he wanted, and after recently turning thirty-one, he was wiser. And he had no intentions of letting Raven Anderson walk out of his life a second time.

THREE

"It's nice to know up front that I'm being used," Raven said, smiling at her good friend Erica Sanders.

The waiter had just shown them to their table at Leo's. The soft lighting and the upbeat sound of reggae music playing in the background helped set the atmosphere of what was expected tonight. One Wednesday a month was Amateur/Open Mike Night, to showcase new and upcoming talent. Raven and Erica had arrived early to get a good table near the stage. It was also the night that one of the owners in particular, Tyrone Hardcastle, usually put in an appearance, since he was responsible for anything having to do with music and entertainment at the supper club. It was no secret that Tyrone was Erica's current love interest.

"Serves you right," Erica said in a huff as she opened her menu. "You should have told me that you knew the Hardcastle twins personally. Instead, I had to find out just how well you knew them this morning at the staff meeting when John mentioned the article you'll be doing about this place and the inside connections you had."

Raven gave Erica a smile before saying, "You fall in and out of love at least once a month. How was I to know that your infatuation with Tyrone would last a little longer than the others?"

"I'd like you to know that this is the real thing," Erica said, grinning, as she leaned forward.

"Yeah, that's what you said last month about Paul Weston," Raven pointed out with a small, faint laugh.

Erica smiled when she glared at Raven for reminding her of that fact. "Let's forget about Paul, shall we?"

Raven shook her head as she looked at her own menu. She and Erica had become good friends after Erica had begun working for Augustan Publishers the same day that she had. Erica was such a likable person and the two of them had hit it off immediately. The thing Raven liked most about her, besides her heart of gold, was that she was a fun person to be around. The thing she disliked most was Erica's constant badgering of Raven for her nonexistent social life.

Like her, Erica was twenty-six years old and not seriously involved with anyone. However, unlike her, Erica dated on a pretty regular basis. Raven much preferred spending her nights at home alone curled up in bed with a good book.

"So, when are you going to start writing the article?"

"In a few days," Raven answered, glancing up only briefly from her close study of the menu. "So I guess I'll be seeing a lot of this place for a while."

"I hope it won't be obvious what you're doing here. Some people may not appreciate being spied on while they're here enjoying themselves."

Raven lifted her head to look at Erica again, this time thoughtfully. "I won't be spying on them, but I can see how some people might think so. I guess I'll have to make it seem like I'm just one of the customers."

"That's not a bad idea. What you need is a man to bring along."

Raven shook her head, grinning. "I don't have a man to bring along."

"You could if you wanted one."

Raven studied Erica for a few moments as she tried to decide whether to respond to her comment. What the heck, she thought, she might as well let Erica give her habitual spiel about having a good man versus having a good job. She reached for her glass of wine and took a sip before casually saying, "I don't want one."

"Oh, yeah, I forgot. You think a good job is more important than a good man."

Raven inhaled sharply, deeply. "I've never said that I thought a good job was more important than a good man. What I have said, on several occasions I might add, is that I'm a firm believer that a woman should not sacrifice her dreams just to be with a man. I have every intention of one day settling down, getting married, and having a family. But only after I've fulfilled *all* my dreams."

Erica stroked her lip with her finger thoughtfully. "Hey, I'd love to fulfill all my dreams, too, especially the ones I have at night," she said, smiling wickedly. "All of them involve a man. Some good man. As far as I'm concerned, anything else can come later. I came to this city looking for a good job, and if things don't work out for me at Augustan Publishers, I'll leave, looking for another good job. But a good man, Raven, a real good man, isn't easy to come by. I've been looking for a good man for years and they are getting snapped up fast. So I still say, give me a good man over a good job any day."

Raven knew Erica just didn't understand. The only people who fully understood her reasons for feeling the way she did were her sisters. "We're different, Erica, with different ideas about things. Our agendas and priorities are different. I like my life just fine and I'm sure you're happy with yours. How's that article you're doing on Smokey Robinson coming along?"

"Don't you ever get lonely?"

Raven exhaled a long breath. So much for trying to change the subject. "I'm too busy to get lonely."

"What you need is more of a social life and a good man in it. When was the last time you had some honest-to-goodness fun with a man? When was the last time you spent some time with a man and truly enjoyed doing so?"

Raven was grateful when the waiter appeared. She was spared

from answering Erica's questions, although she knew what her response would have been. The last time she had had fun with a man and totally enjoyed it had been the time she had spent with Linc during spring break.

After the waiter had taken Raven's order he turned his attention to Erica. "And what would you like tonight?" he asked.

Erica smiled as she considered his question, for all of two seconds. "I'd just love to have Tyrone Hardcastle given to me on a silver platter."

Benjamin Goodman plucked the cherry from his daiquiri and popped it into his mouth before turning surprised raised brows to Linc. "You mean you actually saw Raven? Your Raven? Here?"

Linc leaned back against his stool at the bar. "Yes, I ran into her here one night last week." He knew that although Ben had never met Raven, he had heard enough about her from him. He and Ben had attended college together at Morehouse and then had attended law school at Southern University in Louisiana. Neither of them had ever ventured to Daytona during a spring break; however, since it was their final year of law school and they had a reason to celebrate, they'd decided to do so. They were going to share a hotel room, but because of a family emergency Ben had not gone to Daytona Beach with Linc after all. Things had worked out just fine, since he met Raven that week and she had been the one who ended up sharing the hotel room with him most of the time.

After law school Ben had accepted a job with the state attorney's office in Atlanta and Linc had returned home to work in his family's law practice. Two years ago Ben had moved to D.C. as a federal prosecutor, and since then he had often encouraged Linc to join him there. It was only after things had died down from the scandal involving his father that Linc made the decision to leave Tennessee for the nation's capital.

"So, how did she look, man?" Ben wanted to know.

Linc took a deep breath, thinking of the words he could use to describe how Raven had looked the night he had seen her. Beautiful? Yes, she was that with her perfect oval face of sable brown; her lips, full and rounded over even teeth; her straight nose; and her square chin. Yes, she did look beautiful. But still there had been more. She had looked enchanting, exquisite, and totally feminine.

"Well?" Ben asked impatiently, leaning closer.

Linc moved his shoulders in a shrug. "She looked exactly like the person I fell hard for four years ago, even better. She looked older, more mature, and more sophisticated."

Ben nodded before taking another sip of his drink. Linc knew he really didn't have to explain things to his friend. Ben knew the same thing now that he had concluded four years ago: Raven Anderson must have been one hell of a woman to make such an impact on Lincoln Corbain.

"Did seeing her again bring back memories?"

Linc thought about Ben's question. "Yeah, man, seeing her again brought back memories." He had never been one to kiss and tell, so Ben didn't know everything that had happened between him and Raven that week, although Linc was sure Ben had pretty much reached his own conclusions. After Linc had returned to school after spring break it had been apparent to everyone who knew him, especially Ben, that something monumental had happened to Linc in Daytona.

"Did you get a chance to talk to her?"

Linc looked down in his drink as if studying it. "She was with someone."

A slow smile came to Ben's lips. "So she was with someone. That didn't stop you from making your presence known, did it?"

Linc's dark head came up. He met Ben's gaze and couldn't help grinning. "No, it didn't."

Ben raised his drink in a toast. "Spoken like a true, fearless Alpha man." He then glanced around the room. "Looks like the show is starting. Come on. Let's find a vacant table someplace before it gets too crowded in here."

The two men got up from the bar and headed toward the area where the night's activities were about to get under way.

For this month, Open Mike Night was being held once a week instead of once a month. Raven's eyes had been glued to the raised stage as she enjoyed the first act, a Billie Holiday reincarnation, when something—an instinct, an uncanny force, a powerful soul connection—pulled at her. She swept her gaze from the performer onstage to across the room.

She saw Linc at the same exact moment that he saw her.

Raven felt her heart speed up, her palms go warm, and her breath catch deep in her throat. He was with someone, another man, and upon seeing her he touched the man's shoulder, whispered something to him, and then the two of them began walking her way.

All the sights and sounds around Raven faded into oblivion as her mind and gaze held the two tall men moving in her direction. Both men were good-looking, but her eyes were focused on the one dressed in gray slacks and a nice dark-colored knit suit. Everything about him was potent and sexy. She was in awe that her attraction for him was as strong as it had been the first time she had laid eyes on him four years ago, and as powerful as it had been last week when she'd seen him in this very same place. Nothing about the magnetism she felt toward him had changed.

Four years ago on the day they had met, she had not understood why her inner thighs clenched when he smiled at her, or why her breath got caught in her throat when she took the hand he offered when he introduced himself to her. Then later that night, when they had shared their first kiss, she had not understood the intensity of it. It had been a kiss that had transcended into a language that was only communicated and understood by the two of them. It had been a kiss that deciphered their thoughts, feelings, and emotions into a gigantic ball of fire. That fire had translated itself into particular tongue movements as their mouths mated. Uncanny as it seemed, it was as if each knew and understood what the other was thinking whenever they kissed. A soul connection. Even now she could remember the delicious taste of him, the feel of the interior of his mouth—warm, sleek, moist. She had felt his expertise, had been the recipient of his artistry, and had benefited from his skill in knowing how to pleasure a woman.

She would forever be grateful to him for his unlimited patience and for being an expert teacher and a considerate lover. He had introduced her to her very own body, a body she'd had all her life but a body she'd been unaware could feel such things and could do such things. It was a body that had certain erogenous points and a body that could drive a man to distraction.

If there were such a thing as two individuals having kindred spirits, then she and Linc would definitely qualify. She had left Daytona Beach believing it had been destined for them to meet, just as much as she believed it had been destined for them to go their separate ways in the end with no regrets.

That was the main reason she believed seeing him again now was an unkind turn of events, one she would have to deal with. Carefully. Cautiously.

"Who on earth are you staring at?"

Erica's question cut into Raven's thoughts. Curious, Erica glanced over her shoulder and saw the two good-looking brothers weaving around tables as they moved in their direction. "Do you know them?" she asked Raven in whispered awe.

With her gaze still holding Linc's, Raven inhaled a slow breath and answered, "I know the one with the clean-shaven head."

"Wow! He's good-looking. Both of them are. Who is he?"

My first and only lover. The man who gave me a week of blazing passion four years ago. The man who could get next to me if I were to let my guard down. Instead she answered, "Lincoln Corbain. We met over spring break four years ago during my last year of college."

Erica, Raven knew, wanted to ask more questions. She wanted more details, but time wouldn't allow it. Linc and his friend were now only a few feet away. But if Raven knew Erica, the subject of Lincoln Corbain was far from over.

"Good evening."

His voice, as Raven had known it would, had an underlying sensuality that captivated, then soothed. He smiled and automatically her thighs clenched, her heart rate increased, and her breath caught. She was barely able to respond to his greeting. "Hi, Linc. Seems you like this place."

His smile widened easily and when it did a warming sensation moved from the center of Raven's clenched thighs upward to her stomach. "Seems you do as well," was his smooth reply.

Erica cleared her throat, reminding Raven that she and Linc were not the only persons present. "Linc Corbain, I'd like you to meet Erica Sanders, a good friend of mine."

Linc broke eye contact with Raven and shifted his dark gaze to Erica. He extended his hand to her. "Nice meeting you, Erica."

Erica returned Linc's smile as she accepted his handshake, all the while holding him in her ever-observant gaze. "Likewise, Linc."

Glancing at the man by his side, Linc said, "And this is my friend Ben Goodman. Ben, this is Raven Anderson and Erica Sanders."

Ben stepped closer, giving both Raven and Erica warm handshakes. "I'm honored to meet two such beautiful ladies."

"Would the two of you like to join us?" Erica asked quickly, not really surprising Raven with the invitation.

"We wouldn't want to intrude," Linc was saying.

"You won't be," Erica replied.

Linc's gaze moved to Raven. "Raven?" he asked, seeking her consent also.

"Yes, please join us."

With those words Linc took the chair next to her and Ben took the seat next to Erica. Raven knew all the reasons she should not want Linc and his friend sitting at their table. One was the very obvious sexual vibes radiating between her and Linc. You would have to be a dead person not to have picked up on it. There was no doubt in her mind that both Erica and Ben had noticed it. Then again, she thought glancing at Erica and Ben, maybe they had not picked up on it. It seemed the only thing capturing Erica's and Ben's attention was each other. Raven smiled inwardly. Evidently Erica's love interest of the month, Tyrone Hardcastle, had gotten kicked to the curb.

The waiter came over and took the new drink orders. When that was out of the way Raven knew she could always count on Erica to get the conversation going.

"Before the two of you arrived, Raven and I were having an interesting conversation about the availability of good men. Are either of you married?"

FOUR

"Ben and Erica seem to be hitting it off," Linc said after taking a sip of his drink, then setting it down.

Raven glanced across the room at the couple who had moved away from their table and were now seated together at the bar. They were leaning close with their heads together, laughing and talking like they were two old friends and not two people who had been introduced to each other less than an hour ago. But then, Raven thought, that's how things had been for her and Linc when they first met. They had quickly and easily connected. Their conversations had been comfortable and relaxed, not at all tense and strained like the one they were sharing now.

"Yes, it seems they are" was Raven's stilted response. She shifted in her seat under Linc's quiet, intense gaze, wondering how she could effectively bring the evening to an end before he could bring up anything about the time they had spent together in Daytona. She didn't think she'd be able to handle it if he did. For the first time in her life she was unsure as to how to pull herself out of a situation with a man she was determined would not progress anywhere.

She cleared her throat. "So, you aren't married?"

"No."

"Ever been?" Raven could have bit off her tongue for wanting to know.

"No. What about you?"

"Umm, no, I'm still single." *And I don't even have a lover. The last time I experienced deep-hot passion was in your arms,* she thought as her thighs instinctively tightened in response to the sudden jolt of heat that vibrated between them. She swallowed as his eyes held hers for a moment before moving down to her neck. She wondered if he could see the rapid throb of her pulse in her throat. His gaze then drifted back to her eyes.

"So how do you like publishing books?" he asked her quietly.

She was so held by his magnificent dark eyes that it took her a moment to realize he'd asked her a question. Tiny lines of a frown drew over her forehead. "I'm sorry; what did you ask?"

He smiled as he repeated his question. "I asked how you like publishing books."

"What makes you think I publish books?" she asked, bemused.

Linc's brows lifted and his gaze lingered before he replied, "The other night when I saw you here you were having dinner with your boss from Augustan Publishers. I understand they are a huge book-publishing company."

Raven nodded, understanding how he could have been misled. "Augustan not only publishes books; they also publish a monthly magazine called *The Black Pearl.* I'm one of their reporters."

She watched as the smile on Linc's face suddenly vanished. He leveled her a cold look. The transformation happened so quickly she hadn't had time to prepare herself for it.

"So, you're one of those people who think it's fun going around snooping into people's lives and printing things that are untrue."

Raven's spine stiffened abruptly with Linc's cutting remark and the unwarranted attack on her profession. An angry look flashed in her eyes. "I am not that kind of reporter, Linc. I happen to enjoy the work I do, and the company I write for is not some sleazy two-bit publisher. Augustan Publishers has never been malicious to anyone, and as a reporter employed by them neither have I. And I don't appreciate you insinuating otherwise."

"Raven," Linc began, not knowing what he could say in the way of an apology, and knowing he owed her one as well as an explanation. But how could he explain to her that a magazine reporter had nearly destroyed his family last year?

Raven had no intention of putting up with anyone taking potshots at her profession. Although she had to admit the behavior of some journalists gave a bad rap to the others in the industry, she would not tolerate anyone questioning her integrity. She stood. "Since it's apparent that you're offended by what I do for a living, I think it would be best if you and I parted company."

"No, please stay. I apologize for what I said, Raven. I didn't mean to say it."

His words of apology were incredibly soft and filled with regret. But at the moment they weren't good enough for her. "Then why did you?"

Linc's solemn gaze lifted to hers and his gut clenched at the look in her eyes. His words had hurt her. "Please sit down and I'll explain."

Raven hesitated a moment before returning to her seat. Her eyes, Linc noticed, were flashing fire. Even angry with him he thought she looked beautiful. The dark, fiery look in her eyes reminded him of another time her eyes were filled with dark fire. At that time, instead of conveying her anger it had conveyed her smoldering need while they made love.

"I'm listening."

Linc leaned back in his chair. "I am sorry for what I said, Raven. It's just when you said you were a magazine reporter it caught me off guard."

Raven lifted a brow. "Why would it catch you off guard? You knew I was a journalism major in college."

"Yes, but as a journalism major you could very well have become a book editor."

Raven's eyes narrowed. "What do you have against magazine reporters?"

Linc inclined his head to look at her. "A magazine reporter nearly destroyed my family last year."

Raven was startled by his words, but looking at the grimness in his face she knew they were true. She also knew from the week they had spent together how close he was to his family. She leaned closer, struggling to deal with what he'd just said. "How?"

Linc stared at her, not really surprised by the care and concern he heard in her voice. "My father decided to run for public office as a judge. His opponent had a friend who knew someone who owned a publishing company. They decided to run a series of articles in a particular magazine accusing my father of various deeds ranging from spousal abuse to racketeering. All of them were untrue, but it wore all of us down denying every single charge."

A regretful sigh escaped Raven's lips. As a journalist she knew there was nothing anyone could have done to legally stop the slander. "Your father lost the election?"

"No, their plan backfired and he won. But the stress of dealing with such a negative campaign had gotten to be too much for him. He had a heart attack on election night mere moments before he was declared the winner."

A deep lump formed in Raven's throat. "Did he—"

"No, he survived and is doing fine now and is one of the best judges Memphis has ever had."

Raven nodded. She was glad. "And how is the rest of your family doing after dealing with all of that?"

"We survived. Some better than others."

Raven studied him, wondering if he was talking generally or specifically. She took a deep breath before asking her next question. During their week together in Daytona Beach, he had shared with her his dream to one day enter politics. "And you, Linc? How did you come out?"

"Bitter," he said, his tone level. The look in his eyes was filled with disappointment. "What happened made me rethink my future goals. I don't want to have anything to do with politics. Ever."

The disheartened sound in his voice made the lump in Raven's throat deepen. No wonder he had reacted the way he had when she told him that she was a magazine reporter. "I'm sorry, Linc. I'm truly sorry."

Linc captured the gaze that was looking up at him. He wanted to reach out and smooth the sadness from beneath her eyes. Sadness that was there because of him. "It wasn't your fault, and I had no right to come down on you the way I did just because you're a reporter, too."

"Thanks for sharing that with me. Now I understand." In a way she understood far more than she really wanted to. His dream of one day becoming a congressman from his home state of Tennessee had been destroyed by the actions of someone in her profession.

Neither of them said anything for a while, then Raven glanced at her watch. "It's getting late. I think Erica has forgotten we have to work tomorrow," she added with a tired sigh.

"Did the two of you come together?"

"Yes."

"I'll be glad to take you home if she's not ready to leave yet."

A flutter of nerves rose and twisted in the pit of Raven's stomach with Linc's offer. And at the same time, a caution warning nudged her. The last thing she needed was to share Linc's company any longer than she had to. "That's OK; I can call a cab."

"I can't let you do that. Besides, I'm ready to leave myself, but I don't think Ben is. It seems as far as he and Erica are concerned, the night's still young. I'll be glad to take you home, Raven."

Raven looked straight into Linc's eyes. Again she wanted to refuse his offer, but she was beginning to feel tired. Usually she would be in bed by now. She had never stayed at Leo's this late on a week-night. She took a deep sigh. There was nothing wrong with Linc taking her home, she convinced herself. It would be up to her to make sure that's all he did. "Are you sure you don't mind?"

"I'm positive."

Raven hesitated briefly before finally getting to her feet. "Thanks. I guess we should let Erica and Ben know that we're leaving."

FIVE

The sliver of moonlight that came through the car's window illuminated Linc's profile as he pulled his BMW out of Leo's parking lot.

Even a side view of him had its merits, she thought, liking the way his shirt stretched tight across his broad chest. Both of his hands were on the steering wheel and unlike her gaze, which kept drifting in his direction, his vision remained glued to the road in front of him as he expertly maneuvered the vehicle around the curves heading toward her home, following the directions she'd given him.

Although soft jazzy music was coming from his CD player, a timeless silence hung in the car's interior between them. The windows were lowered midway to take advantage of the October night's cool breeze, and a gust of air that came through pushed Raven's hair into her eyes. She reached up and pushed it back out of the way.

Linc had taken his eyes off the road when he brought the car to a stop at a traffic light. He saw Raven's hair flutter against her face and watched as she pushed it aside. Even with windblown hair he thought she looked perfect.

"When did you decide to stop wearing braids?" he inquired softly.

Startled by the sound of his voice, Raven looked over at him and saw that he was staring at her with eyes that were compelling and seductive. Taking a deep breath before answering, she said, "Right after college. I had a new job and wanted a new look to go along with it."

Linc nodded as he moved the car forward again when the traffic light turned green. "I like the change, although I think you looked good before, too."

"Thank you, Linc," she said, trying not to sound as pleased as she actually felt at his compliment.

His body leaned slightly forward, and without taking his eyes off the road he slipped out the CD that was playing and put in another, one by Kenny G. Then he settled back in the seat while the stirring sultry sound of the man and his saxophone flowed around them. Linc placed his hand back on the steering wheel.

His hands, Raven thought, definitely knew how to operate. She suddenly felt heated when her mind remembered how those hands, big, strong, yet gentle, had operated on her.

"How's your family?" he asked her, interrupting Raven's thoughts and sparing her any further self-inflicted torture from memories. "I recall you mentioning that your mother lives in South Carolina and your two sisters live in New York."

Raven leaned back against the seat. "Mama died a couple of months after I graduated from college."

"I'm sorry to hear that," Linc said, giving her a quick sorrowful look before returning his gaze back to the road.

"Thanks. That was a very difficult time for me and my sisters. We were very close to our mother. Her death was unexpected; at least it was for the three of us. She'd been diagnosed with a rare form of colon cancer the year before and didn't tell anyone."

Raven remembered the hurt and pain she and her sisters had felt upon learning that their mother had gone through that year alone while encouraging them to pursue their dreams. It had all made sense as to why her mother had encouraged her to go to Daytona Beach and enjoy her spring break instead of coming home like she usually did. Willow Anderson hadn't wanted her around to get suspicious of anything.

"My sisters are doing fine," she said after a few brief moments.

"Robin, the one who's a master chef, has been in Paris for six months studying at a renowned culinary school there. Falcon, the one who is a stockbroker, still lives in New York, doing what she does best with stocks and bonds."

"Do you see them often?"

Raven smiled. "Not nearly as often as the three of us would like, since we're extremely close. But we're also extremely dedicated to our professions and know that with that dedication come sacrifices. Robin will be turning twenty-eight in two weeks and is returning to the States so the three of us can celebrate at my place. We always spend our birthdays together."

When Linc stopped at another traffic light, he glanced over at her. "Are husbands invited?"

"There aren't any husbands. Falcon and Robin are still single," she said, thinking how John had almost swept Falcon off her feet and had come awfully close to changing that single status. "And with no marriage plans in their futures," she added. "At least not until they fulfill their lifelong dreams."

"Which are?"

Raven didn't hesitate answering. "Robin wants to open a culinary school in New York, and Falcon wants her own brokerage firm one day."

Linc slowed the car down to turn the corner to the street where her apartment complex was located. He took another quick glance in her direction. "What about you, Raven? What are your plans for the future? What are your dreams?"

Raven thought carefully about the answers to Linc's questions. Not that she had to ponder what they were. Her mind was very clear and straight as to what her future plans and dreams were. She wanted to take her time and respond in such a way as to make certain that Linc would be clear and straight.

"My plans for the future are to continue doing what I've been doing for the past few years, and that is staying focused on my main agenda and working my way up to the top of my profession. More than anything I'd like to write that special exposé that could earn me a shot at a Pulitzer Prize. In the meantime, I'm learning all I can to be ready to start my own publishing company in a few years."

Linc pulled into the driveway of the Eagle's Nest Apartments and brought his car to a stop in front of her building. He turned off the car's ignition and shifted around in his seat to look at her, capturing her with his eyes. "And what role does John Augustan play in all of this?"

Raven gave him a confused look. "John's my boss."

Linc nodded. "You also mentioned when you introduced the two of us that he was a good friend of yours."

Raven dipped her head, trying to remember everything about that night when she'd seen Linc in Leo's that first time. The only thing she remembered with absolute clarity was how good he looked. Any conversations she'd had were totally unclear in her mind. "Yes, he's a good friend of mine."

"How good a friend is he?"

Raven raised her head and looked at Linc, surprised at the tone of his question. His gaze pinned her in place, forcing her to understand exactly what he was asking. Her stomach muscles quivered at the intensity of his gaze as he waited for her answer. She could lie and tell him that she and John were intimately involved and effectively put an end to any ideas he might have of renewing any sort of relationship between them. But then a part of her knew that lying to him would be the coward's way out. She had to believe in her ability to handle every aspect of her life, even someone she didn't particularly want in it at the moment, like Linc. He would be a threat not only to her peace of mind but also to all her future goals and plans. She had to be strong enough to keep her priorities straight around him, and she believed that she could be. She'd been shown too early in life what could happen if she didn't.

She met his gaze head-on when she finally answered him. "John's a very good friend. He's a very close friend."

Raven studied Linc's features to see what impact her words had on him. She watched as his eyes narrowed and his jaw tightened. A part of her body inwardly reacted to the thought that her involvement with another man bothered him.

"But," she continued, "he's an even closer friend to my sister Falcon. At least he was before she turned down his marriage proposal."

Linc frowned. It took him a few moments to catch on to what Raven was telling him. "He asked your sister to marry him?"

"Yes. John loves Falcon very much, and I know she loves him just as much."

Linc's frown deepened. "Then why did she turn down his marriage proposal?"

"Bad timing. She has dreams yet to fulfill."

He lifted a brow, certain he had not heard her correctly. "Are you telling me that your sister loves John Augustan, but she turned down his marriage proposal because he asked her to marry him before she could fulfill her dreams?"

"Yes."

"Is this the sister who wants to one day own her own brokerage firm?"

"Yes."

The right side of Linc's mouth curled up into a half-smile. "Any reason she can't have both, the man and her dreams?"

"Yes. No woman should get seriously involved with anyone until she's fulfilled all her professional dreams. The most important thing that a woman can do is have a career and take care of herself and not have to be dependent on a man."

Linc stared at Raven. He could only assume those words were coming from the lips of a true-blue women's libber. "And you actually believe that?"

"Yes."

"And your sisters? They believe that as well?"

"Of course."

Linc chuckled and shook his head. "Whatever happened to the idea of finding a balance and having both a personal and a professional life? What's wrong with pursuing them both?"

"You can't have both because there is no such thing as a balance. Someone is always expected to compromise and usually it's the woman. We're the ones who're asked to put our careers on hold, to follow our man from pillar to post or wherever his career may take him. We have the responsibility of raising the children and are expected to turn a house into a home for our family. Instead of being our own individual, we become our husband's other half. And if the man decides to up and leave one day, we're the ones who are left with nothing—no future, no career, no dreams. He will have stripped us of all of that."

Linc looked at Raven as lines of confusion showed up on his forehead. "Is there a particular person you know firsthand that this happened to?"

He saw her expression and knew his question had taken her by surprise. He watched as she drew in a sharp breath before slowly nodding. Looking away from him, at an object outside the car window, she answered, "Yes."

"Who?"

She looked back at him. "My mother. My father left her with three kids all under the age of five without ever looking back. She had given up her future, her career, and her dreams for him and he walked away and left her with nothing."

Linc studied Raven for a while and watched how the pain of her father's abandonment shone clearly in her eyes. "No, he left your mother with something. In fact, I believe that he left her with the most precious gifts he could ever have given to her, Raven. He left her with you and your two sisters. And I refuse to believe that at any time in your mother's life she would have preferred having a future, any dreams, or a career without the three of you being a part of it."

Without saying anything else he got out of the car and walked around the vehicle to open the door for her.

SIX

A long moment of silence stretched out between Linc and Raven as he walked her to her door. He hoped her silence meant she was thinking about what he had said. He knew it would not be easy to change her views or how she felt, but if he could give her some food for thought, that would be enough for now.

The problem he saw with Raven Anderson was that the woman was too independent for her own good. There was nothing wrong with wanting to be successful, but the key was being successful on your own terms, without having to make unnecessary sacrifices.

"Thanks for bringing me home, Linc."

Raven's soft voice broke the quietness and invaded his thoughts. His gaze was drawn to hers, then slowly dropped dead-center to her lips, as he remembered the heated bliss he'd found there more than once. Thinking about those hot and heavy kisses sent a ripple of pleasure up his spine. Pure unadulterated male pleasure. He cleared a suddenly tight throat and said, "Anytime."

His gaze must have lingered on her lips much too long for comfort, he thought as he watched her unconsciously moisten them with a nervous sweep of her tongue. His gut clenched and his body experienced an acute craving to feast hungrily on her mouth.

"It's late. I better go in," she said, reaching into her purse to retrieve her door key.

When she pulled out the key he caught her hand in his. "I'll open the door for you," he offered, feeling tingles of desire inch through his veins from touching her.

Raven stared at him for a long, thoughtful minute. She knew his intent. He wanted to kiss her good night, and it wouldn't be the type of kiss that could be given on a doorstep amid possible prying eyes. This kiss would deserve privacy. There was kissing and then there was kissing . . . Lincoln Corbain's style. He had his own special technique. Linc didn't just kiss; he made love to your mouth while he was doing so.

"Do you think that's a good idea?" she asked on a long, deep indrawn breath, wondering why she'd asked such a question. Did she really expect him to answer no?

He smiled and nodded. "I think it's the best idea I've had all night," he said in a husky whisper, easing the key from her hand.

The warmth of his smile flooded Raven's whole being, and she couldn't deny him what he wanted, because deep down it was what she wanted, too. As much as she wanted to deny it, she couldn't.

She watched as he slipped her key into the lock and with a twist of his wrist opened the door. Taking a deep breath to calm her racing heart, she walked inside her apartment on none-too-steady feet. Linc followed her in, closing the door behind him.

Her hand automatically reached up to a nearby light switch, but he captured her hand in his. "Leave it off for now. There's enough light in here for what we need," he whispered, gently pulling her to him.

Despite Raven's best efforts to drum up any sort of resistance to him, her body automatically leaned toward him and felt his arms tighten around her waist, drawing her even closer.

The first touch of his lips on hers sent the pit of her stomach into a wild swirl and set her body aflame. His mouth covered hers hungrily, sending shivers racing from the top of her head to the tips of her painted toes. She would have fallen to her knees with the devouring impact of the sexual hunger she felt if he hadn't tightened his hold on her. His mouth moved deeply over hers, tasting her, feeding on her, drawing her out.

And then he went in for the kill.

His hand around her waist slid to her behind, cupping it and urging her body closer to the hard fit of him at the same time that he inserted his tongue into her mouth, reacquainting it with this special brand of intimacy they'd shared four years ago. Instinctively she captured his tongue with hers, at first shocked at the degree of her own hunger and the magnitude of her smoldering desire. She heard herself purring, then moaning as she melted like butter in his arms. Their tongues mated hotly, profusely, greedily.

And then it happened, that unexplainable, uncanny, but special form of communication they were able to share whenever their mouths met with such intensity. He was the one sending all the silent messages and she was reading them loud and clear. It didn't matter what roadblocks she tried putting in his path or what goals she intended to reach or dreams she wanted to fulfill, he intended on being a part of her life from this night on.

"No," she said, suddenly breaking off the kiss and trying to push him away. She could not let him or any man have this type of control over her. She didn't want to be dependent on any man, not even for this.

"Yes," Linc whispered huskily, knowing she'd deciphered his thoughts. His hold on her tightened, refusing to let her push him away from her. He reached up and traced his finger up her cheek and along the curve of her cheekbone. His gaze was intent, purposeful, challenging. "I'm not going anyplace, so get used to seeing me."

She looked up at him, her dark brown eyes rebellious but still filled with desire. She spread her palms on his chest, seeking distance. "I don't have time for this."

"Then I suggest you make time by adding me to your agenda,"

he said, trailing a feathery touch of his finger down the curve of her neck.

"I have plans, goals, dreams. I'm too busy to get involved with anyone," she implored in a shaky voice.

"I'm not just anyone, Raven," he said softly, stroking her swollen lips with his finger. "I'm the man you became a part of four years ago. The first man to make love to you. We bonded, we connected, and we—"

"Screwed each other silly during a week of fun and games, Linc. That's all it was, nothing more."

Her crude description of what they'd shared didn't faze Linc. He knew she was lying to herself. He could see the mixture of longing and fear in her eyes. She was actually afraid of him, not physically but emotionally. "It was more. You know it as well as I do."

"It was lust," she said in a quivery and unconvincing voice.

"Call it whatever you like for now, but I can guarantee that you'll come to know the right word for it later." He recaptured her mouth in a smooth sweep, intending to block all thoughts from her mind. He wanted her full attention and deep concentration. He would have time to prove to her that that week had been more than just fun and games for him . . . and for her.

He made this kiss even more hot and heavy than the one before. He refused to let her forget what they had once shared, and he refused to let her make it into something sleazy and meaningless.

His tongue became dominant and he made love to her mouth in a slow, sensual mating. He felt her tremble in his arms. He felt the heat of her center through the silky material of her dress as it came in contact with his hardness pressing against her.

When he finally broke off the kiss she clung to his shoulders for support, her breathing unsteady. He pulled her to him. "I have dreams, too, Raven," he whispered in her ear as if there could be others listening. His voice was husky with emotion. "Occasionally at night when I close my eyes I remember seeing you as I saw you that last night we spent together. You on my bed, stretched out, your body trembling while waiting for me. The look in your eyes told me you weren't ready for our week to end any more than I was. But we had agreed that that week would be all we'd ever have. Neither of us was interested in continuing things with a long-distance romance. We both had plans and dreams that didn't include a commitment to each other. We knew and accepted that then."

He breathed deeply as his gaze continued to hold hers and his arms tightened even more around her. "That night, when we made love, it was more special than any of the other times before, and do you know why, Raven?"

Raven was transfixed by the blazing intensity of his eyes. "No," she said quietly.

"Because that night we connected in a way we'd never done before, I never knew that two people could get that close, that united, and could join so deeply."

Raven closed her eyes remembering. His foreplay that night had been torturous and had pitched her body into a frenzy of need, not only to be satisfied but also to become a part of him. He had pulled every single emotion that she possessed from her that night. At one point she'd even been tempted to rip his condom off to feel the very essence of him inside her body. She had wanted it all. She had wanted to share every part of him, even a part that could have put her at risk of becoming an unwed mother. But luckily for them both, she'd retained her sanity and held back.

"Fate has brought us back together," he continued, lacing his fingers through hers. "I regretted letting you walk out of my life. So don't think I'm going to let you do it a second time."

He lowered his head and placed a soft kiss on her lips before releasing her. His mouth curved into a warm smile. "Get a good night's sleep and while you're doing so think about what we once shared and will be sharing again."

Without giving her time to say anything, he opened the door and walked out, gently closing it behind him.

An angry Raven sat pounding away at the keyboard on her computer. She was furious with anybody, everybody, but especially with herself.

Stupid! Stupid! Stupid! How could she have let Linc take control of things like she had last night? She had been putty in his hands and, more specifically, under his lips. The man could have told her that the U.S. capital was being moved to Hawaii and she would have believed him as long as he'd kept his mouth cemented to hers. His kissing abilities had gotten even better, not that they'd needed improving, mind you.

Sighing in disgust, she glanced out the window on the other side of her desk. In the distance she could see the Lincoln Memorial. Today the name "Lincoln" did not sit well with her. At the moment, it was definitely not one of her favorites. She frowned. At least the Lincoln that the memorial was named for had been honest. There was nothing honest about the Lincoln who had taken her home last night. He had played dirty. He'd known she would not be able to resist his kiss, and the man had laid it on thick and heavy.

Raven exhaled and forced herself to return to the document she had just entered into her computer, the opening for the article on Leo's that she was writing for the magazine. She glanced down at the club's schedule that Tyrone Hardcastle had dropped by her office earlier that morning. Leo's was open six days a week from Tuesday through Sunday for after work and dinner. They were open Sundays for brunch. There was live music on Fridays, Saturdays, and Sundays. All other nights you were entertained with taped soft jazz except for once a month on Wednesday nights, which were set aside to showcase new and upcoming talent.

Raven turned back to the document she'd been working on, trying to collect her thoughts on the talent that had been showcased last night. She had been impressed and her attention had been completely captured . . . until she had spotted Linc. Scowling, she started pounding on her keyboard again as she tried to erase the memory of everything that had happened last night.

Raven looked up when she heard the knock on her office door. "Yes?"

A smiling Erica breezed in. "Good morning. Did you get home OK last night?"

Raven frowned as she stared at her friend—the deserter. "Like you care," she said, displaying her wretched mood.

Erica's eyebrows lifted. "Of course I care, but Ben and I thought you and Linc needed time alone to reminisce about old times."

"Well, you and Ben thought wrong." Raven narrowed her eyes. "And speaking of you and Ben, the two of you were awfully chummy last night."

"Oh, yes," Erica replied, her smile widening. "He's a nice guy. I really enjoyed his company." She then came and sat in the chair across from Raven's desk. "What about you, Raven? Did you enjoy Linc's company?"

"Not particularly." Raven would have loved to tell Erica that she had detested Linc's company because things had moved too fast between them last night to suit her. But she decided the less she talked about it the better off she'd be.

"So did he spend the night?"

"Of course not!" Raven snapped angrily.

Grinning, Erica was not put off by Raven's sharp tone. "Mmm, I was hoping that he had."

"Why?"

Erica leaned forward. "Because you, Raven Anderson, need a man in your life to get your mind off work for a while. You are a sistah who definitely needs a brother. A hot-blooded brother at that."

"No, I do not."

Erica smiled. "Trust me, yes, you do, and as your friend I need to tell you these things, since those two sisters of yours won't. They're just as mixed-up and confused as you are. Especially the one John's in love with. I can't imagine any woman in her right mind not wanting to marry him."

Raven didn't want to hear any more. "Don't you have work to do?"

With a small chuckle Erica shook her head and said, "Not at the moment. You don't know how excited I was to discover that you and Linc have a history."

"So what of it?"

"You know what they say: history has a way of repeating itself."

Raven arched her eyebrow and narrowed her gaze. "History can also come back to haunt you. It's my belief that what's in the past should stay in the past."

"Not if it looks anything like Lincoln Corbain."

Before Raven could give a scorching retort there was another knock on her door. "Come in."

Megan, her secretary, opened the door and walked in carrying a beautifully wrapped box. "This was just delivered for you, Raven." She placed the box on Raven's desk and walked back out before a surprised Raven had a chance to thank her.

Raven gazed at the box for a second before picking it up, wondering which one of her sisters had sent it. She began opening it, ignoring Erica's curious gaze. Raven pulled out the white card that had been placed inside the box and began reading it:

Another thing that I occasionally dream about is the memory of our walks on the beach. I hope this package helps you remember those special times, too.

Linc

Stunned, Raven stared at the card and reread it.

"Well, who's it from?" Erica asked without exhibiting the least bit of shame at being nosy.

Raven lifted her head and looked at Erica. Seeing no reason not to tell her, she said, "It's from Linc."

Placing the card on her desk, Raven removed the tissue paper stuffed inside the box. Tucked under it all was a beautiful glass case containing several beautiful seashells.

A breathless astonished sigh escaped Raven's lips as she stared at the gift Linc had sent her. She closed her eyes for a moment, remembering the sound of the ocean as they strolled along the seashore holding hands while looking for seashells.

"Raven, you OK?"

Raven slowly opened her eyes to see Erica staring at her. She looked back down at the item she held in her hands. "It's beautiful, isn't it?"

Erica smiled as she stood up. "Yes, simply beautiful. Umm, I'd even say expensive. That glass looks like real crystal. Not only does Linc Corbain look good, but the brother has good taste. I think I'll leave you alone to think about whatever else he has that's good." She then walked out of the office, closing the door behind her.

Raven leaned back in her chair as she stared down at the gift that had been delivered to her. She pursed her lips as she considered her predicament. Lincoln Corbain was pulling out all the stops to get next to her. He was using the one thing she couldn't fight, and that was the memory of their time together in Daytona Beach.

The man was definitely playing dirty.

SEVEN

Raven sat alone with a glass of wine in her hand as she studied the sights and sounds around her. Soft conversations flowed through the club and mixed in with the smooth sound of jazz music. Her gaze roamed the room, lingering and committing to memory those things she would need to make the article she was writing informative and interesting.

She had selected the right place to use as the basis of her story. Leo's, like so many other supper clubs that were now springing up in different cities around the country, had found its niche. She admired the Hardcastles for operating such an upscale establishment that was both formal and friendly. Supper clubs, which had once been local traditions, had quickly gotten replaced by franchise restaurants, mostly the bar-and-grill types. But those franchises did not provide the novel entertainment, delicious food, and coziness that supper clubs had. Restaurant entrepreneurs, in their haste to become dining giants, had lost sight of those things that were tried-and-true favorites. The Hardcastles had not lost sight of them, which was probably the reason people kept coming back.

"Would you like to order dinner now?"

Raven lifted her head to look up at the waiter who had appeared by her side. "No, not yet, but I'd love to have some more wine."

The older man nodded as he went about refilling her glass. After he left, she took a sip and began thinking about someone she had promised herself she would not think about: Linc.

Today he had sent her another gift, a small potted palm tree. The plant was gorgeous, and she'd found the perfect place in her house for it. The card that had accompanied the plant had said:

Remember the palm trees swaying in the Florida breeze and our picnic under them as we watched the sun dip below the Atlantic Ocean.

Linc

Raven released a deep sigh. The problem she was having was the fact that she *was* remembering, which was something she didn't want to do. Ever since the plant had arrived she'd had memories of her and Linc's picnic on the beach one afternoon.

During the day the beach had been crowded, but in the late afternoon you could usually find a secluded spot. They had found the perfect place under a cluster of palm trees. She remembered Linc spreading a blanket out on the sand. He'd then pulled her down on the blanket next to him. Opening the picnic basket the hotel had prepared for them, he had withdrawn grilled chicken sandwiches, chips, grapes, a bottle of wine, and two wineglasses. After filling both glasses, he had handed one to her and then raised his own. "Here's to graduation in a few months, but more important, here's to what has been a beautiful and special week," he had murmured hoarsely.

"To graduation and to a beautiful and special week," she had repeated, touching her glass to his, then sipping the wine.

Raven shook her head, bringing her thoughts back to the present, not at all happy that she'd had them in the past yet again. Thoughts and memories were intruding into her work time, and she couldn't allow that to continue. No man had ever competed with her attention to her work assignments. And she was determined that Lincoln Corbain wouldn't be the first.

She didn't want to think about their nights together, the warmth and hard feel of his body as it lay atop hers, or the sounds she'd heard in the pitch-black of their hotel room: sounds of their heavy breathing, their moans, groans, and passionate cries. And she refused to think about their mornings and waking up to the brightness of his eyes that still glowed with wanting and inner fire.

Raven picked up her glass to take another sip of her wine. The tingling warmth of the liquid that flowed down her throat matched the tingling warmth that flowed through her limbs and pooled at her core whenever she remembered Linc making love to her.

For the first time in four years she suddenly felt unbearably hungry, but it wasn't food that her body craved.

Sitting across the room at the crowded bar, Linc watched as Raven took another sip of her wine. His steady gaze watched as she lifted the glass to her lips, slightly tipped her head back, and arched her neck. Never before had observing a woman sipping her drink been sensuous enough to send involuntary tremors of arousal through him.

"Do you want a refill?" the bartender asked, intruding on Linc's thoughts. Linc noticed the man wasn't Flint and remembered that Flint only moonlighted a couple of nights of the week and Friday wasn't one of them.

"No, thanks, this is it for me tonight."

"You're planning on sticking around, aren't you?" the bartender asked.

Linc glanced over at the table where Raven was sitting alone. "Possibly. Why?"

"It's Sixties and Seventies Night. There's bound to be a lot of dancing going on."

Linc nodded. A delicious thought drifted through his mind. It was one of him holding Raven in his arms while he danced with her to a very slow tune, with the heat of his body pressing against hers long enough for him to savor the contact.

"In that case I'll definitely be sticking around."

An upbeat selection of sixties and seventies music filled the club as one singing group after another took the stage. First it had been the Commodores, then the Delfonics, and now the Dells. A large number of people crowded the dance floor. Most of them were couples, and others were in groups. There were even a few bold singles dancing anything and everything from swing to the bump, to the whatever-you-want-to-call-it current style of dancing.

Raven smiled as her gaze took in the entire scene. People were really enjoying themselves, as was evident in the laughter and rousing conversations surrounding her. She looked across the room and her gaze came into contact with Linc's. She had seen him earlier sitting at the bar, but other than lifting his glass in a silent greeting to her, he had kept his distance. In a way she was glad, but another part of her felt the least he could do was come over and say hello. Then she could thank him for the gifts he had sent and in a nice way ask him not to send her anything else.

She turned to the stage when the Dells came to the mike and the announcer said they were about to do one of their slow numbers. The dance floor crowd suddenly began thinning out when the groups and singles gave way to the couples.

"I want every man who has a special lady here tonight to use this opportunity to take her into your arms on the dance floor," the announcer said, smiling. Raven watched as more couples began heading forward.

"Raven?"

At the sound of her name, Raven turned and saw Linc standing next to her table. Stunned, she looked at him and watched as he reached his hand out to her. "May I have this dance?"

She tilted her head up, considering his request, knowing she should say no and reinforce her stand that there could not be anything between them. But instead she nodded, placed her hand in his, and stood. He led her to the dance floor.

Raven knew she was a goner the moment he took her into his arms. When he placed his arms around her, she inhaled sharply as their bodies began swaying in time to the music.

"You look good tonight, Raven," he whispered softly in her ear, tightening his hold on her.

"Thank you," she replied in a voice so low she knew he probably had to strain to hear it. "And thanks for the gifts, Linc."

"You're welcome."

"But you're going to have to stop sending things for the sole purpose of recapturing memories of our time in Daytona."

"No, I don't," he said.

He heard her release a long sigh before saying, "You weren't this way before."

He leaned back and met her gaze. "What way?"

"Aggressive."

He smiled. "Thank you."

She frowned. "It wasn't meant to be a compliment, Linc."

His smile turned into a chuckle. "Yeah, I know."

Deciding to drop the subject for now, Raven pressed her cheek against his hard chest as they continued to dance to the slow music. She drew in a deep breath when he pulled her closer to his body and wrapped his arms around her more securely. Her body, so close to his, made her feel every hard part of him. Their movements were slow, charged, stimulating. By the time the last lyric had been sung and the last note played, a moan of pure want had arisen in her throat. She forced herself to swallow it.

"I have to go," she said when he escorted her back to her table. Her voice was trembling.

"I'll follow in my car to make sure you get in OK."

"That's not necessary. I've been going in after dark by myself for quite awhile," she said sharply.

Slowly he smiled. "I'm sure you have, but I prefer doing it anyway."

Raven frowned. "Fine. Do whatever you want."

Linc's arm closed around her shoulder as they walked out of Leo's. He wished he could take her up on her offer to do whatever he wanted, because his body was aching and, more than anything, he wanted to make nonstop love to her tonight.

"Lincoln Corbain is going to be the death of me," Raven said to herself in a low, deep growl of anguish as she looked in her rearview mirror to see the lights of the car following close behind her.

"The bottom line is," she raged on to herself, "the man is *not* going to get next to me. I refuse to let him do that. I have plans and dreams that don't include him. The sooner he realizes that, the better."

Her fingers tightened around the steering wheel. "If the reason he's following me is because he thinks he's going to get another kiss off me like he did a few nights ago, well, he has another thought coming."

Her heart pounded when she pulled into the driveway of her apartment complex. "I won't let him kiss me; I won't," she chanted to herself as she parked her car and got out with her door key in her hand. She wasn't surprised when he parked next to her and got out. But she was surprised when he said, "I'll wait right here until you get in. Flip the light switch twice to let me know you're inside and things are OK."

Raven frowned. *He wasn't going to try to talk his way inside her apartment? He wasn't going to try to kiss her good night? Well, that was just fine with her. That's what she wanted anyway, wasn't it?*

"Raven?"

She looked over at him. He was leaning against his car staring at her. "What?"

"Pleasant dreams." His words came with that megawatt smile that could always cause extreme sensual heat to settle in the lower part of her body, like it was doing now.

She fumed as she walked to her door. Pleasant dreams? In order to dream, one had to sleep, and there was no way she was going to get any sleep tonight.

Glaring at him one last time, she unlocked her door and went inside. And as he had asked her to do, she flipped the light switch twice.

Raven had undressed, showered, and gotten settled in bed when the phone rang. She looked at the digital clock on the nightstand, then back at the phone, wondering if it was Linc. She then thought there was no way it could be him because, as far as she knew, he didn't have her number. She picked up the phone.

"Hello."

"Took you long enough."

Raven smiled at her sister's impatient voice. "I was wondering who would be calling me this late. How are things going, Falcon?"

"They're going. You OK?"

Raven shifted her position in the bed to find a more comfortable spot. "Yeah, I'm OK. What about you?"

"Yeah, I'm fine. Have you heard from Robin lately?"

Raven frowned. Actually, she hadn't, at least not this week, and that was unusual. Robin was the one who made it her business to keep in touch on a rather frequent basis. "No, I haven't. You?"

"She called and left a message on my answering machine a few nights ago saying she's doing OK and to tell you she's been busy but will call you this coming week. I guess she wants to get us to finalize the details for her birthday party."

Raven smiled, shaking her head. Of the three of them, Robin was the one into birthday celebrations big time. "Yes, I suppose."

"How are things at work?"

"They're fine, and before you ask, he's doing OK, Falcon."

"I have no idea who you're talking about."

"Don't play dumb, Falcon. You're too smart. Besides, being coy doesn't become you."

There was a long pause. "I miss him, Raven. It's been a year tonight."

Raven sighed upon hearing the pain and loneliness in her sister's voice. She also had heard the occasional sniffing that indicated Falcon had been crying. "Yeah, I know. I thought about it this morning. It was the week before Robin's birthday last year that John asked you to marry him." She decided not to tell Falcon that John had not come into the office at all today. Chances were he had remembered, too, and the day had been just as miserable for him as it had been for Falcon.

"And I turned him down," Falcon finished. "But I did the right thing. I know I did."

"If you really believe that, then everything will eventually be all right, Falcon," Raven said softly, not knowing what else to say.

"Of course it will be. I think I'll have enough money saved in another year to get things started with the company I plan on opening."

"Oh, Falcon, that's wonderful."

"I can't wait." There was another pause. "That's what it's all about, isn't it, Raven? It's about working hard and fulfilling our dreams. Everything else can wait. Nothing else is important."

Raven sucked in a deep breath as she heard her sister's words. She let it back out slowly. Leave it to Falcon to always remind her of what came first with them. "You're right, Falcon," she said softly. "Nothing else is important."

EIGHT

Raven had just finished tying her shoelaces when there was a knock on her door. She frowned. It was just a little past six in the morning. She wondered who her early-morning visitor could be. She doubted it was Erica, although she had an open invitation to go running with Raven whenever she wanted. Some people weren't morning people, and Erica fell into that category.

Upon reaching the door Raven took a quick glance out the peephole.

Linc!

She immediately opened the door. Given the fact that she didn't get any sleep last night and she blamed him for it, Lincoln Corbain was the last person she wanted to see. "Wh-what are you doing here?"

Raven almost stammered on her words as she looked at the man standing in her doorway. A new kind of awareness pumped furiously through her veins. Oh, she had awakened in a bed with Linc before so she knew all about his sexy-as-sin early-in-the-morning look. And during their week together he had mostly worn tank tops and shorts, so she was well aware of the fact that he had a gorgeous body. But he must have gotten into some bodybuilding program since she'd last seen him. The man looked absolutely stunning in his well-fitted see-how-fine-the-brother-really-is running outfit. Just looking at how he looked made a burning sensation sizzle from the tips of her breasts down to her middle. There it stopped. His body was so taut, so firm, so tight, so unbelievably built. There was not a flabby place anywhere on him. Her gaze automatically went to his midsection. She sucked in a deep breath. Lincoln Corbain was well endowed. As she continued staring, she began remembering one particular morning while they were in bed together, sliding her fingers beneath the waistband of his shorts to feel just how well endowed he was.

Raven swallowed. That same moan that had threatened to erupt from her throat last night when she'd been in his arms while dancing was threatening now. She returned her gaze to his face and saw that he had been watching her ogle him. She cleared her throat. "I asked what you're doing here, Linc?"

His eyes bored into her in a way that seemed to touch every feature on her face. "I thought I'd go running with you."

Raven frowned as she searched her mind in response to what he'd just said. Fairly certain she had never mentioned her early-morning weekend activities to him, she asked, "How did you know I go running on Saturday mornings?"

"Erica mentioned it to Ben, and since Ben knew I also go running early on Saturday mornings he mentioned it to me."

She narrowed her gaze on him. "So you just assumed it would be OK to join me?"

"Yes," he said, giving her a seductive smile. "That's about the shape and size of it."

Instinctively, when he said those words, her gaze went back to his midsection, remembering another time he'd used those same words. She inhaled sharply as she tried to get her mind back on track. She looked back up at him. "I think you assume too much, Linc."

He studied her for a moment. "And what else is it that you think I assume?"

"That you can pick up where we left off four years ago in Daytona."

He cocked his head as if considering her words. He then said, "The only thing that I'm assuming and what I know for a fact, Raven, is that you prefer I left you alone. But I can't do that."

"And why not?"

Linc smiled. "I'll tell you some other time. You ready to go running? I promise to be good company."

You'll be more company than I need, she thought to herself. "If you want to tag along you can. Just as long as you keep up."

Linc let out a smooth chuckle. "I was going to give you the same advice."

"How about something to drink?" she offered after they returned to her apartment from their jog a couple of hours later.

"Water will do fine, thanks."

Linc followed her into the kitchen and sat down on one of the stools at her breakfast bar. "Nice place."

"Thanks." Raven went to the refrigerator to get him a thirty-two-ounce bottle that she always kept on hand full of drinking water. As much as she didn't want to admit it, she had enjoyed Linc's company while running. He had kept up with her pace, and they'd engaged in steady conversation most of the time without losing a beat.

He had told her that he had gotten into a fitness program right after law school and still went to the gym at least twice a week. He enjoyed keeping his body in shape by working out. She'd been tempted to tell him that in her opinion he was doing a super-nice job of it.

She walked back over to the kitchen counter and handed him the bottled water. She watched, fascinated as well as magnetized, as he uncapped the bottle and, tilting his head back, took a huge swallow of the clear liquid.

Raven's gaze was drawn to the muscular expanse of his neck, and she watched as the water flowed down his throat, making his

Adam's apple move. Her body ached to go over to him and take her tongue and lap up the water that was missing his mouth and running freely down his neck. She stood there and watched as he consumed all thirty-two ounces of the water without stopping to take a breath. Amazing.

When he finished he licked his lips and smiled at her. "I guess I was thirsty. It's like that with me sometimes. When I get ahold of something I want bad, I almost become addicted to it."

She nodded as her heart thumped erratically. She thought of the many times they had made love in Daytona. Had he become addicted to her that week? If so, what had been her excuse? Had she been addicted to him as well?

"What are your plans for the rest of the day?" Linc's question broke into her meanderings.

"I'm going to edit an article I'm working on about Leo's."

Linc's brow rose. "You're doing an article on Leo's?"

"Yes. It's an article about the revived popularity of supper clubs. I chose Leo's as my subject since I know the Hardcastles personally."

Linc nodded. "How about dinner and a movie later?"

Raven had known that sooner or later he would get around to asking her out. And just as she'd been prepared for the question, she should have been prepared to give him an answer of "no." But for some reason she held back. She told herself that it would just be a movie and dinner. No big deal. She hadn't been out to a movie in ages, and besides, she would have to eat sometime. As long as she remained in control of the situation there could be no harm in it. She had learned by Falcon's mistakes. The harm came in falling in love, and she had no intentions of doing that.

"Dinner and a movie sounds nice as long you understand that there's nothing between us other than friendship, Linc."

He stared at her quietly. "You want us to go from being former lovers to just being friends? Is that what you really want, Raven?"

"Yes. I won't go out with you otherwise. It's a friendship thing or nothing. No more sending me stuff to remind me of our time together in Daytona. What we shared then is in the past and I want to keep it that way."

After a brief moment he nodded slowly. "If that's the way you want it, then that's the way it will be. Will seven o'clock tonight be OK?" he asked as he stood to leave.

"Yes."

He leaned down and instead of giving her the heated kiss she had come to expect, he tenderly brushed his lips against her cheek. "I'll see you later, friend."

She nodded and drew in a deep breath, knowing she was getting just what she'd asked for, a platonic relationship with him.

Somehow she regretted it already.

NINE

Raven sat in her office at Augustan Publishers and pounded away at the computer keyboard. Never before in her life had she felt so frustrated, and she had only herself to blame.

It was a day short of being a week since Linc had agreed to her stipulation that they be just friends, and ever since then she'd been a basket case. Not that he ever got out of line, mind you. He was playing the role of friend to the hilt. Just like she had asked him to do, he was treating her like a friend and not a former lover. But she found that although he may not be treating her like a former lover, she felt like one just the same.

And that was the crux of her problem.

As much as she tried, she just couldn't see him in a whole new light. She kept seeing him in the old one, where his sensuous beam had once rendered her blind. Each and every time she saw him brought forth emotions from within her that she couldn't explain no matter how many times her mind evoked objective reasoning.

With a frustrated sigh she stopped typing to think about all that had happened during the past week. After dinner Saturday night he had taken her to a movie. It was a romantic comedy that she totally enjoyed. Then he had taken her home, and after walking her to the door and giving her a chaste kiss to her lips he had left. She had lain awake in bed that night hungering for his touch, reliving their last heated kiss, and wondering if she had ruined her chances of ever getting another one.

Linc had evidently reached the conclusion that although she wanted a platonic relationship, he would not be out of sight nor out of mind. He had shown up unexpectedly on Sunday after she had come from early-morning church service, inviting her to brunch at Leo's. After leaving the club they had gone for a walk in the park; then he had returned her home, saying he would call the next day.

On Monday he had called her at work inviting her to dinner at his place. After showing her around his neatly furnished apartment he had fed her a delicious meal that he had cooked himself. After dinner they had sat around talking about how their day had gone and about current events.

On Tuesday they had met for lunch at a sandwich shop not far from her office, and then on Wednesday he had taken her to Open Mike Night at Leo's.

Thursday he had come to her house straight from work bringing Chinese food. After they had eaten, he had sat at her breakfast bar silently reviewing a case he was working on, while she sat at her kitchen table editing her article on Leo's. Although she hated admitting it, she had liked the idea of him being there and hadn't felt threatened by his presence. She couldn't remember the last time since college that any one man had dominated so much of her time. Usually when it came to dates, she rarely went for seconds. Going out once with a person was enough. But she had seen Linc each and every night without any thought of feeling crowded or having her style cramped. She didn't want to dwell on the fact that two people who were trying to have nothing more than a platonic relationship wouldn't be spending as much time together as they were.

The week she had just finished spending with him was totally different from the week they had spent together in Daytona. Then they had been lovers who hadn't been able to keep their hands off each other. Now it appeared that she was the only one suffering from the strong physical attraction she still felt for him, although she was pretending not to be.

And she didn't like playing the role of a pretender.

She didn't like pretending that she didn't notice the way he filled out a pair of jeans like nobody's business, or that when dressed in a suit he looked like the prime candidate for a magazine cover. She didn't like pretending that his smile didn't make her thighs clench, her heart rate increase, or her breath catch. Nor did she like pretending that that morning they had gone running together the scent of his hot sweat and the pure masculinity that clung to him didn't completely arouse her. And she sure as heck didn't like pretending that she preferred sitting across from him on a sofa chatting about world news to sitting in his lap while kissing him senseless. Or better yet, him kissing her senseless.

Raven released a frustrated sigh. Her week had gone from bad to worse, and the prospects of it improving weren't looking too hot. "Something gotta give," she muttered to herself as she closed down her computer to bring her workweek to an end. It was Friday and she and Linc had another date tonight. And she was going to make sure that when the evening was over he was just as miserable as she.

Linc paced the confines of Raven's apartment waiting for her to finish dressing. He had arrived a little earlier than planned, and she had come to the door with a towel wrapped around her all-too-seductive body. His tongue would have fallen out of his mouth had it not been attached.

"You're early," she'd said breathlessly after rushing to open the door for him. "I just got out of the shower. You're going to have to wait a few minutes."

Somehow he'd found his voice to say, "Uh, no problem."

When she turned around to go back into the bathroom he couldn't help noticing that the towel barely covered anything.

Linc stopped pacing and lowered himself onto the sofa, wondering how much more torture he could take. Surely Raven could see that their being just friends wasn't working. The physical attraction they had for each other was too strong.

"I'm ready."

Linc glanced up. His breath immediately got lodged in his throat. A ripple of pure male appreciation ran up his spine. Dressed in a short, curvy black dress, Raven looked fabulous. She had both the body and the legs for the outfit she had chosen to wear. He forced himself to stand, hoping he didn't embarrass himself when he did. "You look great, Raven."

She smiled at him. "Thank you. You look good yourself." That definitely wasn't a lie, she thought. He looked handsome in a white dinner jacket and black pants. They were attending a dinner party that his law firm was giving, and she had wanted to look nice.

A moment of silence stretched out between them before Raven cleared her throat. "Ready?" she asked.

"As ready as I'll ever be." Taking her arm, Linc led her out of the apartment.

"It was a nice party," Raven said to Linc as he walked her to her apartment door.

Linc thought his eyes would pop out of their sockets at seeing the way Raven's dress clung to her body in all the right places with every step she took. He had forgotten just how small her waist was and how curvy her rear end was until tonight. He coughed to clear his throat. "Yeah, it was, wasn't it? And I think you were the most gorgeous woman there."

"Thanks."

"When will your sisters get in tomorrow?"

Raven opened her purse to pull out her door key. "I'm expecting them in the morning."

When she leaned down to look into her purse for the key, he caught a glimpse of a hefty amount of cleavage. The one thing he had

main agenda

not forgotten was how sexy her bare breasts were. He coughed to clear his throat for a second time. "Well, I hope everything with the birthday party goes as planned."

"Me, too." She took a deep breath. "Good night, Linc."

"Good night."

He waited for her to open the door and go in, but Raven hesitated. "Your throat sounds dry. Would you like to come in for something to drink?"

He stared at her for a long, thoughtful minute before saying, "Sure." He followed her inside and to the kitchen, sitting down at the breakfast bar.

"What would you like? I have water, tea, and soda."

"A glass of water will do."

Raven nodded as she opened the cabinet to take down a glass. She then began filling it with water from the pitcher in her refrigerator. After handing him the ice-cold glass of water, she leaned against the counter to watch him take a few sips.

"How's the article you're doing on Leo's coming along?"

"It's almost finished." As though drawn by a sudden thought, she asked, "Would you like to read what I've put together so far?"

"Sure."

"OK. I'll be right back." Like a kid who was eager to show her parent a paper that had been graded with a perfect score, Raven raced out of the kitchen. She didn't want to think about why it was so important to show Linc what she had written. It just was. Maybe it was because a part of her wanted to prove to him that she was not like the other reporters he had come to detest. That had to be the reason, she inwardly told herself, because she had never shared her work with anyone, especially while it was in the prepublication stages.

Raven returned in no time and handed him the papers. He accepted them and sat back down at her breakfast bar and began reading. She tried not to make out his expression while he was reading, but she couldn't help but wonder what he thought of what she had written. It seemed it took forever before he had finished.

His eyes met hers. "This is an outstanding piece, Raven. You have a gift with words. You're a woman with a very special talent."

"Thank you." His opinion meant a lot. She didn't want to question the why of it just yet.

Nor did she want to question why she felt the need to kiss him, especially when he was staring at her with those deep, dark eyes of his. His gaze was seductive and magnetic, drawing her in closer. She suddenly leaned toward him, and bracing her hands on his thigh, she touched her lips to his and accepted that a platonic relationship between them had been doomed from the start. The passion that was always there surrounding them had the ability to consume completely, thoroughly, and burn hot.

Her senses immediately began spinning before she realized that he was not going to help her out with the kiss. *Fine, he can just sit there and be a stone, but I plan on getting my fill,* she thought as she closed her eyes and deepened the kiss. She'd been dying to taste him again. She let her tongue explore the recesses of his mouth as she ravaged it with a hunger that belied her outward calm.

And still he held back his tongue from her.

So she continued to assault his mouth, feeling the shivers racing through him with every stroke of her tongue, giving herself freely to the wantonness she felt and the fiery intimacy she was sharing with him as she feasted on his mouth.

She felt his arms tighten around her. She heard his breathing get heavy, then heavier. And then she felt him easing to his feet, without breaking her hold on his mouth. He pulled her closer to him, and her body felt every hard inch of him. She increased her assault as a sense of urgency drove her on.

She broke off the kiss for mere seconds, just to pull air in, then covered his mouth with hers once more. This time he joined in her attack.

Her senses reeled as if short-circuited when his tongue captured hers, taking over with demanding mastery and savage intensity. Nobody could kiss like Lincoln Corbain, she decided, giving her mouth up to his fiery possession. He took it, sending pleasure radiating through every part of her body.

As he further roused her passion she knew that his own had to be growing just as strong. Her emotions whirled and skidded as to how far she wanted him to go. And then she knew the answer. She wanted him to go all the way. She wanted him to make love to her.

So she relayed that message to him in her kiss.

He got it.

Pulling back, he sucked in a long gulp of air and looked down at her.

She nodded, meeting his unwavering gaze.

His mouth came down on hers at the exact moment he swept her off her feet and into his arms. Carrying her into the bedroom, he gently placed her on the bed. For the hundredth time that night, he thought she looked sexier than any woman had a right to be with the dress she had on. And he knew he hadn't been the only man at the party who had thought so.

Kneeling on the bed, he reached out for her and brought her close to him. Leaning down, he captured her parted lips. Tonight they would create new memories. That thought overwhelmed him. He had never felt such uncontrollable desire before. The other times they had come together, he had claimed her body. Tonight he wanted her heart and soul.

He pulled away long enough to undress her. When that was done he stood back and looked down at her as a growl of need erupted from deep within his throat. He quickly began removing his own clothing. Fumbling with his wallet, he took out a foil packet and ripped it open. Moments later, he went back to her. Driven by want and need, he ran his hands over her body, reacquainting himself with her soft flesh.

brenda jackson

Raven whimpered under his touch. It had been four years since she had been touched this way. It seemed all the heat and passion of her body had lain dormant until Linc had reentered her life. She felt him sliding his hand up and down her stomach, then back up again to her breasts to give them special attention.

Need suddenly tore into her like the rush of a mighty wind when she felt the warmth of his tongue replace his hands on her breasts. Moans escaped her lips as he lavished attention from one tip to the other. Her breath came out in short puffs and her fingers gripped his shoulders as he continued his assault.

"Linc..."

He heard the passionate plea in her voice. He wanted to delay everything and drag it out until the end but knew that would not be possible. Their desire, passion, and need for each other were too strong and too hot. But still he refused to be rushed. Slowly and completely, he continued his assault over every inch of her body, remembering the areas he could touch that would drive her nearly out of her mind.

Finally, when his need became just as great as hers, he placed his body over hers. "Raven." He groaned out her name like a dying man who was about to take his last breath.

Wanting what was about to come, Raven parted her lips and eagerly accepted the invasion of his tongue at the same time the hardness of him entered her. When he found her body tight, too tight, he tore his mouth away from hers and looked down into her eyes. The look in his gaze was questioning, confused.

She was torn between her desire to have him get on with it and finish what he had started and his need for her to explain why her body felt just as tight as it had the first time they'd made love. When she saw he was dead set on not moving...not even another delicious inch, she met his gaze and, drawing in a slow breath, said, "I haven't done this since that time in Daytona with you, Linc."

His gaze was intense as he stared deep into her eyes. He remained still as the meaning of her words sank in. Suddenly a deep sense of pride and elation swept over him. "Raven." Cupping her face in his hands, he whispered her name with deep emotion in his voice as he crushed her to his throbbing body, going deeper inside her. The magnitude of that connection made them both groan out loud as their mouths joined once again.

With tender care, he began moving inside her, savoring each stroke and letting his tongue move inside her mouth in the same slow rhythm. When the tempo of his rhythm increased, so did his lovemaking to her mouth. Their mouths mated just as wildly as their bodies.

He grasped her hips tightly, as if to keep her in one place as he pushed deeper within her. He groaned tightly when he felt the first sign of tremors race through her body. His mouth swallowed each and every moan she made as red-hot passion splintered them both. It was exquisite. It was torture.

It was everything he remembered and had dreamed of having again.

Finally tearing his mouth from hers, Linc gave out a loud growl of male pleasure when he felt himself emptying within her in an explosion that rocked their bodies endlessly. He pulled her closer to him, ignoring the pain of her fingernails as they dug deep into his shoulders.

Recovering after the last tremor left him, he slowly forced himself off Raven so his weight wouldn't hurt her. Sliding to her side, he pulled her against him, closing his arms around her.

"Linc?"

He rose slightly until he could look at her. Her face was flushed, her eyes were glazed, and her lips were swollen from the intensity of his kisses.

"Yes?"

She smiled and whispered, "You're incredible."

"No, sweetheart, you are." He pulled her back into his arms and began kissing her again as passion blazed to life between them once again.

He took her through another round of passionate lovemaking. It was as if he couldn't get enough of her and she, in turn, couldn't get enough of him. The four years that had separated them had dissolved and everything they had meant to each other that week in Daytona had returned tenfold. When there was no way they could survive another bout of lovemaking, he was content to rain kisses all over her face and neck, knowing that he neither could nor would let her out of his life again.

"I love you," he whispered, saying aloud what he had felt in his heart since seeing her again.

Raven's body stiffened, certain she had heard him wrong. Her mind began to spin. Love? He couldn't love her. She didn't want him to love her. She didn't have time for love in her life.

She pulled away from him and took deep intakes of breaths to get her heart rate and breathing back in sync. She looked up at him and the eyes returning her gaze were as soft as a caress.

"What is it, Raven? What's wrong?"

"You just said you loved me."

"Yes, I do love you."

Raven shook her head, not wanting to believe it, although he sounded as if he meant every word. "But you just saw me again two weeks ago."

"I fell in love with you in Daytona. I tried telling myself that there was no way I could have fallen in love with you in such a short amount of time, but I knew after returning to Louisiana that I had. That's the reason I went to Tallahassee looking for you."

She stared at him, surprised by what he had said. "You went to Tallahassee looking for me?"

"Yes, the day after I graduated from law school. But the school officials said you had graduated a few days earlier and had already left. They wouldn't give me information about your whereabouts."

He took a deep breath before continuing. "I went home to Tennessee and began working with my family. But I thought about you often. The only thing I had left was the memories of our time together. After a while I gave up hope of ever seeing you again. When I ran into you at Leo's last week I knew I was being given a second chance."

Raven lowered her gaze. When she raised it moments later she blinked away the moisture that had begun gathering there. "You're mistaken, Linc. You haven't been given a second chance. I don't want any part of a relationship with you or anyone. My work is the most important thing to me. It's all I need."

"What about love?" he asked, frowning.

"Love only complicates things. That's what happened with Falcon and John. They started out being lovers, then they fell in love, and after that everything went wrong."

"Only because you and your sisters think that falling in love is wrong," he said curtly. "It's the most natural thing in the world for a man to want a future with the woman he loves."

"Not if that woman doesn't want to have a future with him." She had to pull her gaze away from his face when she saw the hurt her words put there. "My work is my life and I don't want anything else in it, especially love." She paused and took a deep breath, hoping he had gotten her message loud and clear.

From the look on his face she knew he had. Raven looked at him, struck by the anger she saw there. She wondered if this was how John had handled Falcon's decision not to marry him.

Linc slowly got out of the bed and began getting dressed. Not one time did he look at her. It was only after he had all his clothes back on that he turned to her. He stood there next to the bed, quiet, his eyes dark, his jaws clenched. Finally, gathering his composure, he said softly, "I admire any person, man or woman, who wants to make their mark by being successful in their chosen field. But there will come a time when your work won't be all you need, Raven.

There will come a time when it won't give you everything you want. Without the one you love, life is meaningless, no matter how many goals you achieve. I love you."

"No," she said softly, lowering her head.

"Look at me," he whispered urgently. Leaning down, he took her chin in his hand and lifted it so their eyes could meet. "Can you honestly look me in the eye and say that I mean absolutely nothing to you? That what we shared tonight meant nothing?"

Raven swallowed, knowing that she couldn't, but she refused to admit it to him or anyone. "I want to be successful."

"And you will be. I've no doubt of that. I'll never ask you to give up anything for me."

Raven didn't answer for a brief moment. Then she spoke. "You can't say that for certain, and I can't take the chance that one day you might. Robin, Falcon, and I are a lot like our mother. She was a woman who loved her man with everything she had. She knew her daughters would probably do the same. If I were to love you, I'd gladly give up everything for you. I'd love you just that much. My mother loved my father so much that she gave him the world. In the end he gave her his behind to kiss. I can't and I won't let myself love anyone that much, Linc. I'm sorry."

He looked at her for a long moment before turning and walking out the door.

At the sound of the door closing Raven pressed her face to the pillow, letting her tears flow, knowing that she had done the very thing she had not wanted to do.

She had fallen in love with Lincoln Corbain.

Sweat of anger popped out across Linc's upper lip as he drove away from Raven's apartment. Although he admired her stubborn determination to succeed and not let anything or anyone stand in her way, he felt she was going about obtaining her dreams all wrong.

His hands on the steering wheel tightened. None of this made any sense. From what he'd been told, his own mother had once been a very vocal advocate for women's rights. She still was. She was also a very successful attorney. When she and his father had married they had formed a partnership. Neither one came first. They were both equal partners in their relationship. Why was it so hard for Raven to believe that that sort of relationship between two people who loved each other could exist?

Linc wasn't in the mood to go home just yet and found himself pulling into the parking lot of Leo's. It was an hour before closing, and he needed something a little stronger to drink than coffee.

Entering the establishment, he noted only one other individual sitting at the bar. Sliding onto the stool next to the man who was leaning down over his drink as if in deep thought, Linc waited for the bartender to take his order. "Scotch on the rocks."

Suddenly feeling like he was under someone's microscope, he turned to the man sitting next to him and found him staring. Linc frowned. "You got a problem?" he asked the man in a voice tinged with all the anger he felt.

The man's chuckle surprised him. "No, but it sounds like you do. Let me guess. One of the Anderson sisters has struck again."

Linc lifted his brow as he studied the man. Then it dawned on him as to who he was. John Augustan. Linc hadn't recognized him dressed in casual clothing.

Linc drew in a deep breath. He took a swallow of the drink the bartender had placed in front of him. If anyone understood how he felt it would be John Augustan. "Yeah, one of the Anderson sisters has struck again."

John met Linc's gaze as he lifted his drink and said somberly with a wry smile on his lips, "No pun intended but welcome...to the club."

TEN

Robin Anderson glanced around the room that had been decorated with balloons hanging from the ceiling and banners covering the walls before returning her gaze to her two sisters. They were waiting for her to make a birthday wish and blow out the twenty-eight candles on her birthday cake. Both Falcon and Raven had red puffy eyes that neither had managed to effectively hide behind carefully applied makeup.

Robin closed her eyes to make her wish, knowing what she was really about to do was say a birthday prayer instead. She needed to send up a prayer more than she needed to make a wish. She loved her sisters dearly, but knowing them, she realized they would not be open-minded and accept what she was about to tell them. Drawing in a deep breath, she let it back out over the cake. Hearing her sisters' cheers, she knew she had hit her mark. Opening her eyes, she saw that all twenty-eight candles had been blown out with one mighty breath.

It was only later, when the three of them were sitting on Raven's living room floor Indian-style, that Robin decided to drop the bomb: "I'm in love."

Falcon and Raven stopped eating their cake and drinking their wine and stared at her. By the look of horror on their faces she knew they had taken her news badly. There was no way she could soften the blow because there was more news to come. "I met him in Paris not long after I got there. His name is Franco and he's asked me to marry him and I've accepted." That last statement she knew was the finishing blow. It didn't take long for them to react.

"Whoa, wait just a minute here," Falcon was saying at the top of her voice. "You can't get married yet. You aren't even close to opening that cooking school you want in New York. You're at least three to four years away from doing that, Rob. How can you even think of love and marriage?"

"Falcon's right," Raven chimed in. "How can you?"

A flash of defiance appeared in Robin's eyes. "Haven't either of you heard what I just said? I love him. That's how I can do it. And now, after seeing you two today, I know more than ever that I'm making the right decision."

Both Raven and Falcon set their plates and wineglasses down. "What do you mean by that?" Raven asked, pulling her eyebrows together in a frown.

"Just look at you two. Falcon's been in a state of funk ever since she turned down John's marriage proposal. I found myself not wanting to call her anymore because each time I did she would start crying, and it's been over a year."

Robin then turned her full attention to Raven. "And I don't know who your lover boy is, but by the looks of you, it seems you've also given him the boot, and you're suffering because of—"

"It's Linc," Raven muttered in exasperation, getting to her feet.

Robin lifted her gaze to Raven. "Ooh, you mean to say you've run into Lincoln Corbain again, after all these years?"

Raven thrust her hands into the pockets of her jeans, frowning. "Yes."

Falcon stood and glared at her. "And you didn't tell us? Why?"

Raven sighed. Her sisters knew all about the week she had spent with Linc in Daytona four years ago. And they had known that he must have meant a lot to her for her to have gone to bed with him.

She had always sworn that the first guy she slept with would be someone she loved. "I was hoping he'd go away."

"And he didn't?" Robin asked.

"No." The word got caught in Raven's throat for a moment. She swallowed to let it down before continuing. "Not until last night. I sent him away."

Robin nodded. "So that's why you've been crying."

"She's been crying?" Falcon asked in alarm, walking over to Raven to study her face.

Robin smiled, amused by the question Falcon had asked. "You've been crying so much yourself this past year, Falcon, that it's not obvious to you when someone else has red puffy eyes. To you it's a normal look."

Falcon glared at Robin. "That's not funny."

Robin's smile widened. "You're right; it's not funny. It's pathetic. And that's the reason I have all intentions of marrying Franco. I refuse to go through life miserable and crying like the two of you have decided to do."

"What about your dreams? Your plans?" Raven asked in desperation.

"What about what Mama drilled into us?" Falcon added.

Robin shook her head. Sometimes she thought she should have been the oldest of the three. Falcon could take the smallest piece of information and run with it—usually in the wrong direction. "First of all, I still have every intention of pursing my dreams. Franco is also a master chef, who wants to share my dream. It's our desire to open a school together." She shifted her position to stretch out her legs as she gazed at her two sisters standing over her. "And furthermore, Mama's drilling was not about men in general. It was about the three of us, as individuals, as women who have choices and dreams. She wanted us to fulfill our dreams and not let anyone stop us from doing so. She died believing that she had given us every means in her power for us to be successful. And she did. I'm not giving up my dream to marry Franco. I'm expanding it to include him."

"I don't believe this," Falcon said, her tone tinged with anger. "Just like that, you think you have all the answers. Don't you think that I did a lot of soul-searching before I turned down John's marriage proposal? Don't you think if there was any way I could have made it work I would have?"

Falcon's dark eyes reflected her pain, and Robin knew she had to tread lightly. "I'm sure you did, Falcon. But your situation was a little bit more complicated than mine. John wanted you to move here to D.C. with him, which meant losing the clientele you had worked so hard to build. With Franco, I don't have that problem. We both want to live in New York. But..."

Falcon frowned. "But what?"

"But regardless of the reason, I think if I had loved John as much as I know for certain that you do, I would have figured out a way to make it work."

Falcon's eyes flared from the sting of her sister's remark. "I couldn't do it."

Robin nodded. "Then why are you still crying over spilt milk? Why haven't you gotten over it and moved on?"

Robin knew those questions were stabbing at her sister's heart. She then turned her attention to Raven. "And what about you, Raven? You either want to be with Linc or not. You either love him or you don't. I suggest that you be happy and love him and still be successful, or you can take the advice you *think* Mama gave you and not love him and be miserable but successful."

After a lengthy silence and a sip of her wine, Robin said, "We all saw the movie *Mahogany*. Didn't either of you get anything from it other than a good drool over Billy Dee Williams? The whole moral of the movie was that success is nothing unless you have the person you love to share it with."

Standing up, Robin said, "So, sisters dear, on my twenty-eighth birthday I'm willing to be the first Anderson sister to walk out in faith and love. Our father was heartless. He was a jerk. He was a dog. But I don't believe all men are like him. I'm blessed to have met and fallen in love with one who's not. I believe if Mama was alive, after meeting Franco she would agree. And I also believe that she would have been happy for me."

She walked over to her sisters and took their hands in hers. "I don't need your blessings, nor do I need your permission. But I do want the two of you to be happy for me and accept that I love this man and that I'm putting our future plans in God's hands. And whatever the future holds, thanks to Mama I'll be prepared either way."

She kissed both of her sisters on the cheeks. Smiling softly, she said, "I'll see you guys later."

"Hey, where do you think you're going?" Falcon asked as she watched her sister head for the door, pausing long enough to grab her purse off the couch.

"To the hotel. Franco should have arrived by now and checked in."

"He's here?" Raven asked, amazed at the turn of events. Granted, Robin had always been the most rebellious of the three, but all of them had agreed at one time or another that men and success didn't mix. Looks like Willow Anderson's middle child was now singing a different tune.

"Of course he's here. It's my birthday and I want him to meet my two closest friends—my sisters. But first, he and I have to celebrate my birthday in style, so don't wait up. You can both meet him in the morning. I'm inviting him to breakfast." With that said, Robin left, closing the door behind her.

"Well, what do you think of that?" Raven asked Falcon with utter amazement in her voice.

"I hate to admit it, but what I think is that Robin may have the right idea," Falcon said, shaking her head. "Hell, she has a man. We're the ones who don't."

The corners of Raven's lips lifted in a soft smile. "Are you insinuating that she's a lot smarter than we are?"

"I wouldn't go that far. Robin is just more daring. She's a risk-taker." Falcon couldn't help but laugh. "Always has been, and turning one year older hasn't changed her."

"I still can't believe she actually left her own birthday party," Raven was saying as she and Falcon took down the last banner.

"I can't believe she left the two of us here to clean up this mess," Falcon grumbled. "OK, what's next? And don't you dare suggest that we go to one of those video stores and get a copy of *Mahogany* and watch it again."

Raven grinned as she looked at her sister. "Don't worry; that's the furthest thing from my mind."

With no hesitation Falcon added, "Same here. But I have been thinking about what Robin said."

Raven released a deep sigh. "Me, too. You still love John, don't you?"

"Yes, terribly. Robin was right. I've been miserable this past year. But I think it's too late. He probably hates me. For all I know he may have someone else in his life now."

Raven knew she could at least get her sister out of her misery for one day. "He doesn't. He's turned into a workaholic. Just like you."

Falcon folded up the birthday tablecloth. "What about you and Linc, Raven? Is there any hope there?"

Raven tilted her head, her expression somber. "No. I said some pretty harsh words to him about not wanting a relationship with him. I told him in no uncertain terms that I didn't want him to be a part of my life and that my plans for the future came before anything, including him."

"Do you regret what you said?"

"Yeah, now I do. Robin's got me to thinking, too. I love him so much, Falcon."

At that moment the phone rang and Raven reached out and picked it up. "Hello."

"OK, you guys, here's the deal," Robin said, coming in over the phone line. "I just left Leo's. I thought I'd drop by and say hello to the Hardcastle twins since I had to pass by there to get to the hotel. I saw John and he was dining with another guy, a good-looking brother. When I asked Tyrell who the brother was, he said the guy was your friend Linc, Raven. I left Leo's before either of them saw me."

Raven raised a brow. "You saw John and Linc together at Leo's?"

"What about John?" Falcon asked, rushing over to where Raven stood with the phone glued to her ear. "Who are you talking to?"

"It's Robin," Raven whispered, taking the time to tell her sister. "She stopped by Leo's and claims to have seen John and Linc eating dinner together."

Falcon frowned. "They know each other?"

"I introduced them a couple of weeks ago, but as far as I know they haven't come into contact since then," Raven said. She then turned her attention back to the phone. "Are you sure you saw John and Linc?"

"I'd know John Augustan anywhere, and as for your Linc, I can only go by what Tyrell told me. According to him, John and Linc were at Leo's together late last night. They were the last two customers who left the bar before closing."

Raven nodded. Evidently Linc had left her place and gone straight to Leo's and had run into John there.

"What is she saying?" Falcon wanted to know, so Raven told her.

"So why is she calling us?" Falcon asked.

Raven shrugged. "Why are you calling and telling us about it?" she asked Robin the same question Falcon had asked her.

"Because if either of you are having second thoughts about your future and the men you want to share it with, I suggest you two get your butts in gear and hightail it to Leo's and do whatever you have

main agenda

to do to get your men back before some other sistahs scoop them up." After that blunt suggestion Robin hung up.

Raven placed the receiver back on the hook. "What did she say?" Falcon asked.

Raven relayed her sister's message to Falcon.

Falcon gave her a level stare. "Just who does Robin think she is, suggesting that we do something outrageous like that?" she asked vehemently.

Raven shook her head, grinning. "She's the one who doesn't have the red puffy eyes." Grabbing her sister by the arm, she pulled her toward the bedroom. "Come on; let's get dressed and go to Leo's. And maybe, just maybe, if we're lucky, we'll be able to win the hearts of our men back."

Raven and Falcon entered Leo's. The place was crowded, which was no surprise. It was Saturday night and Earth, Wind & Fire was providing the live entertainment, jamming out their classic hit "Let's Groove."

"I think we should split up," Falcon said, glancing around the room.

Raven gave her a skeptical look. "You think that's a good idea?"

Falcon looked at her sister and nodded slowly and smiled. "Yes. I don't want you around if I have to resort to begging."

Raven chuckled as she laced Falcon's fingers with hers, tightening her hold on them before letting them go. "Good luck, Sis."

"Same to you."

"What if neither of us are successful in meeting our goals here tonight?" Raven asked as she pulled in a deep breath for courage.

"We *will* be successful. If not on the first try, then maybe the second, or the third, or the fiftieth. And the reason is that the Anderson sisters will always be successful in their endeavors. Willow Anderson willed it to be so. Now scat."

Raven sure hoped Falcon was right. Turning, she walked off

alone toward the area where Earth, Wind & Fire had begun performing another of their classic hits, "Saturday Night."

Linc saw Raven the minute she walked in. The deep feeling of love and desire he still felt for her even after what she'd said to him last night didn't stun him. It was the words she hadn't said that had meant a hell of a lot more. She had not been able to look in his eyes and say that she cared nothing for him. That still gave him hope.

Sighing deeply, he turned to the man sharing his table, "Raven just walked in," he said to John. "She came in with another woman who I believe is her sister. Is that the birthday girl or *your* woman?" Linc asked, nodding his head in the direction where the other woman had gone, choosing a table on the other side of the room from Raven.

John's gaze followed Linc's and his eyes lit on Falcon. Pain clutched at his heart. "That's Falcon. And she's *not* my woman." He frowned. "I wonder why they're sitting at separate tables."

Linc shrugged. "A sisters' spat perhaps?"

"Not hardly," John said, taking a sip of his wine. "They might disagree sometime, but never to the point of anything separating them. They stick together like glue."

Linc nodded. "I wonder where the third one is. The birthday girl."

"Who knows about those sisters, and frankly, who cares?"

Linc shook his head, deciding not to remind John that *he* cared. They both did. If they didn't care, the two of them would not have stayed at Leo's until the place closed last night, nursing their pain with drinks. "Well, don't look now, but the one you claim is not *your* woman has seen you and is headed this way."

Linc chuckled at the curse he heard flow from John's lips. A few moments later a very attractive woman with features closely resembling Raven's stood before their table.

"Hi, John. It's good seeing you again."

Something about the way she said the words made John look up from studying his wine. His gut twisted. Falcon Anderson was more beautiful than ever. Then he remembered that this was the woman he had loved but who had chosen a career over his love. "Falcon, I would say 'Likewise,' but it wouldn't be true. It's not good seeing you again. What the hell are you doing here?"

Deciding that this should be a private conversation, Linc stood. "Hello, I'm Linc Corbain." He offered Falcon his hand in a warm handshake. "I was just about to leave, so you can have my seat."

Linc's statement gave Falcon pause. He couldn't leave before Raven got a chance to talk to him.

"Hold up, Corbain; I think I'll call it a night myself. There's no reason for me to stick around," John said coldly, staring at Falcon.

Falcon's eyes reflected pain from John's remark. But then the look in his eyes made her heart ache. She had hurt him and he was retaliating in the only way he knew how, by trying to hurt her in return.

"John, can we talk?" she asked quietly.

"Talk? Why do you want to talk to me?" John asked gruffly, almost growling the words. "I think you said all you needed to say a year ago."

"I thought I had, too."

Something in Falcon's voice made John uneasy, cautious, and curious. "OK, Falcon, you talk and maybe, depending on what you have to say, I might listen."

Linc decided that now was the time to leave the two people alone and headed for the door.

Raven's heart sank as she watched Linc leave the club. She knew he had seen her when, for the briefest of moments, their eyes met across the room before he walked out the door.

"Would you like to order dinner?"

The waiter's question interrupted her thoughts. She looked at the door Linc had walked out of a minute ago. "No, I've changed my mind. I'm leaving."

She glanced across the room and saw Falcon sitting at the table with John. Feeling certain she was not leaving her sister stranded, Raven didn't waste any time as she grabbed her purse and walked out of the club.

On instinct Raven drove to Linc's apartment, hoping that's where he had gone. She released a breath of relief when she pulled into his apartment complex and saw his car parked in the space he usually used.

"You can do this, Raven," she told herself as she parked her car alongside his and got out. "He's worth it and more."

Taking another deep breath, she knocked on his door.

Linc looked startled when he opened the door to find her there. "Raven, what are you doing here?"

Raven breathed in slowly. He had removed his shirt and stood in the doorway. Her gaze dropped from his bare chest and moved lower to his flat, hard stomach, then lower still to the unsnapped top of his pants. She sucked in a deep breath and forced her gaze back to his face. "I need to talk to you."

Linc studied her with an odd expression on his face before moving aside to let her enter, closing the door behind her. "What is it you want to talk about?"

She met his gaze. "It's about last night and—"

"Linc, sweety, where are your towels?" a woman asked, coming into the room. "Oh, sorry, I didn't know someone was here," she said, studying Raven with as much interest as Raven was studying her.

Raven's gaze took in everything about the very beautiful woman, even the fact that she was only wearing a bra and a slip. Raven's anger flared at the thought that the reason Linc had rushed from the club was that he'd had a woman waiting here for him.

"No, I'm the one who's sorry," Raven said before rushing out of the apartment without looking back. She went straight to her car and got in. She tried ignoring Linc's hard knock on her car window as she tried putting her car in reverse. She didn't want him to see her cry.

When another car that was coming into the apartment complex blocked her from backing up, she had no choice but to roll her window down. Her pride dictated that she do so.

"What do you want, Linc?"

He pulled a shirt over his head before stooping down beside the car's open window. "Why did you run out like that?"

Raven was speechless. She would think it would have been pretty obvious to him why she'd left the way she did. Evidently it wasn't, so she decided to tell him. "You had company."

"I don't consider Sydney company, especially when she pops up unexpectedly. But I'd like for you to meet her."

Raven couldn't believe his nerve. "You want me to meet *her*!"

Linc frowned as he stood. "Is there any reason you don't want to meet my sister?"

Raven's mouth dropped open. "Your sister?"

Linc's frown deepened as he studied her. "Yeah, my sister. She arrived this evening from Memphis." He crossed his arms over his chest. "Who did you think she was?"

Raven didn't want to tell him what she had thought. But she didn't have to. The deep coloring of embarrassment on her face gave her away.

Linc leaned over and rested both his hands on the opening in her door. "You actually think I'd leave your bed last night and find another woman to put into mine tonight, Raven? I told you last night that I loved you, and when a man loves one woman he doesn't sleep around with another."

Elation spread through Raven as a rush of air entered her lungs, reminding her to breathe. "You still love me?"

Her question surprised him. "Of course I still love you. When you really love someone you don't fall out of love with them like that," he said, snapping his fingers for effect. "Besides, I have no intentions of giving up on you that easily, Raven. I made a promise to myself to not let you walk out of my life a second time, although I was about ready to do just that until I ran into John last night. Talking to him made me realize his mistakes in dealing with your sister."

"Which were?"

Linc stooped back down to be on eye level with her. "Giving up on Falcon too quickly and too easily. I decided not to make the same mistake with you. I figured that sooner or later I'd succeed in wearing down your resistance."

Raven smiled softly, believing that eventually he would have. "It took Robin's announcement that she's getting married to make me and Falcon see the mistakes we were making. I love you, Linc. I first fell in love with you in Daytona and then fell in love with you all over again that night I saw you in Leo's." She leaned over out the car window and tasted his lips. "I love you and I *will* be successful because I'll have everything I've ever wanted or dreamed of having and more."

Linc stood up and opened her car door. "Slide over, baby," he said huskily, easing into the car as she scooted over into the passenger seat. "Do you know a place where we can go to be alone?"

Raven gave him a sensuous smile. "My place. I doubt either of my sisters will be returning there tonight. What about your sister?"

Linc grinned. "She's a big girl who can take care of herself." He paused before starting the car and turned to her. "Come here and tell me again."

Raven scooted over closer to him, glad that her car had bench seats. "I love you and I want it all—you, my dreams, your babies, the works."

Linc pulled her into his arms. "And I'm going to make sure you get it all. Starting tonight."

EPILOGUE

Six Months Later

Sunlight poured into the room through the curtains. Raven yawned and stretched, still feeling tired and still not wanting to open her eyes just yet. Yesterday had been such a busy day. A beautiful triple wedding had made it understandably so. But she, Falcon, and Robin had survived and were gloriously content with sharing the rest of their lives with the men they loved.

After an elaborate wedding followed by a just as elaborate reception in one of the large rooms set aside for parties at Leo's, Robin and Franco had flown to Europe to honeymoon on the Riviera. French and African-American, Franco Marcus Renoir was a very handsome man, and Raven knew he would make her sister happy.

Raven smiled thinking about Falcon and John, who had left the wedding reception heading for California. After a week of honeymooning there, they were flying to Hawaii for an additional week. Lines of happiness had replaced Falcon's red puffy eyes.

Raven then thought about her and Linc. They had flown into Daytona Beach to spend a few days here before driving to Port Canaveral to catch their cruise ship for a week's cruise in the Caribbean for their honeymoon.

The past six months had been wonderful for them. She had flown to Tennessee with him over the Thanksgiving holiday to meet his family, a family who had welcomed her with open arms. She had also convinced Linc to rethink his decision not to enter politics. She knew his fairness and honesty were assets he could offer the people he would represent. Besides, like she'd told him, she could easily add being a politician's wife to her agenda.

Raven barely caught her breath when she felt the sheet covering her naked body slowly being brushed aside. She didn't want to open her eyes just yet. She preferred just lying there and enjoying the sensations she knew her husband could make her feel whenever he touched her.

Her heart began pounding furiously in her chest when she felt Linc's strong, firm hands slide over her, beginning with the calves of her feet and working their way upward, to her breasts, letting his lips follow the path of his fingers.

She wondered how much longer she could pretend sleep. Undoubtedly she was about to find out when his wet, hot tongue latched onto a nipple and feasted hungrily before moving to the other one.

The assault he was making on her body was one she could not bear any longer. She knew she was a goner when he moved from her breasts and attacked her mouth, making love to it in his own special way. She automatically wound her arms tightly around his neck as she mated her tongue with his.

"Open your eyes and look at me, Raven," he whispered as he pulled back from their kiss and moved his body over hers.

Raven opened her eyes and met his gaze the exact moment he entered her, hard and fast, lifting her hips to receive all of him, joining their bodies as one.

The look of wanting, desire, and love in his eyes inflamed her, making her wrap her legs around him to enjoy the moment of being a part of the man she loved—her husband.

"I love you," she whispered to him as waves of heat consumed her with every thrust he made into her body.

"And I love you," he said huskily before throwing his head back and releasing a deep, guttural sound from his throat as he emptied his seed deep into her womb, glorying in the feel of having unprotected sex with his wife. They tumbled over into the throes of ecstasy together, savoring every moment until at last his mouth moved back over hers, absorbing her whimpers of pleasure.

When it felt like everything had been drained from him, Linc collapsed against the pillows, taking her with him and shifting their positions so his weight would not hurt her. Pulling her closer into his arms, he cradled her to him and kissed the top of her head. "This is where it all began, isn't it, Mrs. Corbain?"

Raven smiled against his chest, liking the sound of her new name. She rose slightly to look down at him, the man who had come to mean everything to her. "Yes, right here in this very room." They had managed to get the same room at the hotel where they had spent one hell of a passionate week four years ago.

"And there's a very good possibility this is even the same bed," she added, grinning. "At least it feels like it. The one thing I remember about the bed is that it had very good springs."

Linc laughed as he reached up and touched her cheek. His eyes then became dark and passionate. "We're making new memories to keep for always."

"Yes, for always. And I have a new main agenda," she said softly.

"Oh, yeah, what is it?"

"Loving you," Raven said, leaning down toward his lips. "My main agenda is loving you, Lincoln Corbain."

strictly business

A man who refuses to admit his mistakes can never be successful.
But if he confesses and forsakes them, he gets another chance.

—PROVERBS 28:13 (THE LIVING BIBLE)

PROLOGUE

Mitchell Farrell was man enough to admit he had made a few mistakes in his lifetime. But he had absolutely no intentions of making the same mistakes twice. With a determined smile he snapped his seat belt in place and settled into the flight that would take him to Houston.

Never in his life had he been so determined to achieve a goal—a goal some would think was impossible with all the obstacles he faced. But he was a man with a plan.

A plan to get his wife back.

As his private jet cleared the Los Angeles runway and tilted its wings toward Texas, he settled back in his seat and remembered the first time he had seen Regina Grant on the campus of Texas Southern University seven years ago; the mere sight of her had taken his breath away. It hadn't been like him to fall hard and fast, but against her he hadn't stood a chance. No other woman had taken such hold of his mind and body like she had. She completely captured his heart.

During his teenage years he had grown up dirt poor, so he'd been determined to one day have wealth and power at his fingertips, determined that nothing and no one would get in the way of his achieving that, especially a woman. He had pretty much kept that resolve until his final year in grad school, when he had met Gina. She had been in her senior year of college. He had been lost the first time they'd made eye contact. That day she'd become as basic to him as breathing.

For the longest while he'd thought he could simply add her to the list of things he wanted in life, which was why he had married her less than a year later. He soon realized that marriage to Gina was more of a challenge than he'd anticipated. He could not get her to understand the driving force of his need to make it to the top at the cost of everything else—including the baby she desperately wanted. Their marriage hadn't worked out, and after four years it had ended. That was a huge mistake. He should never have let that happen.

He had been a fool to let her walk out of his life, an even bigger fool to have placed more emphasis and importance on making it to the top than holding their marriage together. And the main reason he'd walked away so easily was that the amount of love he'd felt for her had disturbed him. He had never counted on loving any woman so intensely that it made him lose his focus.

It had taken him two lonely years after their divorce to accept just how much he had loved her and that success was nothing without her. He wanted and needed her back in his life. For him the tragedy of September 11, 2001, served as a blunt reminder that you could be here one day and gone the next, and that when you left this world you couldn't take anything with you, especially not the material things you had worked hard to accumulate.

He had been in New York that day for a meeting at the World Trade Center with a business associate and friend, Tom Swank. But a phone call that morning from his office in Los Angeles had delayed him at his hotel. Quite frankly, that phone call had saved his life—but nothing had saved Tom's. That had been his first wake-up call to reexamine who he was and what he was. In the end, he'd decided he didn't like himself very much. At thirty-five he'd realized that his priorities were screwed up and knew he had to take whatever measures necessary to get them back in order.

He was no longer the workaholic he used to be; no longer endlessly driven by success. The only thing that drove him now was the tremendous task he faced of convincing Gina to give him another chance. And if given that chance, he would give her every damn thing she had ever asked for: the honeymoon they'd never gotten around to taking, the baby she'd always wanted, and more time for them to spend together since he'd always been constantly on the go. A part of him refused to believe it was too late, that things were completely over between them.

So he was headed to Houston with a plan. And it was a plan he intended to make work, by any means necessary.

ONE

There were certain things that a woman just couldn't forget.

For instance, she could not forget the time she progressed from girl into woman, the time she began wearing her first bra, her first date, the first time she fell in love, and the first time she had made love.

Gina was reminded of the latter two as she sat across from the man who had played an instrumental role in both: her ex-husband, Mitch Farrell. She tried to concentrate on what he was saying and not on the memories invading her mind. Memories of naked bodies and silken sheets, of lovemaking sessions that had seemed to last forever, of orgasms of the highest intensity that had no endings.

Seeing Mitch again reminded her of all those things. It also reminded her of pain still lingering deep within, and was a rude awakening that even two years after their divorce, he was not yet out of her system, not fully out of her heart. That thought made her rather uncomfortable.

"What about it, Gina?" Mitch asked softly after taking a leisurely sip of his wine, interrupting her thoughts. The eyes that met his were curious yet reserved.

They sat at a corner table in Sisters, a well-known restaurant in downtown Houston. On weekends it was usually filled to capacity, but tonight—a weeknight—the amount of people dining was a good number: not too many to be considered crowded and not too few to be considered cozy. The atmosphere was relaxing, comfortable and tranquil.

"Why me, Mitch? Why have you come to me with such a generous offer?" she finally asked him, her brows knit.

He smiled before his gaze shifted to the magazine in front of him, having expected her question. "I think the answer to that is obvious. That piece you did on Jake Madaris and Diamond Swain was outstanding and says it all."

She smiled. "Thank you."

When wealthy rancher Jake Madaris and movie actress Diamond Swain had announced to the world they were married, and had been for nearly two years, everyone had wanted their story. It had been Gina Grant Farrell, a twenty-eight-year-old freelance writer and family friend of the Madaris family, whom the couple had gotten to do the exclusive interview and write the article. Before then, Gina had done a number of jobs for various publications but the piece on Jake and Diamond for *People* magazine had brought her skill as a journalist into the national spotlight.

"And you know how I am when it comes to my privacy, Gina," he continued. "You know me better than anyone, and I think it's time people knew the real Mitch Farrell as well. I want you to be the one to tell my story because I know you'll be fair and objective."

Gina inhaled slowly. Yes, she did know him and at one time she'd felt she had known him better than anyone. But that had been before the demise of their marriage. After that she'd wondered if she'd really known him at all. She silently admitted there were times when she thought there were things about his past that he refused to share with her. But the one thing she did know was that Mitch wasn't the cold, hard, self-made millionaire the media made him out to be. He was fast becoming one of the largest land developers in the country, and everyone wanted to know all they could about the elusive, wealthy divorcé who'd made his mark in real estate.

"People might think I'd be *less* objective since we *were* once married," she finally said.

"Or they may think that since we were married you would have the inside scoop if there were any. I want my story told, Gina, so people can stop speculating."

Again she was surprised. The Mitch she knew wouldn't have cared what anyone thought. She had been a journalist long enough to know that people liked reading whatever they could get their hands on about the rich and famous—regardless of whether the information was true. "The speculation may not stop, Mitch. It may only increase."

"I know, but I want to put it in writing once and for all that I live a very normal and very dull life that doesn't include a different woman in my bed every night."

Gina took a sip of her wine. She was glad to hear that. Although she hadn't wanted to believe what she'd read in the newspapers and tabloids, the thought that he had become a womanizer had bothered her more than it should have.

She sighed as she placed her wineglass down. There was a lot to consider. She had thought about him a lot over the past few weeks after hearing he had returned to Houston on business. He had moved to California within months after their divorce.

He had come to town to discuss a business deal with Madaris Enterprises, a company formed by the Madaris brothers—Justin, Dex, and Clayton—to fulfill their dream of building an exclusive office park that would house the fifteen-story Madaris Building as well as a cluster of upscale shops. She had been surprised to get a call from Mitch yesterday, inviting her to dinner to discuss a business proposition. The last time they had seen or spoken to each other had been at her brother Trevor's wedding reception almost a year ago. She knew Trevor and Mitch had stayed in touch over the past two years.

Her mind went back to the offer he'd made. She knew any journalist would jump at the chance to do an exclusive with Mitch. He was a man who seldom did interviews. And not only was he willing to do one, but he wanted her to be part of it.

And that was the crux of her problem. That was the reason she felt so tense. There was no way she could spend any amount of time with him and not remember what they had once meant to each other. Although they had agreed to remain friends after their divorce, all it took was for her to look at him to know that even after all this time she was still attracted to him. He was still handsome, sexy, and masculine, with eyes so compelling they not only penetrated your soul but had the ability to draw you in. Even now when he looked at her, his eyes went almost black. They were just that intense, dark, and magnetic.

She sighed deeply. The effect Mitch still had on her was startling and played havoc on her raw nerve endings. He could still make her body ache in certain places. The interview would take a good week to complete if she did it in stages, like the one she'd done on Jake and Diamond. How would she survive Mitch Farrell for an entire week?

"Where will the interview take place?" she asked, breaking the silence between them and trying not to notice his hands. They were hands that used to give her hours upon hours of earth-shattering pleasure. Of all the things they used to disagree about while married, sex was never an issue; the both of them had had overpassionate hormones. The main reason they had decided to go ahead and marry so soon after they'd met was that they had found it hard to keep their overheated sexuality under control. It was during those times in his arms, while they were able to bring each other to a second orgasm while still trembling from the effects of the first, that she'd felt so much an integral part of him. Even now, a part of her body tingled just thinking about how they used to make love all night long.

"My ranch."

Gina raised an arched brow when she realized he had answered her question. "Your ranch? In Los Angeles?"

He gave her a smile that had the ability to actually reach out and touch her, which was bad timing after just having thoughts of them making love. "No, the one here in Houston," he murmured softly.

She stared at him through the lingering fog of his words, confused. "You own a ranch here in Houston?"

He knew that information had surprised her. "Yes. Actually it's a few miles out, a hundred acres of land in Fresno. I bought it six months ago. Are you familiar with the area?"

Gina nodded in stunned shock. Yes, she was familiar with the area. It was a beautiful section that was far enough away from the hustle and bustle of downtown Houston but close enough by way of the interstate. The land, rich in dark Texas soil with large oak trees and lush green grass, was beautiful and scenic. She knew Trevor and his wife, Corinthians, were thinking about buying land in the area to build a new home.

"How are your parents, Gina? I understand they're back together."

Gina refused to let him smoothly change subjects, especially after the bomb he'd just dropped. "Yes, after nearly twenty years Mom and Dad are back together and are ecstatic about being grandparents," she said, thinking about her three-month-old nephew. Then, without missing a beat, she asked, frowning, "Why did you buy a ranch in Fresno, Mitch?"

He met her gaze. "Because I'm moving back here."

She frowned some more. "Why?"

Rather than tell her the truth, the absolute truth, Mitch decided to give her the watered-down version. "I miss Texas, Gina. Houston especially. Although I was born in Beaumont, I consider Houston my home since I spent the majority of my time growing up here. Is it so unusual for someone to want to return home?"

She considered his question thoughtfully before responding. "No, but you used to hate Houston because of the things you didn't want to remember." They were things he had never shared with her. "Is it easier to come back now that you've gotten everything you wanted in life?"

A part of Mitch knew that now was not the time to tell her he hadn't gotten everything since he didn't have her. Nor was it the time to tell her that he'd found out the hard way he had never been satisfied. The more he had obtained, the greedier he had become. But in the end he'd realized material possessions and success weren't everything. Having someone you loved and someone who loved you were. And he did love the beautiful woman sitting across from him. He loved everything about her. He loved the way she wore her hair now, an abundance of shoulder-length, precision-cut layers. And he loved her full lips, the high cheekbones on her cocoa-colored complexion, and the dark brown eyes that conveyed sensuality and allurement all rolled into one.

"No, that's not the reason, Gina," he said as the corners of his lips lifted in a smile. "I guess you can say that I've come back to find myself. That's one of the reasons I want you to do the article. Talking about it, getting it out with someone I trust will help. That's one mistake I regret making while married to you. I didn't openly communicate with you as I should have."

Gina said nothing for a long time. This was definitely not the same Mitch. He might look the same, but his views had definitely changed. What he had just confessed was true. He hadn't openly communicated with her because he'd been too busy making it to the top. Being successful and having money and power were all that had mattered. He had wanted those things more than he had wanted her. What had bothered her most about their breakup was how easily he had walked away from their marriage without putting up a fight.

"I need to think about it, Mitch."

"That's fine, but I'd like to know something within a week if possible."

She nodded and glanced at the magazine that was still in front of him. A week was plenty of time for her to really think things through. "All right. I'll let you know something by then."

She then looked up at him and again got caught up in the way he was looking at her. His gaze was touching her; she could feel it through the clothes she was wearing. The deep penetration of his eyes was hot. She let the scope of her vision run lightly over his face, everywhere except the deepness of his dark eyes. She took in the rich chocolate coloring of his skin, the sharp cheekbones, the jutting chin with its dimpled cleft, the full lips. She inhaled deeply when she felt deep sexual awareness and knew she had to make sure his offer was just what it was. She could not fill her head with illusions that it was more than that. For a moment she tried reading his thoughts, but as usual his expression was unreadable.

"This interview is strictly business, right, Mitch?" she decided to ask.

Mitch lifted his wineglass and met her stare before taking a sip. "Yes, Gina, this is strictly business," he said smoothly. He then tipped the wineglass to his lips and while the cool wine slipped down his throat he thought, *Strictly* unfinished *business.*

TWO

Gina heard her phone ring the minute she walked into her home. Locking the door behind her, she quickly crossed the room to answer it. "Hello?"

"How did things go tonight?"

Gina smiled upon hearing her sister-in-law's voice. The woman her brother had married almost a year ago had become the sister she'd never had. With only a three-year difference in their ages, she and Corinthians had quickly formed a bond that was priceless.

Easing onto the sofa, Gina pulled off her earrings and adjusted the phone to a more comfortable position. "They went okay, I imagine, given the fact that I sat across from Mitch hot and bothered the entire time. Isn't that pathetic?"

"No," Corinthians answered softly, not trying to mask the smile in her voice. "Considering that you still love him, I don't think it's pathetic at all."

Gina released a long, deep sigh. "I never said I still loved Mitch."

"You didn't have to. I heard love in your voice the first time you told me about him. And if you'll recall, you were rather upset that Trevor had invited him to our wedding reception."

Gina sighed, remembering that time. "Only because we'd been divorced less than a year and I didn't think I was ready to see him again."

"But you did see him and you survived."

"Yes, but just barely. And now that he's back makes it harder, especially since he mentioned tonight that he's moving back to Houston and wants me to do an exclusive interview with him."

"That's a generous offer. Are you going to do it?"

"I don't know. Financially, it's a great opportunity since a lot of magazines are just dying to get their hands on his story, but I don't know if I could handle being around him long enough to do it."

"If he's moving back to Houston you'll be around him anyway, won't you? The two of you are bound to run into each other occasionally."

"I can deal with occasional sightings. What he's proposing is for me to do the interview at his ranch. A good solid interview will take a week to complete, especially with the angle I plan to use. I can't imagine spending a week alone with him, Corinthians."

"Where's his ranch?"

"He bought one in Fresno."

"Umm, then there's a good possibility we might become neighbors. Trevor and I put a down payment on some land in Fresno today. We hope to start building sometime next year."

Gina smiled, happy for the brother she thought would never marry. Not only did he have a wife he loved completely, but he also had a son he simply adored. Not wanting to talk about Mitch any longer, at least not any more tonight, she changed the subject. "And how is my darling nephew?"

Corinthians laughed. "Right now he's in his father's arms watching a football game. Trask is here and he's explaining the rules of the game to Rio."

Gina shook her head grinning. Trask Maxwell, a family friend and former professional football player, was still considered the greatest running back in NFL history. "Does Trask really believe a three-month-old baby can understand football?"

"Evidently he does since he's been at it since the game started.

Surprisingly, Rio doesn't seemed the least bored and is still awake." Corinthians sighed happily. "Of all my accomplishments I think having Rio is the greatest. He's such a wonderful baby."

Gina shifted slightly in her seat as old tinges of longings rose up within her. Since Trevor had been older than her by ten years, she had spent her adolescent years wanting her parents—who'd separated when she was six years old—to get back together, if for no other reason than to give her a baby sister or brother. And when that hadn't happened, she had grown up looking forward to the day she would marry and have a child of her own. While married to Mitch she had wanted his baby more than anything, but he had staunchly refused to talk about her going off the Pill.

"Gina?"

"Yes?"

"Don't worry. Things will work out. I believe there's a reason Mitch is moving back to Houston."

"There is. He wants to find himself."

"Oh? And where do you fit into all of this?"

"I don't fit anywhere."

"What about the interview he wants you to do?"

Gina released a deep, lingering breath as she remembered Mitch's words. "The interview is strictly business."

"What are you smiling about?" a deep, masculine voice asked from across the table.

Mitch quickly wiped the smile from his face as he looked into the curious gaze of Trevor Grant, the man who had once been his brother-in-law and who, if Mitch succeeded with his plan, would one day again hold that same connection. He had awakened that morning with a smile on his face after a night spent having hot, vividly sensual dreams about Gina. And now it was close to noontime and he was still smiling. He doubted Trevor would want to know the real reason for his jovial expression. After all, Gina was the man's sister.

"No reason," he muttered, looking down at his watch. He then glanced around the restaurant. "What time will the Madarises get here?"

"Soon enough. They had to swing by the airport and pick up Justin, which is just as well since it gives us time to talk."

Mitch allowed himself a minute before reluctantly looking at Trevor. He had an idea just what Trevor wanted to talk to him about but decided to play dumb. "Talk about what?"

"Gina."

Mitch leaned forward and placed his hand on the table. "What about Gina?"

"I want to know what your intentions are, Mitch."

Mitch shrugged. "What makes you think I have any?"

"Mainly because I know the two of you went out to dinner last night and just a few minutes ago you had that same stupid-looking smile on your face that I sometimes get on mine when I'm thinking about Corinthians."

Mitch angled his head. "And you assume my thoughts were on Gina?"

"Weren't they?"

Mitch pulled his gaze away from Trevor knowing the truth was in his eyes. Feeling agitated that he was under cross-examination, he answered, "Yes."

"Then I want to know what your intentions are."

Mitch frowned as he tossed down the scotch, flinching slightly as it burned his throat, and then signaled for a refill. "You're not her father, Trevor," he said angrily after he'd gotten his second drink.

Trevor's expression hardened. "No, I'm her brother, but if you'd prefer I could get my father to ask the question."

Mitch tossed down another mouthful of scotch. That was the last thing he needed, he thought grimly, feeling the hot liquid settle firmly in his stomach. Maurice Grant was a hard man to deal with when it came to his daughter. Mitch still remembered the day he had asked for Gina's hand in marriage. It had been like asking for a piece of the Red Sea. He had to all but prove his worthiness. Both Mr. and Mrs. Grant had felt he and Gina were rushing things and should wait at least another year before considering marriage. But Mitch wouldn't hear of it. He had wanted Gina and since she had been determined to remain a virgin until marriage, he'd had no intentions of waiting another year. There were only so many cold showers a body could take.

Mitch leaned back in his chair, closed his eyes, and rubbed his temple. Dear heavens, he didn't need this. Especially not now. "Why are you giving me grief, Trevor?"

"Because I don't want to see Gina get hurt again, dammit."

Mitch opened his eyes and met the hard, cold-steel ones of Trevor Grant. He stared at his ex-brother-in-law without flinching, something most men wouldn't be able to do. "I made a mistake, man. I love Gina. I always have and I always will."

"Then why did you let her go?"

Mitch winced at the hardness he heard in Trevor's voice. He couldn't help but remember how he had lost his parents before his sixth birthday, and how after that he had gone to live with the grandmother he'd adored, until she had died when he'd turned ten. The three people he had loved the most had left him. After that, for two solid years he had been tossed from one relative to another, never fitting in with any of them and never feeling completely loved. From the age of twelve until he had graduated from high school, he had lived in the worst kind of poverty, having been sent to live with an alcoholic uncle. The man used the money the state gave him each month for his nephew's care on booze and women. There had been many nights that Mitch had gone to bed hungry, and many days he had gone to school wearing the same clothes he had worn the day before. He had made a solemn vow then never to depend on anyone being there for him, and to do whatever he could to never live in poverty again.

"I let her go mainly because I was too stupid to appreciate what I had and too afraid to completely give my heart to anyone again," he said softly.

Trevor leaned toward him; from the look in his eyes Mitch knew the explanation he'd just given hadn't been good enough. But Mitch refused to be more specific. He owed Gina an explanation before giving it to anyone else.

"I always liked you, Mitch," Trevor said in a tone of voice that indicated he was not taking the conversation lightly. "Mainly because deep down in my gut I felt you loved my sister senseless, although things didn't work out between the two of you for whatever reason. She got her life back together after you left and I don't particularly relish the thought of you returning to town messing it back up again. I'd rather you conclude this business with the Madarises as quickly as possible, and go back to California."

Mitch kept his anger in check. After all, Trevor was only trying to protect Gina. "I won't hurt her, Trevor."

"You did once," Trevor accused.

"Yes, but everyone is entitled to make mistakes—just like everyone is entitled to a second chance." He met Trevor's stare. "And I'm asking that you give me that. Both Gina and I made mistakes in our marriage, and we both gave in to the divorce too easily. When push came to shove we forgot about the vows we'd made that said *for better or for worse*. We should have stayed together and worked things out, but we didn't."

"And now?"

The two men stared at each other for a long moment before Mitch finally said in a throaty whisper as something sharp and blunt swirled around his heart, "And now the main reason I've moved back to Houston is to get my wife back. I love her, Trevor, and I hope I can convince her that I've changed and to give me another chance. These two years without her have shown me just how wrong my priorities were. She was the best thing to ever happen to me and in my own selfish and self-centered way, I put my wants and needs before hers. I'm ready to do whatever I have to do to regain her love." Mitch saw belief, then acceptance, in Trevor's dark eyes.

"So," Trevor said as he leaned back in his chair and took a sip of his drink. "I imagine you must have a plan, because you're definitely going to need one."

Mitch nodded. "Yes, I got a plan."

"And you think it's going to work?"

Mitch nodded again. "I pray to God that it does."

Trevor gave him a slow smile and said, "I pray to God that it does, too."

Six days after Mitch made his offer Gina still hadn't made a decision. She had spent most of that time collecting all the recent articles about him she could. Most of them had been sketchy, including the one that had appeared in *Newsweek* four months ago, when Mitch had made news as the first Democratic African-American appointed by a Republican governor to serve on a national committee for land acquisition and development in Washington, D.C., to work with the present administration.

She was proud of all the accomplishments Mitch had made in his life. A part of her knew she and Mitch had wanted different things while they had been married: he had wanted his career, and she had wanted his baby. And neither had been willing to compromise. The only place they had compromised had been in the bedroom, giving in to each other's demands, wants, and desires.

She stood and walked over to the window. She had converted an empty bedroom into an office where she did most of her writing. Presently, she was working on a piece for *Ebony* magazine for Black History Month.

Without realizing she was doing it, Gina gently touched the windowpane. She remembered a day that was very similar to this one, when she had stood by a window and watched as Mitch had loaded the last of his things into the car. It had been the last day they had spent together under the same roof as man and wife.

She would never forget the day she had asked Mitch for a divorce. She slowly removed her hand from the window and placed it on her waist as her mind relived that day.

"What do you mean you want a divorce?" Mitch paused from placing the folders in his briefcase long enough to ask.

"I mean just what I said, Mitch. I'm going to file for a divorce. We no longer have a marriage. You spend more time at the office than you do here. We never spend any time together and I'm tired of it."

He slammed his briefcase shut. "You're tired of it! How in the hell are we supposed to eat around here? How are the bills supposed to be paid? Most women would want their husbands working hard each and every day to take care of those things. They sure as hell wouldn't be standing around whining about it."

She shook her head. "You just don't see it, do you?"

"All I see is a woman used to being pampered by her father and brother who now wants to be pampered by her husband. Well, I think there are more important things to do than spend my time pampering you, like putting food on the table and making sure that we keep a roof over our heads. That's why I work as hard as I do, Gina, so we can have those things we want. I want you taken care of."

"No, that's not it, Mitch. And it's not like I don't have a job, because I do. You work as hard as you do for your own satisfaction. I want a husband who will spend time with me; a person who is my friend as well as my lover. I don't have to have a husband with a prestigious career and a well-thought-of position, or someone making over a hundred thousand a year. All I want is someone I can talk to, someone I can see and spend time with."

Tears filled her eyes. "You don't love me, Mitch. You love whatever it is you're trying to achieve. We have different goals in life; different needs and different dreams. I don't need the huge mansion on the hill, the Mercedes in the driveway, or the bank account that's overflowing with money. All I need is a husband who loves me."

"I do love you, Gina."

"No, you don't, Mitch. At least you don't love me as much as I love you, and I can't take it any longer. Just give me a divorce so I can get on with my life and you can get on with yours. And I hope that the two of us can remain friends."

She had waited, had hoped and prayed that he would cross the room and take her into his arms and tell her that he did love her as much as she loved him, and that he didn't want a divorce . . . but he never did. Instead he just stood there looking at her for a long moment before walking over to the closet to begin packing his things. An hour later he had walked out the door without looking back.

Gina blinked when the sound of a car horn broke into her thoughts. She drew a deep, shuddering breath and slowly went back to her desk. Anything and everything that she and Mitch had ever shared was now in the past. They had been divorced for two years and the only thing they now shared was friendship . . . and possibly a business deal if she agreed to it. He had asked that she give him an answer within a week and time was running out. She hadn't seen or heard from him since that night but knew he was still in town, and could only assume he was staying out at his ranch. She gazed at the piece of paper he had given her at dinner that night, which contained the phone number where he could be reached. Before she could change her mind she picked up the phone and began dialing.

"Hello."

Gina felt every muscle in her stomach constrict at the sound of Mitch's voice. She thought it was everything a male voice should be—deep, throaty, and seductive. She couldn't help remembering that same voice whispering sensuous and sexy words in her ears while he made love to her. She closed her eyes briefly as the impact of those memories swept over her like a warm silken caress.

"Hello."

She blinked her eyes, coming back into awareness when she realized she hadn't responded to his first greeting. "Hello, Mitch. This is Gina."

Mitch silently sighed and allowed himself a moment of profound thanks. At least she had called. When days had passed and he hadn't heard from her, he had gotten worried that maybe she would not accept his offer. Even now he still wasn't sure that she would. "Yes, Gina?" he asked softly.

"About your offer for me to do the interview."

He swallowed hard and tried not to sound too anxious. "Yes, what about it? Are you interested?"

Mitch's gut twisted at the brief pause . . . and then she said, "Yes, I'm interested. I would love to do it and want to thank you for giving me the opportunity."

Mitch felt the tension in his shoulders ease and let out a deep, ragged breath of relief . . . and of thanks. "It's my pleasure, Gina," he said huskily. *And,* he thought, *I can guarantee you that in the end it will be your pleasure as well. You can count on it.*

THREE

Gina was still having misgivings about accepting Mitch's offer when she drove down the long driveway leading to his ranch house. A frown marred her features when just ahead she saw what she thought to be the most dilapidated-looking structure she had ever seen. It resembled an old worn-down farmhouse more than a ranch house.

She blinked twice, thinking she must be seeing things. Surely this building wasn't the ranch house Mitch had purchased. Apparently so, she thought a few seconds later when he got out of a black Durango SUV in front of the house when she brought her car to a stop. She blinked again. He was wearing jeans. Other than that calendar he had posed for last year, she could count on her right hand the number of times she had seen him in something other than business attire. He'd always stressed that a person should always dress for success, so even while lounging around the house he'd worn casual designer slacks and shirts, a totally different look from the well-worn jeans he was sporting now. She couldn't help but appreciate the well-put-together male body, a definite eye-catching look. It was the kind of look that could distract a woman something awful. She shifted her attention to his face and caught her breath at the same time that her heart stuttered. The dark shadow covering his chin, along with the well-worn jeans, made him look like a desperado from yesteryear.

A very handsome desperado at that.

"Good morning, Gina." He greeted her with warm brown eyes and a heart-stopping smile as he opened the car door for her.

"Good morning, Mitch. Are you sure today is a good time to start?" she asked, trying not to concentrate on the deep huskiness she heard in his voice.

"Yeah, I'm sure. We can get started just as soon as I get your opinion of the place."

Gina walked around the side of the car and took a good look at the building that was supposed to be a ranch house. Up close it was worse than she'd thought.

"Well, what do you think?" he asked, coming to stand next to her.

She tried to focus on his question and not on him standing so close beside her. Once again it was beginning to bother her that after two years, he still had the ability to stir her physically. "Well, I guess it has potential," she finally responded. "But it depends on what you plan to do with it."

He smiled. Gina had always been blatantly honest; almost too much at times. "I plan to live here," he said softly.

"You're going to tear it down and rebuild?"

Mitch chuckled. "No, I plan to remodel."

Gina glanced back at the huge house that was barely standing. He had to be kidding. And she told him so.

"No, I'm not kidding. Believe it or not the structure of this place is still good. I've hired a really good team of professionals to assist me in restoring it to how it used to look."

She couldn't help but find that idea amusing. "Back in the eighteen hundreds?"

Mitch shook his head, grinning. "No, not quite that far back, but I have plans for this place. It will take me awhile but I hope to have it livable within a year."

"That will take a lot of time and work."

"I have the time and will enjoy doing the work."

Surprise showed in Gina's face. "You won't be working?" she asked, then clarified by saying, "Your regular job as CEO of your corporation?"

"Yes, I'll still be working. In fact I'm meeting with the Madarises again later today. But I no longer spend all my time working my regular job, Gina. I have a couple of young executives for that. That gives me the time to do some of the things that I enjoy doing."

"Well, that's a switch," she said before she could stop herself. "I remember a time when all you did was work." *And never made time for yourself or for me,* she thought bitterly.

"Yes, I know. And I hate that I did that when I think of all that I lost in trying to be successful."

Gina actually heard regret in his voice but a part of her hardened. Too bad he hadn't realized that two years ago. It would have spared her a lot of heartache and pain. He'd been so quick and eager to make a marriage commitment with her, but hadn't been so quick and eager to do what it took to make their marriage work. In the beginning a part of her had understood his need to do what was necessary to make it to the top. But she could not understand nor accept the degree in which he had done so. First there had been the countless hours of overtime that would extend into the weekends. Then, when he had made operations manager and later operations vice president, there were the business trips that carried him from one part of the country to another. He literally thrived on the hustle and bustle of the business world, and more times than not he was packed and ready to fly out, destination unknown, at a moment's notice. It became a norm for her to come home from work and find a note letting her know he was gone again.

Gina sighed. There was no reason to waste time thinking about their past. The only reason she was here was to talk to him about the interview. But still, she couldn't help glancing around and asking, "So, where are you staying? At a hotel in town?"

"No, I'm staying in that trailer over there through the trees."

Gina looked where his fingers pointed and saw a trailer very much like one of those usually stationed on a construction site, only it was a tad larger. "You're staying in that?" she asked disbelievingly.

"Sure. It has a bath, bed, and a small kitchen. Everything I need."

Gina knew he could afford a hotel room if he wanted one, so that couldn't be the issue. "Why are you staying out here instead of at a hotel?" she couldn't help asking.

He smiled. "I like it here. It's so quiet and peaceful. Out here I'm attuned with nature, my surroundings, and with myself. I think this is the perfect place to be." He met her inquisitive gaze. "This used to be my grandmother's home."

Gina sucked in her breath, shocked at his revelation. "But...but I thought you were born and raised in Beaumont."

"I was. My father was born in this house. He moved to Beaumont when he met and married my mother, and that's where I was born and lived until they were killed. Then I moved here with Gramma Eleanor when I was six."

He smiled warmly upon remembering that time in his life. "She was everything a grandmother should be and I loved her dearly. Together, she and I spent many hours walking this land, taking care of her gardens and farm animals. My life was the happiest until I turned ten. That's the year she got sick and died."

Gina swallowed upon hearing the pain in his voice. He had never shared this part of his life with her. She'd known his childhood had been less than grand, but he'd never shared any intimate details like he was doing now. "Where did you go after your grandmother died?"

"To an aunt and uncle who took great pains to let me know I was a charity case. And because of their attitudes, I rebelled and got into all kinds of trouble. As punishment they sent me to live with my uncle Jasper."

She nodded. He *had* shared stories with her about his uncle Jasper. "He's the one who had a drinking problem, right?"

"Yeah, he's the one," he said angrily through his teeth.

Gina knew his anger was not directed at her but was the result of lingering memories he had of the man who had tormented his life during his teen years. She glanced around the property again, now seeing it through different eyes and accepting it for what it really was. This was the place Mitch had been most happy during his childhood. This was the place that had brought him the most joy.

"Did you inherit this place after your grandmother died?" she asked. If he had, he had never mentioned it during the time they'd been married.

"No, my father had a brother, and when Gramma Eleanor died this place automatically went to him. As you can see he had no use for it and over the years let it run itself down. It was only recently that I was able to negotiate a deal to buy it from my aunt when my uncle passed."

She stared at him, dumbfounded. Aunt? Uncle? He had never, ever mentioned that he had any relatives. In fact, she remembered distinctly asking him about any when she had made out wedding invitations and he'd told her there were none. Evidently he'd not grown up close to them.

Gina suddenly felt rattled. She had learned more about Mitch in the past few minutes than she'd known in the entire four years they had been married. There had been certain things he'd never discussed with her. His family, or lack of one, had been one of those topics he'd avoided. A part of her was surprised at the depth of what he'd revealed.

"So, where do we start?"

His words were casual, soft-spoken, yet they had the effect of something hot and luscious, snapping Gina back to the moment. And the tone, all sexy and sensuous, sank right into her bones. "Where do we start what?"

He gave her a crooked grin. "The interview."

Realizing that her thoughts had gone off in another direction, one that set a tingling in her midsection, she quickly reeled them back in. "How about if we agree on the questions I want to ask you?"

"You can ask me anything, Gina."

"Well, yeah, but I'm sure there are some things you'd want to avoid sharing with the world. Things you hold sacred that you want kept private."

"Like our marriage?"

She lifted her chin. "I said things *you* hold sacred, Mitch. Our marriage was never one of them."

There was a sudden quietness. The only sounds that could be heard were those of insects buzzing about and the distant sound of water flowing in a nearby stream. The smile on his face was gone, replaced by something close to misery. If that were the case, then the saying that misery loved company was true because she was right there with him. For two people who had once loved each other deeply, they had made a complete mess of things.

"I did hold our marriage sacred, Gina," he finally said softly. "Maybe not as much as I should have, but I did. I want very little said about our marriage in this article. There's no reason letting the entire world know what a complete fool I was in letting you go."

"Dammit, Mitch," Gina said, staring up at him and feeling the sudden threat of tears in her throat. How dare he say something so bold, that he realized he'd made a mistake in letting her go? A part of her was glad he did recognize it, but then another part knew the realization had come two years too late.

"Why, Mitch? Why are you saying these things? And why now? Why are you being so repentant?"

His expression went from misery to regret. "Because I am. I'm fully aware of what I lost the day you divorced me. I'm also aware that too much damage was done for any type of repair. I've accepted that, Gina. But that doesn't keep me from acknowledging just how wrong I was and what mistakes I made."

Gina took a breath, full of emotions. He hadn't been the only one who had made mistakes. She had to admit that she had made a number as well. She had gone into their marriage thinking it would be simple and easy. After all, they loved each other and love would certainly be enough; however, the first time she saw that it wasn't enough had been difficult for her to handle.

She sighed. Rehashing the past was a waste of time. Their marriage was over. There was no way they could ever go back. She knew it and hoped that he knew it as well. She decided to ask him to make sure. "You do know that we can never go back, don't you, Mitch?"

He sighed deeply. "Yes, Gina, I know it and I've accepted it. But we can be friends, can't we?"

"We've always been friends, Mitch, even when we weren't in touch. My parents were separated for over twenty years and remained friends because of Trevor and me. And although we didn't have any children together I see no reason to become enemies just because we decided we could no longer live together as man and wife. Things between us just didn't work out and we moved on. End of story."

Mitch knew that this wasn't the end of the story. It was just the beginning. He hadn't been completely truthful with Gina just now when he'd said that he had accepted the fact that they could never go back. He had every intention of winning her back, and he knew it meant patience on his part. Patience had never been one of his strong points, but somehow, someway, he would pull this off. He had to. First, he would strengthen their friendship and then go from there.

He glanced down at his watch. "How about if we decide on those interview questions over lunch?"

"Lunch?"

He smiled. "Yes. I can still fix a mean grilled cheese sandwich if you're interested. And I just might be able to find a few lemons to squeeze while I'm at it. You've always loved my lemonade."

Gina smiled. That was no joke. For the first year of their marriage they had lived on Mitch's grilled cheese sandwiches, lemonade, and love.

Love.

They had been so much in love that first year, she thought. Then things had changed after he'd gotten that promotion he'd always wanted. "I'd love a sandwich and lemonade."

"Come on, then. My modest kitchen awaits you."

He held his hand out to her. She hesitated a brief moment before placing her hand in his. Immediately the touch of his hand on hers made her shiver although the Texas sun was hot and shining bright in the July sky.

Mitch felt her tremor and looked at her. "Are you okay, Gina?"

She nodded that she was okay. However, a part of her doubted she would ever truly be okay again now that Mitch Farrell was back in town.

FOUR

Gina sat on a stool at the kitchen bar and watched Mitch. He was standing at the stove with his back to her, grilling their cheese sandwiches. One word that readily came to mind as she continued to watch him was sensuous. He was such a sensuous-looking man.

She had thought that very thing each and every time they'd made love. At twenty-two she had come to him a virgin; and on their wedding night he had slowly, yet completely, introduced her to all the wonders of a woman and man coming together in love, meshing their minds, bodies, and hearts in a way that took her breath away. In bed, in his arms, there was no right and wrong. Whatever they'd felt comfortable doing and exploring was all right. Sometimes their lovemaking would be slow and easy. At other times he would take her with an urgency of passion so fierce, so demanding, and so frenzied, the effects would last for days, nights, even weeks. While in his arms nothing else mattered; not their problems, differences, or the inner turmoil that plagued their marriage. Whenever he filled her the only thing that mattered was him, and the sensations and ecstasy he was able to share with her.

He would know just where to kiss her, just where to touch her, and just what parts of her to concentrate on to bring her the greatest degree of pleasure. The bed was the only place she had truly felt as one with him, mainly because it was during those times that she knew, without a doubt, that she had his complete attention. Those were the only times when his job and career had played second to her.

She sighed deeply and decided to switch her thoughts. It didn't help matters when she glanced around. The inside of the trailer was cozy. Too cozy. The furnishings were nice for a trailer, especially the bed she had seen on her way to the bathroom to wash her hands. She had tried not to stare, but she couldn't help thinking about all the wicked and wanton things that could be done in that bed with Mitch.

"Gina?"

She blinked, realizing Mitch had turned around and said something to her. Their gazes met and a pulsing heat began gathering low in her body, spreading in a hot, sensuous rush to all parts of her. She wanted him, she silently admitted. Desire was flitting too fast and furious throughout her to *not* admit it. For nearly two solid years the thought of being with a man had never entered her mind, mainly because she hadn't been ready to indulge in any type of a serious relationship with anyone. But now her senses were on full alert. Mitch was too close and too overwhelming for them not to be. Even from across the room she could smell his aftershave—a deep, potent, male scent. Her fingers itched to touch him, her tongue yearned to taste him and her body hungered to have him.

When he repeated her name she blinked, bringing both her breathing and mind under control; or at least trying to. "I'm sorry, I wasn't listening. What did you say?"

He stared at her and she hoped and prayed he hadn't figured out what she'd been thinking.

"I said I ran into Corinthians yesterday at the mall. It was the first time I had seen her since the wedding reception, and just from the brief conversation we had I can tell she's an awesome person. I can see how Trevor fell in love with her."

Gina smiled, remembering both Trevor and Corinthians's tale of how they had hated each other in the beginning, although neither would say exactly how they had met or why they had disliked each other so. It evidently was a secret they shared. "Yes, Corinthians is a sweetheart."

"Trevor is a lucky man."

Gina nodded, thinking that was definitely true; the good thing about it was that her brother knew just how lucky he was and never took his wife for granted. He worked hard but when work time was over he knew how to come home and take care of business. He knew how to balance both work and home life, which was something Mitch never could figure out how to do.

"Don't, Gina."

Gina lifted her gaze and looked directly into Mitch's eyes. "Don't what?"

"Don't remember the bad times."

She swallowed and wondered how he'd known what she'd been thinking. She slowly eased off the stool when he walked toward her, suddenly feeling cornered when he came to stand in front of her.

"There *were* good times in our marriage, weren't there? The memories aren't all bad, are they, Gina?" he asked in an almost whisper, as he gently gripped her upper arms.

Touching her again was a huge mistake. The moment he did so, she gasped as sensations that had been left on hold for two years suddenly rushed straight from the top of her head to the bottom of her feet, making her fully aware of every inch of him and herself as well. Just from his touch, she felt like a woman for the first time in two years.

A woman who ached for the man who used to be her mate.

A shiver of passion aroused her and she knew Mitch felt it. Their gazes held for the longest moment. Then slowly, deliberately, he lowered his head toward hers. A part of her demanded that she step back but she couldn't. The only thing she could do was stand there while he claimed her mouth slowly, tenderly, and thoroughly.

Heat, in various degrees, inflamed her when he slid his tongue between her lips. She took the time to feast on him, to taste him as he sought out her tongue, which she readily gave to him. Her body knew exactly what to expect. It knew what it wanted and just what it was going to get. A deep ache grew inside of her and began spreading to all parts of her body. Mitch made kissing an art form and today he was at his best.

He drew her closer and tightened his hold on her. The lower parts of their bodies touched and she could feel his hard erection through his jeans. It was such a familiar and a missed feeling that she immediately reacted and widened her legs to cradle him between them. Blood pounded fast and furious in her veins at the thought that after all this time she still affected him as much as he affected her.

Mitch heard a moan. He wasn't sure if it had come from him or Gina, but neither did he care. Right now she was where he wanted her to be: in his arms while he kissed her with all the feelings of a man in love. He was lost. Totally and completely out of control … and evidently out of patience. He hadn't meant to kiss her this way so soon. But when he'd looked across the room and saw her watching him, he couldn't help himself. Some things just didn't change, and their deep attraction for each other seemed to be one of them.

Knowing he had to bring them up for air sometime, Mitch slowly broke off the kiss. Then he bent to brush a soft kiss over her lips, wanting to taste her again, even if it was a quick taste.

"That kiss was inevitable," he said quietly, his voice a soft, smooth murmur. "Just like it's inevitable for us to do it again."

He leaned over and closed his mouth completely over hers once more, absorbing the minty flavor right out of her mouth. He hadn't realized just how much he had hungered for her taste until now. And he could tell from the way she returned his kiss that she had hungered for his as well.

It was Gina who finally regained control of the situation and returned back to reality. Breaking her mouth free of his, she placed her hands on his chest and pushed out of his arms. She inhaled a deep breath and released it. He was right. The kiss was inevitable.

At least the first one had been. But not the second, and had she not pulled back there would have been a third. Possibly even a fourth. She and Mitch had always been a fire just waiting to ignite. But that was no excuse—those days were supposed to be long gone…in the past.

She forced her gaze up to Mitch. He was looking at her and saying nothing. Just looking at her. "This was supposed to be business," she said softly, not knowing what else to say. At the moment all other words escaped her.

"It is."

She frowned. "Two people conducting business don't carry on the way we just did, Mitch."

He eyed her with a ferocity that made heat skitter down her spine. "They could if they wanted to."

Gina sighed as she continued to pull herself together. Mitch wasn't helping matters. "Maybe we ought to lay down some ground rules."

And maybe we ought to just lay down, he thought as he continued to watch her. *Mmmm…that had numerous possibilities.* Knowing he had to smooth her over before her feathers got ruffled any further and she decided to call off the interview, he said, "Like I said, the kiss was inevitable, Gina, considering our history." He smiled apologetically. "I got carried away. I promise to control myself in the future."

Knowing he hadn't indulged in the kiss-a-thon by himself, she smiled wryly and said, "Same here. I promise to control myself in the future, too."

He hoped not. He'd always liked her out of control. "Go ahead and sit back down," he said, nodding toward the stool. "Lunch is almost ready. Or instead of sitting you can help by getting a couple of glasses out of the cabinet and filling them with ice for the lemonade. They're in the cabinet over the sink."

She chuckled at his request. "That sounds easy enough."

He shook his head, grinning as he remembered she was definitely not a whiz in the kitchen. But then her capabilities in the bedroom had more than made up for it. "It *is* easy enough."

He watched as she sashayed around him and walked over to the cabinet to take out the glasses. In the pair of slacks she was wearing, her backside seemed to have gotten a bit curvier since the last time he had checked it out. He smiled. He couldn't wait for the chance to check it out again. He could imagine undressing her, removing every stitch of clothing that covered her, then pulling her to him— skin to skin.

He groaned silently, knowing it was time to move on to the next phase of his plan. He just hoped Gina was ready for it. He knew that he definitely was. Slowly, methodically, he intended to break down every barrier she had erected. In the end he was going to have her so dizzy with passion, so saturated in desire, and so full of need that she wouldn't be able to think straight.

And he intended to make sure that happened as quickly as possible.

FIVE

"Are you sure you're fine with the interview questions, Mitch?"

Mitch watched Gina as she placed her writing pad back into her briefcase. After lunch she had immediately developed a strictly business manner. It was one she figured would not be swayed. Boy, did he have news for her.

"Yes, I'm sure," he said, taking another sip of his lemonade. At this point he would be satisfied with just about anything that would provide a chance for them to spend an ample amount of time together. "Now that we have that covered, how about me showing you around?" he said, standing.

She glanced up at him. "All right. But when can we officially get together for the interview?"

Mitch glanced at his watch. He was meeting the Madarises in a few hours. What he needed was to begin breaking down her defenses on her own turf.

"How about if I drop by your place later tonight?" He watched her reaction to his suggestion and could just imagine the wheels that had suddenly begun turning in her head.

"My place?"

"Yes."

"Later tonight?"

"Yes. From what you said earlier it will take approximately a week to finish up the interview. Right?"

"Yes."

"Then we'll need to meet every free chance I get. Unfortunately, getting things off the ground for the construction of the Madaris Building will take up a lot of my time this week."

Gina nodded, understanding the predicament he was in. He probably hadn't counted on it taking her an entire week to do an interview. "All right. Stopping by my place tonight will be fine. What about around seven?"

"Nine o'clock would be better. I have a meeting already scheduled for seven."

She frowned; nine at night was awfully late for them to do business, but she did want to start on the interview. "Okay, nine o'clock will be fine."

Mitch nodded, pleased with himself. "Now, come on and let me show you around. I especially want you to see the places I most enjoyed as a child."

Gina's heart began beating rapidly as she got to her feet. She was eager to see anything that was part of Mitch's past; a past he'd always been reluctant to share with her. "I'd like that."

With his hand on Gina's back, Mitch guided her around his property, sharing with her tidbits of his childhood and how much fun he'd had while living with his grandmother. They came to a stop when they reached a huge pond. Earlier that morning there had been a light drizzle so the ground was still damp. The air smelled of earth and pine and was stirred by a gentle summer breeze.

"You loved your grandmother very much, didn't you?" Gina asked after he'd shared yet another fond memory with her.

He smiled. "Loved, admired, and respected. My grandfather died in the early years of their marriage, but through hard work and dedication she was able to hold on to the ranch with only two young sons for help. And even when those sons later decided ranching wasn't for them, she continued to hold on to the ranch, hiring out seasonal workers and depending on her neighbors only when she really needed to."

He picked up a twig and tossed it into the pond. "When I arrived here I was still mourning the loss of my parents. In time she made my hurt go away; and as I continued to live here, a part of me knew that I'd be the one who would stay and be the rancher. I loved and enjoyed everything about this place just that much. I felt I had everything I needed right here and had no intentions of ever leaving."

Gina nodded, wondering what had happened in his life to make him change his mind. She knew the time he'd spent with various family members after his grandmother's death had had a lot to do with it, especially the time he'd spent with his uncle Jasper. Had there been something else, too? Something he had never shared with her?

"This has always been my favorite spot and it seems fitting that I bring my favorite girl here."

Gina's pulse raced at what he'd said. "Your *favorite* girl?"

He tilted his head back and smiled at her surprised expression. "Yes. You were the first woman I'd gotten serious about during my four years of college and two years of grad school. I had almost made it to the finish line free of any serious involvement with a woman, and then one day I bumped into you coming out of class and wham, my life hasn't been the same since."

Neither had hers, Gina thought as she shook her head, smiling and remembering that day. Mitch Farrell had not only bumped into her that day, he had literally rocked her world. He had shaken it and in a short space of time he'd had it revolving out of control. But still, for him to claim nearly two years after their divorce that she was still his favorite girl was a bit much.

"What about all those other women I read about in the magazines and newspapers whom you've been involved with? Surely they rate much higher on the scale than I do."

Of all the things that could have happened just then, Gina hadn't expected—nor was she prepared—for Mitch to suddenly whirl her around to face him in such a way that brought them chest to chest, and made her tip her head back to see him. She'd barely had time to register what he'd done when she noticed the darkening of his eyes and the firm set of his jaw. When she did, her stomach curled and her nipples tightened. He wasn't smiling, which indicated the intensity of his thoughts; she knew whatever he was about to say was serious.

"I evidently need to make something absolutely clear, Regina Farrell. Divorce or no divorce, no woman rates higher in my life than you do. You're the woman I chose to be my wife, but you were more than that. You were my best friend and my most loyal supporter. And no matter who I may have dated after our divorce, you're the only one I've ever wanted with unadulterated, relentless, and endless passion and never-ending and undying love."

Gina's heart thumped so hard in her chest that it hurt. *Neverending and undying love?* Was he saying what she thought he was saying? She shook her head. *No, he doesn't mean it. At least not the way it sounded,* she thought. *Especially not after all this time. There is no way.*

She sighed deeply. A part of her knew Mitch still loved her; it was the same kind of love she had for him. You couldn't fall madly in love with someone and then expect that love to go away with a mere divorce. A part of her still loved him and cared for him—as someone who had once been a special part of her life, nothing more than that. And she figured that for him it was probably the same. She was the only woman he had ever taken the time from his busy schedule to pursue. And he had done so relentlessly until he had broken down all her barriers, except for one. He had not gotten her to change her mind about them sleeping together before marriage, not that he had tried. Once she had told him of her intentions to wait, he had respected her wishes. But that hadn't stopped things from almost getting out of hand a few times when they had been alone at his apartment. However, he'd always been able to regain control and bring things to an end before they'd gone too far.

The declaration he'd just made about how he felt about her rendered her speechless, and before she could say anything he glanced down at his watch. "It's time for us to start heading back if I'm to meet the Madarises on time."

Gina nodded, glad for the change in subject. "So how are things going with the plans for the Madaris Building?" she asked as they began walking back toward the area where their vehicles were parked.

"What Justin, Dex, and Clayton plan to build is awesome. It's been a dream of theirs for a while and I'm glad to see them move forward with it. And I definitely appreciate them letting me be a part of it."

Gina nodded. "Who will be the builders?"

Mitch chuckled. "I think that was decided before the first piece of land was purchased. Madaris Construction Company will be the ones handling things. They plan to keep it all in the family. At first I thought it was too large an undertaking for two such young men, but Justin, Dex, and Clayton felt comfortable in letting their young cousins do the work. After meeting them I can see why. Those two guys have good heads on their shoulders and there's no doubt in my mind they will do a fantastic job."

Gina smiled. The cousins Mitch was referring to were the twenty-seven-year-old twins, Blade and Slade Madaris. Originally, the construction company had been owned by the twins' grandfather and father, Milton Madaris Sr. and Jr. Milton Sr. had long ago retired; Milton Jr. had recently decided to take early retirement and travel a bit and turned over the running of the operation to his offspring. Already, Blade and Slade were making a name for themselves and had been awarded a number of building contracts.

When they reached her car Mitch opened the door for her. After she slid in he leaned down and reached across her and snapped the seat belt in place. She appreciated his thoughtfulness. "Thanks, Mitch."

"You're welcome." He had to hold back from adding, *I now know the importance of taking care of what's mine.* He was still leaning down and at that angle he was staring straight at her mouth. His gut clenched and he suddenly felt sweat form on his forehead. His control was good, but not good enough to resist moving in just a bit closer to taste her one more time.

He gazed into her eyes and saw the exact moment she realized his intent. He heard her breath catch and heard her gentle sigh. Then he saw her automatically part her lips for him. With such an invitation, whether intentional or not, he leaned closer and stroked his tongue past her parted lips and right into her mouth. Her tongue was there, waiting on his. Sweet, moist, delicious. He wanted to devour her but knew that now was not the time. He had to move cautiously since he didn't want to do anything that would make her want to call off tonight's meeting.

So after tasting her thoroughly for a heart-stopping minute, he retreated and slowly, reluctantly, eased his tongue out of her mouth. "Tonight," he said in a husky whisper. "I'll see you later tonight. At around nine."

Gina swallowed. Mitch's voice was rich with promise. A part of her wanted to tell him that tonight was off, since it appeared that she couldn't trust herself around him. In her book he was the epitome of everything sexual. He was vital, strong and all male. Definitely all male. Even now she could feel moisture gathering between her legs just thinking about how male he was. Somehow and in some way she had to emotionally distance herself from Mitch before…

She didn't want to think about what might happen if she didn't. Every bone in her body was beginning to turn to mush at the very thought. "Mitch?"

"Yes?"

"About tonight."

"Yes, what about it?"

"Ahh..." She tried to speak but couldn't. Never before had she felt at such a loss for words. The only other time she had been this aware of a man had been her first encounter with Mitch. His very presence had taken her by storm, just like he was doing now. But still, she intended to keep things strictly business between them, even if it killed her... which, from the way things looked, it just might. "Nothing," she said softly. "I'll see you later tonight."

Stella Grant glanced across the table at her daughter. Papadeaux was their favorite place for dinner; Gina just loved their seafood. But she couldn't help noticing that Gina had barely touched her food. "Are you are all right, Gina?"

Gina lifted her head and met her mother's concerned gaze. "I met with Mitch today." She knew that about said it all. Of all people, her mother knew just what Mitch Farrell had meant to her at one time. Her mother also knew how much the breakup of their marriage had hurt her.

"So you have decided to do the interview?"

"Yes."

"Why?"

Gina sighed. She hadn't heard censorship in her mother's voice, just blatant, outright concern. When it came to her children, Stella Grant was a fierce protector. But then, on the other hand, she had always allowed them to make decisions for themselves. Gina and her mother had always had a close relationship. Nothing had changed.

"The reason I decided to do it is because it's a good career move for me that will also pay well when some magazine buys it. But I also have an ulterior motive for doing it. While I'm interviewing Mitch, I'm hoping that I can find out some things about him. In fact, I already have," she said softly, thinking about what he'd shared with her about his parents and grandmother. Each time she conversed with him she learned more and more about the man she had once been married to.

"But those are things you should have learned when the two of you were married."

"True, but there was never any time since Mitch spent most of his time working. The only time we communicated was in…" Gina cleared her throat upon deciding that no matter how close they were, she had no intentions of sharing intimate details of her marriage with her mother. Besides, she was more than sure her mother got the picture.

"So, where will all this lead?" Stella asked, concerned.

"I really don't know, Mom. All I'm hoping to get out of this is one fabulous article. Both Mitch and I keep stressing this is strictly business, yet…" She sighed, about to go there again. Why were she and Mitch such passionate, oversensuous people? It seemed the only thing they used to do with their free time was make love, think of making love, or plan to make love.

"Gina?"

She blinked upon realizing her mother had spoken to her. "Yes?"

"What you do with Mitch is your business. I just want you to be careful."

Gina nodded. "Careful that my heart doesn't get broken again."

Stella nodded. "Yes, that, too. But I was really thinking about being careful that you don't end up pregnant."

"Mother!"

Stella waved off Gina's tone of indignation. "I want you to hear me out, Regina Renee Grant Farrell. I've been where you are now, remember? Your father and I were separated for nearly twenty years and during that time I still loved him something fierce. Around Maurice I knew how it felt to be a woman mainly because he was the one who made me into a woman." She smiled. "There were times when he would come and pick you and Trevor up for the weekend, and I had to fight to hold back from throwing myself at him. While I always maintained control, there were times I literally climbed the walls after he left because I had wanted and needed him just that bad." She looked at Gina pointedly and added, "I know all about wants and needs, young lady."

Stella reached across the table. "I know children oftentimes can't imagine their parents as passionate and sensuous beings, but they are. You and Trevor wouldn't be here if Maurice and I weren't. I know firsthand how it is for a woman who's been without love and passion for a while. You haven't seriously dated anyone since your divorce. It's a wonder you aren't pulling your hair out about now. And although you've never mentioned it to me it was no deep, dark secret that you and Mitch had a rather active sex life."

Gina raised a brow. "And how do you know that?"

Stella chuckled. "Because each and every time I phoned to chat the two of you were in bed, getting in bed, or getting out of bed. And let's not forget those unexpected visits when I would interrupt the two of you...doing things."

"Okay, Mom. I get the picture."

"No, dear, I really don't think you do, at least not the one I'm painting. What I'm talking about, Gina, is sexual needs. What kept me from losing it when those sexual needs hit were you and Trevor. The two of you kept me busy and helped to occupy my mind. You don't have a diversion."

"I have my work," Gina said, wondering if her mother had somehow been privy to the recent dreams she'd been having about Mitch.

Stella smiled. "Yes, but now your work includes Mitch. You run the risk of mixing work with pleasure."

"Things are strictly business between us."

"Yeah, right. If you believe that then you probably still believe there's a Santa Claus. Get real, Gina. It's been almost two years. Take my advice and play it safe. Before going home stop by the nearest convenience store and get a pack of condoms since you're no longer on the Pill."

Gina leaned back in her chair, not believing the conversation she was having with her mother. "Trust me, Mom. I won't need condoms or any other type of birth control. I've never indulged in casual sex and I won't start now."

Stella smiled. "There's nothing casual about sleeping with an exhusband, trust me. In fact, it's probably one of the most serious things you can do. The effects of it can possibly leave you in a way you aren't prepared for. Emotionally and physically. You would be sleeping with someone you definitely know, someone you once loved and someone who still has a part of your heart—even if it's a very small part. And last but not least, he is someone who's the very person who taught you everything you know in the bedroom; every itty-bitty little detail and then some."

Gina could feel her face flush. "Ahh, can we change the subject, please?"

"If that's what you want."

"Yes, that's what I want."

"All right. But remember my warning as well as my suggestion."

With her head lowered Gina slowly resumed eating her food. She could feel her insides heat up at the thought of every itty-bitty little detail Mitch had taught her. He had been thorough, absolute, consummate, and outright perfect. In her heart and mind she believed that even if she slept with more than a hundred men, none would ever compare to the way Mitchell Cameron Farrell made love. He'd had other faults but in the bedroom he had reigned supreme in her book. Just thinking about him made her . . .

No, she wouldn't go there . . . again. She had to believe that she was still in control of her mind and body and that her mother was wrong. Casual sex was casual sex no matter who your partner was. And as long as she believed that, she didn't have a thing to worry about.

At least she hoped and prayed that she didn't.

SIX

"Forgive us for boring you, Mitch."

Mitch snapped his head around and looked into four pairs of grinning eyes. He shrugged. "Sorry, guys."

Justin Madaris smiled. "Hey, don't apologize. We've all been there. In fact, we're still there."

Mitch raised a brow. "Where?"

"In love."

Mitch smiled, not really caring that the four men he had joined for drinks at the conclusion of their business meeting had figured things out. "And just what gave me away?"

"Your mood," Justin said easily.

Dex Madaris spoke next. "It was the way you keep looking at your watch."

Clayton Madaris then added, "For me it was the fact that you mentioned three times since we got here that you have a business meeting with Gina at her place tonight at nine."

Mitch's gaze then moved to Trevor to see just what he had to say. "For me it was that silly-looking smile you still have on your face."

"Oh." Mitch chuckled and took another sip of his drink. When he absently checked his watch again a few minutes later, the other men began laughing. And he couldn't help but join them. He had met the Madaris brothers through Trevor after he had become engaged to

Gina. The Grants and the Madarises had grown up in the same neighborhood and were a rather close-knit group.

Deciding to change the subject about his love life, he turned to Clayton. A few months back a demented escaped convict had run Clayton over when he was leaving his office one day. The hit-and-run had been intended for Clayton's wife, Syneda. He had pushed her out of the way and taken the impact himself.

"I'm glad to see you're out and about and back to your old self again, Clayton," Mitch said seriously.

Clayton smiled. "Thanks. You know what they say: you can't keep a good man down."

Mitch nodded, then asked Clayton and Dex how their wives were doing. Syneda and Dex's wife, Caitlin, were both expecting. Mitch was suddenly reminded of the times that Gina had asked him for a baby, and how he'd flatly refused her with the excuse that he wasn't ready to become a father. But now, if given the chance, he would gladly give her fifty babies if that were what she wanted. The thought of becoming a father didn't bother him like it used to. In fact he actually relished the idea of having a son or a daughter if Gina was the child's mother. He could imagine a little girl who was a replica of her mother.

"You got that silly smile on your face again, Mitch."

Mitch took another sip of his drink and rolled his eyes at Trevor. "You know, I could be thinking about all the money I'm going to make off this deal."

Trevor nodded. "Yeah, that could explain the smile, but it doesn't explain why you're looking at your watch every ten minutes." He crossed his arms over his chest and gave Mitch a hard stare. "Now tell me again the reason you're meeting with Gina this late at night."

Dex chuckled. "Leave him alone, Trev. There's nothing wrong with a man who admits to making a mistake and then goes about trying to make things right."

"And you think he plans to meet with Gina, *this late at night,* to make things right?"

Evidently Trevor's question raised some serious doubt in the other men's minds; they suddenly eyed Mitch suspiciously. "Hey, guys, back off. What's going on with me and Gina is our business," Mitch said in an irritated tone. Jeez! It was bad enough he'd felt the need to defend himself to Trevor a few days ago, but now the Madaris brothers were trying to give him grief, too. It was a known fact that they considered Gina as one of their sisters.

"Okay, we'll back off for now," Dex said slowly. "Like I said, there's nothing wrong with a man who admits to making a mistake and tries making things right. Just don't think about making the same mistake twice."

Mitch knew that of the three brothers, Dex was the one he had to worry about. He meant what he said and said what he meant. "Trust me. I don't plan on making the same mistake with Gina."

Evidently satisfied that enough had been said, Clayton Madaris decided to change the subject. "Has anyone noticed that Blade has just as many women as I did when I was his age?"

Justin raised his eyes to the ceiling. "And you think that's something to brag about?"

Clayton smiled. "Hey, it's good to know there's another Madaris out there keeping the ladies happy."

Dex frowned. "Oh, is that what he's supposed to be doing?"

"You bet. If he keeps it up he'll be the one to inherit that case of condoms I've been keeping in my closet, since I won't be needing them anymore."

Mitch chuckled. It was common knowledge that Clayton was Houston's number-one womanizer during his bachelor days. Also, it had been rumored that he'd kept a case of condoms in his closet. Evidently it had been more truth than rumor. Hearing Clayton mention condoms made Mitch wonder if Gina was still on the Pill. He decided not to take any chances—he'd stop by the convenience store on the way over to her place.

He looked at his watch again. The time was close enough for him. "I hate to leave but I got to run," he said, standing and tossing a few bills on the table.

"Maybe the four of us should go over to Gina's place with you."

Mitch frowned at Trevor's suggestion. "Don't even think about it." He then turned and hurriedly walked out of the restaurant.

Gina paced restlessly about her house after checking the clock for the umpteenth time. Was Mitch still coming over? Was he on his way? Why was she so anxious to see him? She had interviewed a dozen people, so what made him any different?

She sighed, knowing the answer to that one. None of them had been a man she had slept with before.

She looked down at the outfit she had chosen to wear for tonight's meeting; a skirt and blouse and there was nothing provocative or tempting about either item. She wanted to set the mood for what their meeting was—strictly business. In fact, instead of them sitting in the living room she had decided to conduct the interview in her office. At no time did she want Mitch to think this was a social call.

Thinking that the lighting in her living room appeared too seductive, she quickly crossed the room and switched on another lamp. The last thing she wanted or needed was for Mitch to get any ideas. They had kissed three times already that day and the last thing she wanted was a repeat performance. Heaven help her if she got one, so she figured the best way to handle the situation was to start out letting him know what she expected and what she would not tolerate.

She took a deep breath when she heard the sound of the doorbell. Taking another large gulp of air for good measure, she slowly crossed the room to the door and glanced out the peephole.

Gina sighed resignedly as she opened the door; she immediately knew she had made a mistake in agreeing to this late-night meeting. When his gaze met hers she felt all the things she had felt the first time they had met.

Sexual chemistry. Instant attraction. Animal lust.

And it certainly didn't help matters that he was now clean-shaven and dressed in a designer business suit that gave him a suave, elegant, and professional appearance. There was an aura of masculine strength in the tall, powerfully built body standing across from her. This was the Mitch Farrell she knew and was used to. He looked nothing like the Mitch who had resembled a desperado earlier that day.

The porch light reflected confidence and an air of sensuality that almost took Gina's breath away. Mitch held her gaze with the compelling force of his. She nervously licked her bottom lip and immediately knew it had been a mistake when his gaze shifted to her mouth, then seconds later shifted back to her eyes.

Finally he spoke. "May I come in?"

Gina tried to ignore the tiny flitters of pulsing heat racing through her body at the sound of his voice, deep and husky. She stepped back. "Yes, of course."

She inhaled deeply when he entered. He was bringing into her house the scent of a man. Her throat felt tight and her insides burned hotter with the masculine aroma. It was earthy, sensuous, and all Mitch. Tension pricked at her nerve endings and she wondered how she would survive being in his presence in such close quarters. She drew a steadying breath, determined to get through it.

Closing the door, she watched him glance around her living room and noted a variety of expressions that crossed his face, admiration and appreciation among them.

"You have a beautiful home, Gina."

"Thanks." It was slightly larger than the one the two of them had shared. She had always wanted for them to get a bigger house so they could start a family, but he'd kept making excuses as to why they couldn't.

"Since the time is already far spent," she said, heading straight into business, not wanting her thoughts to dwell in the past, "we may as well get started. I plan to conduct the interview in my office."

He raised a surprised brow. "Your office?"

"Yes. I thought it would be appropriate since this *is* a business meeting."

He nodded smiling. "That's true, but do I get the offer of something to drink first?"

"Sure, what would you like? I have cola, tea, fruit juice, water, wine…"

"A glass of wine will be fine."

"All right. I'll be back in a minute."

Mitch watched as she walked away and looked at the sensuous body he knew so well from head to toe. He inwardly grinned. If Gina thought tonight would be strictly business she had another thought coming. Oh, sure, things were bound to start off that way, but he planned a totally different ending to the night—and he was determined to make it so. He'd known it the moment she had opened the door. She looked beautiful and he knew that although she probably had not done anything to deliberately get him aroused, just seeing her had effectively done that.

While she was in the kitchen getting his wine, he decided to check out the layout of her home. Specifically, he wanted to know the location of her bedroom. He made a quiet and quick assessment and returned to the living room a few moments before Gina appeared carrying a wineglass.

"Here you are," she said, walking over and handing it to him.

"Aren't you going to join me?"

"No. I prefer not to drink while conducting business."

He nodded. "Oh, I see. Well, in that case, I don't want to take up any more of your time than I have to. So let's get started."

"Thanks, I appreciate it, Mitch."

"Don't mention it. Like I told you that first night at dinner, I want the article done right and I know you'll do that."

She led him across the living room into her office. Again she watched him glance around and saw his satisfied expression. "This is nice. I bet you spend a lot of time in here."

"Only when I have to do a lot of typing and research. I seldom do interviews at home. In fact, you're my first."

"Again?" he asked, turning to her and smiling over the rim of his wineglass. "I was also the first man to ever make love to you. The first guy to ever make you..."

Come. A jab of desire went through Gina at the memory. Although he hadn't finished the sentence it had been very easy for her to supply the missing word. Her body, which was already heated inside, began burning hotter with all the memories.

Deciding not to make a comment, she cleared her throat and said, "You can sit in that chair, Mitch." With trembling fingers she picked a sheet of paper up off her desk. "Here's a copy of the questions I plan to ask tonight. As you can see, there are only six, so you won't be here that long. And to help things run smoothly, I will tape this session. Is that all right with you?"

"Yes, that's fine. When will you get around to asking the other questions?" he asked, accepting the paper she handed him. He knew she had at least twenty questions to ask him for the interview.

"Later this week when your schedule permits. Tomorrow I will replay your responses and work on tonight's segment. For the next group of questions I'd prefer if we were at your ranch. I think a change of location for each session will enhance the interview."

Mitch nodded. "You believe that technique is better than asking all the questions in one session and be done with it?" he asked, not that he was complaining. He liked the thought of spending a lot of time with her.

"Yes, I think so," Gina answered, taking the chair behind her desk.

"This way neither the interviewer nor the interviewee gets tired and fizzles out. I want you to relax and be yourself. And I want you to be open and honest with me."

"Thanks. I intend to." He glanced down at the questions. All six involved his love life.

Seeing his curious expression Gina said quickly, "I thought it would be best if we go ahead and cover these questions first. There are a lot of women who have been fantasizing about you ever since you did that calendar." She decided not to add that she was one of them.

"It was for charity."

"I know, and from what I understand the sales were phenomenal. I'm sure the relief fund for the September eleventh tragedy appreciates you and the other men who participated."

Mitch removed his coat and tie, taking her up on her suggestion that he relax and be himself. Gina leaned back in her chair and crossed her legs to fight the heat forming between them as she watched him. He had such a wonderful body. No wonder the women had gone bonkers when he had appeared in the calendar as Mr. February. Dressed in a pair of tight-fitting jeans and an open shirt that had revealed his beautiful chest, he had definitely been a lot of women's flavor for the month. She had been totally surprised when a friend from college had mailed her a copy of the calendar. The Mitch Gina knew would not have done such a pose, no matter the cause, and she wondered why he'd done it.

Curiosity got the best of her and she found herself asking, "Why did you do it?"

"Do what?" he asked as he eased down in the chair.

"The calendar."

Mitch glanced down at the sheet he held in his hand. "That's not an interview question," he said, smiling.

"No, it's not. I just want to satisfy my own curiosity."

"Like I said, it was for charity," he replied, looking directly into her eyes. But knowing that she knew him better than anyone, he added, "And also for Tom."

"Tom?"

"Yes, Tom Swank, a business associate of mine and also a good friend. He was in the World Trade Center when it went down."

Gina heard the pain in his voice. "I'm sorry, Mitch."

Mitch nodded, accepting her words of regret. "Tom and I had a meeting that morning."

Gina sat up straight in her chair. "You were in New York that day?"

"Yes. And I was to meet with Tom at eight but a phone call from my office delayed me. It saved my life."

"Oh, Mitch," Gina said as a lump formed deep in her throat. She shivered at the thought that Mitch could have been one of the victims and thanked God that he hadn't been. And her heart went out to Tom Swank's family. "Was Tom married?"

"Yes, and he had a six-year-old son. That's when I began examining my life. I thought it was so fortunate that Tom had had a child that he had spent time with; a child who would carry on his legacy. It made me realize what I didn't have."

"I always wanted to give you a child, Mitch, but you didn't want one," Gina said, her voice rising slightly.

"I know," he responded quietly. "But that was then. If I could turn back the hands of time I would get you pregnant in a heartbeat."

Their eyes held. Neither spoke. Both knew they could not turn back the hands of time even if they wanted to.

"Ah, I suggest we go ahead and get started," Gina said, clearing her throat and reaching across her desk to turn on the tape recorder. It was time to move on. "Rumors have been circulating for the past three months that you're having an affair with model Lori Brasco. Is it true?"

"There's no affair. Lori and I are nothing more than friends who share the same interests."

A good reporter would ask just what those interests were, but Gina decided she really didn't want to know. "What about your alleged affair with department store heiress Nicole Lane?"

"Nicole and I dated a few times but that's it," he said as he casually undid the top button on his shirt. Then the second. And the third.

Gina tried not to notice what he was doing but found she was watching him anyway. She swallowed and forced her vision back down to the paper in front of her. "Do you ever plan to remarry?"

"Yes."

Gina's head snapped up, surprised he had answered so quickly and with such conviction. "You think you're good husband material?" she asked curtly. That question was also not on the paper.

"Now that I've learned from my past mistakes, yes."

Gina sighed. The interview was going badly. She wasn't asking the questions she should be asking and was asking some she shouldn't. "And what have you learned, Mitch?"

He smiled. It was a beautiful, rich smile but at the same time it was serious. He stared at her for the longest moment before replying. "I've learned not to ever take a wife for granted again. I also learned that success is just a level of achievement, but a wife is a gift, a beautiful gift to be loved and cherished. She's not a possession to be picked up and played with on a rainy day ... or made love to when the urge to do so strikes you. I've also learned that although it's a very enjoyable part, there's more to a marriage than sex. And I've learned to appreciate the good times in a marriage, as well as the bad. But more importantly, I've learned to appreciate a wife."

Gina's throat was so thick she could barely swallow. She was supposed to remain neutral, unattached, and unbiased, but she was doing a poor job of it. "And what brought on this stunning revelation?"

Mitch held her stare when he said, "Losing my wife, the woman I had loved more than life itself. I had two years to analyze what went wrong with my marriage and what I could have done to make things right. In the end I acknowledged all the mistakes I had made and didn't like myself very much, so it became crystal clear why in the end she didn't like me either."

Gina fought the tears that clouded her eyes and waited a few minutes before asking softly, "Does your wife know that?"

"She does now."

Dragging her eyes from his, Gina fumbled with the paper on her desk. "If you plan to remarry, do you have someone in mind?"

"Yes."

A part of Gina's heart felt crushed with that one single word. She should be happy for him, glad that he had realized the importance of taking care of a wife properly, but she felt saddened that someone else would reap the benefit of that lesson. All she could think was that another woman would wear the name of Mrs. Mitchell C. Farrell.

When seconds ticked by and Gina didn't say anything, Mitch asked, "Aren't you going to ask me who she is, Gina?"

Gina slowly lifted her gaze to his. Hurt and anger filled her eyes. "Why would I want to know that?"

"For the interview."

That single statement made her remember that she was indeed supposed to be conducting an interview with him. She swallowed tightly. "All right. Who is she? Who is the woman you want to marry? I'm sure there are a lot of women who would want to know."

She watched Mitch stand. Then she watched him slowly walk over to her desk. She tried to concentrate on him and not the bare chest revealed by his unbuttoned dress shirt. When he reached her desk she tilted her head back to look up at him. With him standing over her, she was acutely aware of everything about him. He was looking down at her, drawing her in and making her feel cornered, restrained, and desired. There was a hot look in his eyes. One she recognized and had come to know well during the time they were married. The question that suddenly crossed her mind was: how could he want her *that* much but intend to marry someone else?

"How, Mitch?" She voiced the question before she realized she had spoken, but she knew he clearly understood what she was asking. When he reached out and touched her chin with his finger, every nerve ending within her body ignited with heat, which flooded her face at the same time it flooded the area between her legs.

"I would think the answer to your question would be obvious, Gina. *You* are the woman I want to marry."

SEVEN

It took Gina a minute to find her voice, then she exclaimed, "Marry!"

"Maybe the proper word should be remarry." Mitch couldn't help but appreciate the shocked look on Gina's face. It was priceless. She stared up at him with eyes so filled with astonishment he was tempted to kiss the look right off her face. Satisfied he had finally made his intentions clear, he crossed his arms over his chest and waited for the rest of her reaction.

She shook her head as if to clear it, making her hair tumble carelessly around her face before taking her hand and smoothing it back in place. He immediately felt aroused. That simple act was too sexy for his peace of mind. As he continued to look at her, he saw he had successfully boggled her mind and squelched further speech. Then all too soon she got it back.

"You can't really mean that!" she said, coming to her feet, which forced him to take a step back.

"And why can't I?"

"Because it makes no sense, Mitch. Until you came to town last week, I had not seen or heard from you since . . . since . . ."

"Trevor's wedding," he supplied easily.

"Yes, Trevor's wedding, and that was almost a year ago."

"And your point is?"

She stared at him for a long moment thinking her point should have been obvious. "My point is that we don't have a relationship, Mitch. Other than having been married once we no longer share a connection. After our divorce you went your way and I went mine. Although we remained friends, you didn't call me on the holidays, I didn't call you. You didn't send me *I'm thinking of you* cards and I didn't send you any either. In other words, you and I have not shared a life, a thought, a concern, or interest for almost two years, and for you to—"

"There wasn't a day that went by that I didn't think of you, Gina."

She glared at him. "Oh, is that right? I'm sure that will probably come as quite a surprise to all those women you have dated since our divorce."

"They meant nothing."

She frowned, her eyes narrowing. "And you expect me to believe that?"

"Yes, I see no reason why you shouldn't," he replied, meeting her glare with one of his own. "I loved you, Gina. I loved you with all my heart. That kind of love can't be turned off with a divorce."

"You didn't love me, Mitch, not really. You loved your work. You desired me and you wanted me."

Mitch looked at her and got the uneasy feeling that she actually believed what she was saying. "That's not true, Gina."

"It is true," she said venomously.

"If you believe that, then I'll have to prove otherwise."

"I don't think you can."

He saw serious doubt in her eyes and took a step toward her, capturing her in his arms. "The hell I can't," he muttered moments before kissing her with purpose. He opened his mouth fully over hers, effectively absorbing her gasp of surprise and her breath of existence. His tongue slipped inside—tasting deeply, exploring thoroughly, and claiming completely. He heard her soft moan of protest and deliberately ignored it when she wrapped her arms around his neck and returned the kiss with equal intensity.

The kisses they had shared earlier that day were nothing compared to this. The sexual hunger that had been clawing at him since his return to Houston had taken over his mind and body. He could still remember the first time he had kissed her, the first time he had exploded inside of her, and the first time she had screamed out his name in a torrential climax. Those sensuous memories of the past invaded his thoughts and combined with the pleasures of the present, hammering away at the last thread of control he had.

Her hips were moving instinctively against him as he kissed her with an all-consuming hunger. They fitted together perfectly, just as always. Desire flared between them and he knew she was as out of control as he was. No matter what she said or thought, Mitch knew that for him this was love. Love of the purest and richest kind. No other woman had ever made him feel this way.

Only Gina could make him want to give her the sun and the moon and not settle for giving her anything less. Only Gina could make him appreciate being a man because he knew he had her as his woman. And only Gina could make him want to stay locked inside her body—real deep and extremely tight—for the rest of his life.

He eased his hand under her blouse wanting to touch her everywhere and deciding to start with her breasts. He had always loved the feel of them in his hands, especially the feel of her nipples hardening from the caressing brushes of his fingertips. He knew just what type of bra she was wearing—one made of lace with a front closure. He sucked in a ragged breath when he unsnapped it easily, then traced a path with his fingers over her delicate skin.

"Mitch!"

His name was a whimpering sound on her lips. Without responding he leaned forward and gently captured a nipple between his teeth, then began laving it with the relentless stroke of his tongue. First one breast and then the other received his hot attention. He glanced upward and saw her eyes flutter closed as another sound, this one a sweet, delectable groan, escaped her lips. When she looked like she was about to swoon, he pulled his mouth from her breast long enough to lift her so she could wrap her legs around his waist.

Walking over to the chair, he settled her in his lap and kissed her lips again with such urgency that she responded in kind. It was as if he wanted to eat her mouth up, frantic for the taste of her and almost delirious with desire for yet something else. His fingers skimmed her leg moving upward to her thigh. Pushing her skirt aside he sought out bare flesh. He drew in a deep breath when his fingers inched higher. The feel of her electrified every nerve ending in his body and caused additional heat to flood his bloodstream. Two years had been a long time without this, he thought, wanting with every part of his being to bury himself deep inside of her.

His hand came in contact with silky panties and he slowly, methodically, skimmed his fingers over the soft material seeking the easiest opening to slip underneath. He found it and heard her soft gasp when he touched bare skin. Her flesh felt soft, smooth, and delicate. Wet.

He cupped his palm over that area between her legs that he had branded his on their wedding night, feeling the heat of it at the exact same time that he felt a shiver touch her body in response to him touching her so intimately.

She tilted her head back and looked at him through glazed eyes. It had been a long time since he had seen that look, and he suddenly realized just how much he had missed it, had missed her, had wanted her and needed her. Having her in his arms this way and knowing just how much he loved her, he bent his head to hers and kissed her deeply. At the same time his hand shifted the lower part of her body to accommodate the fingers he'd slipped inside of her. He felt the jolt of her body against him but continued to kiss her as his fingers penetrated her beyond the satiny folds of her flesh.

"Mitch!" She freed her mouth from his and her face dropped forward on his chest.

He heard the desperation in her voice. He also heard the urgency. "What do you want, Gina?" he asked, whispering the words in her ear as his fingers continued to intimately caress her. "Tell me what you want, baby."

She slowly lifted her head from his chest. Her gaze was heated but he knew his eyes were just as smoldering. "You. Inside me. Now!"

Sweat dampened Mitch's forehead at her words. But he wasn't ready to put an end to his torment or hers. "No, sweetheart, not yet."

Not yet? Mitch's words whirled around in Gina's head. The urge to mate with him was so strong she didn't want to wait. Her mother had been right. Her body knew this man and it wanted and needed him in the worst possible way. It was letting her know that two years had been a long time. Tonight it had no shame, just outright greed. It wanted it all and was too desperate to offer any type of resistance, not that she wanted to anyway. There was nothing casual about this, nor was this something she could walk away from. Her body and all the elements within it were reacting to the only man it had known, wanted, and loved.

She couldn't help wondering why he was torturing her. Why didn't he give her what she wanted and obviously needed? She bit down as the heated movement of his fingers inside of her continued to arouse her beyond comprehension, escalating her desire.

Leaning forward she kissed his mouth, his throat, and the part of his bare chest exposed through his shirt. If she was going to be tormented then so was he. Her tongue glided over him, licking his salty dark skin. She reached up and undid the rest of the buttons on his shirt, wanting to expand the area where she could taste him.

She heard his groan and sharp intake of breath when her tongue came into contact with his nipples. She could feel him straining beneath her, his erection fully grown and hard. She lifted herself off him just a bit and reached down to unzip his pants. Sticking her hand into the opening she heard his tortured groan and felt his stomach tense when she slipped her fingers beneath the waistband of his briefs to take control of the part of him that she wanted. He felt big, powerful, and hot in her hand. *Oh, so hot and hard.*

"Let go," he growled in her ear in a voice that was fast losing it. She had begun stroking him just the way he had taught her; the way that gave him immense pleasure.

"I'll let go of you when you let go of me," she announced flippantly.

Instead of letting her go, he arched his back and worked his fingers deeper inside of her. He looked up at her to see the play of emotions on her face. He felt her hand tremble, but she did not let go of him. In fact she met his smoldering gaze and continued what she was doing. Her fingers were working their magic on him, very gently and very thoroughly, smoothing his flesh all the way down and up again. When an explosive curse broke forth from his lips she smiled naughtily, and with an arrogance that could only match his own asked softly, "You want to take a bet on how long you'll last, Mitch Farrell?"

He frowned. She knew she was pushing him to the limit and was enjoying every damn hellacious minute of it. "No, I don't want to bet," he rasped, barely able to think straight. He had taught her the art of seduction too well.

"Then give me what I want, Mitch. Now! No more games." She softly whispered her command blatantly clear in his ear.

"Okay, you've convinced me," he said huskily and stood with her in his arms and quickly headed toward her bedroom.

"If I didn't know better, I'd swear you've been here before."

He laughed and looked down at her. "I have. In your dreams."

She shook her head, grinning. "You're kind of sure of yourself, aren't you, Mitch?"

"Do you deny it?"

He placed her on the bed and stepped back. His eyes were dark and hot as he looked at her, waiting for her to answer him. "Do you deny it?" he repeated.

Gina inhaled deeply. He stood before her with his shirt unbuttoned, revealing the most gorgeous chest any man could possibly possess. And due to her brazen handiwork, his pants were unzipped, with the most proud male part of him unashamedly exposed. She thought he was the most virile man she'd ever seen. And he was right. She remembered the dreams she'd had of him just last night, not to mention the ones she'd had occasionally over the past two years. He had been in this bedroom with her before—right in her dreams.

"No, Mitch, I don't deny it."

The thought that she had dreamed about him brought a sexy smile to Mitch's lips. "Well, baby, I'm about to make your dreams come true," he said silkily, slowly removing the belt from his pants.

Gina reclined in bed and watched him strip, definitely enjoying the show. She had always thought he had one hell of an incredible body, and seeing it again only reaffirmed her belief. He was hard and muscular in all the right places; his shoulders were broad and his hips narrow. And she didn't want to even concentrate on his thighs. They were Herculean thighs. Strong, solid, and built. She remembered all too well the feel of those thighs rubbing against hers while he pumped relentlessly into her, bringing her body pleasure beyond measure.

"Now it's your turn to take everything off."

She met his gaze and slowly slid out of bed. "You sure you want to watch this?" she asked, grinning. "It might bore you."

"I doubt that," he said, taking his turn reclining on the bed to watch her.

Trying to drag things out for as long as she could, just to torment Mitch some more, slowly, ever so slowly, Gina removed her skirt. Her blouse followed and then the bra that was half off anyway.

"You are perfect, Gina."

She smiled over at him. "Full of compliments, aren't you, Mr. Farrell?"

He returned her smile. "Among other things." He slid off the bed and stood. "Come here, Gina."

Not hesitating, she walked over to him and took the hand he held out to her. He picked her up in his arms and placed her on the bed. "I don't want to use this until the last possible moment, Gina," he said raspily, displaying the condom he held in his hand. "Is that all right with you?"

Gina remembered her mother's words. There would still be a risk if he waited until the last possible moment to put the condom on. She looked at that part of him, large and hard before her. They had never used a condom when making love since she had always been on the Pill. One of the pleasures she had always gotten while making love to him was the feel of him exploding inside of her while her inner muscles gripped him, and squeezed out of him everything she could get and then some. But still…

"Are you sure about that, Mitch? What if…"

"What if I forget? What if I lose control and don't want to stop and take the time to put it on? What if I'm buried inside of you so deep I don't want to come out?" He paused a moment, then said huskily, "And what if I'm driven beyond reason to make you pregnant?"

Gina wasn't sure just how long she stood there, unable to speak. Then she regained her wits. "But you don't want children. You didn't want them while we were married so why would you possibly want them now that we're divorced?"

Mitch slowly shook his head. Evidently she still didn't buy into his theory that they wouldn't be divorced for long. He had every intention of remarrying her, baby or no baby. She belonged to him and would always belong to him. He loved her and would spend the rest of his life proving that to her if he had to. "But what if I was that driven, Gina?"

Gina drew in a deep breath as she thought about what he was saying. The only thing she'd ever known Mitch to be driven to do was to be successful. Although he hadn't relished the idea of them having a child, she had always believed that he would have made a good father. A hardworking one but a good father nonetheless. And she had always wanted a child, which hadn't changed. But she had never thought about being a single mother. Although her parents had been separated while she was growing up, both had played major roles in her life. Her father had always been there for her, just like her mother. She'd had a close relationship with the both of them. She hadn't missed out on having a father figure in her life just because her parents had not lived under the same roof. However, a part of her had always wanted her parents to get back together because for some reason she'd felt they had still loved each other. Even as a child she had felt love between them, even if they hadn't. But as her mother had explained one day when she had been old enough to understand, it was not a matter of simply kissing and making up. There had been too much hurt and pain for that.

Gina couldn't help but wonder if Mitch understood that the same held true for them. They couldn't kiss and make up. Nor could they make love and make up either. Although she had every intention of making love to him tonight, as far as she was concerned their situation had not changed. At least not enough to rebuild what had been torn down.

"Gina?"

Mitch regained her attention. She fully understood what he was asking, and more specifically, what he was insinuating. Had it been a night where she was not filled with profound need, she would have thought a different way. Her mother had forewarned her about long-denied sexual needs, and tonight Gina wanted and needed Mitch in the most intimate and elemental way. It was the way a woman was meant to want a man. That meant she would have her night with him and her morning, and possibly another day and night, maybe several. But sooner or later he would realize, just like she did, that what they shared was physical. Emotionally, he didn't stand a chance with her because she would not allow him to invade her heart a second time.

Fully understanding her position, even if he didn't, she slowly walked over to him, naked as the day she was born into the world. So was he. Standing on tiptoe she placed her arms around his neck and brought her body close to his, skin-to-skin, flesh-to-flesh, and sensuality-to-sensuality. "If I get pregnant, Mitch, I'll deal with it. I've always wanted a child, anyway."

"And what role will I get to play?"

"The only role you can play. The father."

Mitch nodded. In time he would establish the role he would play in her life as well—her husband. But right now, tonight, he wanted to give her a taste of that role, a sampling she would not forget. He slid his arm around her waist and drew her even closer to his body. Now they were bone-to-bone, hip-to-hip.

He slowly walked her backward to the bed, and when they couldn't go any farther, he eased her down on the bed with him the same moment he took her mouth into his, kissing her wildly as he splayed his hand across her hip and thigh, and sought out the area between her legs.

A fierce rush of sexual need flooded Gina and she could barely get breath into her lungs. Mitch was touching her, tormenting her, and branding her and she was helpless in his arms. Then the next instant he was hovering above her. Ready for him, she widened her legs and lifted her hips the moment he drove his hardness into her.

He felt huge and was inside of her so deep she thought he must have gotten bigger since the last time they had done this. Her body felt tight around him. Tight and incredibly feminine. She groaned deep within her throat when he shifted their bodies and lifted her even more into the cradle of his arms while buried deep inside of her.

The position he had placed her in forced her to look at him. After wrapping her legs around his waist, he braced his hands on either side of her head and stared down at her without moving.

"I love you, Gina."

His words, spoken like a soft caress, penetrated her mind and made her insides quiver. But a part of her refused to accept his declaration. She knew it was lust and not love that was talking.

"No, you don't love me. You love *this*."

"I love *you*."

"No, you love this. Admit it."

He held her gaze for the longest time before saying, "Yes, I love *this* but only because *this* is a part of you. But I love this, too," he said, pressing a kiss to her nose. "And this," he said, kissing an area just above her right eyebrow. "And I'm plumb crazy about this," he said, gently brushing a kiss to her mouth. "There isn't an area on you that I don't love, mainly because I love you, Gina. So damn much."

And then he began moving, slowly, making sure she felt every stroke he made into her body. On and on, back and forth, in and out he moved, rocking into her and setting off shock waves of pleasure throughout both of their bodies.

The sound of Gina's moans increased as she became delirious in desire to the point where she could barely speak. He heard her draw a deep gasping breath with every stroke he made, just as dazed and overcome with passion as he was. His gentle strokes turned into deep thrusts and he fought back his intense need to explode inside of her.

When he felt himself losing control he reached for the condom he had placed on the nightstand next to the bed and ripped it open, intent on pulling out of her and putting it on. But that was before he felt her body quivering uncontrollably as she surrendered to her own release.

"Mitch!"

Her legs tightened around him and his body automatically detonated at the feel of her internal muscles clenching him. He began pumping into her, flooding her insides with enough semen to produce fifty babies.

When the both of them were completely spent and their bodies had begun melting down through a sweltering haze of sensations, Mitch pulled Gina closer into his arms and whispered "I love you" one last time before pulling the covers over their naked bodies and giving in to sleep.

The ringing of the telephone woke Mitch. Disoriented, he glanced around the room, saw it was barely daylight outside, then remembered where he was and who he was with. The sensuous smell of the woman sleeping in his arms was a welcoming reminder.

Without thinking he reached over and picked up the phone before it could ring again. "Hello."

"Good morning, Mitchell."

Ah, hell, Mitch thought, closing his eyes. *Why on earth had he answered the phone?* He slowly reopened his eyes. "Hello, Mrs. Grant."

There was a soft chuckle. "Somehow I just knew you would be there."

Mitch decided not to ask how she'd known. "Gina is asleep," he decided to tell her as a way to hurry up and end the conversation. He could just imagine what Gina's mother thought with him answering the phone this time of morning. And what was so bad, everything she thought was probably true. He and Gina had done a number of wild and wicked things throughout most of the night.

"Please wake Gina up. I need to talk with her."

He started to tell her Gina was probably too tired to talk, but decided that wouldn't be the wisest thing to do. He didn't want to make waves with the woman who would soon be his mother-in-law again; someone he could definitely use as an ally. Shifting positions in the bed, he gently nudged Gina. She looked at him sleepily and before she could say anything he quickly handed her the phone.

Confused, sluggish, and still very drowsy, Gina yawned as she spoke into the receiver. "Ahhh, hello...?"

"And what were you saying just yesterday about things being *strictly business* between you and Mitchell, Regina Renee? If anything, it seems whatever you two are working on is *strictly pleasure.*"

Gina quickly sat straight up in bed. "Mom!"

EIGHT

Mitch lay with his hands behind his head as he watched Gina talk on the phone to her mother. He couldn't take his eyes off of her. She was an extraordinarily beautiful woman.

The sheet had fallen past her waist, leaving the top part of her bare. Deep in conversation, she didn't bother to cover herself. His gaze feasted on her breasts, firm, squeezably soft, and a perfect fit for his hands. His heated vision then blazed a trail lower to the curve of her small waist and the flatness of her belly.

He felt his body become aroused as he continued to watch her, wondering how much longer she would be on the phone. He could tell from her expression that whatever her mother was saying, she wasn't too happy about it. He watched her move the phone to the other ear and waited for the time when he could claim her attention. He wasn't in any hurry since he didn't plan to leave her bed anytime soon.

Finally, she glanced over at him. Her cheeks tinted when she saw he lay uncovered, unashamedly exhibiting a full erection. She tried looking away but a few seconds later her gaze returned to him. He smiled when she unconsciously began licking her lips.

"Uh, Mom, I have to go. Yes, I'll tell Mitch, but the decision will be his." Gina inhaled deeply as she continued to look at him. "Tell Daddy that I love him, too. Good-bye." Taking another deep breath she handed Mitch the phone and watched as he placed it back in the cradle without shifting positions.

"You'll tell me what?" he asked, his voice low and intimate, as he reached up and touched her shoulders. He immediately felt a shiver race through her.

"Dinner," she said, barely getting the word out. She felt herself melting from his touch and the heated look in his eyes.

"What about dinner?"

When she felt his hand move lower toward her breasts, she had to think hard for an answer. "They want you to come to dinner."

"They who?"

A long breath staggered from her lungs when Mitch touched her breasts, slowly caressing one nipple and then the other. His touch felt so good she found herself closing her eyes to . . .

"They who, Gina?"

She reopened them and looked at him. He had shifted positions and was now close to her face. She quickly sucked in a gulp of air when his hand moved lower, to her stomach. How on earth did he expect her to concentrate while touching her this way? "My parents. They want me to bring you to dinner tonight. Can you?"

Mitch gently massaged her stomach. He couldn't help wondering if perhaps he had gotten her pregnant last night, and if even now his child was taking shape and forming into a life inside her womb. That very thought made him want her even more. He leaned up closer to her ear, tasting her right beneath it with the tip of his tongue, before moving to her mouth. "Can I what?"

"Can you come?"

He chuckled against her lips. "After last night how can you even ask such a thing? Yeah, I can come, plenty of times. In fact I'm about ready to come now."

"Mitch," she whispered, her voice straining, her body blazing hot. "Don't misinterpret the question. Mom and Dad want you to come with me to dinner tonight at their place. But you don't have to."

"Thank you," he said, placing butterfly kisses around her mouth and chin. "For letting me know that I don't have to, but I don't mind going."

Gina swallowed. With the way he was kissing her and touching her, overwhelming desire was clouding her mind. "You sure?"

"About what?" he murmured as he traced kisses from her mouth to her shoulders.

"Dinner at my parents' place." Gina was wondering how long she would last before finally going up in flames when he slipped his hand beneath the sheet and found her hot and wet. Her body jolted to awareness when his finger intimately checked her for readiness.

"The only thing I'm sure about," he said, gently easing her on her back, "is that I want to make love to you again."

Moments later, when his body entered hers, the only thing Gina could think was—*Good answer, good answer.*

The interstate into Fresno wasn't the least bit crowded, Gina noticed as Mitch drove them to his ranch. After they had made love once, then twice, they had showered together. He had invited her back to his place, saying she could interview him on the way there. So she had, although it was hard thinking about business when the two of them had had so much pleasure the night before and that morning.

"So, now that you've gotten chummy with our governor, does that mean you will be changing political parties?"

Mitch chuckled, trying to recall if that particular question had been on the list. "No. I plan to remain a Democrat until the day I die and the governor knows that. Appointing me to that national position showed he cares more about what the real issues are than party affiliations."

Gina nodded. "Do you have to travel to Washington often?"

"I did in the beginning. But now the committee only meets twice a year unless there are some major concerns."

That piqued Gina's interest. "Have there been a number of major concerns?"

Mitch smiled over at her when he finally pulled up in front of the ranch house and brought his Durango to a stop. "I know for a fact that that wasn't an interview question, Gina. And I don't think the president or the other committee members would appreciate me telling any secrets."

Gina grinned as she unfastened her seat belt. "I'm not *that* kind of reporter, Mitch."

He raised a dark brow at her. "Any reporter is *that* kind of reporter once they get wind of what they think is a news-breaking story. Come on, you can finish asking me your questions later. I need to talk to that group over there."

The "group" he was referring to were the contractors he'd hired to completely renovate the ranch house. She smiled when she saw it was the twins, Blade and Slade Madaris. Throwing up her hand, she waved to them as she headed for the trailer. They were a year younger than she was, and she remembered the times the three of them often played together as kids while growing up, along with the twins' cousin, Luke Madaris.

Once inside the trailer she glanced around. Mitch had to be one of the neatest men she knew. Everything was in place. When they were married he had nearly driven her crazy with his fetish for being tidy. She smiled. She felt better today than she had in a long time.

Half an hour later, without looking over her shoulder Gina said, "Lunch is ready," as she stood on tiptoe to take some plates out of the cabinet.

"Can I take a chance and eat it and live?"

She turned around with a frown on her face. "I'll have you know, Mitch Farrell, that I've learned to cook."

Mitch leaned against the closed trailer door with his arms crossed over his chest looking skeptical. "Since when?"

Gina smiled. "Since I no longer had you to do it for me," she said, remembering how Mitch enjoyed doing all the cooking. Even those times when he had put in long days at the office, he would get up at the crack of dawn and prepare a four-course meal for dinner before going to work. The only thing she did in the kitchen was to go get a plate.

"Besides," she added, placing bowls and cups on the kitchen table. "You can't go wrong with a can of Campbell's soup and a box of saltine crackers."

Mitch shook his head, smiling. "No, I guess you can't. Give me a second to wash my hands and I'll join you."

"All right."

By the time he returned Gina had set the table. "I didn't want us to eat anything heavy to ruin dinner. Knowing Mom, she's probably preparing a feast. Trevor, Corinthians, and the baby are coming to dinner, too."

Mitch slipped into the chair opposite Gina. For the second time in less than twenty-four hours they had shared a meal together. Yesterday he had prepared lunch for her and today she had prepared lunch for him. He could actually count on his fingers the number of times they had shared a meal together while married. Usually he was so late coming in from work that by the time he got home she would have eaten and gone to bed.

Bed.

Now that was where they had spent most of their time together. No matter how late it had been when he got home, once he went to bed, Gina would willingly come into his arms.

"Now for the next question."

He looked up after saying his grace to see her pull out her writing pad and pencil. He also noted she had the tape recorder sitting on the side. He frowned. "I didn't know this would be a working lunch."

Gina grinned at him. "So now you know. I thought if we got through most of the questions, we wouldn't have to spend our time later tonight discussing them."

A smile tilted the corners of his lips. He knew exactly what he wanted them to do later tonight. "That's a good point."

She laughed. "Yeah, I thought you would agree." She flipped through the pages to find the questions she wanted to ask him. "Now then, what drove you to become successful?"

She could tell the question bothered him, judging from the way he looked when she asked it. "Mitch?" Some sort of struggle was taking place inside of him but she didn't understand why. "Mitch, why does that question bother you? It was on the list."

"Yes, I know, but I wasn't prepared for it yet."

"Surely, you've been asked that before?" she countered.

He stared at her for the longest moment before saying, "No, I haven't ever been asked that. Mainly because no one knows how hard I worked to become successful. And no one knows how I let it become an obsession. I was truly what you'd call a workaholic. I became addicted to work the same way a person becomes addicted to drugs or alcohol. Do you know by the time we got a divorce, I was working well over eighty hours a week?"

Gina shook her head. She hadn't known he'd been working *that* many hours, although she'd known he had been working quite a lot.

"Well, I was. The only time I wasn't thinking about work was when I was making love to you. You were the only distraction I had, Gina."

"But why, Mitch? Why were you driven so?"

He sighed deeply. He wasn't ready to share with her how it was to be a child and go to bed every night hungry. Sometimes the hunger pains were so bad you couldn't function in class the next day. Then you had to deal with teachers who thought you weren't paying attention because you were slow, when in truth you were so hungry you couldn't think straight. The only thing that had kept him going, that had kept him from giving up, was his determination to one day never be hungry and never be thought of as slow again. He had vowed to work hard, study hard, and be successful. There had been nothing wrong with that goal—except somehow he had taken it to the extreme.

He began talking, hoping that Gina would understand without his having to tell her everything. "For the longest time I had convinced myself that the reason I did it was because of what I went through while living with my uncle. I've often told you what a miser he was. I promised myself that I would grow up and become successful and I wouldn't go without anything. And I guess that was partly true. But somewhere along the line I lost focus. Somewhere along the line I began working in order to live and living in order to work. Work became the center of my life, and while other things were important to me, work became number one."

Gina nodded. He wasn't telling her anything she didn't already know. She had realized long before she had finally asked for a divorce that she had been relegated to the bottom of his list.

"So to answer your question, Gina," he said, reclaiming her attention, "I guess you can say that I was first driven because I somehow believed that I *had* to be successful. In my mind not being successful meant being a failure. Then, when I married you, I knew I had a tough act to follow with your father. Although he didn't live with you and your mother and Trevor, he still was able to provide for you. I considered you as high maintenance. Although you didn't ask for much, I knew you were used to having nice things and I wanted to continue to provide you with those things."

"But I had a job, Mitch. I worked every day and had money."

"Yes, but I felt that as your husband *I* was supposed to take care of you and provide you with the things you needed and wanted. I was determined to take care of you, and in order to do that it meant I had to work hard and move up in my career. At some point I became unable to separate work and play. Other than sex, work was what energized me."

"And what about now, Mitch?" she asked softly, wanting to know, needing to know. "What energizes you now?"

He smiled across the table at her. "You. With you I'd rather play than work."

"Why now and not before?"

"Because I've changed and I've allowed my priorities to change. And because I've been so damn miserable without you in my life, Gina."

She wanted to believe him. She wanted to believe that he was no longer working himself to death and that his life was more manageable now than it had been when they were married. She wanted to believe all of that, but a part of her was afraid to. The last thing she wanted was a repeat performance of pain in her life. "When you finish eating, how about we take a walk and I can complete the list of questions I have for today?"

Mitch nodded. He knew that she was deliberately bringing the interview to an end for now. She didn't want to accept that workaholism was a disease just like alcoholism and that people could become bona fide workaholics. One day he would tell her how he had met Ivan Spears, a successful banker, at a gym, and how Ivan, a former workaholic himself, had talked him into attending a Workaholics Anonymous meeting. Ivan had organized a group of men and women—all African-Americans—who were in the same predicament as him. After several meetings they had helped each other realize that, as African-Americans, they shared the belief that giving one hundred percent in the corporate workplace wasn't enough. They had to give one hundred and fifty percent or even more to reach the same success level as their white counterparts. Being supportive of each other had helped. And although they couldn't change the way corporate America operated, at least they knew what they had to do to recover from workaholism.

"Mitch?"

He smiled across the table, bringing his thoughts back to her suggestion. "All right. After lunch we'll go for a walk."

NINE

"Your father still doesn't believe in sugarcoating his words, I see," Mitch said as he opened the door to Gina's house. They were just returning from dinner at her parents'.

Gina smiled. Considering everything, she thought the evening had gone rather well. At least Mitch was still alive and in good health. After their divorce her father had claimed that he would do bodily harm to Mitch if he ever came within five feet of her again. He had behaved himself at Trevor's wedding reception, and had even tolerated the two of them dancing together, but only because at the time he and her mother had reconciled after a twenty-year separation and had been too busy acting like newlyweds themselves to worry about her.

"Dad is Dad, I doubt he'll ever change, Mitch. I'm sure Mom told him that you spent the night, and he's still overprotective where I'm concerned."

Mitch nodded, thinking that was an understatement. However, he had to admit that during his and Gina's marriage, Maurice Grant had never meddled in their affairs. Once he had turned his daughter over to Mitch's care as her husband, that had been that. But Mitch knew he had let the man down. He had promised to love, honor, and cherish Gina and he hadn't always done that. He had loved her with every breath in his body; he also felt he had honored her as well. But he had been sorely lacking with the cherishing part. He had been too busy working long and extended hours to cherish anything. He now regretted every minute he had stayed late at the office instead of going home and spending time with her.

"It's strange seeing your parents together that way," he said, following Gina into her kitchen.

A smile curled her lips as she began making a pot of coffee, remembering how openly affectionate her parents were to each other. "I know. It takes some getting used to. Dad loves Mom and she loves him. Too bad they had all those wasted years when they could have been together."

Mitch nodded. "Yeah, but they're together now and that's what's important."

"You're right and they just love being grandparents. Did you see how they carried on over Rio?" She laughed. "That baby is going to be spoiled rotten."

Mitch chuckled. "Hey, you were doing a pretty good job spoiling him yourself tonight, Aunt Gina. For a while I thought he was glued to your arms."

Gina leaned against the counter knowing that was true. It seemed that every time she held Rio, the desire for a child of her own pierced her heart. He was such a good baby, a beautiful and precious baby who would grow up in his parents' deep love and protection.

"You've gotten quiet, Gina. What are you thinking about?"

She looked up at Mitch and decided to be honest with him. "I was thinking about Rio and how each and every time I hold him I wish I had a child of my own. I've always wanted a baby."

Mitch looked into her eyes and knew he had disappointed her in that department, too. He distinctly remembered the number of times she had asked, almost begged, for them to start a family and how he had refused her on the grounds that he wasn't ready to become a father. He had to be sure he could successfully provide for a child before agreeing to bring one into the world. He hadn't realized until now just how wrong and selfish he had been to withhold from her the very thing that would have made her happy.

With a deep ragged sigh, he reached out and pulled her into his arms. "I'm sorry, Gina."

"For what?" she asked, liking the feel of being held by him, pressed so close to his strong body. His chest felt wonderful against her chin.

"For all those times you asked me for a baby and I refused to give you one."

A tiny, sad smile touched Gina's lips. "That's all right, I understand."

Mitch looked down at her. "Do you, Gina? Do you really understand? I don't think so, because I've yet to give you a reason to understand. And now I think it's time that I do."

Gina saw the intense look on his face and knew whatever he had to tell her would be serious. "All right." She nodded. "Give me a second to pour us a cup of coffee and then we can sit at the table and talk."

"Okay."

A few minutes later they were settled in chairs at her kitchen table. She said nothing as she waited for Mitch to begin speaking.

"I never told you everything about my uncle Jasper. I know I told you he had a drinking problem and that he was stingy, but I never went into the extent of emotional abuse that I had to deal with, too. He wanted me to believe that I was dumb, worthless, and no good, and he spent every day that I lived with him telling me that. Most of the time he didn't feed me. For a while I had to eat scraps anywhere I could find them to survive. Other times I went hungry."

Gina was appalled. "Weren't there agencies around that were supposed to check to make sure you were getting the proper care?"

"Yeah, I suppose there were. But I figured I somehow had fallen through the cracks. Once I ran away, and when I was returned to him, he gave me the beating of my life. In fact it almost ended my life it was so severe. The check he was getting every month was what enabled him to buy his booze and his women, and he wasn't about to let me get away."

"Oh, Mitch."

He sat across from her and saw the deep emotions in her face and the mistiness that appeared in her eyes. She was sad because of what had happened to him. Reaching across the table, he captured her hand in his. "Don't be sad for me, Gina, because I survived. Every night that I went to bed hungry and every day that I went to school ashamed of how I looked made me that much more determined to grow up and make something of myself. I tried so hard, but at times it seemed that no matter how much I studied and tried to do well in school, I couldn't. I would sit in class so hungry that I couldn't concentrate. But I did finish school, and the following day, without taking anything with me, I left Uncle Jasper's house and vowed never to return."

"Good for you."

Mitch smiled. "Yeah, I thought it was good for me, but I still found things hard. Still, I had a determination that no amount of starvation had gotten rid of. I was determined to be successful, no matter what it took. I applied for a loan to go to college and worked two jobs while attending classes, and I kept those same two jobs when I went on to grad school. I had also made up my mind never to become involved with anyone until I had accomplished all my goals. I read every motivational, rags-to-riches book I could get my hands on, and in the end I knew what I had to do. I had to work hard and use my brains."

Gina's heart went out to Mitch for all he had endured. Now she finally understood why he had been so obsessed with making it to the top, why he had been so driven to be successful. She then remembered what he had told her earlier that day. "You really did become a workaholic, didn't you?"

"Yes." He was glad she finally understood things. "I also became a perfectionist. Everything had to be perfect and timed correctly.

The reason I couldn't think about us having a child was because in my mind the timing wasn't right."

She nodded and looked at him. "What about marrying me? Had the time been right for that?"

He released her hand and smoothed his fingers across her bare arm before saying, "No, the timing was all wrong. I hadn't counted on falling in love with you, Gina. But you came into my life and I couldn't get you out. And for the first time I became obsessed with something other than making it to the top. I knew somehow and some way I had to have you and still be successful, and I really thought it would work."

"But it didn't."

He chuckled. "It sure as hell didn't. From the beginning you demanded my time, more time than I had ever given anyone. And I found myself liking it. I enjoyed being in bed with you more than I enjoyed attending some seminar about how to succeed in life. I found myself watching the clock every day at work, counting down the hours, minutes, and seconds when I could leave the office to go home and be with you. I used to sit in board meetings and remember how it had been the night before to slip inside your body and reach an orgasm with your name on my lips." He smiled. "I had it pretty bad."

Gina swallowed the lump in her throat as she remembered the first year of their marriage, when Mitch had given her so much attention and so much love. "When did you realize that?" she asked softly.

"When my boss called me into his office and said that I didn't seem as focused as I had once been, and wasn't as sharp and dedicated as I used to be. He thought that maybe something was wrong at home. I was too obtuse to tell him that it was just the opposite and that everything was right at home—my wife was wonderful and my life was happy and I had found a way to balance both work and home. Instead, in my mind I took his words to be synonymous with what my uncle used to say about me. And a part of me was determined to prove him wrong. So I began working harder and staying at the office later."

He drew a long breath before continuing. "That meant putting you second and my career first. That also meant not giving in to anything I thought would set us back. I had my eye on a house in McGregor Park. It had always been my dream to live there."

Gina nodded. McGregor Park was a very old, established and exclusive area of Houston where the well-to-do lived. "If you felt I was a threat to your career plans, why didn't you just divorce me, Mitch?" she asked, seeing and now understanding the extent of what he'd been going through.

"Because as much as I wanted to be successful, and as much as I wanted all those goals I had been determined to achieve, I loved you and couldn't give you up. I had convinced myself that in time I would be able to handle both you and work. It hadn't dawned on me then that a workaholic is never satisfied. They constantly take personal inventory and come up with other things to aspire to and they buy into the belief that more money will solve all the problems in their life."

He was silent for a brief moment before saying, "After our divorce I realized the mistakes I had made. I had never really given our marriage a chance to work because of the way I was."

He sighed deeply. "I joined Workaholics Anonymous and met other men and women like myself who were suffering from the same affliction. My group consisted of African-Americans who knew that the issues we face in corporate America aren't faced by our white counterparts. We have helped each other tremendously, most of us have since recovered and have found that balance between work and family."

He captured her hand in his again. "I love you, Gina. I know it's a lot to ask, but I'd like you to give us another chance."

Another chance? Gina felt battered from her emotions, she could barely think straight. "Mitch, I don't know. I need time to think. You shared a lot with me tonight. Most were things you should have shared with me long ago. Then I could have been more supportive and understanding. But I don't know if we can put the past behind us."

"We can at least try, can't we? I don't expect you to make a decision tonight, Gina, or even this week or this month. All I want is for you to agree to let me back into your life. I want to see you, be with you, as a friend and a lover. I want you to give me the opportunity to make things up to you, to wipe the slate clean and start fresh. I want to have the chance to prove that I do love you and that I have always loved you and that I will always love you. Will you agree to at least give me a chance, Gina?"

She sat still, unsure of herself and the situation Mitch had placed her in. She looked down at their joined hands. He wanted them to establish a relationship; a very serious and exclusive relationship. He wanted to be her friend and her lover. But what happened if things between them didn't work out? What if . . .

"Gina?"

She slowly lifted her gaze, suddenly ensnarled in the imposing silence that filled the room and the heat that flowed from his eyes to hers. This was the man who had taught her everything she knew about the physical aspects of love. He was the man who had provided so much for her while they were married.

She sighed deeply. As much as she didn't want to admit it, she loved him and wished she had been stronger and had fought harder for him and their marriage. But she had to wonder if love would be enough. It hadn't been the last time, and she didn't think she could go through that again. But a part of her was willing to do what he asked and give him—give them—another chance. They were sleeping together again anyway, and she didn't see that coming to an end any time soon—especially when her body wanted him something fierce. She might as well have a relationship with him, because like she had told her mother, she had never been into casual sex, and without a relationship, that's what sleeping with him would become: casual, a way to appease her sexual hunger. And he meant more to her than just a bed partner.

"All right, Mitch," she finally said. "We'll date and do the relationship thing. But if things don't work out the way we think they should, then we should bring things to an end, before either of us gets hurt. Agreed?"

He looked from her face to their joined hands and then back to her face again. He gave a satisfied nod and said, "Agreed."

TEN

During the following weeks, Mitch and Gina settled into a nice, satisfying routine. She had finished the interview and had given him the rough copy to read and approve. He had told her he had been impressed with what she had written. The article would satisfy the public's curiosity but at the same time keep his privacy—and his secrets—intact.

Work had started on the ranch house and she was astonished with the results. Retaining the structure of the original house, the Madaris Construction Company was fulfilling Mitch's dream of returning his grandmother's home to the place he remembered and loved.

Their relationship blossomed more every day, and on occasion, they would dine with her parents. She had explained her and Mitch's relationship to her family and had been adamant that they understood that just because they were together as a couple did not necessarily mean that they would remarry. At the present what they were trying to do was build a solid relationship, one that could and would withstand anything, especially the pressures of marriage.

She found that she and Mitch were communicating more. She also found herself included in a number of his business decisions, and he often asked her advice and opinions on a lot of issues. They spent every night together, either at her place or his, and Gina had to admit that she was the happiest she had been in a long time.

"You're glowing, Gina."

Gina smiled as she looked up and met Corinthians's smile. The two of them had decided to do lunch together at Sisters when Gina's mother had eagerly volunteered to keep Rio. "Am I?"

Corinthians arched a dark brow and returned Gina's smile. "Yes, you are. In fact you are glowing all over the place." She tilted her head to study her. "You have a certain look about you. It's a happy and a serene look, a satisfied look. I would say Mitch definitely agrees with you."

Gina chuckled. "Thanks, I think I'll keep him around."

Corinthians's smile widened. "Does that mean the two of you have finally decided to remarry?"

Gina frowned. "No, it means just what I said: I think I will keep him around."

Corinthians placed her menu aside and leaned back in her chair. "And how long before you decide to make a decision on your future with him?"

"There's no rush."

"Maybe not for you, but it's obvious that Mitch would remarry you in a heartbeat if you gave the word. What are you afraid of?"

"I'm not afraid of anything."

"Aren't you?"

Gina hesitated for a long moment before finally deciding to be honest with Corinthians. She loved Mitch. She had known that before she had agreed to his offer of giving them another chance. But he was back to working again. Although he was now the boss and made his own hours, a part of her got nervous each and every time he got involved in some business deal. Although he had been doing a good job balancing his time with her and whatever business he needed to take care of, she was afraid he would again find she wasn't enough and would go back to being the workaholic that he used to be.

"Yes," she said softly. "I'm afraid."

"Of loving him?"

"No, I'm afraid of him not loving me, the way I want and need to be loved. I don't think I could handle playing second fiddle to his job again."

Corinthians chuckled. "Honey, I doubt very seriously that you ever will. Everyone can see that you, and only you, have Mitch Farrell's complete attention. Remember that night last week when the two of you were over to our place? He couldn't keep his eyes off you and when he got that call on his beeper, he didn't leave. He stayed right there."

Gina nodded, remembering. "But it shouldn't have bothered me if he *had* left. There will be times when he'll get an unexpected business call and have to take off. I should be at a point in our relationship where I'm fine with it and don't feel threatened."

"Then why do you feel threatened?"

"Because I lost the number-one spot in his life before."

Corinthians reached across the table and captured Gina's hand and squeezed it gently. "I believe Mitch knows the mistake he made doing that and regrets it, Gina. In my heart I believe he doesn't plan on doing it again. But I don't think you're being fair to him. He's trying so hard to make things up to you and still you're remembering the past and holding it against him. At some point you have to forgive him and believe in a future for the two of you. It's going to be up to you, Gina, to put things behind you and move on."

Gina tilted her head to the side and studied her sister-in-law. "Sounds like you're speaking from experience, Corinthians."

A gentle smile touched the corners of Corinthians's mouth. "I am. Your brother and I couldn't stand each other. For nearly three years after we first met we could barely tolerate the sight of each other, and being in the same room for any length of time was a total nightmare."

"Wow," Gina whispered softly, finding that hard to believe.

Corinthians's smile widened. "Believe it or not, but things were just that bad. And only because neither of us would let go of the past, which had a lot to do with how we first met."

Gina nodded. As usual her curiosity was piqued but she knew Corinthians wasn't ready to divulge the details of that quite yet. "So, when did the two of you put things behind you and move on?"

Corinthians chuckled. "Not until my father intervened and sat us down and talked to us. I guess you can say he forced us to see the light and we're so thankful that he did. It was only then I discovered that Trevor loved me and he discovered that I loved him. But I would advise you not to wait for anyone to intervene in your case, Gina. It's going to be up to you to do it. And if you love Mitch as much as I believe you do, then you will."

Gina was still remembering the conversation with Corinthians while taking her shower later that night. Coming out of the bathroom she glanced across the room at the clock. Mitch had called a couple of hours ago and said he would be detained for a while because he was at the trailer waiting on an important business call.

She tried not to think about the fact that his job was keeping him from her. She went into the living room and decided to find something to watch on television. An hour later, after having watched a program she'd found interesting, she turned off the set and went into the kitchen.

The table was still set for the dinner she had prepared for them and she could feel herself getting angry and annoyed. *How dare Mitch do this to me?* She had just opened the refrigerator to start putting the food away when the phone rang. She quickly picked it up. "Hello."

"Hey, baby, sorry I was delayed. I just finished that business call I told you about. Unfortunately, it took longer than I expected. I'm about to leave. I'll be there in half an hour."

"Don't bother."

"What?"

"I said, don't bother. I'm ready for bed."

"So?"

"So, I'm ready for bed. I went to the trouble of cooking you dinner tonight thinking you'd be coming here when you said that you were and now everything is cold."

"Dinner? Oh, I'm sorry, honey, I didn't know. Why didn't you tell me?"

"It was supposed to be a surprise."

"And I ruined it. I'm sorry you're upset."

"Yeah, well, I should have learned my lesson by now, don't you think? It's not the first time your job came before me."

There was silence on the phone, and then Mitch spoke. "I'm on my way, Gina, and your butt better still be up when I get there." Gina could tell from the tone of his voice that what she'd said had really angered him.

"My butt . . . how dare—" She stopped speaking when she heard him hang up the phone on her. She became furious. "I can't believe he had the nerve to do that! Oh, just wait until he gets here. I will *definitely* tell him a thing or two! I don't care if I never see him again. Just wait!"

Gina was still fuming half an hour later when she heard Mitch's car outside. She barely gave him time to knock before snatching the door open. "How dare you say such a thing to me, Mitch Farrell!"

"And how dare you say such a thing to me, Gina!" he said, coming into the house and slamming the door shut behind him. "You are spoiled and selfish!"

"I am not spoiled and selfish!"

"Yes, you are. Case in point: last Monday, you were supposed to meet me at Sisters for dinner at six. You got there at seven-thirty. Did I get upset?"

She glared at him. "No, because I called and told you I was running behind and would be late."

He began pacing the floor to walk off his anger. "And then last Wednesday, you were supposed to meet me at the ranch at four, but you didn't get there until six."

"Yes, well, I got detained. I got a business call at the last minute from a publisher interested in me doing an article for their magazine. I told you that."

"Yes, you did, and I understood, didn't I?"

"Yes."

"Then why can't you afford me the same courtesy, respect, and trust? I called to let you know I was waiting on an important business call and would be a little late. Granted, time went a little beyond what I had expected, but still, I would think being a businessperson yourself that you would have understood. Instead, you got royally and I do mean royally pissed and decided to throw things up in my face about my past deeds. I thought we had gotten beyond all of that. Haven't I proven to you over the past five weeks that you mean everything to me and that I love you? So I'm going to ask you again, Gina. Why can't you afford me the same courtesy, respect, and trust that I give to you?"

When she didn't answer immediately, he walked over to her and stood in front of her. The eyes that glared at her were livid. The corded muscles in his neck were straining, his jaw was clenched hard and his nostrils were flaring. "Why can't you, dammit?"

Gina glared back up at him, not knowing what to say. So she told him the truth. "Because you're right," she said softly, breaking eye contact with him and looking down at her hands. She took a deep breath and met his gaze again. "I am spoiled and selfish." Feeling tears sting her eyes she added, "But when it comes to you, I can't help it. I want you all to myself, Mitch. I had to share you the last time and won't share you that way again." A tear slid down her cheek and she wiped it away.

Mitch swallowed his anger as he looked at her. He saw her hurt and tears, but more importantly, he saw her uncertainty. Four years of playing second fiddle to his job had really done a number on her. It would take time and patience for her to feel she had regained that number-one spot in his life.

He reached out and smoothed a few strands of hair out of her face and leaned down and stroked his tongue across her lips. "Oh, baby," he murmured softly against her mouth, nibbling gently on her lips. "Don't you know that you will never share me again? Work is work. You are you. I know where to draw the line now. I had that pretty well figured out before I returned to Houston. You are the most important thing in my life, Gina. Please believe that." Then he kissed her, his tongue thrusting deep in her mouth, making them both groan.

Kissed out of her mind, Gina felt herself drowning as Mitch sucked the very air from her lungs. She wasn't sure if she would ever breathe again, but if she had to die, then this was just the way to go. His tongue, hot, intimate, and delicious, was inside her mouth mating with hers and sending pleasure waves to all parts of her body, making it ache.

He broke off the kiss and framed her face with his hands. "I love you, Gina. I love *you*."

She closed her eyes and felt herself being lifted into big strong arms. She knew exactly where he was taking her and could barely wait to get there. She reopened her eyes when she felt him place her on the bed. He stood back and for a few minutes he simply stared at her. And then she saw what he had wanted her to see all along. It was there, clearly in his features, especially his eyes. He loved her. He had always loved her and he would always love her.

"Oh, Mitch." She reached out her hand to him and he took it and joined her in bed. With agonizing slowness he removed her gown and then removed his own clothes. As usual he placed a condom on the nightstand next to the bed. He had yet to use one of them, she thought. For a man who used to believe in doing everything at the right time, he hadn't been able to pull himself out of her to put a condom on. But the thought that they had been taking a risk each and every time they'd made love hadn't bothered her. Nor had it seemed to bother him. After each lovemaking session, they would promise themselves that they would get it right the next time; however, they never did. And something deep inside Gina told her that they never would.

First he began tormenting her breasts with his mouth and fingers, and pretty soon she was thrashing about in the bed, begging and pleading for him to stop, to continue, to hurry up... whatever.

Then his fingers, slowly and deliberately, began blazing trails over her body for his mouth to follow. No part of her was left untouched and untasted as desire cascaded over her. Tension was building everywhere, causing every inch of her to throb out of control.

"Now, Mitch!"

"Not yet."

Not yet! What does he plan to do? Torture me to death? "Mitch, please, now!"

He ignored her plea and continued what he was doing, sending the most incredible pleasures racing through her body. She curved her hands around his shoulders to stop him from pushing her over the edge and out of control but it was a waste of her time and effort. He was deliberately driving her insane.

"Mitch!"

It was then and only then that he parted her legs, lifted her hips and entered her, filling her completely and sending a bolt of heat through the most intimate part of her body. He then set the pace, withdrawing slowly and reentering, over and over again, each time going deeper and deeper. Her entire body began trembling from the impact of the sensuous rhythm he had established. Excruciating pleasure shattered her mind as he increased his pace, faster and faster, and adjusted his body to go deeper and deeper. When the explosion came, it was like a torpedo hitting the both of them hard and at the same time, sending them whirling into a space that was void of anything and everything but the two of them. It was an experience so emotional and tender, they clung to each other, soaring together beyond the stars and the moon and then slowly returning to earth and reality.

But not for long.

Mitch suddenly felt fully rejuvenated; the need to have her again rammed into him. He began pumping vigorously into her, over and over, relentlessly.

"Mitch!"

When the second orgasm came crashing down on them both, so soon behind the last, they both screamed out at the top of their lungs as they soared to heights so high, swift, and powerful, they thought death would surely follow.

They lay for a long moment in each other's arms, not saying anything, still in awe at what they had just shared. Finally, Mitch spoke when he saw the unused condom on the nightstand. "We goofed again, baby." He then thought about their bodies' double explosion and added, "Big time."

She smiled as she snuggled close to him. "Don't worry about it. We'll get it right one day."

"I may have gotten you pregnant tonight. You were real hot inside both times, and I filled you up pretty good."

Gina smiled. She had always appreciated the fact that she and Mitch had been able to talk candidly and frankly to each other in the bedroom. That sort of sexual communication only enhanced the sensuality they shared. "Don't worry about it. I didn't get pregnant tonight," she whispered, turning in his arms and looking at him.

"You sound pretty sure of that."

She leaned over and softly kissed his lips. "Trust me, I am."

He lifted a brow, wondering if she had gone on the Pill or if she had used some other type of birth control and had failed to tell him about it. "How can you be so sure?"

She met his gaze and a smile tilted each corner of her lips. "Because a woman can't get pregnant when she's already pregnant."

Gina saw his forehead bunch as he tried figuring out just what she meant. Then she saw the crinkle of happiness that immediately appeared in his eyes and the grin that suddenly shone on his mouth. "You're having a baby?" he asked in awe, barely able to contain his happiness and excitement.

"That's what the doctor said this morning."

"Why didn't you tell me?"

"I had planned to. Tonight. That was the reason for the surprise dinner."

Mitch pulled her into his arms. "Oh, sweetheart, I can't believe it. A baby. We're going to have a baby."

She nodded and wrapped her arms around him. "Are you happy about it, Mitch? I mean, are you truly, really happy?"

He leaned down and gently kissed her lips. "Yes, I am truly, really happy."

She leaned back in his arms, contented with his answer. "I hope you know what this means."

Mitch shook his head smiling. "No, what does this means?"

"It means, Mr. Farrell, that as soon as it can be arranged, you'll have to make me Mrs. Mitchell Farrell all over again."

He pulled her closer to him. "And it will be my pleasure. You've always been Mrs. Mitchell Farrell, Gina. In my heart you were always my wife."

"Oh, Mitch, I love you so much."

He leaned over and kissed her, thanking God for giving him this second chance with her, and believing in his heart that this was how things were meant to be. They were supposed to be together, and this time he was going to make sure it lasted forever.

EPILOGUE

A Month Later

Only family and close friends were invited to witness the marriage of Mitch and Gina. Corinthians's father, the Reverend Nathan Avery, had been more than delighted to perform the ceremony. Trevor had happily served as Mitch's best man and Corinthians had been Gina's matron of honor.

They hadn't told anyone about the baby, deciding to keep it their secret for a while. As Gina glanced around at the number of pregnant women in the room, she knew when the time came she would be in good company.

Syneda, Clayton's wife, was due to have her baby in a few months and Jake's wife, Diamond, was not far behind. Then there was Dex's wife, Caitlin, who had recently found out with an ultrasound that they were having a son. Last, but definitely not least, was Nettie, the owner of Sisters, who was married to Ashton Sinclair, one of Trevor's best friends. Everyone was excited with the news that Nettie was having triplets, all boys.

Gina glanced across the room at Mitch and smiled. He was talking to her brother and just looking at him sent heated desire racing down her spine. She couldn't wait for them to be alone later.

"You look absolutely radiant."

She smiled when Corinthians's compliment snagged her attention.

"Thanks, and I feel radiant as well as very happy. Today has been a very special day."

Corinthians chuckled softly. "The first of many more to come."

Gina's smile widened when she thought of what her future had in store. "Yes, the first of many more to come, and I appreciate everyone who came to celebrate our joyous occasion."

Corinthians took a sip of her punch, then said, "Speaking of joyous occasions, I wonder what's wrong with Alex? He seems bothered about something."

Gina glanced across the room at the man Corinthians was talking about, Alex Maxwell. He was Trask's brother and a close friend of the Grant and Madaris families. Her smooth forehead furrowed. "I don't know, but it looks like he's glaring at Christy Madaris."

"Hmm-mm, I think you're right," Corinthians said as her gaze followed Alex's and lit on the beautiful young woman with vibrant red hair who had arrived moments before and was circling the room. Christy was the Madaris brothers' baby sister and when it came to Christy, the brothers were overprotective.

Gina shook her head smiling. "I can't believe how Christy has grown up, and she'll be graduating from college next spring. I can remember when she was a teenager who had a big-time crush on Alex. I'd often wondered if she would grow out of it, and apparently she has."

Corinthians nodded as she glanced back across the room to Alex. He was still glaring at Christy. She remembered a time Trevor wore a similar expression when he looked at her. A slight smile touched her lips and she wondered if perhaps history was about to repeat itself.

"So, you pulled it off, I see," Trevor said to Mitch, smiling as he glanced across the room to where his sister stood talking to his wife. He could tell from the smile on Gina's face just how happy she was.

Mitch chuckled. "Did you think for one minute that I wouldn't?"

Trevor grinned. "No. That night I talked to you, you were pretty damn determined. I'm glad you're back in the family, Mitch."

"And I'm glad to be back." He glanced across the room to where his father-in-law was standing talking to Reverend Avery. "Excuse me, Trevor, there's something I need to take care of."

He walked over to the two men. "Excuse me, Reverend Avery, but I would like to speak with Mr. Grant privately for a second."

Nathan Avery smiled. "Sure thing, son. We were discussing our grandson there. I'll check out those little sandwiches Stella just put out."

When Mitch found himself alone with Gina's father at first it was hard for him to gather up his thoughts. And it didn't help matters that Maurice Grant was looking at him through dark eyes that reminded Mitch so much of Trevor when he wasn't too pleased about something.

Mitch cleared his throat. "There was a reason I didn't ask for Gina's hand in marriage this time, sir."

"Oh? Were you afraid I wouldn't give it to you a second time?" Maurice Grant said, unsmiling.

Mitch shook his head. "No, I felt it wasn't needed. You had given it to me once and a part of me felt you knew I was doing the right thing by getting her back."

"And have you done the right thing, Mitch?"

"Yes, sir, I have. I love your daughter very much."

Maurice didn't say anything for a long moment. Then he let out a deep sigh. "I know you do. I've always known how you felt and I was fairly certain we hadn't seen the last of you, although Gina was pretty convinced we had. So, I really wasn't surprised when you showed back up in Houston."

"You weren't?"

"No." The older man let out an amused chuckle. "In fact, I had expected you sooner."

"I had a lot of issues to resolve."

"And have you?"

"Yes, sir."

"Good. My daughter loves you very much, but I guess you know that."

"Yes, sir, I know that."

"And I guess I don't have to tell you that I expect you to make her happy."

Mitch shook his head, smiling. "No, sir, you don't have to tell me that."

"Good." He extended his hand out to Mitch. "I'm glad to have you back in the family, son, and I know in my heart that you are the *best* man for her. You are the *only* man for her."

A lump formed in Mitch's throat. It had been important to him to regain this man's trust and confidence. "Thank you."

"Mitch?"

Mitch turned toward the soft, ultra-sexy voice and smiled when he saw Gina. "Yes, sweetheart?"

She glanced from him to her father, then back to him again. Concern showed in her eyes. "Is everything all right?"

He chuckled. "Yes, everything is fine. Come here, Mrs. Farrell."

She closed the distance between them and walked straight into his opened arms. He held her tight and close to his heart. Tonight they would leave on a trip to the U.S. Virgin Islands, St. Thomas, and St. Croix, for a four-week honeymoon. Two weeks for the honeymoon they'd never had the first time around and the other two for this marriage.

From now on everything between them would be *strictly pleasure*.

irresistible attraction

*So teach us to number our days, that we may apply
our hearts unto wisdom.*

—PSALM 90:12

*To my husband, Gerald Jackson Sr.
and
A special young lady, Sydney Rashan Snow*

PROLOGUE

Sydney Corbain smiled as she watched her brother Linc steal a kiss from Raven, his bride, as they waltzed around the room, their first dance together as husband and wife. Tears of happiness shone in her eyes and she took a deep breath, then exhaled. This was how it was supposed to be for two people who loved each other.

Her smile widened as she acknowledged there were actually six people dancing around the room who loved each other, happy and eager to start their new lives together. This was the first triple wedding she had ever attended, and she had to admit it was one of the most beautiful. It was evident that Leigh Walcott Alexander, the professional event planner, along with the owners of Leo's Supper Club, the Hardcastles, had worked hard to make the wedding and the reception special for the three couples.

She didn't think she had seen such beautiful brides as Raven and her two sisters, Robin and Falcon. They were simply glowing for their husbands and there was no doubt in Sydney's mind they were women well loved.

She glanced around the room and her gaze met that of Tyrone Hardcastle, one of the owners of Leo's. This wasn't the first time tonight that their gazes had met... and held. She could feel something between them—interest, curiosity, awareness—as well as something else.

An irresistible attraction.

She sighed deeply, frozen in place, as they continued to look at each other. His gaze began moving slowly over her face, studying her feature by feature. She wanted to look away but could not. Her senses were on high alert and she actually liked the excitement. At twenty-six, a sexual attraction she could handle, an emotional connection she could not.

The two of them had been introduced last year when she'd come from Memphis to D.C. to see her brother Linc, and within seconds she had felt an aura of acute sexual awareness that radiated between them. It was there in the intensity of his gaze whenever he looked at her, making a shiver of heated desire course through her body. Even now she could feel her reactions being triggered. She knew from the psychology classes she'd taken in college that sexual attraction was normal and a part of every human's makeup.

Sydney sighed again. There was nothing normal about the desire she was feeling for Tyrone Hardcastle. She was an attorney, for heaven's sake, programmed to deal with facts—specifics and details. But at that very moment, Tyrone was making her too confused to play the role. The strange thing about it was that she had never felt these strong vibes from his identical twin brother, Tyrell. Her reaction to Tyrone was one sure way to tell them apart, as well as the difference in hairstyle. She hadn't spent enough time with either to know their temperament. Last October, exactly six months ago, she had learned the painful lesson that a person could be one way on the outside and totally different on the inside. Rafe Sutherlin had been the one to educate her. She was glad she had found out what type of inconsiderate person he was before she agreed to marry him.

So here she was, fighting off vibes she had never felt for Rafe, or any man for that matter. Everyone who knew her was aware that she was levelheaded in some things and impulsive in others.

Like now.

She and Tyrone were flirting with each other without saying a single word, yet flirting just the same. But so what? It was fun, spicy, and harmless. Each time they saw each other their attraction became more tempting and enticing, and she felt that Tyrone Hardcastle was worth every minute she was putting into it. Juilliard educated with a doctorate degree, he was responsible for the music and entertainment at Leo's. She had to give him credit for how his skillful selection of music, every noteworthy tune, had enhanced the event. Those in attendance would remember the varied sounds and resonance of the reception as much as they did the wedding itself. Both had been crafted together in a way that made it one unforgettable event.

She could also give him credit for how he looked tonight. He was not dressed like a behind-the-scene worker, detached from the activities. Like the rest of the Hardcastles who felt a definite closeness to the three brides, he was dressed in formal attire like everyone else.

No man, she thought, should look that good in a tux and have such a striking profile. He wore his sandy brown hair in twists that fell to his shoulders. His skin was a golden brown and his eyes, still trained directly on her, were large, slanted, and clear brown. Like his twin, there was a distinctive mole on his left cheekbone and a strong cleft chin.

From what her sister-in-law Raven had told her, Tyrone was very much single, preferred to be called Roni by family and friends, and placed everything, including women, second to his music.

She shrugged. She didn't have a problem with that since she'd also been accused of placing everything second to her career. At least that's what Rafe had claimed. As she took a sip of her punch, thinking that even the fruity drink was first class, she decided to stop this game she was playing with Tyrone Hardcastle for now, since nothing could ever come of it.

But then, maybe, one day…

ONE

Nine Months Later

Tyrone Hardcastle clasped his hands around a mug of hot chocolate while sitting in a café in New York City in the middle of January, with the temperature less than fifteen degrees outside. He almost envied the two brothers and cousin he'd left behind in D.C. to run things at Leo's.

Almost but not quite.

Even with the cold weather, nothing was better than being in New York in the wintertime. He had grown accustomed to New York winters while a student at Juilliard. In spite of the ice, snow, and cold, there was something invigorating about being back in the Big Apple, even for just a short while, especially since he was here to do something he got a lot of pleasure from: sharing his musical talent with others.

He thoroughly enjoyed his job as entertainment director at Leo's Supper Club, a restaurant he owned along with his oldest brother Noah, his twin brother Tyrell, and his cousin Ayanna. During the year he occasionally traveled to a number of places to keep his finger on the pulse of the music industry, which was the reason he was in New York. He had returned to work as a visiting music professor at Columbia University for six weeks.

Tyrone glanced up, looked out the window, and studied the feminine figure moving across the street, then drew in a deep breath

irresistible attraction

as a sudden feeling of heat slithered through his body. This was the second time he had seen her this week, and both times he had gotten this sudden feeling of acute desire. He wondered if she were someone he knew, but both times he'd only managed to catch a glimpse of her from the back. As she was also wearing a huge overcoat and a knitted cap, he hadn't been too sure. Still, a part of him wondered, what was the possibility of two women having that same sensuous walk? As far as he was concerned, Sydney Corbain definitely had a patent on it. She also had a patent on the sudden rush of passion he was feeling. In all his thirty-three years, she was the only woman who could make him feel such an irresistible attraction.

Sydney Corbain.

Thinking of Sydney, he recalled the last time they had seen each other, at her brother's wedding nearly nine months ago. He would never forget that day. They had not exchanged a single word yet somehow managed to take the art of flirtation to a whole new level. They had been rather creative, and she had definitely gotten a rise out of him . . . literally.

She'd had all the qualities needed to attract a man's attention that day, and had definitely attracted his. From the moment she walked down the aisle as a bridesmaid his libido had gone into overdrive. Instead of the long gowns that most attendants wore, the three brides had decided to go with short bridesmaids' dresses. There was nothing like seeing a great pair of legs to turbocharge a man's mating instincts, and his had nearly overloaded. He couldn't forget the perfume he'd gotten a whiff of when she passed him on her way to the altar. It had been soft, sultry, and sexy as hell.

At the reception things had gotten even more interesting. After posing for enough pictures to last the brides and grooms until their silver anniversaries, Sydney had changed into an outfit that showed not only a lot of leg but also a nice amount of cleavage. He hadn't been the only man watching her, but he'd been the only man whose interest she had reciprocated.

Since he'd been technically working that day to make sure the music at the reception was everything the brides had wanted, he did not get a chance to speak to Sydney, but he had definitely enjoyed their flirting game. He had asked her brother Linc about her a few months ago when the newlyweds had patronized Leo's one Sunday morning for brunch. According to Linc, she was doing fine and was busy back in Memphis working on an important court case.

Tyrone sighed deeply and made a quick decision to solve the mystery of the woman across the street and why she had made him think of Sydney. When he saw her enter a neighboring shop, he stood, threw more than enough money on the table for his bill, placed the straps to his saxophone case on his shoulder, left the café, and quickly crossed the street.

The evening was still young, and for once he didn't have anything else to do.

Sydney smiled the moment she stepped across the threshold of Victoria's Secret. Closing her eyes, she inhaled the subtle scent of everything feminine, a trademark of every Victoria's Secret store she patronized. She liked feeling sexy as well as looking the part.

Opening her eyes, she walked into the store and immediately went over to a table where panties were on display. She was beginning to develop a fetish for sexy underwear, and before her were some of the sexiest. She picked up a pair of cotton low-rise V-string panties and definitely liked the feel of the material. She had begun wearing the scanty undies, liking the way they fit, the freedom of movement they provided, and the naughtiness of wearing almost nothing.

Her smile widened as she glanced at the tag. They were on sale! Deciding that a dozen or so were definitely a must-buy, she concentrated on selecting the size and the colors she wanted, then quickly decided that, while she was at it, she might as well buy the colorful sexy-looking bras to match.

"Can I help you, Miss Corbain?"

Sydney inhaled sharply, startled at the deep, masculine voice behind her, very close to her ear. Her heart started pumping enough blood to bring a dead man back to life, and a sizzle of awareness coursed rapidly through her body. She blinked to bring herself out of her sexy haze. Only one man had the power to make her feel overloaded from so much sensuous heat. However, *that* man was supposed to be in Washington, D.C.

Her arms filled with at least fifteen pairs of panties, she slowly turned around, tilting her head back to take a good look. Her eyes grew wide in surprise, and for a brief moment her words stuck in her throat as she tried to speak. Finally, after swallowing deeply, she found her voice.

"Tyrone Hardcastle! What are you doing in New York?" She allowed her gaze to soak up just how good he looked in his black leather overcoat, a sax case over his shoulder. And as always, his features were calm, composed, and utterly handsome.

Tyrone smiled and crossed his arms over his chest. "I should be asking you the same question, although I think it's obvious," he said, indicating the bundle of brightly colored panties she cradled tightly in her arms.

Sydney shook her head. There was no point in getting embarrassed, although it wasn't every day a man was present when she purchased her underwear. Even Rafe would not have dared.

She continued to hold Tyrone's gaze, transfixed. His smile was a complete turn-on, vibrantly alive, sensuous, and blatantly male. She had always appreciated his smile, but found that she appreciated it even more today. The weather was rather cold outside, but he was definitely thawing her out. "Well, these purchases are only part of the reason. They're an added perk, I guess you can say," she finally answered. "There's nothing like a Victoria's Secret sale."

Tyrone glanced around at all the scantily clad mannequins, then tilted his head at her. "You like shopping at this place, do you?" In his mind he was imagining her wearing some of the items he saw on display.

"Yes." She decided to quickly change the subject. "You never told me what you're doing in New York." She wondered what he would think if he knew that since her brother's wedding, he had been the object of her fantasies and a participant in many of her heated dreams.

"I'm in town for six weeks as a visiting music professor at Columbia University. And you?"

She smiled. "I'm getting much-needed rest. For the past four months I've been involved in a very taxing litigation case. I'm proud to say that I won, but it took a lot out of me. When a friend who's a television news correspondent asked me to come here and stay in her apartment and watch her dog for three weeks while she did an assignment in Barcelona, I jumped at the chance."

She glanced at the snowflakes falling lightly outside the store's display window and added, "Although I wish it could have been summer instead of winter."

Tyrone shook his head and laughed. "Sweetheart, winter is the best time to be in New York."

Sweetheart. Although she knew he hadn't meant anything by the use of the endearment, it sent shivers up her body just the same. And then it started happening—the attraction she'd come to expect intensified. She knew the exact moment that he picked up on it as well. Her long sigh echoed simultaneously with his, and his eyes darkened as her gaze was drawn to his lips. He had such a pretty mouth for a man, one that was meant to kiss and be kissed. Then there was everything else about him: tall, muscular build, very nice features, and sandy brown hair. A woman couldn't do much better, unless she happened to meet his identical twin.

Sydney blinked upon realizing he had said something. "I'm sorry, could you repeat that?" she asked, embarrassed he had caught her staring.

A grin tilted both corners of his mouth. "I asked what were your plans for later. Would you like to have dinner with me?"

His grin did things to her insides. "Dinner?"

"Yes, dinner. And since I know that you like French food, an evening at Au Petit Beurre would be nice."

She raised a brow. "And how do you know I like French food?" she asked, although she already knew the answer.

He laughed then said, "A little birdie told me."

She couldn't help but laugh along with him. Since one of the grooms at the wedding, Franco Renoir, was part French and part African-American, a number of tasty French dishes had been prepared, compliments of Tyrone's twin Tyrell, who was Leo's master chef. Sydney had spent a lot of time at the buffet table and, as Tyrone had watched her closely that night, he would have definitely noticed all her activities.

But then, she had watched him that night as much as he had watched her.

"So, what about dinner, Sydney?" More than anything he wanted to take her out. The attraction that had been there between them from the first still burned, and there was no way he could walk away from it this time.

She sighed deeply, knowing there was no way she could turn him down. "What time do you have in mind? I'd like to finish my shopping first, then go home and change."

He nodded. "All right. I need to go back to the hotel and change as well. And I want to call my parents. Today is their fortieth wedding anniversary."

Sydney smiled. "Oh, that's wonderful." And she really meant it. She was proud of the number of years her own parents had been happily married. They would be celebrating their thirty-fifth anniversary later that year, and she and her three brothers knew their parents were still very much in love. She always planned to have that sort of happy ending for herself. It had been her goal after finishing law school to meet the perfect man, get married, and have his children. She had thought she'd found him in Rafe only to discover that was not the case. But she refused to give up. She truly believed there was a man out there somewhere who believed in love and marriage as much as she did.

"Thanks. I think it's wonderful how long they've been married, too," Tyrone said, although he'd never really given the longevity of his parents' marriage much thought. However, her words made him stop and appreciate what they had together.

He checked his watch and asked, "Would seven o'clock be okay?"

She smiled. "Yes, seven will be fine."

He nodded. "Give me your address."

She rattled it off to him and he wrote it down on a piece of paper. "Strivers Row? That's a real nice part of Harlem," he commented.

"Yes, it is. My friend is doing quite well for herself."

Tyrone shifted his sax strap to the other shoulder. "Well then, I'll see you at seven. He started to walk off, then turned around, smiled, and added, "You may as well get a purple pair, too. I think that color would look good on you."

She couldn't help but laugh again. "I'll think about it, Mr. Hardcastle." She watched as he left the store, keeping her eyes glued to him until he was no longer in sight. His nearness had really scrambled her brain. Before walking off to where the bras were located, she snatched an additional pair of panties off the table—purple—thinking it was a shame he would never see her in them.

TWO

Sydney checked her appearance once again in the mirror. She had no qualms about going out with Tyrone, in fact she was rather excited. Chalk it up to her still being on a high after winning that court case, as well as the fact that she was away from Memphis, where her behavior would not be scrutinized and used as a possible weapon against her father's reelection bid.

She smiled and for a brief moment thought how in New York she could do just about anything she wanted. Being the only daughter of Judge Warren Cobain was pretty difficult at times, especially when wanna-be politicians didn't play fair, ran dirty campaigns, and thought nothing of smearing someone's reputation. Such was the case in the last election, when her father's opponent had spread vicious rumors about her parents' marriage. Sydney had found out the hard way that no one was spared when someone was obsessed with winning.

She also had to confess there was another reason why she looked forward to her date with Tyrone, one she had only owned up to while getting dressed. She liked challenges, and Tyrone Hardcastle was definitely a challenge.

Raven had been full of information about him since her sister Robin had dated Tyrone's twin brother Tyrell a few years back. Tyrone was known to date a lot of women but would not hesitate to put the brakes on any involvement that started taking precedence over his music. He was a born musician, a gifted artist, whose first love was his music.

Sydney tossed her hair back to apply her lipstick. Music or no music, the bottom line was that the two of them were deeply attracted to each other. He knew it and she knew it, and in that way the two of them had forged some sort of intimate bond. Whenever he looked at her she felt passionate, wild, filled with the most wanton kind of lust.

In a way, his attraction to her was comforting, especially after Rafe made it seem like she'd been lacking in the bedroom. He thought she had been criticizing him one night when she'd tried suggesting ways to boost their sexual pleasure—specifically hers. She'd read an article in a women's magazine about how a woman should be able to openly communicate with her mate and tell him what she wanted in the bedroom, especially if the pleasure was becoming one-sided. She had noticed that their lovemaking had started getting rushed and was usually over before she'd even reached sexual fulfillment. He would roll away, satisfied, and she'd be left wanting.

After reading the article, she decided to broach the subject with Rafe, and all she'd ended up doing was crushing his male ego. He'd said that if she wasn't getting anything out of their sex life, it meant she wasn't putting enough into it, which was her fault and not his. He further declared after a somewhat heated and downright nasty exchange, that he had no intentions of altering his style of doing things. As far as he was concerned, there was nothing wrong with his technique. He had left angry and had not called her for four days. That night had shown her he really didn't care about her feelings. The world revolved around Rafe and his wants. It had also shown her it was time to wise up and do something about her situation. Life was too short to have to put up with unnecessary foolishness.

The next time he'd shown up at her place, she had asked for her key and told him to get the hell out of her life. That had been over

irresistible attraction

a year ago. In the beginning, he had called constantly and sent her flowers numerous times as an apology, but she hadn't felt inclined to forgive him for being selfish and inconsiderate. He had learned a hard lesson—that he had his ego, but she also had her pride.

Rafe had been the first guy she'd slept with. At the time, she thought they had a promising future together, not knowing then that he was the type of man stamped "Fragile, handle with care, and proceed with caution." She was grateful that she had too much confidence in herself to believe what Rafe had said about her being totally lacking. She may not have been a pro in the bedroom, but she hadn't been a complete failure, either. She believed there was a man out there whose buttons she could push and who could definitely push hers, and she needed to do some button-pushing, fast. Ever since her breakup with Rafe she had poured all her time and energy into her work. Now it was time to try and relax, loosen up, live a little, and have fun.

Her thoughts immediately went to Tyrone Hardcastle and the attraction they felt whenever they saw each other. He could make her toes curl and her breathing unsteady just by looking at her. No matter how tired she was at night, as soon as her head hit the pillow she had fantasies about him. It had been that way since their encounter at her brother's wedding last April. She didn't want to think of how her bedroom experience with him would be, if the real thing came even close to her fantasies.

She would give just about anything to find out.

Swallowing hard, she wondered if she had totally lost her mind. She'd never been one to engage in casual sex. She knew a lot of her friends were into it, but for her, sleeping with a man meant love and a deep commitment, not to mention marriage and family.

A frown drew her brows together. After a year of avoiding any involvement with the opposite sex, the woman in her needed assurance that she was still desired and had what it took not only to capture a man's interest but to hold it as well. And for that reason alone, Tyrone Hardcastle—the man and his music—would be her biggest test since music and not any sort of relationship with a woman was his focus. She needed to know just where she would rank next to a saxophone. The big question of the hour was, did she have the guts to find out?

Tyrone leaned against a white column on the porch after walking up the steps and ringing the doorbell. Seeing Sydney earlier definitely had him looking forward to tonight.

Since arriving in New York a few weeks ago, he had spent the first couple of days with a few friends from college, but after that he had pretty much kept to himself. Unlike the other visiting professors he'd met, who usually went out on the town most evenings, he'd been satisfied just to go back to the hotel where he was staying in Manhattan and chill.

While waiting for Sydney to answer the door, he considered what he knew about her; information he'd been able to obtain over a period of time from Linc. She was twenty-six years old, a graduate of Spellman as well as the University of Tennessee law school. She came from a family of attorneys. Her mother, her two older brothers, Adam and Linc, and her younger brother Grant were all practicing attorneys. A couple of years ago, her father had stopped practicing law to enter the political arena.

Although Tyrone had never spent any time alone with Sydney, she came across as someone who appreciated having a good time, and since Linc was someone whom he considered a friend, he knew he had to watch his step. Besides, an involvement with any woman was the last thing on his mind. He went to great pains to keep his relationships commitment-free. The last woman he'd been with had proven to be rather clingy and had questioned his comings and goings too often to suit him.

But he couldn't discount the attraction that he and Sydney shared. It was there when he saw her and at times when she wasn't there—like in his dreams. He had to admit, something had happened between them at her brother's wedding that had shaken him to the core. Never before had he felt such an intense need and desire for a woman. He grew warm just thinking about what had happened between them— from a distance and without any words being exchanged. For a man who prided himself on being relaxed, he'd been anything but relaxed that day. He had been gripped in a kind of tension that made his body tight, heavy, and hard.

When Sydney opened the door he drank in her scent, part store-bought fragrance and part natural. Together they formed a luscious aroma that was most definitely female. He held her gaze for a moment without saying anything. The only thought that came to his mind was that she was simply beautiful.

Gone was the knitted cap from earlier that day. Now her dark brown shoulder-length hair was parted in the middle and shimmered with reddish streaks of highlight that enhanced her cocoa-colored complexion as well as the vibrancy of her dark brown eyes. Her brows were perfectly arched, and her lips were covered in a delectable shade of strawberry that made him want to lean down and taste the fruit right from her mouth. A black wool pantsuit clung to her shapely curves.

His gaze shifted back to her mouth when she moistened her lips with her tongue. At that moment, a vision of kissing that mouth entered his mind in the most provocative way. He was tempted to kiss her right then and there, but he held himself back, somehow found his voice, and said, "Your hair. I like what you've done to it."

She smiled at his compliment, pleased that he liked the highlights she'd let her beautician talk her into since the wedding. "Thanks."

She took a step back. "Would you like to come in and meet Denzel?"

He blinked and forced his gaze from her hair to her eyes, then raised a dark brow. "Denzel?"

Her smile widened. "Yes, the dog I'm watching for the next three weeks."

Tyrone shook his head, grinning. "Your friend named her dog Denzel?"

Sydney returned his grin. "Yes."

"Why?"

Her lips flashed him a playful smile. "Because she knew that he was the only Denzel she'd get in her bedroom," she replied, grinning. "And," Sydney couldn't help but add, "he's the only Denzel she'll have at her beck and call."

Tyrone chuckled. "Sure, I'd like to meet him."

He had taken one step over the threshold when a little black terrier appeared out of another room. He immediately came over and began sniffing at his shoes and circling his legs a few times. Having a love for dogs, Tyrone bent down, picked up the little terrier, and held him in his arms. "Hey, little guy, how's it going?" he asked, giving him a playful scratch behind the ear. In response, the dog barked and began wagging his tail.

"I'll be ready to go as soon as I grab my coat."

Tyrone watched Sydney as she left the room, admiring the way she looked and feeling again the fierce tug of awareness that always consumed him whenever the two of them were anywhere near each other.

Putting the dog down, he decided to check out the framed pictures on the walls. He recognized the woman in the photograph immediately as Donna Burbank, someone he'd seen reporting the national news a number of times. The different photos showed her with well-known people. There were two of her with presidents, both present and past, one with Colin Powell, another with Samuel L. Jackson on one side of her and Will Smith on the other, and one with news reporter, the late Ed Bradley. Then there was a photograph of a much younger Donna and Sydney together, dressed in caps and gowns in what appeared to be a high school graduation photo.

"So, you and Donna Burbank went to high school together?" he asked when he heard Sydney reenter the room.

"Yes, even further back than that. We've been friends since we were babies. Our parents went to law school together, and I've always considered her mom and dad as my second set of parents while growing up. At least I did until they got divorced."

Tyrone turned around. "And how long ago was that?"

"When Donna and I turned twelve. Her mother caught her father in an affair, but they got back together. Then less than a year later her father caught her mother in one. Her father moved to Atlanta and married the woman he'd been having the affair with and her mother remained in Memphis. Donna was close to her parents, and more than once she was caught in the middle when they played her against each other."

Tyrone shook his head. He'd had a friend who had gone through a similar situation with his parents while growing up. "That was unfair to her."

"Yes, it was. Since then, both her parents have had numerous marriages. They're both on their third."

For the second time that day, Tyrone thought about his own parents' marriage. His father, Leo Hardcastle, would not hesitate to let everyone know that his wife meant everything to him. Not too many women, Leo would say, would have willingly traveled around the world for over twenty years with her military husband and not complain about it. "Just like you said earlier today, Sydney, it's wonderful that our parents have stayed together for so long," he said in a tone filled with solemn conviction.

She nodded in agreement as she gazed up at him. His twisted hair style looked good on him, but then, everything did. He also had long eyelashes, the kind most women would kill for.

Sydney swallowed hard and her heart nearly missed a beat when he met her gaze with his own. In that short time, desire shimmered through her, and she had a feeling it shimmered through him as well.

She cleared her throat and clasped her coat in front of her to still a trembling that came over her, suddenly feeling unsure of herself where he was concerned. "Are you ready to leave?"

He smiled. "Yes."

Tyrone took her coat out of her hands and helped her put it on. Her skin suddenly felt hot with his nearness, and when he smoothed and straightened the coat on her shoulders, she shivered at his touch. Her breathing was becoming difficult and her breasts ached.

"Think we can handle things tonight, Sydney?"

Sydney quickly met his gaze. She knew what he was asking and why. He was being up front and honest with her, and with each other, by acknowledging the strong attraction between them. The question of the hour was whether or not they would let it get the best of them.

This preoccupation was new, and troubling. After her first time making love with Rafe, she had thought that sex had been all right, but definitely not worthy of the hoopla she'd heard in college. She had a deep feeling that with Tyrone, things would be different. For some reason, she believed that he would not be a conceited and selfish lover, that with him she would experience the type of passion she'd only read about in those women's magazines.

She tied her coat belt around her waist, tilted her head, and looked up at him. "Yes, I think we can handle things between us tonight, Tyrone. We have no other choice."

He met her gaze and the glint in his eyes, as well as the expression he wore, told her that he wasn't as confident about that as she was.

THREE

The restaurant was quiet, quaint, and upscale, and the aroma of French food reached Sydney as soon as they entered. She felt the heat of Tyrone's hand in the center of her back when he touched her as they followed the waiter to their table. Just being with him made her appreciate being a woman.

"Would you like some wine?" Tyrone asked when they had been seated.

She wanted to tell him that she thought she needed something a bit stronger than wine, but refrained from doing so. "Yes, please."

Tyrone gave the waiter their drink request. After the waiter returned with their drinks and they gave him their meal selections, Sydney eased back in her chair and relaxed somewhat. She noted Tyrone did the same.

"So, what else have you been doing since the weddings, other than winning court cases?" Although he'd asked her a rather simple question, the heat in his eyes almost unnerved her. She cleared her throat and took a sip of her wine, hoping the liquid would somehow calm her nerves and cool her insides. "That particular court case took up the majority of my time," she finally found her voice to say. "It was a long, bitter battle and I'm glad we won."

He nodded. "What type of case was it?" he asked with genuine interest.

Sydney appreciated his response. She really liked her job, and with everyone in her family being attorneys, it was hard for anyone to want to talk shop at the end of the day. Even Rafe, who was also an attorney, used to get annoyed when she'd tell him how her day went or attempt to discuss some of her court cases, just to get another opinion.

"It was a David versus Goliath case, a little woman going after a major corporation that dropped the ball and didn't want to admit it. My client is a working mother of two girls, and for years she'd been tucking away money into one of these educational plans that guaranteed the money would be there when she needed it to fund her daughters' college expenses. Well, when her daughter turned eighteen and applied to colleges, evidently some of the rules for dispersement had changed without my client being notified, which included the fact that now only certain colleges and universities fell under their umbrella. As far as I was concerned, it was an outright case of a conflict of interest, since the majority of those schools somehow benefited from the company in the long run, as well as the fact that none of the schools on that list were ones my client's daughter wanted to attend. They made it seemed like she didn't have a choice. As her attorney, I had to send a message out there that she did have a choice. If she had one when she took out the plan then she had one at the end, especially if their change of policy wasn't dictated to her."

Tyrone nodded. While she'd been talking, he'd kept his gaze glued to her mouth. He liked the firm fullness of her lips and was turned on by the color of her lipstick. He'd never been so attracted to a woman's mouth before. And when she stopped talking and nervously licked her lips before taking another sip of her wine, he knew that if he ever got a chance, he planned to feast on that mouth until he got his fill, then wondered if such a thing were possible. He had a feeling that across from him sat a hot-blooded woman, filled with passion of the highest degree.

He could feel it. And he wanted it.

Tyrone blinked when he realized that Sydney had asked him a question.

"I'm sorry, could you repeat that?" he asked.

She smiled, and the way that smile touched her lips made heat settle in the pit of his stomach. "I asked what you've been doing since the weddings."

Nothing much, other than fantasizing about you, he wanted to say. Dreams of making love to her had been the norm for months following the wedding. He would wake up at night in a cold sweat with visions of her naked silky flesh entwining his. He could even hear her tiny cries of pleasure when they both came. He didn't think he would ever forget his vision of her moving beneath his thrusting body. On some nights, the only thing he could do to calm himself was to get out of bed and belt out a few, slow melodic tunes on his sax, or play a soothing number or two on his piano. One night things had gotten so heated he felt the need to beat out his frustrations on his drums, but in consideration of his neighbors hadn't done so.

Tyrone shifted in his seat and decided to give her what he considered a watered-down version of what he'd been doing since they'd last seen each other. "Most of my time has been spent booking entertainment for Leo's for the rest of the year. Wednesday nights will continue to be Amateur/Open-Mike Night, when we showcase new and upcoming talent, but we'll like to continue to bring class acts on Fridays and Saturdays, when we do live entertainment."

Sydney nodded. One weekend before Linc's marriage, the two of them had had dinner at Leo's, and Smokey Robinson had made a rare appearance. It had been a wonderful show. "Sounds like you've been busy," she said smiling. "Who's running things while you're away?"

"Clyde Burrell. He's the entertainment manager for the club. Normally when I'm in town we work together, and when I'm away I leave things in his capable hands."

"Do you get away a lot?"

"I take extended trips two or three times a year. Any dedicated musician needs to keep his fingers on the pulse of the music industry."

Sydney tugged on her bottom lip with her teeth as she listened. She could imagine those same fingers keeping a pulse on something else, too. She'd studied his hands earlier while he'd been taking a sip of his wine. They were firm hands, strong and beautiful, and she believed they were capable of giving a woman all kinds of pleasure. Her heart began beating relentlessly at the thought when suddenly she was reminded of the last time she'd had pleasure. It had been the kind she had with Rafe Sutherlin, the kind that had left her still wanting.

Suddenly she wanted to make love to Tyrone. She craved it with a desire so deep it almost took her breath away, and the way he was looking at her didn't help matters. She opened her mouth to say something, then closed it when the waiter appeared with their food.

She sighed, thankful for the timely interruption, since she'd been tempted to act more brazen than she'd ever been with a man by asking Tyrone to make love to her tonight.

"It was a lovely evening, Tyrone, thanks for taking me to dinner." They stood in front of her door and she tried not to stare at him too much and too long. But when he nodded and let his gaze drift to her mouth, she knew he wanted to kiss her, that he would kiss her, and the kind of kiss he would give her needed to be done inside.

"Would you like to come in for a while?" She didn't include the phrase "for a drink" because she knew he would be coming in for something other than that. There was no use pretending otherwise. Curiosity between them had reached its peak, and they needed to sample this unusual, mind-blowing attraction before it got the best of them.

"Yes, I'd like to come in for a while," he responded in a voice that sent sensuous chills down her spine.

Sydney knew that if she'd had the presence of mind, she would have told him good night after thanking him for dinner. But she didn't have the presence of mind. The only thing on her mind was finding out if he tasted as good as he looked.

She slowly unlocked the door and opened it, all the while feeling the heat of his body standing close to her. Her breathing was irregular and her breasts ached. She didn't need anyone to tell her she was turned on to the third degree and had been all evening.

She heard him close the door behind her and turned around expectantly. Tyrone was glancing around the room.

"Where's Denzel?" he asked.

She lifted a brow. Her thoughts were focused on kissing him and his were on a dog? He evidently understood what she was thinking. "I don't want any interruptions, Sydney."

Her skin suddenly felt hot when she realized what he was saying. She swallowed deeply and then answered, "It's late. Denzel has probably turned in for the night. Not too much will wake him after that." She couldn't help but smile when she added, "He's not a very good watchdog."

Tyrone chuckled lightly. "Maybe that's a good thing, because I'm not sure I'd want him to watch this," he said, reaching out, taking her hand, and pulling her toward him. He gently eased the coat off her shoulders, then did the same for his, tossing both garments across a nearby chair.

When he met her gaze again, she felt her pulse increase its racing. As if he knew, he slid his hand up her wrist and touched the area that was beating out of control. While she watched him, he slowly lifted it to his lips and placed a kissed there.

It took everything Sydney possessed not to swoon. The touch of his lips to her wrist was hot.

"Do you remember the first time we met, Sydney?" he asked huskily.

She didn't have to rack her brain to remember that day. She and

Rafe had broken up and, needing to lick her wounds, she'd shown up unexpectedly in D.C. At first it hadn't seemed like good timing on her part since Linc had had an argument with Raven. When Raven had shown up at Linc's apartment to make up and had seen her standing in the living room with nothing on but her slip and bra, she'd gotten the wrong idea. Needless to say, things had gotten straightened out and the three of them, along with Raven's two sisters and the men they loved, had met the next day at Leo's for brunch. That Sunday she'd been introduced to Tyrone.

"Yes, Tyrone, I remember when we first met."

He smiled. "And do you know the first thing that went through my mind when I saw you?"

She shook her head. "No."

He took a step closer; so close she could feel the firm peaks of her breasts touching his shirt.

"I had two thoughts. My first thought was that you had to be the most beautiful woman I'd ever seen. And I mean that sincerely, Sydney. It's not just another line a man would say to a woman."

He then placed his hands at her waist. "My second thought was that one day I wanted to taste you in every way."

The fire that had been smoldering in Sydney's veins all evening suddenly escalated into a blaze. Maybe it was the fact that that same thought had gone through her mind when she'd first seen him, too. Whatever the reason, they were in a position, a very good position, to find out.

Boldly she reached out and placed her arms around his neck. "Now you have your chance, Tyrone Hardcastle, and I have mine, since I had the same thought," she said honestly, too far gone to play games with him.

Sydney wasn't all that clear as to what happened next. All she knew was that Tyrone's mouth was slanted on hers, kissing her in a way she had never been kissed before, not even during the year she had dated Rafe. With the tip of his tongue Tyrone traced every part of the insides of her mouth before capturing her tongue with his own, mating with it and driving her wild.

His hand shifted from her waist to her hips. Holding her body against his, she felt his erection against her middle, leaving little doubt in her mind of how much he wanted her. By the same token, she could feel the heat between her legs intensify and the firmness of the tips of her breasts against him. He was rock-solid against her, and she imagined that hardness inside of her in a way she had only dreamed about for months.

She felt an immediate sense of loss the moment he ended the kiss, but not for long. After a deep breath of air, he was back at her mouth, kissing her relentlessly. In spite of the heat, she was shivering in his arms. Grasping his shoulders for support, she met the gentle rotation of his hips against hers, grind for grind. The musician in him had created a tempo, and the woman in her was stroking the tune he was playing.

Tyrone was determined to give in to the desire that had been driving him mad since first meeting Sydney. Her body's response to him was making him that much hotter. She was pure temptation, and he wanted nothing better than to take her to the nearest bedroom and get inside of her. No woman had ever made him this out of control, and he had to slow down. He forced himself to think about her brother. Their relationship dictated that he not take advantage of her. Then he thought about Ayanna. He didn't have a sister, but he thought the world of his cousin. He would be mad as hell if any man wanted to use Ayanna's body just to satisfy an urge. He was determined to show Sydney the same courtesy and respect, even if it killed him... and walking away tonight, turning down what she was so blatantly offering, just might.

He reluctantly pulled his mouth away, but not before his tongue traced the wetness it had generated from around her lips. When she stretched her neck and groaned, he couldn't resist brushing his lips against her neck, tasting her there.

"I'd better go before we do something we'll both regret later, Sydney," he whispered hoarsely against her ear.

Sydney nodded, knowing what he said was true. She appreciated and admired his willpower, because at that moment she didn't have any. She'd never felt so out of control in her life. Never had kissing a man made her feel this way. If he'd had the mind to pick her up and take her to the nearest bedroom, she was so far gone in desire that she would have gladly participated in anything he had planned.

"I usually don't get this carried away," she murmured. She didn't want him to think of her as a loose woman, although at present she was not at all together.

"I know. I think the two of us bring out a certain degree of lust in each other," he said smoothly, still kissing her softly around her eyes and cheeks.

"Why do you think we do?" she asked curiously, since he seemed to understand more of what was happening between them than she did.

"We're deeply attracted to each other."

She chuckled good-naturedly. "Tell me something I don't know, Tyrone."

He grinned. "All right, when was the last time you slept with a man?"

She lifted a brow but answered anyway. "About fifteen months ago." Wondering where his line of questioning was going, she asked, "And when was the last time you slept with a woman?"

He frowned as he thought about her question. When it dawned on him that he also hadn't been with anyone since then, almost fifteen months, he decided to be as honest with her as she'd been with him. "I haven't slept with anyone since I first met you, Sydney."

Sydney's eyes widened. "Why?" she asked on a breathless sigh.

Again he decided to tell her the truth. "Because I'd made up in my mind that you were the woman I wanted."

Sydney shook her head. "If it's true that there was more than the obvious attraction between us, why didn't you say anything to let me know you were interested?"

He met her gaze. "Because I'd overheard Linc mention to Ayanna that the reason you showed up in D.C. unexpectedly that weekend was because of an argument you'd had with your boyfriend. For all I knew, once you returned to Memphis, the two of you worked things out and got back together."

"We didn't," she said quickly.

He continued holding her gaze. "Yes, I know. I asked Linc about you a few months later, and although I tried asking in the way of small talk, I think he picked up on the fact that I may have been interested in you." He smiled wryly. "So, I believe out of pity, every time he'd come into Leo's he would tell me some tidbit or two about you and how you were doing."

Sydney nodded, meeting his warm gaze. "Why didn't you make an attempt to talk to me six months later, at the rehearsal dinner?"

"Because I still wasn't sure if you and that guy would get back together," he said quietly. "According to Linc, the two of you had dated for over a year, and that's a lot of history."

And a lot of selfishness on Rafe's part, she thought. She had finally seen just how inconsiderate he'd been to her. "There's no way Rafe and I can get back together," she said firmly.

Tyrone's deep voice filled her senses. "Although I pity the guy, I'm glad he's out of the picture."

Sydney was stunned by the seriousness in his voice and marveled at the thought that he felt that way. But a part of her needed to know the reason. Her throat tightened with emotion when she asked, "Why?"

He took her hand and folded it gently into his. "Because nothing has changed. I still want you."

"Oh." She was speechless. She and Tyrone barely knew each other and they definitely weren't in love. Yet from the first, something monumental and totally unexpected had taken place between them. Seemingly they had been drawn together by something irresistible that went beyond common sense . . . at least her own.

"I really don't know what to say, Tyrone," she said softly. Even now she couldn't take her eyes away from his.

He reached up and skimmed his thumb against the softness of her cheek. "You don't have to say anything. Just consider it a 'tell me where you're coming from' night. And because I want you as much as I do, I won't take advantage of the situation. We've waited over a year to finally put these desires out there on the table, and I think that we'd be doing each other a disservice if we rushed into anything because of overloaded hormones."

He smiled warmly. "You never seemed to be the kind of woman who did anything without first thinking it through."

Sydney nodded. Her family had often accused her of analyzing things to death. Yet when it came to Tyrone Hardcastle, she felt wildly impulsive.

"If we ever decide to take things further, I want to know without any doubt that you understand what the relationship will be and also what it won't be."

She raised a confused brow. "Which is?"

His hold on her hand tightened. "What it will be is sharing mindless passion by two people who are irresistibly attracted to each other. And what it won't be is a prelude to love or to a commitment. I'm not interested in either."

Sydney understood what he was saying. She couldn't remember how many men she had walked away from who'd offered her the same thing. It wasn't in her makeup to accept so little out of a relationship, but Tyrone was making her rethink that position. Even now, she felt her resistance to his offer melt away.

She was too confused to give him an answer about anything tonight. "You're right. I need time to think about all of this, Tyrone."

He smiled into her eyes. "Take all the time you need, and if you feel you can't handle the type of relationship I'm offering, then I understand."

She nodded. His tone was sincere, and she knew he meant what he said. Whatever they shared would be physical and not emotional. The big question of the hour was whether she could handle that sort of relationship with him. It seemed so detached. But then, she'd been in what she'd considered an *attached* relationship with Rafe, and look where it had gotten her.

"Can I leave you with something else to think about, Sydney?"

Tyrone's deep, sexy voice pulled her back in and she gazed into his eyes. Her heart began pounding furiously when she saw the deep desire in his gaze. "Yes," she said softly, and wondered why in heaven's name she was playing with fire.

He smiled and leaned down closer to her, and her mind suddenly cleared of everything except him. She opened her mouth under his, and again he took the time to kiss her. The intensity of his desire for her was still evident in the way he was kissing her, and she couldn't do anything but return the passion that seemed to be uniquely his.

Moments later, he slowly lifted his head to end their kiss and stared down at her. A frown knotted his forehead, and for a minute she wondered if he were as confused about what was taking place between them as she was.

He took a step back and got his coat off the chair that he'd thrown it across earlier. "What are you doing tomorrow?" he asked, in deep thought about something.

She shrugged, trying to regain the senses that his kiss had knocked right out of her. "I hadn't planned on doing anything special. Why?"

"Tomorrow is one of my free days, and I thought the two of us could spend some time together, starting with lunch. And if you're free tomorrow night, we could go to dinner, then attend a play afterward."

She didn't say anything for a while. It had been a long time since she'd allowed a man to monopolize her time. She also made a quick decision about lunch and dinner. "And I'd enjoy spending time with you tomorrow."

He smiled. "Good. I'll be by to pick you up at noon."

She nodded. "All right."

He then took a step toward her, leaned down, and placed another kiss on her lips, taking his tongue and tracing the sweet seam of her mouth, reveling in her taste as if he needed the memory until he saw her again. "I'd better go while I still have the good mind to do so," he said huskily, finally pulling away.

He turned to leave. Before reaching the door, he turned around again, and after taking a long, hard look at her, he opened it and walked out.

FOUR

"The food here is wonderful, Tyrone. Thanks for bringing me," Sydney said after taking the last sip of her iced tea. He had picked her up exactly at noon and had taken her to a restaurant near Times Square. She couldn't help but admire how he had braved the New York traffic to reach their destination.

"I'm glad you liked it. The Monetts have owned this restaurant for years. This place was a favorite of mine when I was a student at Juilliard."

Sydney nodded. Over lunch he told her about the years he had lived in New York while attending college, and the many friends he'd made. He also told her about his older brother Noah, his twin Tyrell, and his female cousin Ayanna. He described enthusiastically their decision a few years back to open a supper club in D.C. and name it after his father, Leo, a man the four of them admired and deeply respected, who had encouraged them to fulfill their dreams from the time they were still in diapers.

Tyrone checked his watch and said, "Do you need to return to your place and check on Denzel?"

Sydney smiled and shook her head. "No, he'll be fine until we go back and change for dinner." At first she'd been surprised when Tyrone had arrived with a garment bag, then realized it made perfect sense for him to use one of Donna's guest bedrooms to change for dinner instead of driving all the way back to his hotel.

"Do you want to walk off lunch?"

Tyrone's question interrupted her thoughts. "Sure, why not?"

Upon leaving the restaurant, he took her hand and desire flooded her insides. She was completely astonished that she could feel the heat of him through the leather gloves she wore, and from the way he was looking at her, she knew he was astonished, too. Instead of releasing her hand, he tightened his hold.

Then he smiled down at her and that gesture sent even more heat shooting through her body. Together they started walking, quickly merging with the pedestrian traffic at a pace a lot more hurried than their own.

The first place they decided to go was to Macy's, where Tyrone wanted to purchase another dress shirt. She sat on a sofa in a men's designer clothes department and watched the salesman help Tyrone with his selection, thinking of how easily she got aroused just from looking at him.

She let out a frustrating sigh. This arousal thing was completely new to her. Rafe could turn her on, true enough, but only when that was his intent. With Tyrone, he was able to get her hot and bothered without even trying.

Sydney sucked in a quick breath as she watched Tyrone remove his pullover sweater so the salesman could take measurements of his chest. Her hands suddenly began itching. She wanted to walk over to him, touch his muscular shoulders, and bury her face in his chest to inhale his scent.

He pulled his sweater back over his head and then, as if sensing her gaze on him, he glanced over in her direction, then stopped what he was doing. Evidently he read something in her eyes, because he stood there staring at her as if glued to the spot.

Sydney's heart began racing. Tyrone was the only man who'd ever looked at her like she was something he just had to have. That thought was so delicious, she felt her erect nipples straining against her blouse. The tips were so sensitive it was as if she wasn't even wearing a bra. And then there was the monumental heat settling between her legs.

She took a deep breath and continued to hold his gaze as the vibration of heated desire flowed across the room and enveloped them. Only when the salesman reclaimed his attention did Tyrone break the connection. Sydney took another deep breath, trying to regain control.

Moments later Tyrone appeared before her with a Macy's bag in his hand. They stood, not saying anything, since there was really nothing to be said, as they waited for an elevator. The doors opened and they stepped inside. They were alone. The moment the door closed, without wasting any time, Tyrone reached out for her. She went willingly into his arms, needing the feel and the taste of him.

His mouth met hers, mating his tongue with her own, feeding her desire, then reached beneath her coat and touched her backside, pulling her closer to him.

They were interrupted by an electronic peep, reminding them to press a button for their floor, which they ignored. "I couldn't wait," he whispered against her lips.

"And I didn't want you to wait," she responded honestly. She dropped her head to his chest to inhale his scent.

When the elevator began descending, she lifted her head and met his gaze, a question in her eyes she couldn't bring herself to ask. From the way he was looking at her, she could tell he knew what that question was.

He tightened his hold around her waist and they stepped back when the elevator stopped to let others on. As soon as they reached the main floor and stepped out of the car he pulled her close to him. Her mouth went suddenly dry, scorched by the look in his eyes. He reached out and touched her cheek, caressing it lightly, and chills of pleasure coursed throughout her body.

"The answer is yes, and if you want what I believe you're asking for, then come with me, Sydney," he said in the sexiest voice she'd ever heard. "Come with me to my hotel room."

Tyrone pulled his card key from his coat pocket as they entered the lobby of the Hyatt Regency Hotel, knowing that once he stepped inside his room with Sydney, things for him wouldn't be the same. He had a strong feeling that she was the type of woman who would leave a mark on him, and that was dangerous. No woman had ever branded him, but he knew without a doubt that Sydney would. Even knowing that, he still wanted to make love to her so much it was almost painful. He glanced down at her, wondering if they were still of the same mind. She hadn't said much after they'd left Macy's, or while they had walked holding hands to his car.

She hadn't said anything on the drive over, either. Neither of them had. He'd been too afraid that if he had spoken, whatever spell they were caught up in would shatter and she would change her mind. He didn't know how he could handle it if she did. But still, he wanted to be fair to her. Only last night he'd told her he was willing to take things slow, that he didn't want her to feel rushed. When they reached the elevator to his room, he stopped and turned to her.

"Are you sure about this, Sydney?" he asked softly. "If you prefer, we can go someplace else, take in a movie or something."

She met his gaze, squelching the urge to tell him that the only thing she wanted to take in was him, that she had a passionate need to feel him inside of her, that she wanted to reach the highest peak of sexual fulfillment with him. While in New York she wanted to forget that she was the type of woman who needed love and commitment from a relationship. The only thing she wanted—what she felt she had to have—was to make love with Tyrone Hardcastle.

Deep down she wasn't surprised. The attraction between them had always been too potent for things to end otherwise. It would be their secret, and no matter what, she would always have her memories of the intimacy they would share.

"Yes, I'm sure," she finally answered.

He nodded with relief upon hearing her response and punched the elevator button. This time they were not alone, and in a way they were glad. The need to keep their hands off each other only added to their excitement.

When the elevator came to a stop on the twelfth floor, he again held her eyes to make sure she hadn't changed her mind. To show him that she hadn't, she quickly stepped out of the elevator. They walked in silence, holding hands, down the carpeted hall toward his room. Words weren't needed. They both knew what they wanted and what they intended to get there.

When they reached his room at the very end of the hall, he leaned his shoulder against the door and took in all of her. Before him stood the most beautiful woman he had ever seen, clutching his Macy's bag in front of her like it was the only defense she had against this irresistible attraction they had for each other.

He cleared his throat and asked gently. "Are you okay?"

She quickly nodded. "Yes, but I think I'll be a lot better once I'm with you inside this room."

She watched him take a deep breath as his eyes darkened. Without hesitating any longer, he inserted the card key into its slot, turned the knob, and opened the door, then stepped aside for her to enter. She did so, knowing from this moment on her life was about to change.

FIVE

The first thing Sydney noticed was that Tyrone's hotel suite had a separate spacious sitting area, a bedroom, and another room with a computer that he could use for an office. There was also a nice eat-in kitchen area with a bar.

The second thing she noticed was that he was leaning against the closed door, looking at her like she was something delicious to eat.

"Nice place," she said when it became apparent he preferred looking at her to talking. She removed her coat and placed it over a chair. "No wonder this room is at the end of the hall. I didn't know this hotel had rooms so large."

He nodded but didn't say anything.

"I guess, since you'll be here six weeks, you need all this space."

Again he nodded but still didn't say anything. He just continued looking at her.

He evidently liked what she had on—a short, purple wool dress, flesh-tone pantyhose, and a pair of short black leather boots. His expression when he had first seen her that day had indicated as much. The dress clung to her curves like a second skin.

It was then that she noted how short her outfit was and how much thigh was showing. Pretending to smooth out the winkles in the dress, she tried to pull it down to cover more of her, she glanced up as Tyrone moved away from the door. His gaze was intense, deeply penetrating, profoundly predatory, and definitely hungry. And it was communicating a message to her that sent chills all through her body.

He came within three feet of her, then stopped. "I consider your brother a friend," he said huskily.

She lifted a brow. "And?"

He frowned and gazed at her several long seconds before he finally responded. "And I'm not sure he would appreciate knowing what I intend to do to you."

She shrugged. "Do you plan to tell him?"

"No."

"Well then, why worry about it? Besides, if you haven't noticed, Tyrone, I'm a grown woman and old enough to make my own decisions about what I want."

He crossed his arms over his chest. "I got the impression that he liked your ex-boyfriend and was hoping the two of you would work things out."

Sydney shrugged. She knew her family liked Rafe and was clinging to that hope. "And I believe I told you that won't happen."

She decided to be completely honest with him so he would know why she was so certain of that. "Rafe wasn't satisfying me in bed like I figured he should be, and I thought we had the kind of relationship where we could talk about it, and be open to trying new and different things. So I suggested a few."

Tyrone nodded. "And I gather that he didn't go along with your suggestions?"

"No. In fact, he got upset over my having the gall to think that anything in our sex life needed improving. He had no complaints, so he felt if there was a problem, it had to be mine."

Tyrone shook his head, not believing that any man would be that inconsiderate to his woman. "What a selfish bas—"

"My sentiments exactly. I ended our relationship after that. He said a lot of things to me that were unforgivable. And when he showed up at my place like everything was peachy-keen between us, I was ready to tell him just where he could go."

Tyrone grinned. "Good for you."

She chuckled. "Yeah, I think so."

He took the remaining steps to stand directly in front of her. "And it's good for me, too, since I consider myself a very generous man. If I feel good, then I can guarantee that you'll feel even better," he said huskily, placing his arms around her waist and bringing her against his already hard body.

"Then I hope, Mr. Hardcastle, that you feel good," she said with labored breathing.

"I have no doubt that I will."

He lowered his mouth to hers, and Sydney immediately forgot Rafe's selfishness and everything else except Tyrone. All her mind could concentrate on was how good he tasted and how wonderful it felt being in his arms and being kissed by him. He might be a master artist with his musical skills, but that mastery also extended to his tongue and how well he used it.

He was stroking, teasing, and tasting her to oblivion, and she was driven by her desire to give him anything he wanted. From the way he was kissing her, he wanted a whole lot. He deepened the kiss to show her how much. His mouth tasted like the strawberry daiquiri he had at lunch, a sweet, fruity flavor that was making heat coil deep within her lower belly; where she could feel his hard and solid erection pressing against her. He pulled her closer to his strong, muscular body.

When he finally released her mouth, she grasped the lapels of his leather coat to keep from sinking to her knees, she felt that weak. Moments later, he removed his coat and tossed it on the chair with hers, then pulled her back into his arms.

Once again he succeeded in sweeping her away in mindless passion. He lifted up her dress to caress her backside, then he broke the kiss, lifted her into his arms, and set her down on the bar's countertop.

He leaned down and removed her boots, then straightened his tall frame to look at her. "Lift up so I can take off those pantyhose," he whispered. Without thinking twice about it, she raised her bottom while he eased the silky hose down her legs, caressing and massaging them as he went, then dropped the pantyhose on the floor.

"You have beautiful legs, Sydney," he said, lifting her right leg and letting it come to rest in his midsection, propped up on his hardness.

She swallowed. "Thanks. I think you have beautiful legs, too."

He lifted a curious brow and smiled. "And when did you see my legs?"

"That Sunday we met. You rode your bike to Leo's."

He nodded. "I like staying in good shape."

"As a woman I can appreciate that."

His smile widened as he placed her back on her feet. "Now for your dress," he said as he reached behind her for the zipper. He found it without any trouble and began easing it down. When he slowly removed the dress from her body, he exposed a purple bra and a matching pair of purple V-string panties.

He caught his breath as he stared at her, seeing the purple dress in a heap at her feet and the purple underwear she was wearing. "Did you know that purple is my favorite color?"

She grinned. "Yes, I figured as much, especially after what you suggested that day in Victoria's Secret. And to think when I bought this set I thought it was a pity that you would never see me in them." She chuckled. "Boy, was I wrong."

Tyrone nodded, thinking she didn't know how wrong she was. A part of him had known he would see her this way, eventually.

"Now it's my turn," she said. She tugged his shirt out of his jeans and rubbed her hand over his bare stomach. The crisp hair there sent a thrumming sensation throughout her body.

She captured his gaze when she began removing his belt. "I've never undressed a man before," she said, thinking how most of the time Rafe was naked in bed, waiting for her, before she could bat an eye. "I think I like doing this," she added, tossing his belt aside.

"I happen to think you're pretty good at it," Tyrone managed to say when she went to the snap of his jeans and began easing his zipper down, grateful that she was taking her time. The bulge of his erection was so large, he didn't want her to cause him any permanent damage.

"You're amazing," she said in astonishment when he stepped out of his jeans and kicked them aside. He was now down to his shirt and briefs.

"Now it's my turn again," he said, pulling her into his arms, and liking the feel of having her there. He reached behind her and unhooked her bra, took the time to toss it with the rest of their discarded things, then fastened his gaze on her. Seeing her naked chest was nearly too much for him. Her breasts were perfect, and he couldn't help but reach out and cup them. He liked the way her breasts felt in his hand and the way the nipples hardened against his caressing fingers. Soon he felt an urge to taste her and he leaned down to capture a budding tip in his mouth.

With the feel of Tyrone's mouth on her breasts, Sydney became so aroused she begged him to stop, then begged him for more. His tongue was driving her insane with pleasure. Lifting her by the waist, he set her back on the bar, then began removing his shirt.

A lump formed in Sydney's throat. She'd never participated in this part of lovemaking with Rafe, and found that simply watching Tyrone undress was so arousing it only added to her sweet torture. He was in perfect condition, with a well-muscled chest, and she was tempted to rub her bare breasts against it.

She watched as he finally rid himself of his last piece of garment and let out a deep admiring sigh. The man was so beautifully made in every way it overwhelmed her senses.

"Now, take off your panties," he said heatedly. "I want to know all your hidden feminine secrets and I want to see them as well."

He lifted her off the bar, stood her on her feet, and slowly began tracing the outline of her panties with his fingertips. The sensuous caress made her moan with desire.

"These are so skimpy, it's like you aren't wearing anything," he whispered near her ear, his breath ragged. "This barely covers you."

Sydney shuddered from his touch. Her senses were approaching overload, and she didn't think she could handle much more of his mind-blowing stimulation. "Tyrone, I—"

His finger slipped past the edge of her panties to find just what she wanted. Instinctively she widened her legs for him. Her smoldering groan was all the invitation he needed to slip his finger into the dewy essence of her heat and stroke her even hotter.

When she swooned, Tyrone picked her up in his arms and carried her to the bedroom. No sooner had he placed her on the bed than he joined her and removed the last barrier that shielded her body from him. Before she could react, his mouth replaced where his finger had been earlier and she all but screamed as he worshipped her body in a way no man had ever done before. His mouth knew the exact spot to increase the sensuous torture she was going through, and she couldn't do anything but enjoy the sensations.

When she thought there was no way she could possibly take anymore, he reached into the nightstand drawer and pull out a condom packet. With one hand still covering the heat of her mound, he used his mouth to rip open the packet.

"Let me," she found herself saying, then wondered how it was done. She'd never put a condom on a man before. Rafe always went into the bathroom to put his on, saying it was something a man did in private. Evidently Tyrone didn't believe in that theory.

After he nodded his consent, she took the packet from his mouth. Easing herself up in the bed, her gaze went to his erection. She sucked in a sharp breath, wondering how she was going to get something that big into a condom that looked so small.

"I'll instruct you," Tyrone said huskily.

She glanced up at him. Evidently he sensed her distress over not knowing what to do. She breathed in deeply. His masculine scent was overpowering and was driving her out of her mind. She reached out and splayed her fingers on his stomach before moving lower and capturing him in her hand.

Following his instructions, she slowly sheathed him, liking the way the solid hardness of him felt in her hand. And for some reason she wasn't embarrassed by what she was doing. Tyrone had a way of making her feel that anything they did in the bedroom together was all right, and she appreciated his letting her share in such an intimate part of their lovemaking.

When she finished, she eased back down on the bed and he positioned himself above her, his legs on either side of her waist and his hard erection directly over her feminine mound.

He held her gaze for a long moment. "I want you more than I've ever wanted any woman, Sydney," he said huskily, easing his body down on top of hers just a little. "From the moment I saw you I knew I wanted you," he said as he placed his hands under her hips and lifted her while he continued to gaze deep into her eyes.

She held his gaze and watched his eyes grow darker and darker and she released a trembling sigh. She had to admit that although she hadn't wanted to think about him that way, she had dreamed of them making love since she first met him. Something about the way he had looked at her that day had made her wonder about all the possibilities.

She sucked in a deep breath the moment she felt the tip of his erection, hard and hot, press against the very essence of her womanhood. She spread her legs as he eased down and, inch by inch, began filling her body and becoming a part of her. He went deeper and deeper until it seemed there was no place left for him to go. He was inside of her, snug, tight, and her body began clenching him, sending waves of pleasure escalating through her.

"Tyrone!"

As soon as his name left her lips, he began moving, slowly at first to let her acquaint her body with his, to let her savor the feel of him inside of her. Then he began pumping hard and steady, making her body rock with his, sharing the rhythm he was creating for them. Each thrust he made into her took her closer and closer to something she had never experienced before, at least not in the magnitude that she knew awaited her.

She sucked in a deep breath and held it when he increased the tempo. She knew he was playing her as expertly and skillfully as he would a musical instrument, and whatever tune he was playing for them was rocking and rolling her world. In the back of her mind, she could hear cymbals clashing, a drum beating, and a horn blasting, all at once. And she knew that only someone like Tyrone could let her experience such a thing. He made love the same way he made his music—all knowing, all caring, and all gifted. It was hard for her to believe that two people who supposedly didn't love each other could share something this beautiful, this special and profound.

She didn't have time to dwell on that thought when she felt Tyrone's hand lift her hips even higher to him and locked down on her in a circular motion that became more erotic than anything she'd ever experienced. He touched areas inside of her that had never been touched before.

Her pulse pounded and her body suddenly exploded so hard and deep, she screamed. Tyrone's answering deep, guttural groan made her realize that he was experiencing the same intense pleasure as she when he sank deeper and deeper inside of her.

Another groan rumbled deep within his chest as he clutched her body tighter into the fit of his and shuddered from the force of his own climax. Instinctively she wrapped her legs tighter around him as he continued to thrust into her, causing her body to be swept up in an earth-shattering release for a second time. And she knew as the waves came crashing down on her yet again, that she wasn't alone. The man who'd been an active participant in her dreams for over a year was there with her, once again tumbling through the boundaries of total fulfillment.

SIX

Tyrone stared up at the ceiling, physically sated and mentally drained. Sydney slept peacefully beside him with one of her legs thrown over his. He had watched her face during her first orgasm, and the expression there had been so utterly and incredibly beautiful, he had wondered how any man could deny her such a rapturous moment. He had been overwhelmed by the depth of her pleasure. Clearly her needs had not been met for far too long. Even now he was tempted to wake her up and make love to her again but decided she needed her rest.

And he needed to think.

He would never admit it, but making love with Sydney had scared the daylights out of him. He didn't think he had ever felt that way with another woman. He'd been so caught up in the scent and feel of her that he'd almost forgotten to use a second condom. If she hadn't mentioned it, he would have engaged in unprotected lovemaking, something he had never done with any woman.

And he had never allowed a woman to put a condom on him before. He preferred doing something that important himself just in case his partner didn't do it right. He didn't believe in careless accidents, and the last thing he wanted was to father a child, at least not at this stage in his life. But for once in his life the desire to have a woman was overriding his common sense, and all he could think about was making love to Sydney, over and over again. As a matter of fact, he was just waiting for her to wake up so he could get back inside of her.

He scrubbed a hand across his face. The last thing he needed was to complicate his life by becoming attached to any woman. Having Sydney in his dreams was one thing, but dallying with the real McCoy was another. He had to make sure he got things back in perspective and didn't let his emotions get wrapped up in what was nothing more than great sex.

He closed his eyes and wondered what had pushed him over the edge. God knows his body had suddenly seemed to become addicted to her. It was as if being inside of her with her body clenching him was the way things should be. After making love to her, the thought of making love to another woman was sacrilegious. He wanted Sydney and no other woman would do.

He released a deep sigh, knowing he needed time alone to think. Easing her leg off his, he slipped out of bed, left the room, closing the door behind him, and went into the sitting room. Picking his jeans up off the floor, he put them on, went into the office, and closed the door. He picked up his sax, needing to hear the sound of it. Sitting in a chair, he began playing a soft tune, one he had composed over a year ago. He closed his eyes thinking, this is what he needed to clear his mind. His music always had a way of soothing him, of helping put things in perspective.

He couldn't recall just how long he'd been playing when suddenly, Sydney's scent wrapped itself around him. He opened his eyes and saw her standing naked in the doorway. He wondered how long she'd been there, watching him and listening to him play. He ended the tune, placed the sax on the desk, and watched her watching him. His gaze swept her from head to toe. She was a beautiful woman and he appreciated the fact that she didn't have any hang-ups about being nude in front of him. He liked a woman who wasn't ashamed of her body, who wasn't embarrassed for her man to see her in all her natural glory.

Her man.

He shook his head. He was getting way ahead of himself.

"That was a beautiful piece, Tyrone," she said softly, breaking the silence that had engulfed them. "I don't think I've ever heard it before."

He smiled. "And you wouldn't have," he answered. "It's a number I composed over a year ago."

She nodded, her gaze lighted up in admiration for his skill as a musician. "What's it called?"

Tyrone's gaze left hers and went to the sax on his desk. It was one of his prized possessions, a gift on his eighteenth birthday from his parents. It was on that sax, the very night of the day they'd met, that he had sat in his darkened bedroom, closed his eyes, and composed the piece that he had simply titled "Sydney."

When he met Sydney's gaze again, he didn't want to think about the significance of what he'd done that night and he didn't want to give her false ideas by sharing it with her. "The name of it isn't important. I'm just glad you liked it."

She nodded. "I do. It has such a soothing and romantic melody. While listening to it I could imagine being swept away in peaceful surrender," she said breathlessly.

"In peaceful surrender?" A heady rush of need flooded him as his gaze moved over her nude body.

"Yes, it has that sort of an effect on me. It reminds me of some sort of love ballad. I can imagine a man playing that tune to the woman he loves, telling her with music just how much she means to him and just how much he wants her in his life."

Tyrone nodded and then, unable to help himself, he crossed the room to her, pulled her into his arms, held her close. Her naked body felt warm and soft against his, and he wondered what would become of him when their time in New York ended and they went their separate ways.

Not wanting to dwell on that, he stepped back, unsnapped his jeans, pushed them down his legs, and stepped out of them. He reached out for her and pulled her back into his arms. He kissed her as if he were a starving man and her mouth was the only food he'd had in months.

Moments later he pulled back, needing to be joined with her in another way. He reached out to gather her into his arms and she quickly placed a condom packet into his hand.

"You almost forgot again," she said smiling sensuously at him. "It's a good thing I brought one out of the bedroom."

Tyrone could only nod and then took the time to do what was needed to protect her, again thinking how little control he had around her. He would hate for her to think that he wasn't a responsible person, because he was.

Picking her up in his arms, he carried her to the bar stool and placed her on it, widening her legs as he did so. As soon as her bottom touched the seat he was there between her legs, seeking entry inside her. He clenched his jaw as he slid into her, leaning her back in his arms so he could go deeper, wanting to feel his body flush with hers.

She wrapped her legs around him, locking him in place when he began moving. "Sydney," he said her name as he pushed hard and began thrusting deep inside of her.

When he felt her body milking him the only thing he could do was press forward and let her take whatever she wanted from him.

He tried holding back, not ready for it to end, but she was clenching him too tight, her body's demand was too forceful. Then in a deep, shuddering release, he gave her just what she wanted, what he wanted. And when he felt her come apart in his arms, he pulled her closer to him and his mouth devoured hers as sensation after sensation washed over him.

A soft whine and an insistent scratching outside her bedroom door woke Sydney. She blinked, then realized that she was in her own bed and Denzel was on the other side of the door, letting her know that he needed to go out. She blinked again. It was barely morning, and Tyrone was sound asleep next to her.

After making love again at his hotel, they had dressed and gone home to take care of Denzel's needs. Then they had changed for dinner and, later that night had gone to a play. Afterward, they had stopped by his hotel only long enough for him to throw a few things into an overnight bag.

As she slipped out of bed, everything they had done yesterday and last night came back to her in full force. She inhaled deeply as she put on her robe, thinking that if she never made love again to a man, Tyrone had definitely given her enough to last her a lifetime. Last night she had slept soundly—relaxed, sated, and peaceful.

Now she realized with full clarity just what she had been missing during the year she had spent with Rafe. Even in the beginning, when their relationship was new and passionate, she had never felt the way Tyrone had made her feel yesterday and last night. Tyrone had shown her what a monumental mistake she'd made by letting Rafe control things in the bedroom. That was not how lovemaking worked. A woman was supposed to reap just as many benefits out of it as a man.

Each time she had been with Tyrone, he had gone out of his way to make sure that she was right there, sharing in the pleasure with him.

When she reached the dresser, she glanced at herself in the mirror. Her hair was tumbled in disarray around her shoulders, her cheeks were flushed, and her mouth looked as if it had been thoroughly kissed. She looked just like the woman she was, a woman who'd been made love to practically all night by the man she loved.

Sydney whirled away from the mirror, her heart pounding. Love? There was no way she could use that word to describe what she felt for Tyrone. They had only spent two days together, so there was no way she could love him. Hadn't she decided after Rafe that she would not fall in love again, at least not for a long time? What she was sharing with Tyrone was just a fling, nothing more. Now was not the time to get lust confused with love.

Yet, as she slipped out of the bedroom and reached down to pick up Denzel, she knew she was only fooling herself if she denied her true feelings. She did love him, she had fallen in love with him the day they had first met. In a burst of clarity she knew that she had fought having any feelings for him because of Rafe and how he had disappointed her. She also didn't want to admit how quickly she had fallen in love with Tyrone. Truthfully, she had stopped loving Rafe months before she'd given him the boot. His overinflated ego had begun playing on her nerves and she had begun losing whatever feelings she thought she'd had for him.

Sydney glanced at the clock on the dresser. She needed time away from Tyrone to think, and walking Denzel was just what the doctor ordered. Tyrone had told her last night that he had a class at ten this morning. She decided to prepare breakfast for him so that he wouldn't have to worry about making a stop along the way. That was the least she could do for him.

And there was no way she would let him know how she felt about him. He had told her up front that what they shared was not a prelude to love or to a commitment since he wasn't interested in either. No matter how she felt, she had to respect his wishes and his feelings.

SEVEN

Tyrone leaned in the kitchen doorway and watched Sydney as she stood at the stove doing something that looked very much like cooking pancakes. He smiled, liking what he saw of her from behind. Need was like a living, breathing thing inside of him as his gaze centered on the curvaceous body beneath her short silk robe.

He decided he could stand here and watch her like this all day. However, Denzel let out a rambunctious bark and raced over to him and Sydney quickly turned around and smiled.

"Good morning."

He returned her smile and crossed the floor to her. "Good morning."

She automatically tilted up her face and he leaned down and kissed her. He had intended to just brush his lips across hers, but the moment she opened her mouth beneath his, the kiss turned heated as he savored her taste while running his hand down the smooth valley of her spine, pressing her closer to him.

He released her when Denzel barked again. "What's his problem?" he asked, nibbling at the corners of her mouth. "Hasn't he been fed yet?"

Sydney chuckled against his moist lips. "Yes. I guess he's jealous."

Tyrone smiled. "Then I guess he'd better find himself a female of his own. Do you know if there're any available ones in this neighborhood?"

Sydney shook her head. "No, and besides I think he's been fixed."

"Ouch!"

Sydney burst out laughing. "Yes, a typical man would say that." She then returned to the stove. "I hope you like pancakes."

He cradled her from behind, enclosing her gently in his arms. "I do. I also like making love to you."

She turned around to him. "And I like making love to you, too. Thank you."

He raised a dark brow. "For what?"

"For making it special and for proving that all men aren't inconsiderate like Rafe."

Tyrone's gaze hardened at the mention of her ex-boyfriend. "Most of us aren't. You just picked a bad apple with that guy."

"Yes, I see that now."

His expression softened and he stroked her cheek tenderly. "Good, and let's not talk about him anymore. All right?"

"All right. If you'll have a seat I'll serve you."

He shook his head. "No, let's serve each other. Tell me what I can do to help."

She smiled. "Okay, since you're so eager to help, you can take down the glasses and pour the orange juice."

She drew in a shaky breath when he left her to walk over to the cabinets. She wondered how in the world she was going to handle downplaying the feelings she had for him for the next two weeks before going back to Memphis. A heavy feeling settled in her stomach.

"Sydney?"

She glanced over at him. Their gazes met. "Yes?"

"Thank *you* for yesterday and last night."

She chuckled. "And just what did I do?"

He leaned against the counter. "After a solid fifteen months of celibacy, I got just what I needed and from the person I wanted it from. You're some kind of a lady."

She remembered all they had done and laughed. "A lady?"

His smiled widened as those same memories flickered through his mind. "Yes, a lady. A very sensuous lady."

Sydney's heart leapt at Tyrone's words. Rafe had never complimented her in bed although she'd known she'd pleased him. Words were important and evidently Tyrone knew that. "Thank you."

"You're welcome."

Sydney discovered that even after their day and night of wild abandon, there was no awkwardness between them. Together they set up breakfast, then sat down to eat, chatting amiably about Linc and Raven's plans to leave D.C. so Linc could return to Memphis and pursue a political career.

"My family is excited that he's returning home," Sydney said. "Everyone in the family works in our law firm, and when he left there was a huge void."

After breakfast Tyrone helped clean up the kitchen. Somehow, something as simple as sharing breakfast had been a complete turn-on. Sitting across the table from her and knowing she had nothing on underneath her robe had almost driven him out of his mind.

When he watched her reach up and place the last dish back in the cabinet, he pulled her into his arms, wanting her again. Their mouths met, the kiss was hot and explosive, carnal. Picking her up into his arms, he carried her to the bedroom and placed her down on the un-made bed. Immediately his hand began fumbling with the opening of her robe, and when he opened it and saw her naked body, his mind and his senses suddenly went over the edge.

He wanted to touch her everywhere and he did, making her moan with pleasure. His hands explored her, stroking her to a fever pitch. Then he leaned down and kissed her again. She returned his kiss hungrily, greedily, which made him that much hotter for her.

"Sydney." He breathed her name and forced himself to pull back, remove his jeans, and prepare himself for her when he felt his sanity and control begin to slip again.

He quickly returned to her and gathered her into his arms, placing her beneath his throbbing body. He almost went weak in the knees when she grabbed hold of his erection and led him to her warm, moist center.

When she raised her hips to him, he flexed his body to go deeper into hers, wanting all of her, needing to claim every part of her as his. He reached out and caught her face in his hands and forced her to look at him, to marvel at what they were sharing.

"Look at me, Sydney," he whispered huskily, needing to see her reaction each time he thrust inside of her, wanting to see her features contort with a passion he knew no other man had given her, and wanting to know from the look in her eyes that she enjoyed his being inside of her as much as he did.

When she tightened her feminine muscles around him, clenching him with all her might, he growled in pleasure.

"You like this, don't you?" he asked as he slowly moved his body inside of her, setting a rhythm dictated by a particular tune that played inside of his head.

She sucked in her breath as he went still deeper. "Yes," she said breathlessly, straining to hold herself back as Tyrone's body leisurely pumped into hers, almost driving her crazy.

"Good, because I like this, too."

He thrust into her deeper, relentlessly, almost taking her over the brink, then slowed the pace again to prolong their pleasure. When it became so overpowering that her eyes fluttered and closed with desire, he urged her again to look at him so he could know just how his lovemaking was making her feel.

When they couldn't handle the exquisite sensations anymore, he sped up the rhythm, thrusting with a manic urgency. She cried out his name. Her face lit up with a climax so intense, the spasms that racked her body also racked his, pulling everything out of him and giving her more of himself than he'd ever given a woman. He screamed her name over and over, and when he thrust into her one last time, determined to go deeper than before, his world exploded and he knew that he could never get enough of Sydney, even if they were to make love every day for the rest of their lives.

A thought came to his mind as his body succumbed to the delight of her; how on earth was he ever going to walk away?

A while later, when he could find the strength to move, Tyrone eased onto his elbows and looked down at Sydney. She was looking at him with glazed eyes, flushed features, and a smile tilting her lips. "You are something else," she managed to say in a breathless sigh.

He leaned down and kissed her lips. "No, *you're* something else. I could make love to you all day and all night."

The smile on her lips widened. "I'm up for it if you are."

He chuckled. "Don't tempt me." He glanced over at the clock on the nightstand. "Besides, I need to get out of here if I'm going to make it to class on time. I don't want my students to think I've gone soft."

Sydney grinned when she felt his erection, hard as ever, pressing against her thigh. "Soft? I don't think you know the meaning of the word."

He laughed. "It's all your fault. I'm going to have to shower again before I leave, or I'll have the scent of you clinging to me all day, and I'll never get any work done."

Moments later, when he came out of the now steamy bathroom, Sydney was just where he'd left her, naked in bed. Her eyes were closed and he figured she had fallen asleep. He leaned against the dresser and stared at her, thinking once again that she was the most beautiful, senuous woman he had ever seen.

He knelt beside the bed and kissed her lips. Her eyes slowly opened. "You're leaving now?"

He smiled down at her, liking the way her features still reflected the pleasures he'd shared with her earlier. "Yes. What are your plans for today?"

She smiled. "I'd thought about catching the subway downtown to do some shopping. But I don't think I have the strength to move."

He leaned down and placed another kiss on her lips. "Well, when you get your strength back, how about dropping by the Cotton Club later? A group of friends from Juilliard who live here in New York and I will be this evening's entertainment. We're trying to raise money for the Harlem Music Festival."

She nodded. "What time?"

"Around five."

She smiled. "I'll be there."

"Good," he said, liking her quick response, and he knew she would be on his mind until he saw her again. He also knew that getting all wrapped up in Sydney was not the smartest thing to do, but for now he couldn't help it. The woman had totally bewitched him.

He stood, knowing that if he didn't leave now, he would climb back in that bed with her and make love to her all over again. "I'll see you later."

As he forced himself to leave her, he realized it was the hardest thing he'd had to do in a long time.

EIGHT

Sydney tapped lightly upon the glossy surface of her table at the Cotton Club. Several groups had performed, but the one Tyrone was a part of had yet to come on stage.

She glanced at her watch. She'd been here an hour already but couldn't complain, as she was enjoying herself. She had felt joyful all day. After Tyrone had left that morning she had gone back to sleep. When she woke up she felt rejuvenated and energized. A day and night spent making love with Tyrone had certainly been the thing she needed.

The lights in the club dimmed, signaling that the matinee was over and the next show was about to begin. She took a sip of her drink, leaned back in her chair, and waited. Her heart raced when four men and a woman appeared on stage. Everyone gave them a big applause, and moments later the emcee introduced them.

"Most of you will remember this group of dedicated musicians," he said. "Years ago, while students at Juilliard, they used to come play for free each week to benefit the Harlem Youth Choir and other charitable events. Tonight they have returned on behalf of the Harlem Music Festival that will be held this summer. Let's give them another round of applause."

And the audience did just that. Sydney joined them, proud of the dedication of Tyrone and his friends on behalf of the Harlem community.

The lone female in the group went to the drums. Sydney lifted a brow when Tyrone went to the piano instead of the saxophone. Their first number was "A Fifth of Beethoven," Walter Murphy's upbeat jazzy style.

She tried ignoring a group of women sitting at the table behind her who were whispering loudly about Tyrone. They all agreed that he was the best-looking man on stage. "Look at that great body." One of the women crooned. "I bet he knows just how to use it in bed."

Sydney tried to force the woman's words from her mind but couldn't, especially since she knew firsthand how Tyrone could use his body to pleasure a woman. Just thinking about what they had shared yesterday and this morning sent sharp sexual awareness through her.

Then the music took over and she joined the audience that was rocking to the beat. She caught Tyrone's eye and her heart fluttered when he smiled at her. The women behind her squealed, thinking his look had been directed at them. Sydney smiled back at him, enjoying the moment, confident that she had been the recipient of that smile. After a few other numbers, most of them soft jazz, they turned the heat up again with a fast-paced number.

The emcee called for a break and the group left the stage to prepare for their final two numbers. Sydney raised her hand to get a waiter's attention for another drink, and he had just left her table when she heard the women burst into excited chatter behind her. Tyrone was heading in their direction. She couldn't help but admire his looks as she watched him walk toward her. Her smile widened when she heard the women's disappointed sighs when he stopped at her table. She could just imagine the envious looks they were probably giving her.

"Hi. Enjoying yourself?" he asked, snagging the empty chair at her table.

"Yes," she said, beaming, the luckiest woman in the place. "I'm impressed. Just how many instruments do you know how to play?" she asked. "You played just about every one on stage. I've heard you play the sax, but it's incredible how you handle the piano *and* the guitar. You're really gifted, Tyrone."

He grinned. "I can play just about any instrument that's put in front of me. I love music."

Sydney nodded, believing him. She could tell from the expression on his face while performing.

"Are you hungry?" he asked her. "If you are, we can grab something when we leave here."

"I ate before I came but if you're hungry we can certainly go somewhere later."

"I'd like that. There's an all-night restaurant in my hotel." He lowered his voice and leaned over and whispered seductively, "And if you stay with me tonight, I promise to have you back in the morning to take care of Denzel's needs."

She agreed quickly since there was no way she could resist his invitation.

He leaned across the table and kissed the tip of her nose, then leaned in closer to kiss her lips as the women behind her sighed in unison. "I have to get back."

She watched him walk away, astonished once again at how anytime he came within two feet of her, her body came alive with wanting. She took a deep breath, knowing she was in trouble by letting herself be drawn to a man who had made it clear from the beginning that he couldn't commit to any woman. But, for her, what had started as merely a short fling was no longer casual in her mind, which proved that she was a woman who could only sleep with a man if her heart was in it. And her heart was in this so deep that it was beginning to get downright scary.

After leaving the club they had stopped at the restaurant in his hotel. She drank coffee while he ate a hearty meal of steak and potatoes. Then, barely keeping their hands off each other, they rode up in the elevator to his hotel room.

Once inside his suite, he had begun taking her clothes off. Then, not bothering to take off his own, he had picked her up in his arms and carried her into the bedroom, kissing her with a passion that had taken her breath away and had sent sensation after sensation rippling through her. After placing her on the bed, he removed his clothes.

She would never forget the look in his eyes just moments before he had entered her. For long moments they remained perfectly still, caressing each other with their eyes. Then he had slowly pressed himself inside of her, joining their bodies.

A look of satisfaction had spread across his face as he entered her to the hilt, and then the action began. He had literally rocked her world—her body, the bed, her mind—as he established a rhythm that was destined to drive them both to the edge. However, before the inevitable free-fall, he would slow down to extend the agony.

She begged him to give her what she craved, but he kept prolonging the moment until his control broke and he growled her name through clenched teeth, taking one final, hard and deep thrust inside of her, letting them explode in mutual ecstasy as they toppled over the edge together, yet another heightened pleasure she experienced for the first time with Tyrone.

"Tyrone!"

His name came out as a whispered gasp on Sydney's lips as he pushed deeper into her. She felt as if she were on fire.

They had fallen asleep in each other's arms. The next morning, she opened her eyes to the sight of his sleeping features. She drew in a deep breath, not regretting what they had shared the last two days.

He opened his eyes, as if he could read her mind, and pulled her closer into his arms. Leaning over, he kissed her lips. "You're something else, Sydney."

She shook her head. "No, Tyrone, you're the one who's something else. I'm just glad we're both here. In this place and at this time."

He gently pushed a strand of hair away from her face. "No regrets?"

She shook her head. "No regrets."

Sydney knew that the odds were that when she left New York she wouldn't be seeing him again, as Linc and Raven were moving to Memphis. That meant she would have no reason to visit the nation's capital. It also meant that this New York trip was the only time the two of them would share such intimacies like this.

When she felt Tyrone shift in bed, she noted that all signs of sleep had suddenly disappeared from his face. Instinctively she went into his arms when he reached for her. As his mouth covered hers she knew she had meant just what she'd said. For her there would be no regrets.

NINE

Over the next two weeks Tyrone and Sydney settled into a satisfying and pleasurable routine. On the days he taught classes, Sydney kept busy touring Harlem or catching the subway into Queens, Brooklyn, and the Bronx. There was so much to see and do. She shopped at some of her favorite stores and went to museums. On the days Tyrone didn't have a class, he would join her. As he had lived in New York, he became her personal tour guide.

In the afternoon they would attend a play, go to some hot entertainment spot, or just enjoy a nice cozy dinner at a restaurant. Better yet were those evenings when they didn't make any plans but stayed in at his place or hers and talked. Then at night, they enjoyed each other. They had taken their intimacy to a new level, and it became the norm for them to wake up every morning cuddled in each other's arms. Neither discussed what would happen when the fling was over since it was understood that in the end, she would go her way and he would go his. But Tyrone knew that the degree of intimacy they shared would stay with him forever. A culmination of three weeks of mindless, earth-shattering pleasure guaranteed that.

Tyrone heard Denzel scratching against the door. Deciding that Sydney needed her rest, he silently closed the door behind him as memories of the intensity of their lovemaking the night before flooded his mind. After making unforgettable love, they hadn't had energy to do more than fall asleep in each other's arms.

As he slipped into the clothes he had hastily tossed on the sofa the night before, he tried not to think about how he and Sydney had only two more days together. Her friend Donna was due back tomorrow and Sydney would be leaving for Memphis the following day. He had planned something special for her final night in New York, but now, as he thought about it, he decided it would not be enough.

What could you do for a woman who in three weeks had shown you a side of passion you'd never seen before? What did you give a woman who made you appreciate the fact that you were born a man? A woman who made multiple orgasms appear like a common achievement?

Tyrone sighed deeply, not believing he was that much into a woman. Since he had discovered there was a difference between the sexes, he had taken pleasure in dodging every beautiful woman who'd been intent on finding some definite place in his life. He always figured it must have been a "twin thing" because Tyrell was of the same mind, dodging them right along with him. Both saw a serious commitment as something to avoid. And he couldn't leave out his older brother Noah, who had been such a good role model for him and Tyrell. For years they'd watched Noah enjoy his life as a bachelor, much to the chagrin of their mother. She complained that it seemed her three sons would never settle down with wives, which was robbing her of grandchildren. Her complaints had fallen on deaf ears since none of them were serious enough about a woman to contemplate marriage.

His mother's obsession with grandchildren suddenly made him think of the two times he'd almost slipped in the protection department with Sydney on the first night they'd made love. Somehow the magnitude of what they'd shared hit him on an emotional level.

Tyrone shook his head. This can't be happening, he told himself.

The two of them were having a fling, nothing more. He'd had flings with women before, although he'd be the first to admit this one with Sydney was different. However, he couldn't lose sight of what was between them, which was nothing more than satisfying overactive hormones and an attraction that was more irresistible than any he'd ever known.

But even with all the intensity they shared, he was convinced that he was getting her out of his system, and confident that all the time they had spent together would do the trick. When she left for Memphis, he would remain in New York an additional week before heading back to D.C. to resume his daily routine. Their time together here would soon be fond memories.

He rubbed his hand across his face. Then why in the hell was he feeling so damn bad at the thought that in two days she would be leaving? Why did the possibility of not seeing her again once Linc and Raven moved to Memphis bother him?

He frowned, refusing to get emotional again. That wasn't his way. He buttoned up his coat while Denzel danced impatiently around his feet, reassured himself that he would make their last night together special, and when he watched her board that plane to go back to Tennessee, he would be okay with it. There was no reason for him not to be.

"Well, what do you think?"

Tyrone's slow, hot gaze traveled down the length of Sydney's body, as he gave her his hand to assist her out of the car. He took in the way the short, clingy dress hugged every curve on her body and how well it showed off her gorgeous legs. "I think you're tantalizing, Miss Corbain."

Sydney chuckled. "Thanks, but that's not what I was asking you. I meant what did you think of Donna."

"Oh." He shrugged. "She's nice, but then I figured she would be since she's such a good friend of yours."

Tyrone had met Donna when he picked her up at five o'clock.

She had raised a curious brow when Sydney announced that she would not be returning that night and would see her tomorrow. Donna knew better than anyone that a casual relationship with a man was not the norm for Sydney.

The plans were that Tyrone would return her to Donna's place to pack in the morning and around noontime, when his class was over, he would take her to the airport. From the look on Donna's face Sydney knew that she and her best friend had a lot to talk about tomorrow while she packed.

After sitting and chatting with Donna for more than an hour, they had left for dinner.

Sydney smiled, thinking of their time together. For some reason she was glad Tyrone liked her friend. "So, are you going to tell me where we're going tonight?"

"No, I thought I'd let it be a surprise." Since his hotel was located in the heart of Manhattan, he left the car in the parking garage so they could walk the few blocks to their destination. He had made special plans for them to dine at one of the most elegant restaurants in the city, located on the sixty-fifth floor of Rockefeller Center, the Rainbow Room.

They entered the beautiful lobby of Rockefeller Center and caught an elevator to the sixty-fifth floor. She leaned back against a paneled wall on the long ride up and considered everything she now knew about Tyrone Hardcastle. Over the past three weeks they had made love plenty of times, but he had also shared a side of him that she had appreciated getting to know. The term "the man and his music" suited him. She had also discovered that he was a warm and caring person who spent time giving free music lessons to underprivileged kids at a couple of the youth centers in the D.C. and Maryland areas. She also found out that he had played at the White House when President and Mrs. Clinton had been in residence, and he had been part of a group that had performed for President Bush's inauguration. What she had discovered most of all was just how giving he was. No matter how many times they had made love, and no matter how fierce a sexual hunger had raged within him, he had withheld his pleasure until he was sure she had gotten hers.

"Here we are."

Tyrone's words broke into Sydney's thoughts and she noted they were at the entrance of a very elegant restaurant. They stepped out of the elevator and her breath caught in her throat, in awe over how posh the place was. The walls were made of glass.

"Oh, Tyrone, this place is simply beautiful and the view of New York City at night from up here is incredible."

He smiled warmly, taking her hand in his. "I wanted to make our last night together special," he said, pleased with the unabashed look of happiness on her face.

"And you have." For Sydney, not only tonight, but the past three weeks she had spent with Tyrone were already special, a time she would not forget.

Dining with him at the Rainbow Room was nothing short of a dream. The food was excellent, the atmosphere elegant, but nothing could compare to the company she kept.

Tyrone was the most gracious of dinner companions. She sat across from him and marveled at just how sinfully, incredibly sexy he looked dressed in his dark suit.

A few hours later, Sydney sighed as she entered Tyrone's hotel room. When he closed the door behind them, he would be hers alone, their final night together. Since he had made dinner special for her, she wanted to make this part of their night special for him.

"I want to thank you again for tonight, Tyrone. Everything was wonderful."

"Like I said earlier, I wanted it to be special." His voice was a deep, soft rumble of sound that immediately made Sydney's entire body tingle from the irresistible attraction they had given into for three weeks, and despite the hunger they had continually fed over those weeks, it was now at its sharpest.

"If I live to be over a hundred years old, I'll never come to understand this sexual chemistry that exists between us, Sydney," he said, placing his hands at her waist. "I've never experienced anything like it in all my days."

She met his gaze while red-hot desire pooled in her body, and knew that she would never love another man the way she loved him. It would be a love she would take to her grave.

She moistened her bottom lip with her tongue as she eased her short leather jacket off her shoulders, then slid the thin straps of the little slinky black dress she was wearing, and within seconds it had slithered down her body to join her leather jacket on the floor. She then stepped out of her high-heeled shoes and stood before him wearing nothing but a black lacy bra-and-panty set and silky black thigh-high stockings with a lacy top.

Tyrone's breath caught in his throat as he gazed at Sydney. During the past three weeks, he had come to expect that what she wore underneath her clothes was just as sexy as what she wore on the outside, which only made him anticipate what was to come. He had gotten more than a glimpse of her passion for sexy, skimpy, and revealing underthings, and her curvaceous body was made for them.

Like his body was made just for hers. She constantly made him remember what a hot-blooded male he was, a man who appreciated the sight of a gorgeous woman.

"Strip for me," he said silkily, hoping that she would. All the other times he had been the one to undress her, but now, tonight, he wanted to see her bare it all for him. Her breath rushed from her lungs and she flushed. Although over the past weeks the two of them had shared one wild sexual fling, in essence there was an innocence about Sydney that always touched him. He was well aware that having casual sex wasn't anything she normally did, and a part of him was grateful to be the man she felt comfortable enough with to have this onetime liaison.

For some reason, the idea bothered him that she might one day decide to engage in this sort of activity with someone else. His heart thundered in his chest at the mere thought that some other man would one day share the same pleasures.

He pushed that idea to the back of his mind, and when Sydney began to slowly unfasten the front hook of her bra and her lush breasts spilled from their confinement, he became excited beyond reason. His tongue tingled in anticipation of devouring the generous swell of flesh exposed before him.

He tensed and his breathing became labored as he watched her hand move slowly down her belly toward the waistband of her panties. She was wearing a pair of the sexiest, most provocative pair he had ever seen on a woman, and the flimsy, itty-bitty garment was contoured just for her shape. It teased more than it covered.

His erection hardened at the thought of what was beneath that scrap of material and just how much he wanted it. He lifted his gaze to meet her eyes and without speaking a word, he told her blatantly what he wanted to do to her. He silently told her how he wanted to use his mouth on her, and how he wanted to get between those long, gorgeous legs of hers.

He saw her flush of excitement as she slowly began easing the panties over her hips and down her legs. He gritted his teeth at the sight of the bounty she was uncovering and his body ached to touch it, taste it, and get connected with it in the most primal way. When she had finally stepped out of her panties and kicked them aside, she stood before him completely nude and completely gorgeous.

A satisfied smile touched his lips and his nostrils flared at the womanly scent she emitted. His gaze dropped to that part of her and his vision caressed it as intimately as his tongue soon would.

He began removing his clothes, giving her the same strip show she had given him, although he took off his clothing a little more hurriedly.

He heard her huge sigh of anticipation when he began removing his briefs. Her reaction to seeing his erection was sensuous and he knew he wanted her with a passion that overrode any common sense he had left.

Tyrone felt a compelling need to take her now, to sink his body into hers, as a hunger more fierce than he'd ever experienced before tore through him.

His control snapped when a desperate need to brand her as his own filled his head. He lifted her into his arms, carried her into the bedroom, placed her in the middle of the bed, and immediately joined her there.

"I have to get inside of you," he groaned against her ear, too filled with emotions he had never felt before and too out of control to think straight. Hunger for her gripped him. Intense. Enthralling. Wild.

Automatically she spread her legs open for him and when she took her soft fingers and wrapped around his throbbing erection, his entire body shook. He knew if he waited even a second longer before possessing her, he would go mad.

As soon as the velvety tip of him touched her wet opening, he thrust deeply inside of her while her moans of pleasure filled his head. Her inner muscles had him in a tight grip and she did some branding of her own when her fingertips raked his back, urging him to move.

And he did.

The thought that this would be the last time he experienced passion this rich, mind-boggling, and provocative made him move faster and thrust deeper. Never before had he been filled with such raw desire for a woman, and with a growl of need that rumbled through his clenched teeth, he relentlessly pumped his body into hers.

She clutched a fistful of his twisted hair and the pain was overshadowed by the intense spurts of pleasure that ripped through him each time her muscles tightened around him.

"Tyrone!"

Her scream of pleasure as she climaxed sent sensations tearing through his insides, and when she went for a second round he re-leased another growl, this one of extreme satisfaction.

Lifting her hips, he gave one final, deep thrust into her, and with that powerful thrust he met her gaze. Over the past three weeks they had given into the irresistible attraction that had over-whelmed them from the first, and now, with an unexpected surge of emotions that had consumed him from the moment she had dropped that final piece of clothing, he lowered his head and kissed her at the same moment that he exploded inside of her, sending his release deep within her womb.

His heart turned over in his chest upon realizing what he'd done, but there was nothing he could do to stop it. Then the thought that he was possibly giving her a part of him that he had never dared share with another woman sent a surge of unexpected tenderness through him. And for a moment, the idea that she could get preg-nant filled him in a way he didn't think he could ever be filled.

And when another orgasm approached its crest, he clenched the muscles of his buttocks, wanting his release to go into the deepest part of her, as yet another wave of pleasure consumed them both.

TEN

Sydney glanced down at her watch. "I have another hour before my plane leaves. You don't have to wait with me if you have something else to do."

Tyrone tipped his head back as he studied her. Even now, that all-too-familiar irresistibility flared between them. Last night had done nothing to tame it. Not that they had tried taming it. They had ridden its crest to get their fill of each other, only to discover their hunger was never ending.

He let out a deep sigh. "We need to talk, Sydney," he said huskily.

Sydney lowered her gaze, knowing what he wanted to say. They had made love last night, numerous times, without protection. While one part of her wanted to assure him it was all right, that the chances were she hadn't gotten pregnant because the timing was wrong, another part wished she had. It was the part of her that loved him and had decided that if she couldn't have his heart, then his baby would do. The thought that she would have a part of the man she would forever love touched her deeply, although she knew the ramifications.

"About last night, Sydney," Tyrone began, breaking into her thoughts. "I owe you an apology for not acting responsibly, and I will—"

She suddenly reached up and placed a finger to his lips to stop any further words. "We promised, Tyrone, no regrets."

He met her gaze. "This isn't about regrets, Sydney. It's about being man enough to admit a mistake and taking a stand to do the right thing. I should have used protection, and if you're pregnant I want to know."

She saw deep concern in his eyes. "Tyrone, I don't—"

He cupped her shoulders. "No, Sydney. If you're pregnant it will be *my* baby. *Our* baby. And I will take full responsibility for our child and for you."

Sydney swallowed hard, fighting the tears that threatened to fall. Tyrone Hardcastle was such an honorable man in every sense of the word, which was why she had fallen so helplessly in love with him. And although he didn't love her, even now his actions proved that he did care.

"You will let me know one way or the other, won't you?"

He moved closer and tucked a stray strand of hair away from her face. The look of tenderness in his features caused her heart to ache. "I'm probably not pregnant. The timing isn't good," she said softly, trying to reassure him.

"But still, there's a possibility, and I want to know one way or the other." He pulled one of his business cards out of his wallet and flipped it over, then took a pen from the top pocket of his coat and wrote a phone number on the back.

"This is my home number. If you can't reach me there, I'll probably be at Leo's." He handed her the card and met her gaze intently. "Promise that you'll call me."

She took the card and slowly nodded. "I promise."

A smile tilted the corners of his lips and he gently pulled her into his arms and kissed her, deeply, hungrily, and she returned the kiss in equal measure.

He released her but kept her close to him and whispered, "I will never forget these three weeks, Sydney."

She forced herself to smile at him. "And neither will I."

Then she caught his face between her palms and kissed him, a

irresistible attraction

kiss she felt all the way to her heart. And for a moment, she wanted him to feel it, too, and to know just how much he had come to mean to her.

And to know that, no matter what, she would never have any regrets.

Three weeks after her return to Memphis, Sydney placed a call to Tyrone to let him know she was not pregnant. She could not reach him at his home or at Leo's and called his home again and left a message on his answering machine, merely telling him, "I'm fine and everything worked out the way you wanted." She hadn't been able to say "the way *we* wanted," because a part of her had held out until the last, hoping she was pregnant.

When a week passed and she didn't hear back from him to acknowledge he had received her message, a part of her felt hurt at the thought that he could so easily toss aside what they had shared in New York. To rid herself of that pain, she became absorbed in her work and lost herself in a new case. Several times she had caught her parents looking at her with concern over what was causing her dismal mood, but it was something she could not talk about to them, although she had come close to confiding in Raven a few times when they talked on the phone.

Sydney, who'd never had a sister, had bonded with her sister-in-law, thanking God for not only giving her brother a wonderful wife but also for providing her with the sister friendship she needed. Although she and her mother shared a rather close relationship, telling one's mother about an intense three-week fling wasn't something she felt comfortable doing.

Although she tried not to think about Tyrone, each day she missed him fiercely, and when she went to bed at night she was reminded of all the things they had done together, and not just the sexual things, but other things as well, the conversations they'd shared and the places they had visited. He was a talented musician and a very intelligent man. He knew a lot about law, and she had discovered that talking to him about some of the cases she'd handled had fascinated him.

She checked her watch. Her mother and brothers had left the office over an hour ago with instructions that she close up shop within fifteen minutes. She tossed aside the file she'd been reading as she thought about her plans for that night. It was Friday and although she had gotten a call from Rafe earlier, inviting her to dinner, she had turned him down flat, not wanting to see him again. After Tyrone, Rafe no longer had a place in her mind or her heart. Besides, Tyrone had shown her how a real man treated his lady in the bedroom.

She stood, stretched, and decided to stop by the bookstore on her way home and pick up Walter Mosley's latest novel. After preparing something quick for dinner, she would spend the rest of her evening in bed, reading.

Sydney turned another page. Already she was up to page one hundred. The story held her spellbound. She had come home and taken some leftover spaghetti out of the freezer, fixed a salad, and enjoyed a tasty dinner. Then she had taken a relaxing shower before slipping into her nightgown and getting settled for the night.

She had been curled up in bed with her book for a few hours when she heard her doorbell ring. At first she didn't want to answer it, thinking it was one of her brothers, whom she adored, then decided she was really in a bad way if she wanted to avoid them, although she didn't think she would be good company for anyone tonight.

Slipping out of bed, she put on a robe and made her way to the door, flicking on a light as she moved around the room. Taking precaution, she looked through her peephole—and her heart stopped.

She held her hand to her heart and quickly opened the door,

barely able to catch her breath. "Tyrone, what are you doing here," she asked breathlessly, not believing he was really there. Her throat felt tight and her eyes burned with tears she refused to let fall.

He looked so good, so darn good. And seeing him standing there, under the soft lighting of her apartment doorway, she became even more aware of just how handsome he was. He was dressed casually in a pair of jeans and a pullover Washington Redskins sweater, and she thought that no man deserved to look that good.

"May I come in?"

She nodded and took a step back to let him enter. When she closed the door and turned to face him, her throat went dry at the way he was staring at her, and that all-too-familiar shiver of sexual arousal coursed through her once more. She took a deep breath and cleared her throat. "Didn't you get the message I left for you last week?"

He nodded slowly, not taking his eyes off her. "Yeah, I got it, but something you said bothered me."

Sydney looked confused, trying to remember just what she'd said that could have bothered him.

"I don't understand. What did I say?" she asked.

"You said that everything worked out the way I wanted."

She nodded. "Well, didn't it work out the way you wanted?"

"No."

His response threw her off balance. She brought her hand to her heart. "And why didn't it?" she asked softly.

For a long moment he didn't say anything. He just stood there and studied her as if he were trying to find the right words. Finally he spoke. "I lost my control that night and unintentionally placed you at risk of getting pregnant, Sydney. But once you left New York, I discovered that I lost something else that night as well."

Sydney's pulse began beating rapidly. "What?"

"My heart. And because I lost my heart to you, a part of me wanted you to be pregnant. It may have been wrong and unfair to you, but I wanted to get a phone call from you saying that you were carrying my baby inside of you."

Sydney leaned back against the door as her knees went to jelly. "What are you saying, Tyrone?"

He took a step toward her. "I'm saying that I love you more than I thought was possible for a man to love a woman. I'm saying that I wanted you to be pregnant with my child. And what I haven't said yet is that I don't want things to end between us."

Sydney nodded, still confused. "Are you saying that you want us to continue our fling?"

He shook his head. "No. I want it to become something else, like a very serious relationship that will eventually lead to us getting married." A gentle smile touched his lips. "Although it would suit me fine if we skip the serious-relationship part and move on to marriage."

He took another step toward her, until he was so close that her back was pressed against the door. "But you can only say yes if you love me as deeply as I love you. I may be wrong, but I think you do. I believe that only a woman who truly loves a man could give herself to him the way you gave yourself to me. And a part of me wants to believe . . . has to believe . . . that you love me. Do you, Sydney?"

Sydney couldn't hold back her tears any longer. The man she loved had just told her that he loved her and wanted her to have his baby.

"Sydney?" He tenderly lifted up her chin with his finger and met her wet gaze.

"Yes," she said softly. "I love you, but I didn't think I could tell you since we had agreed not to take things seriously. But I couldn't help loving you. I even admit that I fell in love with you that same day we met in Leo's."

Tyrone smiled. "It took me a bit longer to admit it, but I fell in love with you that day we met, too. I stayed up most of the night writing that piece of music you heard me play on my sax in my hotel room. I had composed that entire piece while thoughts of you filled my mind. Even when you asked me the name of it, I couldn't let myself tell you that I had named it 'Sydney,' after you."

A huge smiled spread across her face. "Oh, Tyrone, you did?"

"Yes. So you were right, it *was* a love ballad. Without realizing it, I was telling you with my music just how much you meant to me and how much I wanted you in my life."

His expression then grew serious. "After you left New York, I kept thinking about everything, all my feelings and emotions, and I was forced to put two and two together. Then I knew that I loved you and began missing you something fierce. Over the last three weeks I haven't been able to eat, sleep, or think straight."

She nodded. "I've been missing you something fierce, too."

His smile widened at her admission. "So what do you think we should do to get out of our misery?"

Instead of answering him, she rose on tiptoes and brought her mouth to his, slipping her tongue between his lips. His mouth opened wide over hers, taking everything she was offering.

Moments later he pulled back, breaking the kiss, reached into his pocket, and pulled out a small white jewelry box. "This is for you."

With shaking fingers she took the box from him and opened it, then let out a gasp of happiness when she saw the beautiful diamond engagement ring. "Oh, Tyrone," she said as more tears filled her eyes.

"Will you marry me, Sydney, and be my best friend, lover, confidante, wife, and the mother of my babies?"

Sydney's heart soared with all the love and happiness she felt. "Yes!" she said through misty eyes as he placed the ring on her finger.

"And I don't want a long engagement," he said immediately.

"Neither do I," she agreed.

Smiling, he met her gaze. "Do you have any qualms about moving to D.C.?"

She shook her head happily. "No, none."

"Good." He took a step closer, bringing their bodies in contact, and she felt the largeness of his erection pressed against her. "Do you have any qualms about my carrying you into your bedroom and making hot passionate love to you?"

"No, none whatsoever," she said in a deep, sultry voice.

"All night?"

"Yes, all night," she said, wrapping her arms around his neck. "We have a lot of lost time to make up for."

"I agree." Tyrone picked her up in his arms, she pointed out the direction he needed to take, and he carried her into the bedroom, knowing that the irresistible attraction that had once consumed them had transformed into a love that would sustain them for the rest of their days.

He placed her on the bed, then joined her there. "Let me love you, Sydney," he pleaded in a deep, raspy voice that was filled with emotions, the same heartfelt emotions that were shining in his eyes.

And she did. She let him love her with all the love the two of them could generate as they sealed their future and reaffirmed their love in a very special way.

EPILOGUE

Six Months Later

Flashbulbs went off as Tyrone and Sydney stepped out of the huge brick church where her parents had gotten married over thirty-five years ago.

Cheers went up from the multitude who had come to see the beautiful bride emerge on the arm of her handsome groom. Sydney glanced up at the man who was now her husband and didn't think she had ever felt as happy as she did that very moment.

The wedding had been beautiful, and no doubt the society column of tomorrow's paper would boast of the forty-piece orchestra, all friends of Tyrone, who had performed "Irresistible Attraction," a special musical piece that the groom had composed and dedicated to his wife.

Tyrone turned to Sydney. Although he hadn't liked the idea of waiting six months to get married, he had to admit that it had been well worth it. Rosalind Corbain, Sydney's mother, had gone all out to make sure their wedding day had the perfect fairy-tale ending, including the horse-drawn carriage that awaited them in front of the church.

He leaned down and kissed her as more cheers went up from the crowd. He brushed his fingers against her cheek. "I love you, Mrs. Hardcastle."

Sydney's smile was radiant. "And I love you, Mr. Hardcastle."

His hand tightened on hers as he glanced at the crowd. It seemed the Corbain family was popular in Memphis, because a lot of people had come to see the judge's beautiful daughter get married. "Are you ready?" he asked her softly.

She nodded as she glanced around at the crowd. "Yes, I'm as ready as I'll ever be."

Tyrone nodded. "All right then." He reached down and tightened his hand around hers. "Hold on tight. We're going to make a run for it." Tyrone and Sydney raced down the steps toward the waiting carriage as pelts of rice showered down on them.

Once inside the carriage, he pulled Sydney into his arms and kissed her, thanking God for bringing her into his life and for providing that irresistible attraction that had pulled them together—permanently.

When he slowly and reluctantly removed his mouth from hers, he met a gaze that was glazed with desire. They both knew they had a huge reception to endure before they could finally sneak off to start their honeymoon, a week in Hawaii, compliments of her parents, followed by another week in the Virgin Islands, compliments of his. It seemed that both sets of parents were eager for them to start making babies.

Not able to help himself, Tyrone's lips sought possession of her mouth once more, and when he heard the soft moan that rose within her throat he was tempted to strip her naked then and there.

Reluctantly he pulled away and blew out a frustrated breath. The wait was killing him.

Sydney's hand covered his, understanding how he felt. They had agreed to stop being intimate three months before the wedding to make their wedding night extra special. And now the two of them were burning up in anticipation. "Just think, sweetheart, two weeks all alone, together."

He smiled and looked at her lips with yearning. They were slightly swollen from the enthusiastic kiss he had given her when the minister

irresistible attraction

had proclaimed them man and wife, as well all the kisses that had followed. He shifted his gaze away from her lips to look into her eyes. "No," he murmured softly. "We have the rest of our lives together."

Then he pulled her into his arms and kissed her yet again.

the hunter

For we cannot but speak the things
which we have seen and heard.

—ACTS 4:20 (NKJV)

ONE

Hunter Sloan wondered if a man could die from horniness, and if so, he was about to take his last breath.

His sexually intense affair with Mallory Standish had ended six months ago, but still, as he watched her pace back and forth in his office after arriving unexpectedly less than ten minutes ago, he couldn't help but admit the time he'd spent with her had been unforgettable, which was one of the main reasons for his present sexually deprived state. Since they had split he had not been attracted to any other female.

Mallory was everything a man could want in a woman. She was intelligent, sensitive, witty, and passionate with a capital *P*. The latter is what he remembered the most. It was hard to think about anything else while his gaze took in everything about her. She was too damn good-looking for her own good, not to mention his. Everything about her was a total turn-on, especially her walk...even when she was clearly agitated about something.

At thirty-four he was a man who avoided commitments, and Mallory had decided at some point during their four-month affair that she wanted more. Unfortunately, more was the one thing he could not give her or any other woman. It had been a mutually agreed-upon decision, that since they wanted different things out of the relationship, the best thing to do was to go their separate ways. So they had, and this was the first time they had seen each other since that time.

And he was definitely seeing her.

His gaze scanned her from head to toe, taking in the dark chocolate coloring of her skin, her pert nose, high cheekbones, and bright red lips. Then there were the dark brown spiral curls that crowned her face and bathed her shoulders, giving her a radiant look. And he definitely liked the business suit she was wearing. It was chic, stylish, and fit the curves on her body as if it had been designed just for her.

There wasn't a time she didn't look good in anything she'd worn, even jeans . . . especially jeans. His favorite outfit had been tight jeans with a low-cut top. But he had to admit the outfit she was wearing now was running a close second. The skirt was short, stopping way above her knees and showing off long, gorgeous legs—legs he distinctively remembered having the ability to wrap tightly around him while he thrust in and out of her with quick and deep strokes. Then there were her breasts. He couldn't help but recall how it felt to caress them, cup their fullness in the palm of his hands, and tease her nipples with the tip of his tongue. There also were those times when he used to lick around her navel before his lips would nuzzle lower to give her an intimate kiss between her . . .

"Hunter! Are you listening to me?"

He quickly met her gaze. She was annoyed with his distraction, but he was glad she was clueless as to why his mind had shifted elsewhere. With tremendous mental as well as a physical effort, Hunter forced his attention back to what Mallory had been saying, and away from the enormous erection that was straining against his zipper. Sitting behind his desk, he shifted in his chair, grateful that she had no idea as to the torture she was putting him through, and even more grateful that she didn't know that he hadn't slept with another woman since their breakup.

"Let me get this straight, Mallory," he said in a somewhat strained voice. "You are accusing your brother-in-law of being unfaithful?"

Hunter saw her uncertainty when she answered. "Yes and no. All I know is what I saw."

Hunter nodded. "How about telling me again what you saw." He hated admitting it, but he hadn't heard a word she'd said. Instead, he had been wondering how long it would take to strip her naked, like he'd done once before when she'd come to his office unexpectedly. He would never forget how he had taken her on this very desk. "And maybe it will be better if you sit down," he added, not knowing how much longer he could handle seeing the sway of her hips as she paced back and forth wearing out his carpet, not to mention his libido.

Thankfully, she nodded and took the chair across from him. But then he almost groaned when she crossed her legs, which made the already short skirt inch a little higher, showing a better glimpse of her thighs. They were thighs he used to ride, from the front, from the back, right to left, any way and every way he could. Even now he could hear in his mind the sound of flesh slapping against flesh.

His attention was drawn to the gold ankle bracelet on her right ankle. He had given it to her after they had dated a couple of months. It had been a gift for her twenty-eighth birthday. He was surprised she was still wearing it and a part of him was glad that she was. He would never forget the night he had given it to her and how she hadn't wasted any time thanking him in some of the most provocative ways. It was definitely a pleasant memory.

He shifted in his chair again and decided it would be safer to concentrate on something that was not pleasant, like going to dinner at his aunt Judith's house that evening, where she would relentlessly remind him that he needed to settle down, get married, and have a lot of babies for her and his mother to spoil. In fact it was his aunt's fault that he had met Mallory in the first place.

Aunt Judith had convinced him that he needed to hire an event planner for his parents' fortieth wedding anniversary party. He had delegated the task of finding someone to his aunt and would never forget the day she showed up at his office with Mallory in tow. The attraction between them had been quick and immediate and his life hadn't been the same since.

Hunter sighed as he brought his thoughts back to the present and his gut clenched when Mallory nervously swept her lips with the tip or her tongue. Boy, he used to thoroughly enjoy that tongue. Forcing his mind back to the business at hand, he again prompted her. "Now, what makes you think he's cheating?"

"Because I saw him yesterday at a hotel. I was there and I saw him."

Hunter raised a brow. The first question that immediately came to his mind was why was she at a hotel? And who had she been there with? His heart began beating like a jackhammer and he forced himself to calm down. He had no right to question what she did and with whom she did it. But still, the possibility that she'd been at a hotel with someone didn't sit too well with him. He, of all people, knew just how passionate she was. He'd had quite a few sizzling nights with her, but it was either at her place or his . . . never a hotel. He hoped she hadn't gotten involved with a married man. A part of him refused to believe that. One thing Mallory possessed was a high sense of what was moral, and besides, her father had relentlessly cheated on her mother, so she would never do that to another woman or herself.

He cleared his throat. "You were at a hotel yesterday?" he asked as casually as he could.

She leaned back in her chair unaware of the chaos going on in his head. "Yes. I had an appointment at the Hilton on Monroe Street. I'm planning a client's daughter's wedding and we're holding the reception there. I needed to check the location to make sure the banquet room would be adequate."

He nodded his head. Relieved. "And while you were there, you saw your brother-in-law?" He had met her sister and brother-in-law only once during their four-month affair. From what he remembered, the man seemed to be a likable guy who was very devoted to Mallory's sister, Barbara. Barbara was two years older than Mallory and if he remembered correctly, she and her husband had been married for five years. He also recalled Mallory once sharing with him the couple's desire to have a child, but the last he'd heard Barbara hadn't gotten pregnant.

"Yes, I saw Lewis," Mallory answered, breaking into his thoughts. "I tried to get his attention, but he didn't see me. He was too busy trying to get on the elevator without being seen. I noted it had stopped on the fourth floor before coming back down. I went up to the fourth floor thinking there was probably a conference room on that floor and Lewis was attending some sort of business meeting, but all I saw were rooms. Hotel rooms. That meant he was meeting someone in one of those rooms."

"Yes, but that doesn't necessary mean he was doing anything illicit, Mallory," Hunter pointed out. "People do hold business meetings in their suites at hotels."

He watched her nervously chew on her bottom lip before saying, "I know that, Hunter, but I have a funny feeling about this. A few weeks ago Barbara mentioned that she and Lewis were having marital problems. I think it has something to do with the both of them wanting so desperately to have a baby and not being able to have one."

He shook his head. There were a lot of things he desperately wanted, but a baby wasn't one of them. Over the years he had learned to turn a deaf ear to his aunt whenever she brought up the subject of babies. She was quick to remind him that he was the last of the Sloans unless he produced a child to carry on the family name.

When Mallory shifted positions in her seat, Hunter's gaze followed the hem of her skirt and saw even more thigh. "Have they consulted a doctor to see what the problem is?" he asked more because she seemed so concerned about it than of any real interest on his part.

"Yes, but according to all the tests results, there's nothing wrong with either of them."

"Then I'm sure things will happen when it's time."

"Yes, that's what I keep telling Barbara, but she thinks the problem is with her."

Hunter picked up a paper clip from his desktop and began fiddling with it. He didn't want to talk about people wanting babies any longer. "What do you want me to do, Mallory? Why are you here?"

She gave him an exasperated look like it should have been obvious. "I want to hire you, Hunter. I need to know for sure whether or not Lewis is having an affair."

"And if he is?"

"Then Barbara should know about it."

"And you're going to tell her?"

"Of course, she's my sister."

He sighed. Knowing Standish family history from what she had shared with him once, he could see her thinking that way. "But why me, Mallory? There are plenty of private investigators here in San Diego."

"Because I want to keep this private, Hunter. I'll feel a lot better if you're the investigator handling this for me. Will you do it?"

Hunter stared at her long and hard as he thought of the problems that could arise if he associated himself with Mallory again, even for a business reason. She would always remind him of sharing a bed, enjoying nights of passion and excitement that culminated in orgasms that came back-to-back for hours. No other woman had the ability to do that.

And no other woman had made him imagine going to bed with her every night and waking up beside her every morning on a permanent basis. When those thoughts had begun formulating in his mind he'd known it was time to cut out, and when she'd thrown out the words "a committed relationship," he hadn't wasted any time putting distance between them. He didn't do committed relationships. What she was asking him to do would bring them back in contact again, and a part of him wasn't sure he could handle that.

He took a shaky breath. Hell, he was about to go bonkers just from the twenty minutes they had spent together already. "I don't know, Mallory. Considering our history, maybe you should—"

"No, Hunter. There's no one else I'd trust. If Lewis is cheating on Barbara you're the only one I'd want to know about it. I really do need your help."

Hunter knew if he lived a whole lifetime, he would always be drawn in by Mallory's dark brown eyes, which were now pleading with him. And for the life of him, he couldn't turn her down.

"Okay, Mallory, I'll do it."

Relief spread across her face. "Thanks, Hunter."

He glanced down at his watch. "There's some information I need to get from you before I can start, but I have another appointment in a few minutes. Is there any way we can meet again later today?"

He watched as she quickly pulled her PalmPilot out of her leather purse. Less than a minute later, she said, "My last appointment is at five. Do you want me to stop back by here before going home?"

He frowned. He had an appointment on the other side of town that would last until around five, and then he was to join his aunt for dinner at seven, which didn't give them much time in between. The best solution, although he didn't want to suggest it, would be for him to drop by her place on the way to his aunt's house. Bad move if he wanted to keep things strictly business.

Then he thought of another idea. "How about if we met at Rowdy's at five-thirty? I have dinner plans for later and that way we can talk and I won't be late for my seven o'clock dinner date." She didn't have to know that his dinner date was with his aunt. It might be best for the both of them if she thought he was involved with someone.

The expression on her face indicated that she didn't care one way or the other. He wasn't sure if he should be relieved or monumentally pissed. "All right, that's fine. I'll be at Rowdy's at five-thirty," she said, standing. "And I really do appreciate this."

He stood and came around his desk to walk her to the door. When they got to the door, he considered locking it and throwing away the key and having his way with her. He knew she liked wearing colorful undies and wondered just what color panties she had on. And he knew that whatever color they were, she was wearing a matching bra.

She reached out her hand to him. "Thanks again, Hunter."

He took her hand and immediately felt a sexual pull in his groin. For a moment he forgot to breathe. The intense attraction, the sensuous connection was still there, and although she remained expressionless, he knew she had to have felt it as well.

"You're welcome and I'll see you later this evening, Mallory." The words sounded a lot more intimate than he had wanted them to.

She nodded, then opened the door and quickly slipped out. When the door closed behind her, he leaned against it and drew in a deep breath, then let it out slowly. It shouldn't take long to find out if Lewis Townsend was cheating on his wife. Once that was done Mallory would be out of his life again and he could regain the harmony he had worked so hard to achieve over the past six months, although the horniness was almost killing him. In his present state, if he hung around her too much there was no telling what would happen.

Engaging in another passionate and thrilling affair with Mallory Standish was definitely out of the question.

TWO

Mallory Standish stepped onto the elevator and was grateful it was empty. After the doors closed behind her, she pushed the button that would take her down to the first floor and expelled the breath she hadn't realized she'd been holding.

It had been hard seeing Hunter again, and if it weren't for Barbara, she would not have come. But her sister was all the family she had and she was determined to find out the truth one way or the other, and like she had told Hunter, she trusted only him to find out.

Hunter.

He was still the tall, dark, and handsome predator. His name suited him well. That had been her initial thought when they had first met. She had walked into his office with his aunt, and the moment their gazes connected, she had discovered there was such a phenomena as instant attraction.

One of the first things she had noticed about him when they met was just how tall he was, way over six feet, with powerfully built shoulders, tapered thighs, and muscular legs. He had returned to the office after playing a game of tennis with a business associate and hadn't yet showered and changed back into his suit. He'd possessed a physique that left her insides tingling, and she had quickly reached the conclusion that no man should have been blessed to have it good in both the looks and the body departments.

His dark brown hair was cut low and neatly trimmed, and his face, the color of semisweet chocolate, had the most arresting features of any man she had ever met. He was so startlingly handsome that it was both a sin and a shame. The eyes that had locked with hers were stark black, intense, and predatory. Since he'd been intent on giving her the same thorough once-over she had given him, it had taken a full two minutes after his aunt had made the introductions before either of them spoke.

In just that span of time her emotions had gone from relatively calm to veering on the edge of turbulent. There was no way she could have ignored the electrifying attraction or the sizzle along her nerve endings when she'd seen him. And when he had taken her hand in his in the appropriate handshake, a tingling warm, pulsing heat had quickly settled between her legs.

She had never had such a physical reaction to a man, and it had been the most bizarre thing she'd ever encountered, instant heat had been fueled by a sexual need that she hadn't known could exist. From that first blazing encounter, the die had been cast. It was a foregone conclusion that the two of them would eventually hook up.

And they did.

Although she had been determined to keep things strictly business while working on his parents' anniversary party, she'd been fully aware that he was a man waiting patiently, biding his time. However, as the time came closer to the date of the party, he had become impatient and more than once tried coming on to her. She'd known without a doubt that he'd been anxious to make his move.

And when the time had come, the night of the anniversary party, he had done so in a very smooth and suave manner. He had not left the country club, where the festivities had been held, when the party was over. Instead, he had hung around while she finalized the very last detail…waiting for her. And they left together, ending up at her place where he spent the night.

Yes, she had known all she needed to know about Hunter and his reputation. There were those who referred to him as the untamable Hunter and claimed he had a wild side when it came to women. His reputation was legendary. He was a ladies' man, although indiscriminately so. She'd also heard that he avoided commitments and had often said he didn't plan to settle down until he was well into his forties, and since he hadn't yet reached the age of thirty-five, he had a few more years to go.

But regardless of all that, she thought she could handle Hunter Sloan since she was too caught up in her own work to get serious about anyone. However, fate had dealt her a reality check when by their third date she'd found herself falling head over heels in love with him. And by the fourth month of their affair she had gained enough courage to test the waters to see if he reciprocated her feelings and had voiced them aloud. Unfortunately, he made it clear what his position was as to a serious relationship with any woman: he wasn't interested.

That was not good news for her since she was interested, extremely so. However, Olivia Standish hadn't raised either of her daughters to be fools, and Mallory had known that the best thing to do was to walk away with her pride intact although her heart was in shambles.

Over the past six months she had managed to survive the pain and heartache, but now it seemed that fate had brought them back together, even if it was for business. Seeing Hunter again made her realize that she still loved him, although she wished it were otherwise.

When the elevator reached her floor and the doors opened, she took a deep breath as she stepped out. She knew that dealing with Hunter would not be easy, but she was determined to do it. Even if it killed her.

Hours later Hunter walked into Rowdy's and glanced around. He immediately saw Mallory sitting at a table by the window. She was

the hunter

so absorbed in the ocean view that she hadn't noticed he had arrived. It was just as well since he needed to get his bearings.

For as long as he could remember, cars and women had been the only two things that had held his attention after he graduated from Grambling College. Then he had opened his company and it had become part of the mix. He enjoyed being footloose and fancy free, although he knew his parents and his aunt Judith were hoping he would settle down, get married, and have kids. For some reason they couldn't quite understand that he wasn't in a hurry. There were a lot of things yet for him to experience—places to go, women to do, and he definitely enjoyed doing women. At least he *had* enjoyed doing women until Mallory had ruined that for him. He couldn't seem to think about sleeping with another woman for fear he would find her lacking. In his mind, no other woman could hold a candle to Mallory Standish in any way. And no matter how many times he had tried convincing himself to move beyond that assumption, he couldn't.

Sighing deeply, he began walking toward her and had just reached the table when she lifted a glass of water to her lips. Immediately, his guts clenched when he remembered all the naughty things he'd taught her to do with those lips.

Heated thoughts flooded his mind. Wicked thoughts. Sexually intense thoughts. He felt his erection beginning to rise and harden and thought it was best to sit down as soon as he could. "Mallory," he said.

She glanced up. Surprised. "Hunter I wasn't expecting you for another ten minutes or so."

He nodded as he took the chair across from her. "My appointment finished up early." His heart began beating faster, so he glanced around, trying to look at anything but her. This was crazy. Absolutely nuts. Why in the hell was he feeling this way? The nervousness. The tension. She was just a woman. Someone he used to sleep with. The last woman he'd slept with. No big deal.

But when he finally brought his gaze back to her and met her eyes, he knew it was a big deal. There was something about her that he just couldn't shake. Even after six months.

He shook his head, determined to shake it anyway, or at least try. "Is water the only thing you're drinking?" he decided to ask.

"Yes. I have a dinner engagement later, too."

Luckily for him, she shifted her gaze to look back out of the window. Otherwise she would have seen the jealousy that flared in his eyes. She would be meeting a man later? For dinner?

To keep his hands from hitting something, he grabbed the menu that sat in a rack on the table. He had to be realistic even if he didn't want to be. It had been six months. Had he really expected her to not get on with her life because he hadn't been able to get on with his?

He had thrown himself in his work, he had convinced himself that the only reason he hadn't been dating was because he'd been too busy. Six months was a long time for a man to go without, especially a man who'd been used to getting it on a pretty regular basis.

"How's your aunt?"

Her question interrupted his thoughts and he glanced up from the menu he was pretending to study and met her gaze. Her expression was cool and he wondered how she could sit so calmly and appear so detached. Whenever he thought of her the one word that always came to mind was hot. That was followed by sexy, beautiful, and passionate.

He decided to answer her question. "Aunt Judith is doing well. She asks about you often."

She smiled as she began fiddling with her water glass, and all he could do was sit there and stare at that smile while his need for her escalated another notch.

"I always liked your aunt," she said, before taking another sip of water.

He almost said "and she likes you, too," before deciding that wouldn't be a good idea. The last thing he wanted to do was give

the hunter

her any ideas. Besides, although he loved his aunt dearly, what she liked or didn't like really didn't matter to him, although he had to admit that Mallory had been the first woman he'd gotten involved with that both his mother and aunt had approved of. That should have been the first warning sign, and it would have been if he hadn't been so focused on getting Mallory into his bed. And once he had gotten her there, he hadn't been in any hurry to get her out.

Thank goodness a waiter came at that moment to take their order and the only thing the two of them wanted was coffee. He stared at her for a long moment when her mobile phone went off and she answered it. Moments later, he sat back, relieved. He had listened to enough of her conversation to know the person she would be meeting later for dinner was a girlfriend.

"So what do you want to know about Lewis that could possibly help the investigation?"

Hunter drew in a deep breath and let it out slowly. Although he had been watching her every move he hadn't realized she had ended her conversation and had placed the mobile phone back in her purse until she had spoken. "Does he still work for the IRS?" he asked.

"Yes."

Hunter nodded. That had been another reason he hadn't been overly eager to make friends with Mallory's brother-in-law. Although Hunter paid his fair share of taxes like the next guy, people who worked for the Internal Revenue Service made him nervous. "Do you know if he's been going out a lot at night lately? More so than usual?"

He watched as a frown marred Mallory's forehead as she thought about his questions. "No," she said moments later. "Lewis is a homebody and I can't recall Barbara mentioning that he's started going out at night. In fact, Barbara and I usually talk every night and he's always home in bed already."

"Has he begun talking any business trips?"

"No."

Hunter nodded. "That means if he is involved with someone, he's doing it on his lunch hour."

Mallory brow raised. "His lunch hour? That wouldn't give him enough time, would it?"

His lips curled into a lazy smile. The reason she had probably asked was because whenever they'd made love they would stay in bed for hours and hours. Sixty minutes had not been enough time for them. "It might. Depending on what all he's doing."

He watched as she swallowed hard and saw her lips tremble when she said, "I hope for Barbara's sake that he's not doing anything."

"Well, that's what you've hired me to find out. Starting tomorrow I'll watch how he spends his lunchtime."

Mallory nodded. "Anything else you need to know?"

There was something else he needed to know, but it had nothing to do with business. It was a question that had been gnawing at him since he had seen her earlier that day, and his mind just wouldn't let it go. It was as if he was driven beyond reason to know the answer, like his very life depended on it. "Yes, there is one other thing I need to know, Mallory."

He leaned forward across the table so his next words could not be heard by anyone else. It brought him so close to her, he could clearly see the darkness of her eyes, and when she also leaned forward to hear what he had to ask, their mouths almost touched.

When he hesitated, she raised a brow and quietly breathed out her next words through water-damp lips. "What is it, Hunter? What else do you need to know?"

He swallowed and felt his sexual frustrations come to a head when he again remembered that sex with Mallory had been absolutely mind-blowing fantastic every single time. He felt a shiver of desire go up his spine and the erection straining against his zipper harden even more. And when she tilted her head slightly, which only inched her lips even closer to his, he couldn't hold back his question any longer.

"I need to know what color panties you're wearing," he whispered.

THREE

Mallory went still.

Her hand, which had been reaching for her coffee cup, dropped to the table as a small gasp escaped her lips. Of all the questions she had anticipated Hunter asking her, the color of her underwear was definitely not one of them.

She met his gaze, not sure she had heard him right and that she must have imagined his question. However, the heated look in his eyes indicated she had heard him correctly and that he was actually waiting on an answer.

Mallory's eyes went wide. Only the untamable Hunter Sloan thought he could ask such a thing. She sat back in her chair and straightened her spine. "Is there a reason you want to know?" she asked coolly, thinking that he really had a lot of nerve.

He shrugged. "Just curious."

Mallory frowned wondering why he was "just curious." It wasn't like he would be getting into them, so why the interest? He was the one who'd decided to end their relationship six months ago; so the way she saw it, the color of her panties was no business of his.

When she saw the intensity of his gaze she couldn't help but remember a time when what she wore under her dress *had* been his business. She had vivid memories of how his dark gaze would sweep over her and his breathing would quicken whenever she would strip down to her panties and bra. And likewise, her body would flare in heat anticipating what was to come.

In the back of her mind she could actually hear the moans she made when he removed her bra and then knelt before her to remove the matching pair of colorful, scanty panties she'd worn. But before he would take them off, he would take his hand and stroke her through the material, making her panties soaked as the scent of aroused woman filled the room. He would ease the scrap of lace down her legs and continued to stroke her in such a way that would leave her quivering and gulping for air. Then he would look up at her and give her that damn untamable Hunter smile and proceed to show her just how much he loved that particular area of her body by cupping her hips into his hands and leaning forward, kissing her intimately, letting his tongue thrust deep. She would nearly pass out from his lusty enjoyment of her, eliciting her cry of release and giving her one hell of an orgasm even before they reached the bed.

Bringing her thoughts back to the present, Mallory breathed in deeply, inwardly admitting that she missed those times with him. Hunter was definitely a man who brought fantasies to life. Sex with him had always been incredible, devastatingly wild, and bone-curling, desire-filling good.

He had found out rather early in their relationship—that first night to be exact—that he was her first lover. And he had set out to make sure he would be her only lover by raising the bar and her expectations too high for anyone who followed. When it came to making love to her, his delivery had always been intense, overwhelming, and very gratifying.

Mallory knew that any woman who had an affair with Hunter would be getting the best. That thought reminded her that she was no longer that woman, and in fact, in a few hours he would be meeting another woman for dinner. The thought that he wanted to know the color of her panties when he would be seeing someone else later didn't sit too well with her, and she became downright angry. She placed her hand in her lap, fighting the impulse to lean over and slap him silly. But then she was too dignified to let any man bring out the worse in her, no matter how much she wanted to lash out in pain.

Deciding she didn't owe him an answer to his question and that they had finished the only business between them for now, Mallory picked up her purse and stood. "Enjoy your dinner date, Hunter, and I would think *she* would be the one whose panties you would be interested in."

Without saying another word Mallory walked out of the restaurant.

"You don't seem to be in a good mood tonight, Hunter."

Hunter glanced up from his meal to stare into the concerned face of his aunt. He knew if he didn't give her a reason for his surly mood she would only continue digging. "I had a rough day," he said, and then, as he resumed eating his food, he realized it wasn't far from the truth. He had wanted Mallory to think he'd had dinner plans with another woman. No sooner had Mallory walked out of Rowdy's than he had felt the impact of his deception.

"So when was the last time you saw Mallory?"

Drawing in a slow breath, Hunter lifted his gaze and stared across the table at his aunt. Not for the first time in his life he wondered if she had ESP or something. "Why do you ask?"

She smiled at him. "Just curious."

He swallowed hard. Those had been the same words he'd given Mallory when she had asked why he wanted to know the color of her panties. Even now he couldn't believe he had actually asked her that, and far worse was the fact that he still wanted to know. It was as if it was privileged information that he felt he was entitled to. But he had to be realistic enough to know that when it came to Mallory Standish, he was no longer entitled to anything.

He placed his fork down, knowing his aunt was waiting on an

answer. As casually as he could, he said, "I saw Mallory earlier today." There was no need to tell his aunt that he and Mallory had also shared coffee less then a few hours ago. He leaned back in his chair when he saw his aunt's eyes fill with speculation.

"Really?"

"Yes, and before you ask the answer is no. Mallory and I are not getting back together. It was strictly a business meeting. She thinks her brother-in-law may be messing around on her sister and has hired me to find out if he is or isn't."

"Oh."

He looked at his aunt uneasily. "And what does that mean?"

She smiled that same smile his mother would often give him. And not for the first time he thought that she should have been his mother's sister instead of his father's since the two women had similar mannerisms and thought so much alike. "I meant nothing by it, Hunter. You're a grown man and I think a fairly smart one. It's been six months, and if you haven't realized by now that Mallory Standish was the best thing to happen to you then that's your loss." She pushed back her chair and stood. "Now, if you'll excuse me, I'll go into the kitchen to get our dessert. I tried out a new recipe. It's called the 'better than sex' cake, and I want you to let me know what you think."

Hunter leaned back in his chair as he watched his aunt leave the room. He didn't have to eat a piece of cake to know there was nothing on this earth that was better than sex, especially if it was with Mallory. Just the thought of kissing her made him hot, because locking lips with her always led to other things, intimate and erotic. The woman was so irresistibly sexy he couldn't think straight. And the thought that he had been her first lover still left him in awe. She had been an eager student, a quick learner, a woman who'd taken in everything he had taught her and had put it to good use.

Before he could dwell on his intimate encounters with Mallory any further, his aunt returned with a huge slice of cake on a plate. "Here you are, Hunter. I hope you like it."

He took the plate from his aunt. "I'm sure I will." He took his fork and after tasting the cake, he thought it was good. But not as good as Mallory, and by the time he had finished half of it he had concluded that, although it was delicious, it wasn't better than sex.

"It's a shame about that lunatic on the loose isn't it?"

He looked up from eating his cake and met his aunt's concerned expression. "What lunatic?"

"That man who's going around calling himself The Mighty Charger and attacking all those women."

Hunter frowned. He had remembered reading something about it in the papers. "They haven't caught him yet?"

"No, and I'm concerned that most of the attacks have taken place not far from where Mallory lives. I hope she's taken every precaution to stay safe."

He finished off the last of his cake before responding. "I'm sure she has." He then remembered that she was meeting a girlfriend tonight. Had she returned home safely?

He stood quickly knowing he wouldn't rest until he knew for sure. "Look, Aunt Judith, I hate to rush off, but I just remembered something I need to do." He walked around the table and gave his aunt a kiss on the cheek. "Lock the door behind me."

And then he was gone.

So much for getting Mallory out of my life and keeping her there, Hunter thought, a half-hour later while parked in the yard of a vacant house directly across the street from where she lived. Her car was not in the driveway, which meant she hadn't come home yet.

If anyone had told him that he would be spending a good portion of the night waiting for a woman to arrive back home, just to make sure she got into her house safely, he wouldn't have believed them.

the hunter

He eased his car seat back for better comfort and folded his hands across his chest. He had turned off the radio awhile ago when nothing was playing that he wanted to hear. He glanced around thinking that he actually liked this older neighborhood of homes, and knew that Mallory had bought the house a few years ago, not long after her sister had gotten married. Up until that time, she and Barbara had lived together in an apartment while they had worked and attended college.

He straightened when he recognized her car as it pulled into the driveway of her yard. He exhaled a sigh of relief and watched as she got out and walked up to her door. Moments later she went inside and closed the door behind her.

He cursed softly when he felt an overwhelming urge to march up to that house and force her to answer the question he had asked her earlier. He'd never had a fetish for women's underwear until he'd made love to Mallory. She used to wear some of the sexiest and most colorful panties and he enjoyed taking them off of her. For months after their breakup he would still fantasize about her. In fact he still did.

Hunter lost track of time as he just sat there in his car and stared at Mallory's house. Then he figured he had done the gentlemanly thing tonight by making sure she had gotten into her house safely. As he turned on the ignition to start up his car he decided that he would handle the case involving her brother-in-law as quickly as possible so that his life could return to normal.

But for some reason the prospect of that happening didn't seem real.

FOUR

"Boy, don't you look serious."

Mallory glanced up from the huge calendar spread out on her desk and gazed into the smiling face of her sister, Barbara. She couldn't help but smile back. Evidently her emotional state was so apparent that Barbara sensed that something was wrong.

As always her sister's appearance in her office always brought a ray of sunshine. At five foot six in stocking feet yet with a somewhat petite build, which they had both inherited from their mother, Barbara took great pride in the way she looked and always had the ability to garner a lot of men's attention. In fact, they both had, only Barbara was always the one with the willingness to return that attention. She had been able to balance with ease getting her schoolwork done and dating.

Not only was Barbara her sibling, but she was also her best friend. With only a two-year difference in their ages, they had grown up as playmates and confidantes in the constant chaos that seemed to inhabit the Standish household.

Her father, a financial adviser with a major bank, went on numerous business trips and always returned home with sloppy evidence that the trips had been more pleasure than business. Instead of getting fed up with her husband's unfaithfulness, Olivia Standish was the dutiful wife, intent on making her marriage work and providing her daughters with a roof over their heads. However, their father finally took the decision out of their mother's hands when he arrived home one day and announced he wanted a divorce to marry his "young" assistant. Mallory would never forget that day for as long as she lived since it just happened to be on her twelfth birthday.

Although their mother had been devastated by her husband's departure, both Mallory and Barbara had thought, *Good riddance,* and had tried moving on with their lives. It didn't help matters when, less than a year later, their mother, still suffering from a broken heart, had gotten killed in a car accident.

For Mallory, the moral of the story had been to never grow up and fall in love with a man who had "playboy" tendencies. Yet she had done that very thing after meeting Hunter Sloan.

Barbara, on the other hand, had always looked at things through rose-colored glasses. Her take on the entire Standish family affair was that their father had been a class-ass jerk and that not all men were like him, and had been determined to fall in love with one who wasn't. She and Lewis had met four years ago after Barbara had completed college and gone to work for a huge marketing firm in San Diego. They had met one night at a nightclub and, according to her sister, it had been love at first sight. Their courtship had been short and sweet and they had gotten married less than a year later.

Mallory had always liked her brother-in-law, although she did consider him somewhat too serious at times, the complete opposite of Barbara. But it always appeared that he loved Barbara immensely and went out of his way to make her happy. Other than their desperate desire to have a baby, she always considered Barbara and Lewis a happy couple and perfect for each other.

At least she had until that day she'd seen Lewis at the hotel. Like their mother, Barbara would be devastated if she ever discovered Lewis was cheating on her, and Mallory hoped and prayed that was not the case.

Standing, Mallory quickly rounded her desk and crossed the room to give her sister a huge hug. "I'm always serious, Barb. You're the playful one. Besides, it's different when you run your own business." She glanced back at the calendar on her desk. "Although business is good for the remainder of the year, I often wonder how I'm going to pull things off. For instance, in two weeks I have three big parties planned on the same day. Luckily, they're at staggered times, but still that's almost stretching me thin."

Barbara raised a concerned brow. "Then why did you do it, Mal?"

Mallory smiled. "To stay busy."

From the look on Barbara's face they both knew there was a lot more behind her response. Every since her breakup with Hunter she had been working extremely hard to keep him off her mind. Now it seemed her attempt to do so had been a waste of time since he was definitely back on her mind and had been there since she'd seen him yesterday.

And then there was the question he'd asked her . . .

"You need a life, Mallory," Barbara said, interrupting her thoughts. "Let me introduce you to this guy I was telling you about who works with Lewis. He moved to town recently from Atlanta and—"

"Forget it, Barbara. I'm not interested."

Barbara took Mallory's hand in hers. "I wish you would get interested. I think he would be perfect for you."

Mallory sighed. As far as she was concerned the only perfect guy in her book was Hunter. Although she knew their breakup was the smartest move for the both of them, she had to give him his due. There was an out-and-out sexiness that made any woman want to tumble between the sheets with him. Hunter Sloan was fabulous in and out of bed.

Deciding she needed to change the subject and quick, she asked. "And what brought you by today? Although I'm always glad to see you, I wasn't expecting you. When we talked last night you didn't mention that you would be stopping by."

the hunter

Barbara folded her arms across her chest. "I took some time off from work today to do a few things and decided to visit. I was worried about you. I didn't like the way you sounded last night. It was as if you were keeping something from me."

If only you knew, Mallory thought, feeling somewhat guilty, and wondering what Barbara would think if she knew that Mallory was having her husband investigated. She sighed, not wanting to think about that since she felt that she was doing the right thing, and that it was for Barbara's benefit and future happiness. She didn't want Barbara to become like their mother.

"I'm fine," Mallory tried to assure her. "Like I said a few moments ago, I've been busy a lot lately."

"There is more to what's going on with you than work, Mal, so don't pretend otherwise and I know it's all because of Hunter Sloan. The way I see it, if you're going to be miserable without him in your life then you may as well be miserable with Hunter and go back to him."

Mallory's eyebrows lifted. "What are you talking about?"

Barbara grinned. "I'm talking about you being sexually deprived. I bet you haven't slept with a man since Hunter."

Mallory frowned. "There is more to a relationship than sex, Barbara."

Barbara's grin widened. "And I agree, but I also think a person shouldn't be alone and miserable. You were always the uptight one, not me. I know you aren't into casual relationships, and that's cool, but you loved Hunter. I can't believe he didn't have any feelings for you, no matter what he said."

Mallory shook her head as she gazed at Barbara. This was her sister who thought everyone should be in love and happy. "Well, he didn't have feelings for me and I've accepted it and moved on. I admit that even after six months it's hard, but I'll survive."

An hour or so after Barbara had left, Mallory was still thinking about what her sister had said. Yes, she would survive and eventually she would get over Hunter. However, in the meantime, she would continue to be sexually deprived and was determined to get over that as well.

There was more to a relationship than sex, but at the moment it was a part she definitely missed.

Hunter sat in his parked car and watched as Lewis Townsend walked out of the Federal Building where he worked and strolled across the parking lot to his dark blue sedan.

Keeping at a comfortable distance, Hunter started his car to follow behind Lewis when he pulled into traffic. It was lunchtime and it seemed the man had a destination in mind, and Hunter had a feeling it wasn't Burger King. Nor did it appear that he was headed for the same hotel Mallory had seen him at yesterday. He took the interstate and that led in an entirely different direction.

Hunter sighed. He wasn't crazy about getting involved in Mallory's family's affairs, but then it was a job. He cursed softly knowing that when it came to Mallory there was nothing he considered as business, even this, as much as he wanted to. During the four months of their affair they had shared an intense physical desire for each other and he had begun getting petrified that it would lead to something more serious. The last thing he had wanted was to begin developing deep feelings for a woman, and when he'd discovered he was doing just that, he had thought the best thing to do was to cut out, which is precisely what he'd done. But now, six months later, after seeing Mallory again, he was finding out that out of sight had not been out of mind. He had thought of her a lot, he had craved her a lot. And last night, like a number of other nights, the memories of her had filled his dreams.

His thoughts were momentarily interrupted when Lewis pulled into the parking lot of the Marriott Hotel. Making sure he wasn't seen, Hunter parked in a space across from where Lewis parked his car, then watched as the man got out of the vehicle and, after glancing around a few times, went inside.

It didn't take long for Hunter to get out of his car and follow, still maintaining a safe distance. He hated admitting it, but the way Lewis was nervously glancing around and making sure he wasn't recognized by anyone would lead anyone to believe he was definitely doing something he shouldn't. You could tell the man was an amateur at being discreet. If he wasn't in the process of being unfaithful to his wife, he was certainly giving the appearance that he was. No wonder Mallory's suspicions had been raised.

Hunter pulled what appeared to be an ink pen from his top pocket. In truth, the instrument he held in his hand was a miniature digital camera that could pick up a subject as far away as a hundred feet. It had been costly, but over the past year had proven to be highly effective. He decided to take a few shots of Lewis to show Mallory later.

Moments later Hunter stood behind a huge planter and watched as Lewis was given a passkey without signing in, which meant someone was already waiting for him in one of the rooms. Hunter folded the newspaper he was holding and watched further as the man crossed the lobby and entered the gift shop. Lewis emerged a few minutes later with a bouquet of flowers in his hand. He glanced around again before stepping into the elevator.

It would have been too risky to get on the elevator with the man since they had met once before. Hunter knew the only thing he could do for now was to sit and wait. All Mallory had asked for was evidence that the man was cheating on her sister, and so far in Hunter's book the man's actions were definitely suspect, although he felt he needed more proof. The next step would be getting pictures of him and the woman together. Today, he would merely report back to Mallory on what he'd seen and let her decide if she needed for him to investigate things further.

Hunter went into the coffee shop to wait out his time. An hour or so later, a smiling Lewis Townsend stepped off the elevator. After glancing at his watch the man quickly made his way out of the hotel.

Some men have all the luck. What a way to spend your lunch hour, Hunter thought as he stood. There was no need to follow Lewis, since chances were he would be returning to work. Knowing there was a strong possibility that Lewis had been involved in some sort of a sexual romp reminded Hunter of what he wasn't getting and hadn't gotten in over six months.

Automatically, his thoughts fell on Mallory.

Damn, he wanted her, and just thinking of how he wanted her made him go hard. He needed to call her to set up a meeting to discuss what he'd seen today. But he intended for their meeting to be more than that. He couldn't ignore his intense desire for her any longer. Fate had her stumbling back into his life and he wasn't exactly sure what to do about it. He shrugged, knowing that wasn't entirely true. The one thing he was sure of doing was making love to her again. His sanity depended on it.

Squinting his eyes against the sharpness of the midday sun, Hunter walked out of the hotel planning the seduction of Mallory Standish.

FIVE

As Mallory brought her car to a stop in front of Hunter's home she thought she needed to have her head examined. Why on earth had she agreed to meet with him here instead of at his office or some other neutral place?

The thought of being alone with him in such close quarters didn't sit too well with her. But he had taken pictures of Lewis that he wanted her to see, and since her last appointment had been with someone who lived within a mile of his home, his suggestion of meeting here had sounded logical.

However, as she got out of her car she knew there was nothing logical when it came to Hunter Sloan or her love for him. Considering everything, she should have gotten over him months ago, but she hadn't and now he was back in her life, even if it was just on a temporary basis.

When she reached his door she felt heat sizzle down her spine. Her body was remembering other times she had shown up here and what she'd always gotten once she crossed over the threshold. Trying to convince her anatomy of what not to expect was a job in itself and the way her breathing was quickening meant she wasn't being convincing enough. Taking a deep breath she rang his doorbell and listened while it echoed through his home.

He opened the door on the second ring. Mallory almost stopped breathing when her gaze met those of the strikingly handsome man standing less than a few feet in front of her. With his shirt unbuttoned and his belt hanging out of the loops, it was apparent he was just about to change clothes. But still he looked so smooth and suave that she felt her toes curl in her shoes.

She stared at him for a moment then released a long-suffering sigh. "I hope I'm not too early."

The corners of his eyes creased in a way she'd always found irresistibly sexy as he stood back to let her enter. "No, you're right on time," he said smiling, closing the door behind her. "I got home a few minutes ago and hadn't had time to set things up. I thought you could view the pictures from my computer."

She unconsciously slid her tongue over her lips. "All right."

"Do you mind if I shower first?"

She blinked at him. "Excuse me?"

"I said that I'd like to take a shower before showing you the pictures."

His statement nearly paralyzed her. There had never been a time when she had been in his home when he'd taken a shower and she hadn't joined him, whether she needed one or not. Vivid scenes of them in the shower stall began playing around in her head. Blood pounded through her body, especially the parts he had once touched, which meant she was tingling everywhere.

She knew the sensible thing to do was to tell him his shower needed to wait and that she wanted to see the pictures now so that she could leave. But there was a part of her that didn't want to be sensible, and it was reminding her that he had graciously taken this case on very short notice and she should be more appreciative. However, sexual need was replacing appreciation and she knew if she hung around she could get into trouble.

"Maybe I should come back later," she said and wondered if he could hear the frustration in her words.

"There's no need. My shower will only take a minute."

Mallory doubted that. Nothing Hunter did only took a minute. He could take the word "slow" to a whole other level and put the word "anticipation" right up there with it. No one had ever kissed her the way Hunter kissed her: slow and thorough. He would take his time like he had all day and all night. She cleared her throat. "Yes, but if you're busy then—"

"I'm not busy, Mallory, I'm just hot and sweaty. Come sit in the living room and make yourself comfortable. I'll be back before you know it."

A confusing mixture of emotions swept through her. "Okay, I'll wait for you to finish," she finally said.

He smiled. "Thanks."

He led the way and she followed, appreciating how good he looked from behind. And if she remembered correctly...and she was sure that she did, she knew that his front wasn't so bad either. In fact it was the best, although she hadn't had anything else to compare it with. But she couldn't imagine anyone being better than Hunter. From the first time they had made love he made her feel completely sexy; he could arouse every inch of her with just one heated look.

She blinked, noticed he had stopped to turn around and his mouth was moving. She blinked again. "I'm sorry, what did you say?"

He looked at her for a long moment and then he smiled again. "I said I want to clear the air about something else. About yesterday..."

She swallowed deeply before asking, "What about yesterday?"

"That question I asked you at Rowdy's that upset you."

Mallory stiffened, recalling exactly what he'd asked her. "Yes, what about it?"

"I need to apologize. I was out of line. I had no right asking you something like that and I knew it. I guess six months going without can make a person kind of crazy."

Mallory raised a brow. "What are you talking about?"

"Nothing more than the simple fact that I haven't slept with a woman since we broke up and I'm still going through withdrawal."

Mallory sucked in a breath. Hunter's words caught her off guard. She lifted her chin and narrowed her eyes at him. "Are you trying to tell me that you haven't slept with anyone in six months?"

"Yes, that's exactly what I'm telling you."

She shook her head, not believing a word he'd said. Hunter was too much of a passionate man to go without sex for that long. "And what about your dinner date the other night?"

"My date was my aunt Judith, Mallory. She had invited me to dinner and I accepted. Like I said, I haven't shared a bed with anyone since we split."

Mallory's skin began sizzling beneath the blouse she was wearing and fire began stirring in her stomach as she held his gaze. "B-but why?"

He leaned against the sofa and crossed his arms over his chest and stood in a pose that looked as serious as it could get. "I haven't gotten over you yet," he said as if those words explained everything.

Well, they didn't. Her eyes widened. "You haven't gotten over me yet?"

"No."

Mallory stared across the room at him, not knowing what to say. The dark, brooding eyes holding hers were not happy, and a part of her felt giddy at the thought that although he had been the one to make the decision to end their affair, memories of how good they'd been together plagued him.

"And I wouldn't get all that happy about it if I were you."

She tilted her head to the side and gazed at him. "Excuse me?"

"I said don't get all that happy about the fact that I haven't gotten over you yet, because I have a very strong feeling you haven't gotten over me either."

With those final words he turned and walked out of the room.

Hunter walked into his bedroom, closed the door behind him, and squeezed his eyes shut for a moment. He hadn't meant to say those things to Mallory. He should have thought clearly before opening his mouth and telling her he still hadn't gotten over her. Now she would think he definitely had a thing for her.

He cursed softly when he had to inwardly admit that he did have a thing for her. He wanted her more than he had ever wanted any woman, and since their breakup, he had literally lost his appetite for anyone other than her. His shoulders relaxed as he let his breath out. Maybe it wasn't so bad to let her know where he stood. That way she would know exactly where he was coming from and right where he intended to go. He began stripping off his clothes as he headed for the shower. He glanced at the bed before entering his bathroom and thought that would be a great place to start.

Like he had told her, he believed she wasn't over him yet either. It was there in her eyes whenever she looked at him. He had been her lover long enough to know deep longing and desire within her when he saw it. He hadn't paid any attention to it yesterday at Rowdy's but here in his house, in his domain where he had made love to her many times, he felt it and was attuned to it. There was no way he was over-reacting to the situation. Mallory wanted him as much as he wanted her and as soon as he took his shower he intended to prove it. Oh yeah, he would show her those pictures, and then he would show her something else. He wanted her to see just what a bad state he was in. He needed to make love to her. She needed to make love to him.

They needed to make love to each other.

Mallory nervously paced around Hunter's living room. She paused for a moment and blew out a breath as she tried to steady her emotions. Hunter had been able to read her so clearly. He could tell that she had not gotten over him but what he didn't know was why. She loved him.

She couldn't help but wonder what was his reason for not getting over her. Oh sure, the sex between them had been good but he had dated plenty of other women before her and she hadn't been much of an expert in the bedroom. In fact he had taught her a lot of his preferred techniques. So what was the deal with him? She wasn't the one who had run away from a relationship that had started getting serious. He had.

Deciding Hunter was a puzzle she didn't want to figure out at the moment, she made a vain attempt to distract herself from the tingling that was going on throughout her body. She glanced around the room to see if he had changed anything since the last time she had visited.

Everything looked the same. She remembered the first time she had spent the night with him here. They had gone to a movie and he had invited her back to his home for ice cream. They never did eat the ice cream, because the moment the door had closed behind them they had begun stripping naked.

"Sorry, if I took too long."

She quickly glanced up when Hunter reentered the room. She studied him, accessed him. He had changed into a pair of cutoff jeans and a tank top and boy did he look good. He radiated, energy, vitality, and sensuality. She knew at that moment she needed to take care of what she'd come for and leave as quickly as possible.

"You weren't long at all. Can I see the pictures now?"

"Sure, let's go into my office."

Again, he led the way and she followed. He pulled out the chair to his desk. "Come on and sit down. I'll turn on the computer and get things started."

She nodded and took a seat at his desk. When he leaned over her to boot up the computer she took a deep breath. The aroma of his aftershave was doing crazy things to her body parts. Her heart began beating faster. He appeared big leaning down so close to her like he was. He was so close all she'd had to do was to stick out her tongue to lick the side of his face, and she was tempted to do just that.

"That should do it," he said softly, close to her ear.

She blinked and noticed his computer was now on and several

pictures were on the screen, all of Lewis. One showed him walking into the hotel, the other of him at the check-in desk with the receptionist handing him a passkey. Then there was the one of him walking out of the gift shop with a bouquet of flowers in his hand, and the last frame showed him getting out of the elevator minus the flowers with a huge smile on his face.

Mallory frowned, disappointed, and leaned back in her chair. "So, what do you think?"

"Umm, what I think doesn't matter. What do *you* think?" Hunter asked her.

She glanced back at the pictures. "I would say it looks like he's involved in an affair."

Hunter raised his eyes to the ceiling. "You need more evidence than this, Mallory. There still may be a plausible reason behind what he's doing."

She rubbed her upper arms as if to ward off a chill when in essence the room felt hot, especially with Hunter's close proximity. And it didn't help matters that her heart was pumping hard. He hadn't moved an inch and was still standing next to the chair. "Come on, Hunter, the hotel, the flowers, the smile. What other proof do I need?" she asked, tipping her head back to look at him.

"The identity of the woman would be nice." He moved to sit down on the edge of the desk. "Look, Mallory, I know those photos look pretty damaging, but until you actually see him and this alleged woman together you really don't have a case. If he's involved in an affair it's apparent this female is in a hotel room waiting when he arrives. And it seems he's not using the same hotel, maybe for fear of being seen or recognized. That will make it hard to set any kind of trap for him beforehand since I have no idea what hotel he may be using next or when he'll be using it."

Mallory nodded, knowing Hunter was right. She needed a female's face to go along with her accusations, otherwise it would continue to be sheer speculation on her part. "I want to be there when it's discovered who she is, Hunter."

He lifted a brow and looked surprised. "Why?"

"Because it might be someone Barbara knows—a neighbor, a coworker, a person she considers a friend."

Hunter wondered if her request had anything to do with what her father had done to her mother. She had shared with him one night that the woman her father had had an affair with had been a coworker, a person who had befriended her mother. "I'm not sure that's a good idea, Mallory."

She frowned. "Why?"

"Things could get messy."

Mallory's eyes narrowed. "The way I see it, things are going to get messy anyway when I tell Barbara what I've found out."

"Which at the moment is nothing," Hunter reminded her.

Anger fired through her. "I happen to think it's something."

He leaned toward her, so close their lips almost touched. "Are you willing to destroy your sister's happiness on these few pictures, Mallory? What if there's a good reason for what he's doing and it has nothing to do with being unfaithful to your sister? There're too many what-ifs until you have more proof," he said angling his mouth a little closer to hers. His hand fell to her nape and his fingers skimmed softly through her hair.

"I know how much finding out the truth means to you and you've hired me to find out what you need to know. I think doing things my way is best," he murmured softly.

Mallory inhaled deep and found herself saying. "All right, I will." His touch was electric and her mind was more on what he was doing than what he was saying. Her brain was becoming muddled as heat skittered up her spine. At that moment she became keenly aware of just how close their faces were. They were so close she could feel the tantalizing sweetness of his breath fan across her lips. He slowly inched a little closer and she couldn't help herself when her lips parted and he slipped his tongue inside her mouth.

He immediately went after her tongue, tasting it, gently sucking, taking control of it and sending desire all through her body. Hunter was an ace at doing wicked things with his tongue and he was doing them now. He was proving a point. He hadn't gotten over her yet. It was there in the way he was kissing her, making a combination of pleasure and heat rip into her. And when he stood and pulled her up from the chair, her eyes fluttered close and she wrapped her arms around his waist. He began exploring her body as his hands moved over the lower part of her back, her hips, and her behind. His arousal was huge and pressed hard against her middle and when she moved her hips against him and felt the heat continue to build in intensity between her legs, she realized he was proving another point.

She hadn't gotten over him either.

The kiss was destined to last forever, and when she began whimpering in need, he let go of her mouth and moved his lips to her ear. "I want you. I need you, Mallory," he whispered. His words, as well as his hot breath, made her shiver in his arms.

Mallory sighed deeply and tipped her head back to gaze into his eyes. She might regret her decision in the morning but at that moment, she needed him like she had never needed him before. She wanted to touch him, run her hands all over him, especially along the hard erection that was pressing against her belly. She wanted him on top of her, inside of her, thrusting in and out. She needed the degree of ecstasy she could find only with him. When his hips moved deliberately against her, letting her feel what she was doing to him, she knew she had to have him the same way he had to have her. Total and complete.

Her pulse quickened and she groaned inwardly. Tonight, for a few brief hours, she longed to be the woman to tame the untamable Hunter.

Deciding to be daring and handle him the same way she'd always done, which was to meet him on his turbulent and oftentimes naughty level, she reached up and cupped his face in her palms and began teasing at his lips with her tongue. She felt his erection get harder, bigger, and took some satisfaction in knowing she was driving him as crazy as he was driving her.

Her hands moved from his face and slowly grazed over his shoulders. As she continued licking his lips, she was surrounded by his scent. It was a scent she had missed, a scent that was pushing her off the edge by sending shivers through her and turning her on even more.

Then suddenly, as if his restraint broke, he took things over and kissed her, putting an end to her teasing. He kissed her like doing so was his top priority, the only thing he wanted in life. The feeling was great, intoxicating, and she began trembling with anticipation. When he suddenly pulled back, the deep chocolate-colored eyes that met hers made her shudder that much more.

"Stay with me tonight," he whispered in a voice so sexy, more heat began flowing around in her belly. "Please, say you'll stay."

She swallowed hard, her decision made. Leaning up on tiptoes she met his gaze and whispered, "Yes, Hunter, I'll stay."

SIX

Upon hearing Mallory's words, Hunter released a low, throaty groan and swept her off her feet and up into his arms, wasting no time carrying her to his bedroom. Not wanting to place her on the bed just yet, he placed her back on her feet, loving the feel of her body sliding down his.

He reached down and grabbed her thigh, pulling her body closer to him, wanting her to again feel his need for her. He had never wanted a woman with this much intensity in his life, and a part of him wanted her to know that. He wanted to do more than just seduce her, or satisfy his desires with her, he wanted to take her, heart to heart, body to body, and soul to soul, and as mad as it sounded for him, Hunter Sloan, a man known to take what he wanted and not look back, it was a revelation he didn't understand. He was beginning to realize that when it came to Mallory Standish he had a crazy streak. And the craziest thing at the moment was his need to see the color of her panties.

He leaned down and began kissing her, as his hand got busy raising her skirt up her hips. He then slid his hand underneath and pulled her backside to him as his hand touched her lacy panties.

A growl erupted in his throat when his fingers came into contact with the scrap of lace and when she began moving against him, heat began building at the tip of his erection and going all the way to the bottom of his feet. In a desperate need, his fingers tugged at the lace at her hip and when he dragged his mouth from hers he took a step back.

She was wearing a pair of mint-green panties.

His breath caught. "You are so beautiful," he said, barely able to breathe as he got down on his knees to remove her skirt and then her panties. He was aching to touch her, was desperate to taste her. After she was completely bare below the waist, he leaned forward and rested his forehead against her stomach and inhaled deeply, needing the scent of her in his nostrils.

He heard the tiny sigh that slipped from her lips when he began dragging his mouth across her stomach, tasting her with the tip of his tongue. His mouth moved lower, to the very essence of her and he kissed her there as if the taste of her could somehow satisfy the hunger that was raging within him.

It seemed that his brain shut down to the sounds she was making—her groans, her whimpers. The only thing he could concentrate on was ravishing her over and over again as his hand, tight and firm on her legs, held her to him greedily devouring all of her. He wanted Mallory to feel everything he was feeling. By the time their bodies joined he wanted her to know how much he had missed this, had missed her.

When he heard her scream out her orgasm he tightened his hold on her, his kiss plunging deeper, harder, and more intense. Only when he felt she was too weak to stand did he pull back, taking his mouth away and tilting his head back to meet her gaze.

"Now I want to get inside of you," he whispered, slowly standing. "And I want to stay there all night. My body has been starving for you, Mallory, and it wants to be fed."

He reached down and touched the area between her legs where he had kissed. "You're wet and hot and we haven't even gotten started yet," he said as he began removing her blouse to reveal, not surprisingly, a mint-green lace bra. Without wasting any time he removed that as well and smiled when he saw how the tips of her breasts were firm and ready for him to devour. He leaned forward, opened his mouth, and captured one nipple in his grasp, making provocative sounds of enjoyment while he did so, determined to get his fill.

"Hunter." The sound from her lips was soft; it trembled with a need he totally recognized and had definitely missed hearing.

He stopped his torment and met her gaze. "Let me make love to you all night long, Mallory. Let me give you pleasure by loving you in every way known to man, in ways man hasn't discovered yet." He leaned down and whispered in her ear, "I want you bad, Mallory. Feel me."

He heard her soft gasp when he leaned forward and his erection pressed against her naked body as if seeking a way out of his jeans and inside of her. Satisfied she'd gotten a good idea of the degree of his desire, he stepped back and they stared at each other for a long moment.

"It's not fair," Mallory finally said, leaning closer to him, her bare breast brushing against his arm. "You still have on clothes."

He smiled, giving her a slow once-over. "You look good naked."

She returned his smile. "If I remember correctly, so do you." She reached up and ran her hand beneath his tank top, letting her fingers skim across his hairy chest. He released a sharp intake of breath with her touch. Talk about not playing fair.

Deciding not to waste time he took a step back and whipped the shirt over his head. The only things left were his jeans and boxer shorts, and he planned on dispensing with both quickly. However, it seemed that Mallory had other ideas when she slowly unzipped his pants and eased her hand inside.

It took every ounce of restraint he possessed not to come right then and there the moment she touched him. It had been a long time since any woman had touched him and no woman could touch him the way Mallory could. Her fingers were soft on his hardness, and each time she stroked him, she increased the risk of pushing him over the edge. When he did he wanted to be inside of her.

Heat began simmering through his veins and he briefly closed his eyes when he felt her push back the opening to his jeans to pull his shaft out. He reopened his eyes, aware of the shallowness of his own breathing as Mallory's capable hands continued on the path of total destruction, unrequited pleasure, sliding her fingers over him, pulling on him, letting the tips of her fingernails gently scrape along his hypersensitive skin.

He tipped his head back and gloried in how her touch was making him feel, wanting to get inside of her with a force that had him nearly gasping for breath. He had to stop her since he was less than a heartbeat away from climaxing just where he stood. "Now who isn't playing fair?" he said in a throaty whisper, taking a step back out of her reach and quickly removing his jeans and boxers.

He watched as she licked her bottom lip. "Umm, I feel extremely naughty."

He gazed into her beautiful face while standing before her stark naked. "And I feel extremely horny and I know of a way to take care of both."

He watched her eyes darken and knew she was dying to find out what he had in mind. The one thing he'd always liked and enjoyed about Mallory was her willingness to trust him on all levels when it came to giving her pleasure. Whenever they shared a bed, making love had always been an adventure, and they had enjoyed the activity with wild abandonment each and every time. Just thinking about some of the things they'd done made his blood boil.

He reached out, picked her up in his arms, walked over to the bed, and placed her in the center of it. Desire, the likes he'd never experienced before, suddenly overwhelmed him and some unnamed emotion that was new to him took control. For a brief moment he thought of how good she looked in his bed, and he admitted that she had always looked like she belonged there.

the hunter

Suddenly, a part of his brain hurled the question at him as to why he had ever let her leave in the first place, and he knew the answer. Fear. He had gotten scared when she had begun getting under his skin. His heart thundered at the memory of how he had turned possessive and how the thought of seeing her each day would send shivers of excitement up his spine.

"Hunter."

The sound of her calling his name made his chest tightened and he marveled at how she could still affect him. Mallory Standish was the most fascinating woman he had ever met as well as the sexiest.

And he wanted her and was driven by a need to have her.

He made a small sound in his throat as he slowly joined her on the bed. And as he gently reached for her he realized that he had her back where she belonged, in his bed, and that he wouldn't ever let her go again. Hunter caught his breath at the depths of his thoughts. He wasn't exactly sure why that revelation had come to him at this particular time; all he knew was that it had, and he meant it.

Instead of teetering precariously on the edge, he had definitely fallen over.

Mallory's heart began pounding deep within her chest as Hunter's predatory gaze slammed into her, making her feel things she had never felt before. Her sexual appetite was high, and from the look in his deep brown, she knew his was, too.

They had not made any promises to each other; the notion of anything beyond this night hadn't even been discussed, yet she was willing to go all the way with him, sleep with him again, in a way that made her breathing ragged.

"You're hot, Mallory."

His observation brought a heated smile to her face. She was more than hot, she was burning to a sexual crisp.

"I can tell by your scent," Hunter said further, leaning over her and whispering the words in her ear. "You're hot for me, aren't you?" he asked, positioning his body over her in way that kept their middle parts from touching.

"Yes" was the only response she was able to give before he slanted his mouth over hers, tasting her with the skillful stroke of his tongue. He was kissing her in a way that made flames race through every part of her body, especially between her legs, making her wetter.

"Ahh," she whispered moments later when he finally released her mouth. She could actually hear the thumping of her heart as his tongue feasted on her breasts. Moments later he moved his mouth to the center of her chest to lick off the beads of moisture that had gathered there.

"Hunter…"

He then pressed his forehead against hers, holding her gaze hostage, demanding her full attention, which was hard to do when his fingers had made their way between her legs, intent on stroking her sensitive flesh.

"Are you still on the Pill?" he whispered the question against her ear.

Mallory grasped his shoulders thinking if she didn't hold on to something she would surely pass out from the feelings he was evoking within her. "Yes." She could barely get the single word out.

"Good. And I meant what I said, Mallory, I haven't made love to another woman since, so you don't have to worry about me not being safe, okay?"

"Okay." Again the word was forced from her lips. "And I haven't been with anyone else either."

Her words touched him, pleased him tremendously. "Then lead me home," he whispered, in what sounded like a strained voice. "Take me inside of you, Mallory. Please."

Mallory's breath caught as she squeezed her fingers around Hunter's hard arousal. His flesh felt hot to the touch and the moment the tip of him touched her opening, he threw his head back and

the hunter

released a deep-in-the-gut groan that could be heard throughout the room.

She tried ignoring the sound as she continued to take him into her, almost losing it the moment his shaft touched her womanly core. Her muscles greedily clenched him, tightened, while he pushed forward, filling her to the hilt. She reached up and wiped the sweat from his brow as she fought to catch her own breath.

"This is what I've been wanting the past six months, so much so that I haven't been able to think straight," he whispered through clenched teeth as he slowly began thrusting in and out, withdrawing then surging back inside of her again as if he could not get enough, at least not in this lifetime.

Mallory lifted her hips to his, meeting him stroke for stroke, glorying in the feel of his length and thickness as it slid in and out of her, pushing her out of control at the sensations that were ramming through her body. Whether they had another encounter after tonight or not didn't matter to her at the moment. What mattered was that her body was getting satisfied and her wants fulfilled.

She wrapped her legs around him, feeling incredibly dizzy with desire as he continued to thrust into her. And when he threw his head back and let out a torturous groan at the same moment that her body tightened when a climax roared through her, he tightened his grip on her hips and pushed deep into her as he, too, was consumed within the throes of passion.

She felt his release inside of her as he furiously bucked into her while aftershocks quaked through her and went directly to him, toppling them both over the edge. She tightened her legs around him, wanting everything he was giving and then some.

For long moments, after the explosion subsided, they lay there, unable to move, their breathing labored, their bodies still connected. Then slowly Hunter leaned up and kissed her, deeply, passionately. She felt him getting hard inside of her again and her feminine muscles reacted, tightening, clenching, and cradling his hard growing erection.

"Ready for another round?" he whispered huskily, nipping at a sensitive area of her neck.

The room had the aroma of sex, intoxicating and potent. Mallory wondered just how many more rounds they could go and knew that the sky was the limit. Tonight he would be her all-night man and she would be his all-night woman. And tomorrow she would not have any regrets, just more memories to add to all the others.

"Yes, I'm ready," she murmured, barely able to speak.

"Good." And he began thrusting into her all over again.

SEVEN

Hunter slowly opened his eyes when he felt Mallory stirring beside him. He groaned heavily and wondered if he'd ever be able to get his body into anything other than a bucking position again.

They had made love all through the night, nearly nonstop, and if the truth were told he would gladly, without much thought, make love to her again. He gazed over at her body, uncovered above the waist. Passion marks were everywhere and her nipples perked, as if ready to be licked and sucked.

He closed his eyes against his renewed desire, as if that would help, yet knowing that it wouldn't. He reopened his eyes and gazed at Mallory. As he continued to watch her, another kind of sensation began taking over him and it had nothing to do with sex.

He shifted positions as he tried to rationalize what he was feeling, and the one question that had haunted him all last night returned. Each and every time he had made love to Mallory he inwardly questioned why he would settle for a commitment-free life when he could have this every night. It was clearly obvious that he cared about her, and it was also pretty damn blatant that he felt a connection to her that he hadn't felt to another woman.

Mental images of what they had done over the past ten hours flitted through his mind. Every aspect of their night had been incredible, not just the physical releases they had shared but the emotional release as well. He had to be completely honest and admit that he'd been dealing with more than the desires of the flesh. He had to finally admit that he'd also been dealing with the desires of the heart.

His heart.

It was the heart he could now admit that Mallory possessed. The mere thought of not being able to share another night like this with her was too difficult to imagine.

He loved her.

His breath caught at the thought that Hunter Sloan could love any woman, but he knew he loved Mallory. What other reason could there for him not wanting another woman since their breakup? What other reason could there be for him desiring her with a desperation that bordered on obsession?

Reaching out, he gathered her close while she continued sleeping. His lips tilted into a smile. Mallory Standish had conquered the untamable Hunter Sloan and his body felt a satisfying warmth at the thought.

As he closed his eyes and snuggled her closer into his arms, he knew that the mighty Hunter had fallen and he had fallen hard.

Mallory opened her eyes and groaned softly into the hairy chest that cushioned her face, loving the manly scent of the man holding her in his arms.

She shifted her body and felt an ache everywhere, especially between her legs. She didn't think she would ever be able to walk again and was glad it was Saturday; otherwise, she would not have made any of her appointments today.

Hunter had definitely proven to be an all-night man. He had the stamina of a bull and had literally driven her wild over and over again. At some point she had stopped counting how many orgasms she'd had and enjoyed each and every one he'd given her. She had wanted a night of passion and had gotten more than she'd bargained for.

She wondered what category last night would fall into. Since they had made love numerous times before, it probably wouldn't be considered a one-night stand, especially since they weren't really involved anymore. The first time they had made love, the night of his parents' anniversary party, it had started out as a one-night stand and had ended up lasting for four months.

Mallory closed her eyes, knowing that would not be the case this time around. Hunter had made it pretty clear that he was not interested in anything beyond sex with any woman. She reopened her eyes and released a mental sigh when she thought of what had brought her and Hunter back together—even for a short while—which was her brother-in-law's unfaithfulness. She didn't care what Hunter said, those photographs he had taken of Lewis spoke volumes, and she had to deal with how she would break the news to Barbara.

She wondered why serious relationships, especially those between married people, always ended in pain. Maybe breaking up with Hunter had been the right thing to do six months ago. At the time she had been willing to take a chance and give her heart to a man, but now she realized that would have been the ultimate mistake, considering how the men the Standish women had a tendency to fall for seemed to let them down. First it had been her father and now Lewis.

She was intent on putting any thoughts of ever indulging in a serious involvement with a man out of her mind. Although she hated admitting it, it appeared that Hunter had the right attitude involving relationships—get physical but stay emotion-free. She hadn't understood his attitude six months ago, but she understood it now.

"Good morning, sweetheart."

She glanced over at him and saw that he was awake. Without allowing her a chance to return his greeting, he leaned over and kissed her hard and deep. Moments later he pulled back and smiled at her. "How do you feel?"

How she was feeling could be summed up in one word. "Sore."

He nodded. "Then it's time for me to take care of you. I'll be back in a second."

She watched as he threw off the covers, got out of the bed, and walked naked into the adjoining bathroom. She slowly shifted her body when she heard the sound of water running and knew he was filling up the bathtub for her to soak in. He had done that very same thing the first time they had made love and he'd discovered she'd been a virgin. If the truth were known she would readily admit she had fallen in love with him that very night. There had been something about the tender and delicate way he had treated her both before and after their sexual encounter that had endeared him to her for life. Although she knew she still loved him, she would be satisfied with things not moving beyond this—the bedroom.

She should have listened to her coworker, Gail Turner, who used to brag about her sexual exploits and say you should take a man to bed but never let him go to your head.

She glanced up when she heard Hunter return. "Ready for a soak?" he asked coming over to the bed.

"Yes."

Effortlessly, he brushed the covers aside, picked her up in his arms, and carried her into the bathroom. After placing her in the warm, sudsy water he knelt down and, using skillful hands and expert fingers, began massaging the soreness from her body.

Mallory closed her eyes and leaned back against the tub when he freed one hand to brush his fingers through the thickness of her hair, actually making her moan.

"How about if we get dressed and go somewhere for breakfast?" he asked, leaning down close to her ear.

Without opening her eyes, she smiled. "That would be wonderful if I had more clothes to put on, but all I have is what I wore over here yesterday."

He nodded. "Then how about I go out and grab us something and bring it back?"

the hunter

She opened her eyes and met his gaze. "Or I could fix you something here," she said softly.

Like a little kid, Hunter's dark eyes widened. "Some of your mouth-watering pancakes?"

Mallory chuckled, glad he remembered the breakfasts they'd shared. "Umm, yes, there is that possibility. In fact, I—"

She never finished the rest of her sentence when he leaned over and captured her mouth in one hell of a mind-blowing kiss.

Hunter anxiously tapped his fingers on the kitchen table to a beat buried deep in his head while watching Mallory stack pancakes onto the platter. Merely watching her was turning him on big time and it wasn't helping matters that all she was wearing was one of his T-shirts that hit her mid-thigh, and he knew for a fact she didn't have a stitch of underwear on underneath.

Sexual hunger was riding him with the need to ride her once again. He was having anticipation attacks right and left, especially during those times when she would bend over to look into the oven to check on the sweet rolls she had decided to bake. Her behind was definitely a real nice piece to look at.

His heart was hammering in his chest at the thought of just how much he loved her and how he had finally admitted that fact to himself. She was exquisite, gorgeous, and everything he wanted in a woman. His aunt had been right. Mallory was the best thing to ever happen to him, and he couldn't wait until she brought up the subject of where they would go from here now that they had gotten back together. When she did, he would tell her of his feelings for her and that he wanted them to move into a committed relationship.

"I hope you have an appetite, Hunter."

Her comment recaptured his attention and he flashed her a quick grin. "Oh, you wouldn't believe the appetite I have, sweetheart," he said huskily, watching as she walked over to the table carrying the tray filled with pancakes in one hand and the container of syrup in the other.

She placed everything on the table and looked at him. "Why do I have a feeling that these pancakes aren't the only thing on your mind?"

His gaze drifted over her body, then he stared intently into her eyes as he reached out and took hold of her hand. "Because they aren't. But since I plan to give your body a rest, you're safe for a while."

She smiled as she leaned down and placed a feather-light kiss on his lips. "Thanks for being considerate."

"For you, always."

When she tried pulling her hand from his, he didn't release it. Instead he pushed his chair back and pulled her down into his lap. "But that doesn't mean I won't taste my fill," he murmured, threading his fingers through her hair and then capturing her lips with his. He kissed her long and hard, doing what he'd wanted to do ever since she had joined him in the kitchen.

Incredible, he thought moments later, releasing her mouth. The taste of her was incredible and would remain with him for quite some time. It was amazing just how she affected him, how much she suddenly made him think of marriage and babies.

Marriage! Babies!

He swallowed hard. He'd never been able to formulate thoughts of either before, but now he did. And only with her. "I could kiss you all day," he whispered against her moist lips.

"And I can kiss you all day as well," she whispered softly. "But that won't get rid of the sound of our stomachs growling. We need food."

He chuckled as she slid off his lap. "That's true." He watched as she walked across the room to open the refrigerator to pull out a carton of orange juice, wondering when she would bring up the subject of them getting back together and decided to be patient.

A few moments later, as she sat across from him enjoying breakfast, he decided that he couldn't wait any longer. Patience had never been one of his strong points. He leaned back in his chair looking at her after wolfing down all four of his pancakes and drinking a tall, cold glass of juice. "My mother and my aunt will be ecstatic to know we're back together, Mallory."

He watched as the fork she'd been using slipped from her fingers. She met his gaze. "We aren't back together, Hunter," she said softly.

He lifted a gaze wondering why she would think such a thing. "Sure we are. Last night we—"

"Had sex. Plenty of times but still it was sex. How many times have you said that you have sex with women, you do not make love?"

He frowned. "But that was before."

Now it was her time to lift a brow. "Before what?"

"Before last night."

Mallory slowly shook her head, confused. "What was so special about last night?"

Smiling, Hunter reached out and tenderly stroked her cheek. "I discovered that I've missed you and want you back in my life."

Mallory shook her head again. "No, you want me back in your bed."

"Yeah, that, too, but I want you in my life more than anything. I don't want a woman who'll just be available for me to sleep with. I want to have a committed relationship with you."

Mallory's eyes widened, clearly shocked. "A committed relationship? Since when? Have you forgotten why we broke up in the first place? I mentioned the word 'commitment' and you hauled ass so fast it left my head spinning."

He shifted uneasily in his chair, remembering that night. "I've changed."

"Yeah, right. And you want me to believe that all it took was several romps in bed for you to change your way of thinking? I'm not buying it, Hunter."

He crossed his arms over his chest. This was clearly not going the way he had figured it would. Six months ago she was the one who was pushing for a committed relationship and now that he was ready it seemed she was no longer interested. "And what will it take for you to buy it?"

"Nothing, since I doubt that I will, especially with what's going on with Lewis."

Confusion settled in Hunter's features. "What does Lewis have to do with us?"

Mallory stood and began gathering up the dishes. "He reminded me that relationships hurt, especially the committed kind. Men are all alike. They can't be trusted."

Her statement angered Hunter and he quickly stood. "Now wait just a damn minute. I don't appreciate being grouped with other men that way. I make it clear with any woman I date what the score is. But with you things have always been different. Not once did I see other women while we dated, Mallory." He rubbed a hand over his face. "Hell, I wouldn't have had energy to bed anyone other than you anyway. You were all the woman I needed. How can you even think that I was unfaithful to you while we were together?"

Mallory released a deep sigh. "I'm not accusing you of that, Hunter. All I'm staying is that at some point in a relationship things can happen, no matter how much the two people loved each other in the beginning. Loss of interest sets in. It happened with my parents and now it's happening with Barbara and Lewis."

He glared at her. "You don't know that. You're making assumptions and jumping to conclusions."

She glared right back. "Maybe so, but that doesn't explain why you've had a change of heart all of a sudden, Hunter. Six months ago a committed relationship was the last thing you wanted, and now I understand why. I'm buying into what you believe."

"But I don't want you to buy into it, because I don't think that way anymore. Like I said, I've changed." He could tell from her expression that she didn't believe him. He also knew at that moment there was no point in telling her that he loved her since she probably wouldn't believe that either. He sighed deeply, deciding to use another approach. "If you don't want a serious relationship with me, then what is it that you do want?"

Mallory shrugged as she thought about his question. "What we had before and what we shared last night. I don't want anything serious. I want to be your bed partner on occasion."

Bed partner? His heart thudded in disappointment. What he'd shared with her last night had been more than that, but he decided to hold back from telling her that. He would have to operate under the theory that actions spoke louder than words. "Exclusive bed partners?" he asked, crossing his arms over his chest once more.

"Yes, that'll work."

Maybe it would work for her but it certainly wouldn't work for him. "All right, we can go that route if that's the way you want things to be."

"It is."

He nodded. He planned to change her thinking on a lot of things. Given even the slightest opportunity, he intended to show her that no matter what her father or Lewis did, it had no bearing on their relationship. He had to prove that he loved her and she was a woman worth loving and worth being faithful to.

"How about if we go to your place for you to pack a bag," he said, taking the dishes out of her hands to place them back on the table and then pulling her into his arms.

She tilted her head back to look at him. "Why?"

"I'd like for you to spend the rest of the weekend with me. Say you'll do it."

His lips came down on hers with a hunger that he knew she felt. Her body began shivering from the thrust of his tongue into her mouth as it swept her breath away. And he knew the feel of his hands squeezing her backside wasn't helping matters. He had Seduction 101 down pat.

"Say you'll stay," he whispered against her moist lips after breaking off the kiss.

Mallory momentarily closed her eyes as she remembered what they had shared last night. He would give her body possibly a brief reprieve but then he planned to make love to her again.

She reopened her eyes thinking she didn't have a problem with that. Hunter Sloan was a man created for sex and she was overjoyed that she was the woman he wanted in his bed. She might be planning to avoid serious relationships, but like she'd told him, she had nothing against being his bed partner, since concentrating on the physical and not the emotional was safer.

"Mallory?"

She glanced up at him, knowing he was waiting on her answer. She moved her hand down his chest and then purposely stepped closer. She met his gaze. "Yes, Hunter, I'll spend the rest of the weekend with you."

EIGHT

A week later Hunter was sitting in his car in the parking lot of the Federal Building. It was Friday and so far he had shown up here for the last four days and the only thing Lewis Townsend had done for lunch was to go to McDonald's or run errands. Either he had ended his supposed fling or this was an off week for him.

Hunter sighed as he rested his head against the seat. He still wasn't as convinced as Mallory that the man was engaging in an affair, although his actions that other day had hinted otherwise. For some reason there was something that Hunter felt he was missing, something vital.

He tapped his fingers on the steering wheel, anticipating seeing Mallory again. They had spent time together three times that week, and as much as it almost killed him, he hadn't made love to her again. He wanted to prove to her that there was more to their relationship than sex. He had taken her to the movies, to dinner, and they had even gone to a concert. And he was glad he hadn't had anything new to report to her about Lewis. She had had dinner with her sister and brother-in-law two nights ago, and according to Mallory, the two appeared to be more in love than ever.

Hunter glanced at his watch. It was way past the noon hour, and it appeared that Lewis wouldn't be doing lunch today, which was fine and dandy with Hunter. He had other things on his mind, like doing Mallory. His body was hot and aroused, which clearly meant that he had reached his limit.

He picked up his cell phone, clicked it on, and punched in her phone number. She answered it on the second ring. "Standish Event Planning. I aim to please."

He smiled, liking her greeting. "So do I," he whispered huskily. "How about meeting me at my place in half an hour?"

Without waiting for her to respond he clicked off the phone.

Mallory raised a brow when Hunter opened his front door. "What's that smile for?" she asked when he moved aside for her to come in. Her body was tingling from head to toe and had been ever since his call. Her nipples felt tight and sensitive against her blouse and the deep throb between her legs was enough to make her scream.

She hoped that he had invited her over for a little afternoon delight, which she badly needed. This had been the week from hell. One of her clients, a high-society dame, had called on Monday to inform her that her daughter and her fiancé had had a huge argument over the weekend and for the moment the wedding was off. Then she had received a call on Wednesday informing her that it was on again. Then she'd received a call that morning saying it was off again. That meant all her plans were on hold until the couple got things together.

"You seemed frustrated about something," Hunter said, interrupting her thoughts.

She smiled and walked over to him when he closed the door behind them. The sound of the lock clicking into place sent anticipatory chills up her body. She had a feeling they were about to get naughty, and naughtiness was something she definitely needed today.

"I was frustrated before I got here," she said, raking her hands down his chest, toying with the buttons on his shirt with her fingertips. "I'm depending on you to make sure I'm frustration-free when I leave. And you never did answer my question about what the smile is for."

"It's for you and the good news I have for you."

"Which is?"

"I have nothing new to report."

Mallory nodded. In a way it was good news, but it didn't mean just because there was nothing new to report that Lewis hadn't been unfaithful. Hunter must have read her thought because he then said, "The man is innocent until proven guilty."

She frowned. "And what if he's never proven guilty, Hunter? It'll be hard for me to completely trust him until I know for sure."

He nodded as he pulled her into his arms. "I didn't invite you here for us to argue, Mallory."

She had figured as much and had hoped as much as well. She tipped her head back and met his gaze. "And why did you invite me over here?"

"I'm horny."

A huge smile touched the corners of Mallory's lips. "I like a man who's straight and to the point, Hunter."

"That's not all I am," he said, pulling her body closer and letting her feel the hardness of his erection.

"I'm just as bad off as you are," she whispered, easing her legs apart so the firmness of him could settle comfortably in her middle.

"You're wet?" he asked softly against her lips.

"Practically drenched."

He smiled. "Exactly the way I want you."

"And you're exactly the way I want you," she said, as her hands moved down to his belt, unbuckled it, snapped open his pants, and then eased his zipper down. "You've been holding out on me the last three times we were together, so if you're horny it's your own fault."

"I was trying to be nice."

Her smile widened. "Don't you know by now that I prefer

naughty to nice?" Her hands slipped into the opening of his pants and his briefs and began stroking him.

"Umm, I'm getting the picture," he said, barely able to get the words out.

"And I'm getting something else," she said as her thumb flicked over the hot tip of his shaft and liking the feel of him getting harder in her hands.

"No fair," Hunter said moments later, almost losing the little bit of control he had, especially when he began inhaling her intimate fragrance. There was nothing like the scent of an aroused woman. A woman ready to spread her legs and mate with her man. And he was definitely ready for that to happen. He had issued the invitation. It was his bash and he intended to provide the party treats, the fun, and all the excitement.

He took a step back, which meant she had to release him, and he immediately felt the loss of her hands on him. He also felt somewhat light-headed and unmistakingly aroused. He smiled, wanting to see her naked. "Undress for me, Mallory."

"Are you sure that's what you want me to do?"

"I'm positive."

She reached under her skirt to tug her panties down her legs and shimmied out of them. They were black lace. He watched as she kicked them aside. Then she removed her short skirt, which left her completely bare below the waist. He licked his lips when his tongue tingled, wanting the taste of her but deciding his aroused body needed something else right now.

He watched as she removed her blouse to reveal a matching black lace bra. The moment she took it off he felt heat swirl around in his belly. She stood in the middle of his living room stark naked, looking sexy and feminine, provocative. The urge to have her clogged his throat and he quickly began removing his own clothes.

"Come here, baby." His voice was low and unsteady but it couldn't be helped. He loved this woman to distraction and wanted her equally as much. And his libido kicked up a notch when she didn't waste any time crossing the room to him.

When she came to a stop in front of him, she placed her hands on his shoulders. "What do you want, Hunter?" she asked, moving her hand slowly back and forth across his shoulder blades.

He leaned down, taking his fingers and stroking between her legs. She was right. She was drenched. "I want this," he said as he gently moved his fingers inside of her when she eased her legs farther apart to accommodate him. He felt her hold on his shoulders tighten and knew she was enjoying the feel of him stroking her. "For starters, I want to take you in my kitchen, on the counter."

Of all the places they had done it before, his kitchen counter hadn't been one of them. Swallowing hard, she whispered, "The kitchen counter?"

"Yes. I've been fantisizing about getting you on the kitchen counter all week."

Consuming desire was taking over every part of her body. "And what's stopping you?"

He smiled before swooping her up into his arms. Crossing the room to the kitchen, he didn't stop until he had placed her naked bottom on the edge of the counter. Then he separated her knees, parting her legs and stepping between them, readying things by placing the tip of his erection against her entrance.

Every nerve ending, every sensation in Mallory's body was prepared for what was about to happen. She looked deep into Hunter's eyes, and for this one time, she wanted him to know just how much she cared for him. For a moment it seemed that everything got silent, even the sound of their breathing appeared to have stopped as their gazes locked. The very air between them seemed to sizzle with fierce sexual need as well as with something else. Love. Neither of them blinked and she knew the exact moment he saw love and not lust in her eyes.

"Why didn't you tell me?" he asked in a whisper.

"Would it have mattered, Hunter?"

A deep sigh escaped him when he realized that no, it probably would not have, and would have made him put distance between them that much sooner. Realizing what he had almost lost completely, he leaned down and began nibbling the corners of her mouth while he ran his hands along her thighs, making a flood of intense love and desire course through her body. Then his tongue began licking the lining of her lips with a slow, deliberate pace.

"I love you, too, Mallory," he murmured, moving his hands from her thighs to her belly. "I only recently realized just how much. I didn't think you would believe me if I told you, but now that I know how you feel about me, I believe in my heart that things will work out."

She shook her head, needing to make him see that things couldn't work out for them. A committed relationship wasn't what they needed, no matter how they felt about each other. But all thoughts of debating the issue with him escaped her mind when she felt his shaft pressing against her womanly core, eager to get inside. She shuddered with need when he parted her legs a little more.

And then he stopped teasing her mouth and took it with a fierce hunger that had her moaning. The feel of his tongue tangling with hers sent shock waves all through her body. The sensation of him tasting her mouth with such torrid intensity made a deep groan escape her throat.

The sensations intensified when she felt him pushing himself into her, overwhelming her, possessing her. What little control she had snapped like a rubber band when she felt the hard and thick length of him pushing deeper inside of her, stretching her, finding her wet and hot, her womanly muscles straining for release.

Her breath came out in short gasps and her sensitive breasts were pressed against his bare chest. She clutched his shoulders, her fingers bit deep into his blades as he continued to push forward, taking his hand and pulling her hips as close as he could. Automatically, she wrapped her legs around his waist as the intensity of their kiss continued.

"I could die inside you this way," he said softly, beginning to thrust in and out while holding her hips tight in his hands. Each stroke he made gripped her, sent her closer to the edge, and her entire body quivered from the pending orgasm. And when it happened, when her climax ripped through her with the force of a volcano, she pulled her mouth from his and screamed.

It seemed her climax gave him renewed urgency and he began pumping into her, over and over, picking up the tempo of their mating, almost bringing her off the counter as a fierce, deep growl erupted from deep in his throat. He threw his head back and hollered out her name as he spilled into her, saturating her already drenched body, filling the kitchen with the scent of sex.

He began kissing her again with light, passionate kisses. She was crying, unable to help herself, and he kissed away her tears. When the explosion inside of them subsided, he placed his hands under her hips and keeping their bodies locked, he carried her to a straight-backed chair and sat down with her legs dangling off the sides.

He pressed her face against his chest, holding her while she continued to cry.

"I love you," she sobbed, wetting his chest. "And you love me, but it doesn't matter now."

He tightened his arms around her. "Shh, it's okay and yes it does matter, sweetheart."

"But I don't want to love you. I don't want us to get together. I don't want a serious relationship with you. Not anymore."

He heard her words but refused to buy them. He refused to believe that she would base what they felt for each other on the actions of others.

"But I do want you to love me," he whispered back. "I do want us to get together. And I want a serious relationship with you more than anything. I was a fool for giving you up. Don't expect me to do it a second time, Mallory."

"But—"

"No buts." He kissed her and groaned heavily when he felt his body starting to get hard again. He stood and her legs automatically locked around his waist. "I'm going to take you into the bedroom and make love to you all afternoon and all through the night. I hope you don't have any more appointments scheduled for today."

"I don't," she said, liking the feel of him growing long and hard inside of her. She tightened her arms around his neck as he maneuvered his way from the kitchen, through the living room, and into the bedroom.

He smiled down at her. "Good. I want you to spend the night with me again. And in the morning, I want you to wake up knowing I've made love to you all night long. And every time my body strokes into yours, I want you to know I am reaffirming my love for you."

Hours later, Mallory sighed deeply as a worn-out Hunter slept, holding her close. One of his muscled legs was thrown over hers as if holding her hostage. Letting Hunter know that she loved him had been a big mistake, but at the moment she didn't want to think about it.

She would have time to regret what she'd done in the morning. At the moment, the only thing she wanted to think about was the man resting next to her who was beautiful even when he slept.

Her all-night man.

It would be merely minutes before he woke up again with the fierce sexual appetite he was known for. She leaned over and placed a gentle kiss on his cheek, wishing the night would never end and that they could love each other this way forever.

NINE

For the following two weeks Hunter and Mallory's relationship continued to blossom, although she made a point not to use words such as serious or committed to describe what they were sharing. As far as he was concerned, they never had to because their actions spoke louder than words. They did things together and his parents as well as his aunt knew his feelings for her ran deep.

Also, during that time Hunter continued to keep tabs on Lewis only to report nothing new to Mallory. Then, when it appeared Mallory was about ready for him to close the case, Lewis left for lunch one Friday and it didn't take long for Hunter to realize he was headed to a hotel again.

After pulling into the hotel's parking lot behind Lewis, Hunter parked the car and watched as Lewis got out and walked into the Sheraton Hotel, whistling as if he definitely looked forward to getting with whomever he was supposed to meet there.

Hunter followed a safe distance behind and saw Lewis as he quickly crossed the lobby and walked straight over to the woman who was walking out of the gift shop with a huge shopping bag.

Hunter watched as the couple kissed passionately before holding hands to catch the elevator. He shook his head. Lewis was definitely having an affair.

Mallory checked her watch as she walked into the Sheraton Hotel. She had received a call on her mobile phone from Hunter asking that she meet him here and to catch the elevator up to room 560 where he would be waiting. The only other thing he'd said before quickly ending the call was that the meeting involved Lewis.

It didn't take her long to reach the room and Hunter opened the door on the first knock. "You didn't waste any time getting here," he said, stepping aside to let her in.

She glanced around. It was a beautiful suite with teakwood-colored furnishings. "You said it was about Lewis. Is he here at this hotel?"

Hunter closed the door and locked it before turning around to answer her "Yes, he's in the room next door. These are connecting rooms."

Her eyes widened. "You mean he's actually in the room next door to us in bed with someone?"

Hunter shrugged. "I have no idea if he's in bed with anyone or not, Mallory, but I figured you would want to know what I found out. And I figured you would want to take a look at the woman as well as letting your brother-in-law know he'd been found out. I normally don't do things this way but the least I can do is to serve as a witness in case one is needed."

Mallory nodded. Hunter's suggestion wasn't a bad idea. She shook her head not wanting to believe any of this. How was she supposed to act knowing her brother-in-law was probably in the connecting room being unfaithful to her sister? "How long have they been here?"

"Less than thirty minutes and it's been pretty quiet over there."

Mallory thought of all the times she and Hunter had made love and all the noise they made and decided on a hopeful note that maybe, just maybe, her brother-in-law was involved in some sort of business meeting after all. She glanced over at Hunter. He had loosened his tie and was in the process of taking it off. "Did you see him with a woman, Hunter?"

He nodded. "Yes."

Disappointment set in and her next question was cut off by a knock at the door. She arched a questioning brow at Hunter.

"I ordered lunch. I figure you had probably missed it and would be hungry."

Mallory nodded, appreciating his thoughtfulness. She was hungry but she doubted she could eat anything. Anger began replacing the hunger in her stomach. Didn't Lewis care how much Barbara loved him and that she would be deeply hurt by what he was doing?

The waiter who wheeled in the cart was efficient and didn't waste any time setting things up and leaving. Mallory took in a deep breath and let it out slowly, watching as Hunter uncovered the food. "I don't think I'm going to be able to eat anything."

He glanced up at her. "Why not?"

"I've lost my appetite."

He nodded as he recovered the dishes. She then watched as he began removing his shirt and it was then that she noticed just how huge the bed was. Colossal was a better name for it.

Confused, she watched as Hunter proceeded to take off his pants then climbed on the bed to lay in the center with his hands underneath his neck wearing nothing but his briefs. "What do you think you're doing?" she asked, barely able to get the words out.

He smiled. "Waiting for you."

She looked appalled. "Waiting for me?" At his nod she placed her hands on her hips as a frown covered her face. "Do you think there's any way I can think of making love with you with what's going on in the room next door?"

Hunter lifted a brow. "Sounds pretty quiet over there. I suggest we make some noise."

"This isn't funny, Hunter."

"And you don't see me laughing. Now relax and come here for a minute. You're all tense. Let me rub your back."

Mallory sighed. He was right. She was tense and agitated and when it came to giving body massages, Hunter was the best. Besides, it wasn't fair for her to take the anger she had for Lewis out on him. She slowly moved to the bed but didn't sit down.

"You're going to have to sit down for me to help you, Mallory."

She slowly eased down on the edge of the bed and when she heard him move when he got on his knees behind her, she felt her breath catch. "Why did you take off your clothes?" she asked, barely able to get the words out when he pulled her blouse over her head to massage her back.

"The room comes with the job and since I'm billing you for it I thought we might as well use it."

"I can't, Hunter. I can't make love to you in here knowing Lewis could be next door cheating on my sister."

He leaned over and kissed the side of her face. "Forget about what's going on next door, Mallory, since there is nothing you can do about it. But there is something you can do about this," he said, straightening and letting his erection press against the center of her back.

"Hunter…"

The name was breathed from her lips when he reached around front and unsnapped her bra and then began massaging her breasts. Too weak to resist him, she let him pull her back on the bed with him and he immediately went after her bare breasts as his entire body shifted in place over hers.

Her brain was torn in two. One part wanted to concentrate on what was going on in the room next door and another part wanted this, another chance to be with Hunter. And when he pulled her skirt up to her waist and began removing her panty hose then fumbling with her panties, the latter part of her won out. Especially when he reached down and parted her with his fingers and began stroking her.

"I love you, Mallory," he said, while simultaneously nibbling at her lips. "And you love me. No matter what your father did to your mother, and no matter what Lewis is or is not doing to your sister, it doesn't take away from the fact that we love each other, right?"

Mallory shuddered. It wasn't fair for him to ask her a question like that while doing this to her.

"Right?" he repeated.

When he sank his fingers deeper, she whispered breathlessly. "Right."

"And we're going to have a committed relationship, aren't we? One that ends with marriage and babies, right?" His mouth skimmed over hers slowly, provocatively as his fingers continued stroking her mindlessly. Her belly was quivering and her nipples felt tender to the feel of his chest rubbing against them.

"Right," she responded again, squirming beneath his hand as delicious sensations flooded her.

"And no matter who stays together and who doesn't stay together won't concern us. We may sympathize but we won't assume it will happen to us. Our love is solid and it will be stronger than that, won't it?" he asked, growling his words in a whisper.

She lifted her hips toward his hand and moaned, "Yes! Yes, it will."

Hunter smiled. "I'm glad we're in agreement on all things." He then scooted his body downward. "And now I want the taste of my future bride, the woman who will be the mother of my children, in my mouth."

She came the moment his tongue replaced his fingers and the orgasm that tore through her almost ripped her in two, and she began trembling uncontrollably. And the more she shivered the more he locked his mouth to her taking the quakes that rocked her body.

"That was nice," he said, moments later as he gathered her sated body in his arms. He held her tight like he never wanted to let her go. "How would you like to be the person to plan my wedding?" he asked, lovingly stroking her cheek.

"I won't have a problem with it as long as I'm the bride," she said, finally accepting her love for him and his love for her. In doing so all the insecurities she felt suddenly faded away. Hunter was right.

Although she had to deal with the issues of her father and Lewis, it didn't mean what they felt for each meant less. If anything it meant more because they were determined to love in spite of it.

She was about to open her mouth to say something else when a woman let out a loud scream in the connecting room. She stilled, recognizing just what kind of scream it was. Then she was off the bed in a flash, trying to put her clothes back on. The more she tried putting them on the quicker Hunter was trying to take them off her.

"Hunter, stop it! I need to get dressed. I'm going to demand that Lewis open that door. I intend to catch him red-handed."

"Then put on one of the hotel robes from the closet because I intend to keep you in here naked for a while."

Mallory looked at him like he had gone mad. How could he think of sex at a time like this? "Get up and have your camera ready, Hunter. I want pictures. Barbara will need them when she files for a divorce."

Hunter shook his head as he slowly got out of the bed. "I'm charging you overtime for this. This job is going past Lewis's lunch hour."

Mallory raised her eyes to the ceiling, not believing Hunter's attitude but decided she couldn't worry about it now as she raced to the closet to get a robe and tossed the other one over to him. She quickly crossed the room to the connecting door. "Okay, open it."

Hunter didn't move. In fact to Mallory's way of thinking he stood in the middle of the room looking somewhat bored. "We can only unlock it from this side," he said. "In order to get inside the other room, they will have to unlock it from their side as well."

Mallory nodded. "All right then, I'll make him open it and just in case the woman he's with tries to split and run, I want you to be in the hallway to snap pictures."

He crossed his arms over his chest. "I doubt if she's going anywhere."

Mallory frowned, wondering how he figured that, but didn't

waste time asking him as she began taking the lock off the connecting door. Then she raised her hand and gave two sharp knocks on the door and yelled at the top of her voice. "Lewis Townsend, I know you're in there so open this door immediately!"

Mallory heard people scrambling about in the other room and glanced over at Hunter before turning to raise her hand to beat on the door again. Hunter quickly crossed the room and caught her hand in his. "The least you can do is to give them time to put their clothes back on or at least time to grab a robe, Mallory."

She glared at him. "Why should I?"

Before he could answer, the connecting door was snatched open and a half-dressed Lewis Townsend stood in the doorway looking furious, as if he was pissed off at being interrupted. He was bare-chested and only wearing his pants. "Mallory? What the hell are you doing here?"

Mallory didn't answer right away. It was apparent that Lewis's question had thrown her for a loop but she recovered quickly. "How dare you ask me that! I should be asking that question of you. You're a married man. I don't know the identity of the woman you've been screwing around with for the past month, but need I remind you that you're married to my sister and I don't appreciate you being unfaithful to her and—"

"Hi, Mallory."

Mallory stopped talking and stared at the woman who was standing behind Lewis and peeping over his shoulder at her and smiling. "Barbara? But . . . but what are you doing here?"

Barbara chuckled as she came to stand beside her husband wearing the hotel's thick velour robe. "I'm the woman Lewis has been screwing around with for the past month."

"Come to bed, Mallory."

Mallory shifted her gaze from looking out of the window to glare across the room at Hunter. "You think this whole thing is funny, don't you?"

Hunter grinned. "Yes. You should have seen the look on your face when you discovered Lewis had been having an affair with his own wife. And you should have seen the look on Lewis's face when he discovered you had paid me to nail him for adultery."

Mallory winced remembering Lewis's brief period of anger. She was thankful that Barbara had made light of the whole thing and made Lewis see how such a wrong assumption could have been made. It seemed their doctor had suggested that to take their mind off making love mainly to create a baby, they should get back into the routine of making love just for the enjoyment and pleasure of it. He figured with the stress eliminated, pregnancy would come easy.

It had been Barbara's idea for them to role-play and engage in lunchtime romantic romps at different hotels just for the sheer fun of it. The idea had worked. Today they had met at the hotel to celebrate the news that Barbara was pregnant.

"I'm so happy for them," Mallory said softly, thinking of how radiant her sister looked.

"Me, too," Hunter said. "Now come back to bed."

Mallory smiled as she walked back over to the bed. They had decided to spend the night at the hotel since they had paid the price for a full night anyway. She tossed back the covers and slipped between the sheets and right into Hunter's arms. He had explained that he'd known who the woman was that Lewis was having an affair with the moment he'd seen her that day in the lobby, which was the only reason he had summoned Mallory to the hotel. He had been determined to make her face her insecurities about them no matter what was going on in the room next door. And she had.

She snuggled in Hunter's arms and smiled proudly. "I'm going to be an aunt, Hunter."

He raked his hand through her hair. "You're also going to be a bride, and I want you a bride before you become an aunt. Let's set a date."

She glanced up at him. "Are you serious?"

"Yes. I want you in my life permanently. Your all-night man wants to become your forever man. Make it happen."

Mallory's smile widened through her tears. She would make it happen and she knew she would spend the rest of her life loving him.

The untamable Hunter had been tamed.

extreme satisfaction

Love endures long and is patient and kind . . . it takes
no account of the evil done to it, it pays
no attention to a suffered wrong.

—I CORINTHIANS 13:4–5

PROLOGUE

"I need a man."

When Cathleen McAlister voiced that thought aloud, she was glad the only person around to hear her was her best friend and business partner, Lisa Meadows.

Now that she had Lisa's attention, she figured she might as well continue her tirade. The office had closed an hour ago, and their staff was probably home by now. The two of them were working late to prepare for a financial seminar they would be presenting tomorrow at one of Birmingham's largest employers, the Myers-Hansel Corporation.

"What good is all of this without a good man to go home to at night?" she asked, waving her hand at the beautiful office that the two of them shared. To say the office was plush was an understatement. Even the reception area was downright luxurious.

Lisa chuckled. "Hey, I *do* have a man to go home to when I leave here, Cat. You're the one who decided not to get seriously involved with anyone while climbing the ladder of success. You saw a man in your life as a distraction. I saw one in my life, while climbing that same ladder, as extreme satisfaction."

After rolling her eyes at Lisa, Cat did something she'd seldom done in all her twenty-eight years: admitted to being wrong. "Okay, stop gloating, will you? I admit I made a mistake. I had a good thing and I blew it."

"No," Lisa said quickly, and with a pointed look. "You did more than just blow it. You shattered it into a thousand pieces when you told Rory just where he could go that night."

Just hearing her ex-boyfriend's name made certain parts of Cat's body tingle. As much as she'd tried, it had been hard, during the past year, to banish Rory Dawkins's gorgeous image from her mind. Even now she could see him vividly—tall, bowlegged, and in a pair of jeans. She didn't know of any man who could wear them better or get out of them quicker. Then there were his broad shoulders, narrow waist, fine-as-a-dime butt, and a too-handsome-for-his-own-good face. And she couldn't forget his performance in bed. She hadn't known what the big O was until she'd hooked up with him. When it came to making love, he had it down to an art form.

Good grief, she mentally chided and stubbornly admitted, she had been celibate since their breakup; desperately missing the best thing she'd ever had, and foolishly given up, all because she'd started seeing Rory as a threat. He endangered all the goals she had laid out for herself in life.

She could now confess to being downright stupid for letting him walk out of her life. He had started talking about marriage and babies, and she was still thinking of ways to expand her business and make it the most sought-after financial consulting firm in Birmingham—no, the entire state of Alabama.

The word "commitment" hadn't been in her vocabulary, and the moment he began hinting at such a thing, she'd sent him packing and told him not to return. Since then, she had discovered how wrong she had been in focusing solely on making it to the top. During her climb, her life had gotten lonelier, and it had lost the meaning it once had. And on top of everything else, her body was going through months of sexual withdrawal, and even the mere mention of Rory's name got her panties wet.

brenda jackson

"I know I screwed up with Rory, and I regret everything I said. That's why I'm placing him on my wish list."

Lisa lifted a brow as she turned away from the computer and the PowerPoint document she'd been working on. "What wish list?"

"It's a list of the things I want, and Rory is at the top of the list. In fact, he's the *only* thing on the list, which means I'm going to have to think of a plan to get him back."

"Well, good luck on that one. The last few times he was over to our place, he didn't even ask about you. In fact, he hasn't in quite a while. And like I told you, according to Peyton, he's seeing some woman who works for Cochrane Enterprises. And although I haven't met her yet, Peyton has, and he said she's a cutie, so it seems your loss was her gain."

Cat frowned. "Do you have to rub it in?"

"It serves you right for letting a good man get away. I tried to warn you, but you wouldn't listen. You were in love with him, Cat. That much was obvious, but you had to have things your way or no way. You hurt him deeply, and some men can be unforgiving about things like that. Peyton would be, and the reason they're best friends is because they usually act and think alike."

Lisa then glanced at her watch. "And speaking of Peyton, let's finish up here so I can leave within the next twenty minutes. He's picking me up, and we're going to Mangos for dinner."

"I *will* get Rory back, Lisa."

Lisa gave her a doubtful look. "You're welcome to try."

"I'll do more than try. I'll succeed."

"Good luck, because after the way you dumped him, you're definitely going to need all the luck you can get."

Rory Dawkins had heard enough. He stepped back from the door and quickly left the reception area to head out of the building. His best friend had asked him to come inside to let his wife know he'd arrived a little early and was outside circling the block. They had tried reaching Lisa on her cell phone but discovered she didn't have it on, and her office number had defaulted to voice mail.

At first Rory had hesitated, knowing there was a strong chance he would run into the one woman he had never stopped loving. But he was determined to face Cat and pretend he was over her, just as he'd assumed she was over him.

Evidently that had been a false assumption.

He had overheard Cat and Lisa's entire conversation. Once Cat had declared she needed a man, his ears had perked up, and he decided to listen. Shamelessly so. And he was glad that he had. Now he was torn between laughing and punching a hole in the nearest wall. So, the woman who had kicked him to the curb because he was becoming too "habit forming," as she'd so elegantly put it, had placed him on, of all things, her wish list. And she intended to try to get him back?

Hell, he agreed with Lisa. Let her try. He would love for her to try to get him back. He had wondered how long it would take for Cat to wake up and finally realize that the two of them belonged together. But now that she'd come to that conclusion, did she think she could just waltz back into his life? He needed to show the spirited, successful, and sexy Cat McAlister a thing or two about men. Nobody liked being dropped like a hot potato and then picked up later like a hot fudge sundae.

He might be on Cat's wish list, but he couldn't forget that this same time last year he'd been on her ditch list. And for that very reason he was determined to prove to her, once and for all, that mega success was nothing without... What was the phrase Lisa had used? Oh yeah, "extreme satisfaction."

Cat definitely had a lesson coming, and he would enjoy being the one to teach it. And it would be a while before he told her that he hadn't been involved with a woman at Cochrane Enterprises. It was a story that he and Peyton had fabricated for Lisa's benefit, since they knew she would occasionally try pumping him for information to feed to Cat regarding his love life or lack of one.

He and Peyton had agreed it was better for Cat to believe he had moved on with his life and was not somewhere pining over her, as he'd actually been doing. A man did have his pride, after all, and at thirty-three, he was too old to play games. But this was one game he intended to play, since Cat had unknowingly placed the ball in his court.

As he stepped onto the elevator, he thought that twelve months was a long time for the woman he had always considered his future wife to finally come to her senses, and he wondered just what her strategy was going to be. But no matter what her overconfident and goal-oriented mind came up with, at least he would be prepared.

A full smile touched his lips. Cat McAlister was going to find out that a prepared Rory Dawkins was a force to reckon with.

ONE

A Week Later.

Something made Rory glance up, and he couldn't help inwardly smiling when he did so. Now that Cat knew what she wanted, she wasn't wasting any time going after it.

She'd known he would be here, at Colin and Melody's party. After all, it was an annual event, this year celebrating the couple's marriage of four years, especially since their families hadn't thought it would last. Colin was the epitome of an introvert, and Mel was as extroverted as one could get.

Another thing Rory couldn't forget was that it was after the party last year, when he'd taken Cat home, and after they'd made passionate love—as passionate as it could get—that she had dumped him. So he guessed in a way tonight marked their anniversary as well.

Although he wasn't surprised to see her, the impact of her presence jolted him, and he quickly turned back around and tried to focus on the conversation going on with Peyton and a couple of their friends. But still, he had seen enough of her already, and she looked stunning.

Her hair was hanging in soft waves over the creamy skin of her shoulders, and dark brown eyes, a pert nose, and a pair of kissable lips were attached to a gorgeous coffee-colored face. Then there was her body. The dress she was wearing, with a scarf around the middle, placed a lot of emphasis on her tiny waistline and her curvy hips. They were hips he had ridden a number of times. And just thinking about all the positions they'd tried got him all heated inside, and he felt his groin tighten. Damn, if he kept this up, he would have to take a step outside to let the night air cool him off. This was only the second time he'd seen her since their breakup. It hadn't been easy, since they shared a lot of the same friends, but he had worked hard to keep distance between them and had succeeded in doing so.

He met Peyton's gaze. His best friend had seen her, too. They smiled in silent acknowledgment. There was nothing more beautiful than a sexy woman on the prowl for one particular man.

The moment Cat saw Rory standing across the room talking to a bunch of guys, her knees felt wobbly. It didn't matter that his back was to her. She would recognize that gorgeous butt and those sharply defined muscles anywhere, in or out of clothes.

She glanced to the opposite side of the room, met Lisa's eyes, and smiled. Her best friend knew her plans and had even agreed to go along with them, and for that Cat was grateful. Everyone made mistakes, and although a year ago on this very night she had practically made her bed, she refused to just lie in it...not alone, and not when she could have Rory back in it. As she watched further, Lisa nodded, letting her know that Rory had come alone and hadn't brought the woman he was presently seeing. A bubble of hope swelled in Cat's chest. If Rory hadn't brought his new girlfriend to a party where he knew the majority of his friends would be, maybe things weren't as serious between them as Lisa thought.

Cat shrugged. In a way it didn't matter, since whoever the woman was, she would find out soon enough that Rory was meant for someone else. Unfortunately, Cat had been late in realizing that she was meant for him, too. But now that she had and she knew how much she loved him, she wanted him back. And she wouldn't stop until he was back in her life on a permanent basis. All was fair in love and war, and she was on full attack.

Deciding she needed to circulate, she moved around the room, knowing that pretty soon Rory would know she was there. Whether he cared or not was a different story. But she hoped he at least noticed. She had taken extreme care with her appearance tonight and noticed more than one single man (as well as a few married ones) glancing her way, checking her out. She knew most everyone there since she had known Melody since high school. Cat had moved back to Birmingham three years ago, after being gone for ten years, and she had met Rory at Lisa and Peyton's wedding. Rory and Peyton's friendship had begun in college, and they had remained the best of friends and were partners in a landscaping business that was doing quite well on a national scale.

From the moment she and Rory had met, the attraction between them was instantaneous, explosive, and passionate. In no time at all, she'd discovered he was a rarity—a combination of good looks and all-around Mr. Nice Guy. She had never given a thought to not dating him, although she'd known that her plans to relocate back home to start a business with Lisa meant a lot of hard work and time-consuming devotion. But no matter how crazy her days got, there had been Rory, who'd kept her nights sane and well balanced. And no matter how good things were between them, she remained focused on her goals and kept sight of her priorities. Their ten-month affair was doing just great...until he'd mentioned the word "marriage."

"Cat, how are you?"

Cat forced herself not to roll her eyes upon hearing the sound of Danielle Stockman's voice. The woman could grate on her last nerve and had always done so, even in high school. Although Danielle and Mel were good friends, Lisa and Cat could barely tolerate her. Danielle's father had been a wealthy attorney around town who'd given his daughter the best. Danielle hadn't hesitated to flaunt what she had to all her classmates, especially those from lower-income families who were less well-off.

Cat and Lisa had been labeled have-nots, whose parents could barely make ends meet. And Danielle could never understand why Mel, whose father was Danielle's father's law partner, had made friends with Cat and Lisa, girls not in their social class. Cat could credit people like Danielle for making her so hard-driven to accomplish so much in life: to prove that a McAlister could rise above poverty level and become a success.

Cat turned and plastered a phony smile on her face. "Hello, Danielle. I'm fine. What about you?"

"Umm, I'm fine, too," she said, checking out Cat's outfit. Cat knew it would kill the woman to give her a compliment about how she looked. Instead, she was looking for some fault, which was a typical Danielle way. "Your dress is simply divine, and it's such a beautiful color. But it makes you look—"

"Cat, glad you came, and you look incredible." Mel's comment, as well as her sistah hug, drowned out whatever it was Danielle said or was going to say.

Cat smiled. "You know I wouldn't miss it, and thanks." She glanced around. "It looks like everyone's here."

"Yes, even Rory," Danielle threw out in a snotty tone. "I hear he has a new girlfriend."

Amazingly, Cat managed to hold her smile. "Really? Then I'm happy for him. Now if you two will excuse me, I want to go over there and say hello to Lisa."

Mel squeezed her hand in understanding. No one could tolerate Danielle in large doses. "Okay. Just enjoy yourself and don't forget that me, you, and Lisa have a lunch date next week."

Cat nodded. "I won't."

As she walked over to where Lisa was standing talking to Mr. and

Mrs. Combs, Mel's parents, she made it a point to cross Rory's line of vision. She refused to look his way but walked at a pace that would give him a pretty good view. When she reached Lisa, she smiled. There was no way Rory hadn't seen her, which meant she had accomplished the first phase of her plan, and before the night was over, she intended to put the rest into action. She had deliberately caught a cab to the party with the full intention of Rory taking her home. And once they got there . . .

"Cathleen, it's good to see you," Mel's mother said, giving her a huge hug. She then received hugs from Mel's father and Lisa, as well. The four of them spent the next fifteen minutes talking about the possibility of Mr. Combs running for mayor next year before Mel's parents got called away.

"Well, what was Rory's reaction when he saw me?" she asked Lisa excitedly once they were alone. She knew her friend had been watching.

Lisa shrugged. "It was hard to tell. He glanced up, but then he resumed listening to what the guys were saying."

Cat frowned, disappointed. "You mean his gaze didn't linger?"

Lisa shook her head. "No, sorry, but he seemed more interested in what Robert Hull was saying than in noticing you."

Cat wished Lisa wouldn't be so brutally honest at times, but then that's what made her a special friend. Unlike Danielle, she was genuine and not phony.

"Okay, then, that means I'm going to have to turn up the heat." She looked over in the direction where he'd been standing and saw him open the glass patio door to slip outside. Now was her chance. "Excuse me for a second, Lisa. It's time for me and Mr. Dawkins to come face-to-face, don't you think?"

Rory leaned against the brick post and pulled in a shallow breath. He had needed to get out of there to get a grip and to regain control.

When Cat had walked by, she had moved with such a sensuous grace that he quickly had to take his eyes off her. But still, through his peripheral vision, he hadn't missed the feminine sway of her hips that had made his groin go tight again. He knew then that he had to escape to the outside before a telltale sign of how much he wanted her began to show.

And his present frame of mind wasn't helping matters. He felt downright horny and had a definite need to get laid. Going without for a year had been murder on his hormones, but he'd refused to get intimate with anyone other than the woman he loved.

But he couldn't go there with Cat even if he wanted to. His future wife had a lesson to learn first, and no matter how much the wait killed him, she would have to accept things on his terms and not on hers. Wanting to have things her way was the reason they were apart now. And he didn't plan to go through this type of separation from her again. Any relationship with Cat meant forever, and she needed to understand that clearly. He needed to be sure she was ready for them to move forward, and he wanted to know what had made her change her mind. If this was nothing more than a spurt of hormonal need, then he wanted no part of it.

Before meeting her, he'd never been involved in a relationship that lasted more than a few months, had never given any thought to falling in love. But he had taken one look at her that day at Peyton and Lisa's wedding, and that rare phenomenon called love had ripped through him. And he'd known she was the one woman for him without them exchanging even a single word.

They dated for four months before they slept together, so although she could turn him on like nobody's business, it hadn't been just sex between them. The sex was better than hot, but then there was also something special about sitting down with her and talking for hours about how his life as a child had been while in and out of foster homes, and sharing information about his workdays. And she had been open about her past, too. He knew she came from a family of six and how her parents had made the ultimate sacrifice of sending all their offspring to college. He'd had nothing against the driving force that pushed her to achieve, and had admired her for it. What he had been against was her willingness to throw away what they'd had because of it.

He heard the patio door opening and hoped to God it wasn't Danielle. The woman had been hitting on him ever since he'd arrived. Didn't she have any shame? he wondered. And what about loyalty? After all, she was also Cat's friend.

"Beautiful night, isn't it?"

The sound of that voice made the erection he'd gotten under control suddenly spring to life again. He was grateful the patio was dark except for one lone light fixture whose beam wasn't hitting him. But still he decided to wait a few seconds before turning around and spoke over his shoulder. "Yes, it is." After a few moments, he slowly turned around. "How have you been, Cat?" he asked smoothly.

Although the light wasn't hitting him, it was hitting her, and he had to forcibly quell his body's response to seeing her and being outside and alone with her. Even from across the distance, he could smell her perfume, a sensuous scent that was uniquely her.

"I've been fine. What about you?"

"It's mid-March, the beginning of spring, our busiest time of the year, but it's all good." After a brief pause, he said, "I understand you and Lisa have moved into your new building. Peyton says it's nice."

"It is. You have to drop by one day, and I'll be glad to give you a tour."

She had no idea that he had dropped by already, and rather recently. "Thanks."

"Rory, I—"

"Well, I'd better go back inside now," he said quickly, not ready for anything else she had to say. The serious look in her eyes communicated what was coming, but as far as he was concerned, a pat

extreme satisfaction

apology just wouldn't cut it for him right now. He had suffered for twelve long months.

"It was nice seeing you tonight, Cat, and I'm glad to know you're doing well. I'll be seeing you around."

Not giving her a chance to say anything else, he quickly walked past her and went back inside.

TWO

"I guess I didn't turn up the heat enough," Cat said quietly, looking into her wineglass. Disappointment etched in every word as she, Melody, and Lisa sat at a table in their favorite restaurant for lunch a few days later.

Lisa and Mel shared a look before Lisa said, grinning, "Oh, I think you did. Mel and I couldn't help noticing when Rory came back that he was turned on as all get-out. That's probably why he left the party so soon."

Cat snapped her head up. "Are the two of you serious?" Hope was in her eyes and her voice.

"Yes, we're serious, Cat, so I wouldn't throw in the towel yet if I were you," Mel said, taking a sip of her own wine. "If nothing else, you proved one thing. Rory is still attracted to you."

"Yes, it definitely appeared that way," Lisa tacked on.

Suddenly in a much better mood, Cat leaned back in her chair and smiled. That was definitely news she'd needed to hear. She had been down in the dumps since seeing him that night. "Now if I can get him to stay in my presence more than five minutes to let him know how I feel. The only way we can really repair our relationship is for us to spend time together. That's the only way I can seek his forgiveness for what I did. I didn't realize just how much I loved him until he wasn't in my life anymore. It seemed like a part of me was missing.

I'm sorry it took me almost a year to discover he'd been right all along and that the two of us were meant for each other."

"So what are you going to do now?" Mel asked.

"Think of a way to get him off somewhere, without any interruptions."

Lisa's eyes lit mischievously. "I think I have an idea how you can accomplish that."

"How?"

"Peyton and Rory have planned a fishing trip to the cabin this coming weekend. What if I come up with a reason for Peyton not to go, which means Rory will be there all alone?"

"Mmm," Cat said thoughtfully, already liking the idea as numerous possibilities flowed through her mind. Then one she didn't like suddenly popped up. "What if he asks his new girlfriend to go with him if Peyton backs out?"

Lisa pursed her lips, considering, and then spoke. "Her name is Shari, and a few weeks ago I asked Rory for her phone number, so I could invite her to do something with me that weekend since he would be away. That would give me the chance to get to know her."

At Cat's glare, Lisa quickly added, "That was before I knew you had come to your senses and wanted him back. Anyway, he said she would be out of town herself that weekend. In that case, I doubt she'll be there."

Cat felt better in knowing that. However if her plan worked, Rory would be faced with making a choice—her or Shari—and Cat was going to make sure she did everything to reconcile things between them. She had actually thought being a success was everything, but now she understood what Rory had tried to make her see. Success wouldn't be there with her on those cold nights, nor was success something she could count on when she needed a friend to talk to. She could tell from their brief conversation that past weekend that Rory had his guard up with her and he would continue to keep it up. She had to try more than ever to breach it.

"Okay," she said, looking at Lisa. "You come up with a reason to keep Peyton at home, and I'll think of a way to make sure this weekend turns out to be one that Rory will remember for a long time."

Mel held up her wineglass. "Here's to getting your man back," she toasted.

Cat laughed and raised her glass along with Mel and Lisa. "Getting Rory back," they all chimed.

The Next Day

Peyton waited until he knew his wife had pulled out of the driveway and then called Rory on his cell phone. He smiled. "Hey man, just thought I'd give you a heads-up. Our women are cooking something behind our backs."

Rory, who had been outside cutting his yard, leaned against his kitchen counter after taking a huge gulp of water straight from an icy cold bottle. "How can you be so sure?"

"Because Lisa convinced me not to go fishing with you this weekend," he said smugly. "She wants me to go with her this weekend to visit her cousin in Atlanta."

"And you're giving up fishing for that?"

"Hey, man, what can I say? She put her persuasive skills to work, and before I knew it, I was agreeing to anything she wanted. You can call me weak—I don't give a damn. However, I prefer to be called satisfied instead."

Rory chuckled. "Okay, man, I get the picture."

"You know this is a setup don't you?" Peyton then said. "And how much do you want to bet that Cat is going to show up at the cabin now that I'm out of the picture."

Desire raced through Rory's body. He definitely liked the thought of hanging out with her alone at the cabin for an entire weekend. Yes, it sounded like a setup, and if it was, little did the woman he loved know that he had his own personal agenda. He planned to teach her a lesson that she wouldn't forget.

Cat left work early on Friday to go home and pack, a chore she found easy, since she was taking as little clothing as possible. Although she knew that it would take more than seduction to bring Rory around, she believed when all else failed, hit a man right below the gut.

And she planned to hit hard.

The question of what his initial reaction would be upon seeing her at the door lingered in her mind. Would he get upset and close the door in her face, or would he pull her into his arms and kiss her? The thought of him doing the latter filled her with all kinds of anticipation. She could actually feel the hard demanding mouth on hers, tasting, promising, but more important, surrendering.

Cat's entire body hummed at the thought, and she allowed herself to indulge further as images of those deep, chocolate brown eyes latching on her just moments before Rory picked her up in his arms to carry her off to the bedroom to make intense love to her. Adrenaline, excitement, love laced with lust flared within her stomach, and she knew if any of the scenarios she'd imagined took place, then this Shari would be old news.

An hour later, Cat was on the road, heading toward Georgia and a section of land near Blairsville that Peyton's parents had given the couple as a wedding gift. The area was rich with prestigious horse farms, large country estates, riverfront homes, and breathtaking mountain views that opened not only your eyes, but also your soul. She would always remember the first time Rory had brought her here alone. They had cruised the back roads leading to the cabin, taking in the beauty of the mountains. And once they'd reached their destination and unpacked, they had taken in the splendor of each other when they had made love for the first time.

So for her and Rory, this would be coming full circle, going back to the place where their intimate life together had begun, and she hoped to mend the tear she had placed in their relationship. Based on the information Lisa had given her yesterday, if her calculations were right, Rory would reach their destination four hours before she did, and Cat hoped that Lisa's claim that he would be alone was an accurate one. She didn't want to think about her embarrassment if it wasn't.

Scratch that. Wipe that thought out completely.

She refused to think of that possibility. Her hopes for this weekend were too high. For the past twelve months she'd been like a woman trapped underwater, and now that she was finally coming up for air, she planned to breathe in as much of it as she could. Already in the deep recesses of her mind, Rory's manly scent was filling her nostrils, and she couldn't help remembering that scent mingling with his taste whenever they kissed.

Sensations suddenly swamped her senses, and as she took the interstate that crossed the Alabama line into Georgia, everything faded from her mind, except thoughts of her and Rory spending time together.

Rory glanced down at his watch. It was almost six in the afternoon. He'd been at the cabin only a few hours and already he was champing at the bit, wondering when Cat would show up. What if Peyton's assumptions were all wrong and she had no intention of coming? Hell, he didn't want to think of that possibility, since he had spent the past two days thinking of an angle he could use that would really throw her for a loop.

According to Peyton, Lisa and Cat's plan was for Cat to arrive, claiming there was some sort of a mix-up, since Lisa had given her the okay to use the cabin for that same weekend. And now since the two of them were stuck here together ... Oh, well ...

Rory snorted. Cat would get what she wanted, but on his terms,

extreme satisfaction

and she would have to be the one to prove that a future, and not just a temporary sexual fix, was what she really wanted.

His ears picked up the sound of a car pulling in outside. He swallowed, knowing the time to playact had arrived. He hated being deceitful, but then, there was a reason for this madness.

He had deliberately parked his SUV in the garage out back to make the story Cat would tell seem even more plausible. Thanks to Lisa, Cat had her own key and was supposed to walk into the cabin and act surprised to see him. He would play as dumbfounded as she while she explained there must have been a mix-up on cabin dates.

Yeah. Right.

He glanced around. The cabin looked cozy enough with the wood burning in the fireplace. He had unpacked and unloaded the food in the refrigerator. He had showered earlier and changed into another pair of jeans and a T-shirt. And now he waited for her to walk through the door. As he watched the doorknob slowly turn, he knew this weekend they would either get their act together or end things completely.

THREE

With her overnight bag in her hand, Cat slowly opened the door, and immediately her eyes connected with Rory's, who was standing across the room next to a lit fireplace.

Silence stretched out for a moment as their gazes held. She closed the door behind her as she tried collecting herself to act surprised to see him, but at the moment the only thought that filled her mind was that he was there...alone with her. But still, she knew she had to become the actress she and Lisa had cooked up.

"So," she tried to say calmly. "What are you doing here?" His eyes on her seemed hot and focused. Or was she just imagining things?

"I should ask you the same thing, Cat."

His words barely registered, but the sound of his voice did. It was low, sexy, a total turn-on. And then there was that wonderful-looking mouth of his that could do so many naughty and wicked things to her. "Lisa," she said softly.

He stared at her. "What about Lisa?"

Her lashes flickered as she held Rory's gaze and hoped he'd buy what she was about to say, since she was not a very good liar. "She thought you and Peyton were canceling the fishing trip this weekend, and when I told her that I needed to get away and asked if I could use this place, she said it would be okay."

Rory leaned back against the mantel. "Peyton backed out. I decided to come ahead alone. Evidently Lisa didn't know that."

"I guess not," she said faintly, barely following their conversation. Her concentration was on Rory's body. The tightness of his muscles looked good in the pair of close-fitting, sexy jeans he was wearing, which emphasized every physical line in his body, his every bulge. As usual, her pulse quickened in appreciation whenever she saw him in a pair of jeans. He looked so compelling, so handsome, and the magnetism radiating from him was so intense, she was losing her train of thought. It was only when she noticed his mouth move that she realized he'd said something.

"I'm sorry, could you repeat that?" she asked.

He nodded. "You said the reason you asked Lisa about coming here was because you needed to get away. Why?"

Cat knew that now would be the perfect moment to level with him and tell him the truth. And although she believed that honesty was the best policy, this was one of those rare times she would have to make an exception to that rule. She had hurt Rory that night. She'd said things that she had later regretted. And now she was filled with uncertainty over whether the seduction she planned to orchestrate would work. Lisa and Mel were convinced that Rory still wanted her. But did he still love her?

"Cat?"

Hearing him call her name made her inhale a deep breath. She didn't want to play games with him. She make a quick decision to come right out and tell him just what was bothering her and what a complete fool she'd been, and that she now wanted all those things he had wanted, all those things he had offered her a year ago: love, commitment, marriage, babies . . .

Dropping her bag by the door, she walked to the middle of the room to start speaking from her heart. "The reason I needed to get away, Rory, is because I've been torn and miserable since we broke up and—"

"I've been torn and miserable since we broke up, too," he said, interrupting her words.

Hope flared within Cat. "You have?"

"Yes." Rory discovered that holding a conversation with her wasn't easy, especially since his gaze seemed glued to the soft material of her blouse and the short, short skirt that showed long gorgeous bare legs and hugged her curvy hips in all the right places. But then he doubted there were any wrong places anywhere on Cat.

And it didn't take much to see that she wasn't wearing a bra. Whether she had on panties was a mystery in itself. But it would stand to reason that if she had planned to seduce him, Cat would have dispensed with the small stuff. Her favorite way of getting it on was quick and hard, especially when she was in an extremely sexually hungry state.

And he could tell from the way she was looking at him, the way her gaze was traveling over him slowly, taking in every piece of his clothing and the body underneath, that she was intensely stimulated. If Peyton's claim was true and she hadn't been with anyone else since their breakup, then she was probably in one hell of an erotic dilemma. Cat was one hell of a highly charged sexual being. There were times he could make her come just from kissing her, and the look she had in her eyes was making his skin heat up. But he knew he had to slow things up a bit, to initiate his own plan and give her something to think about, to mull over . . . to set right.

He moved, crossing the room to come stand before her. "You were right, Cat, and although it took me awhile, I finally realized that everything you said that night was true. Marriage isn't for everyone, and it wasn't fair for me to push you into doing something you weren't ready for. And from the way things have been going in my life, it seems that I really wasn't ready for such a move either. I had only thought I wanted to marry you."

Cat's heart suddenly dropped down into her knees, and she had to hold herself up to stop from falling. "You only thought you wanted to marry me?"

"Yes. I saw what Mel, Colin, and Lisa and Peyton had, and assumed that I wanted it for myself. For us."

"But you realized later that you didn't?" she asked, the words forming a tight knot in her chest. A huge disappointment in her heart.

"Yes. And I agree with everything you said. Why mess up a good thing with a commitment? You and I were doing okay having an affair, and I should have left well enough alone. But no, I didn't do that. I had this vision of us getting married, having babies, and living happily ever after. But there's more to life than falling in love, isn't there? And you made me see that."

"I did?" she asked, not knowing what else to say.

"Yes," he said, reaching out and taking her hands in his, stroking a palm with his thumb, sending pleasure radiating through her body. "I wanted to talk to you last week at Colin and Mel's party, but couldn't. The timing wasn't right. But it looks like fate brought us together this weekend, and I want you to know how I feel, how I've been feeling. I want us to get back together, Cat, pick up where we left off a year ago."

She took a deep breath and pulled her hands away from his and placed them in the pockets of her skirt. Things definitely weren't going the way she had planned. He was using all the words she had spoken a year ago in anger, in fear of entrusting her life to a committed relationship, to end things between them.

"By picking up where we left off, you mean you want us to engage in another affair? One that has no promise of ever leading elsewhere?" she asked quietly.

He nodded, watching her closely. "Yes. That sort of relationship seems to work between us the best. We won't date others like before, but then we won't bring up certain words, like 'love' and 'marriage,' ever again. That way neither of us will feel pressured about anything. It will be just like you wanted. No strings attached and no expectations."

He had hated lying to her, but those had been the words she had thrown in his face that night, the words that had caused him twelve months of heartache. And it would be up to her to set things right between them, and he hoped to God that she did so before the weekend was over. He didn't want either of them to leave Sunday until they knew for sure that their future was dead set with each other and that it included love and marriage.

No strings attached and no expectations. A part of Cat had heard Rory's words and wanted to cry out that she might have wanted things that way then, but now she wanted love and marriage. A part of her felt angry, frustrated, caught in a trap of her own making. His offer of a loveless relationship was something she would have been glad to agree to last year, but now . . .

Suddenly remembering something, she tilted her head and gave him a pointed look. "What about your new girlfriend?"

"My new girlfriend?"

"Yes, her name was Shari or something."

"We broke up last month."

She stared at him. Confused. Lisa must not have known that. "You broke up with your girlfriend a month ago?"

"Yes." Moments later he asked, "Are you seeing anyone?"

A part of her wanted to tell him that although he had sought out someone else after their breakup, she had not. But then she had to remember she was the one who'd decided that she no longer wanted him as part of her life. "No, I'm not seeing anyone."

"Then is there any reason we can't resume what we once had?"

For the moment Cat kept her expression noncommittal, thinking that yes, there was a reason. She loved him, and she now wanted those things he had wanted back then. But it seemed he had moved on. It would be hard to maintain the type of relationship he wanted, knowing what her feelings were. But then, she had gotten herself into this mess; it was up to her to get herself out of it.

She could either tell him that she'd been wrong and wanted more than what he was offering, or she could go along with him for now and formulate another plan to make him fall head over heels in love with her again, make him crave commitment and marriage.

Hoping she wasn't making a mistake, she lowered her lashes and then slowly raised them provocatively, until she met his gaze and said, "It depends on what kind of weekend you want."

They held each other's eyes, and then he leaned over close and spoke in a low, sexy tone. His lips were just inches from hers. "How about an unforgettable one?"

"I think—" She made her decision and wrapped her arms around his neck. Her body was beginning to tingle, her nerve endings were sizzling, and her senses were reeling. "—that it will work."

She then pulled his mouth to hers and began kissing him deeply.

FOUR

Rory's entire body immediately responded. And when Cat sucked his tongue into her mouth, he growled deep within his throat and slanted his mouth across hers, suddenly becoming unbearably aroused.

He felt seared by the kiss she was giving him, and already her fingers were working at the fastening of his jeans, pulling down his zipper. He could taste the urgency of her kiss. She was hungry and hot. He thought of suggesting that she slow down, but when she reached inside his jeans, discovered he wasn't wearing any underwear, and immediately took hold of his shaft, any such words died on his lips.

All the while, her mouth continued to devour his.

"I want you, Rory," she whispered, breaking off the kiss and taking a step back. He watched as she quickly pulled her blouse over her head and tossed it aside. Just as he'd thought. She wasn't wearing a bra. And then her hand went to the side zipper of her skirt, and within seconds it slid down her legs into a pool at her feet, leaving her totally and completely naked. His suspicions about the panties had been right also. She wasn't wearing any.

His chest began vibrating with uncontrollable desire, and he ripped his own shirt over his head. And since she had already unfastened and unzipped his jeans, it didn't take much to finish removing them. It seemed that she intended to jump his bones, when she came back into his arms, and holding on tightly to his shoulders, she wrapped her legs around his waist. He sucked in a deep breath when he felt the dampness between her legs brush against his huge erection.

She claimed his mouth again, and he knew it was his time to take charge and lead them into something that was uninhibited and unadulterated. When it came to making love, there was no limitations, no dos and don'ts. Whenever passion flared this out of control between them, there was no gentleness or politeness. Those were the times when they both liked being aggressive and uncivilized.

And this would be one of those times they took it to the max.

"Take me, Rory, hard, fast. Now!"

He didn't have to be told twice and quickly headed for the nearest wall and pressed her body against it. Sexual energy crackled between them, and seemingly of their own accord, the legs wrapped around his waist widened, undeniably ready for him to take possession.

"Are you sure you want this?" he asked, his tongue darting out to lick the area around her lips.

"Oh, yes." Cat reached down and took him into her hand. The moment she touched him there again, heat flared through every point in his body, building a blazing fire within him.

"Then get ready, because here I come . . . one of many."

"Oh, that sounds good, and this feels good, too," she said, running her hand over the iron-ridged hardness of his erection, the smoothness of its head, stroking him into oblivion.

Rory was about to lose it, but somehow he managed to ask, "You're still on the Pill?"

She met his gaze. "Yes." Her words came out as a whisper. "And I haven't done this with anyone else since you."

His gaze burned into hers when he said, "I haven't done this with anyone else since you either."

He watched the slow lifting of her brow and knew now would be a perfect time to tell her there was never a Shari. There had never been anyone but her. But he knew to do so would mean divulging other things, providing explanations, and even now although he knew she wanted this, she wanted him, he wasn't sure she wanted a future.

"You and Shari never made love?" She asked, like the information had left her breathless and dizzy. She of all people knew how sexual he was.

"No. We never got that far. Besides, I couldn't imagine going inside any woman's body other than yours." And that had been the truth. No other woman could turn him on as quickly and as completely.

"Oh, Rory. That means..."

"Yeah." He shuddered at the same time she did at the thought. That meant he would definitely be keeping her on her back this weekend, against the wall, on the table, on the floor, in the shower. Whenever. Wherever. They had twelve months to make up for. But somehow during those intimate moments he would break through her mind's defenses, as well as her heart's, and make her realize an affair was the last thing the two of them wanted to share. There had to be something more solid and concrete between them.

Something more permanent.

When he leaned forward to kiss her, the thought of forever was on his mind, and when he felt her place the tip of him against her wet opening, he entered her in one hard stroke.

He released a low growl when he felt her muscles clamp tight on his throbbing erection. He sank in deeper, with the intent of going to the hilt. And to accommodate him, she spread her legs wider, seemingly needing him as much as he needed her.

And this weekend, he intended for her to get as much of him as she could take. He intended to have his Cat purring one minute and scratching heatedly the next. He intended for her to see that in bed or out, they were meant to be together.

Cat pulled back from Rory's kiss and met his intense gaze when a torrent of sensations overtook her at being completely filled by him. They were so closely connected that the firm and solid plane of his

extreme satisfaction

stomach rested smack up against the flatness of hers. And she could feel the thick width and length of him, throbbing inside her. Her inner muscles gently squeezed him, and she heard another low growl come from deep within his throat. And when he began to move, in and out, she grabbed hold of his shoulders as the lower part of her body picked up the rhythm he was creating.

When he went in, their bodies would automatically lock tight while he grinded her almost into the wall, forcing her body to arch into him for even deeper penetration. Then he would pull out. Almost. The friction of flesh sliding against flesh made sensation after sensation roll through her. An urgency for more was creeping up her spine, rushing blood through her veins, and making more heat settle in the area where their bodies connected.

And then he increased the tempo and went faster, harder. Cat wondered if it was possible for a person's body to shatter into a thousand pieces, because hers was definitely heading there. He was wringing her out wet. She gasped when he went deeper, harder still, and wondered if her body would make a permanent impression on the wall.

His movements became even more frantic, urgent, his breathing that much more forced. And the dark eyes that dared her to look away filled her to overflowing. She loved him. She would always love him. And she was determined that before they left the cabin, he would know just how much and that an affair would not work for them.

Then she felt him stiffen, felt the first sign of a release shoot inside her. And the moment she felt it—the hot, sticky substance his body had created—she shuddered, and his name slipped from her lips just moments before he captured them in his.

He rocked into her, time and time again, then the big O hit both of them, throwing their bodies into long, deep, mind-blowing spasms. Of all the times they'd made love, she'd never known a time that had been so powerful or so intense. She couldn't hold back the convulsions that began overtaking her as another intense and fiery orgasm ripped through her.

He hollered out her name, and she felt it again, a thick stream of release shooting inside her, making their connection that much more profound, intimate, and urgent. And when he gripped her hips to get the full effect, she knew if she hadn't been on the Pill, there was no way she wouldn't be getting pregnant at this very moment.

When he released another hard groan, his shaft tightened inside her. She held hard to his shoulders and knew round two was about to begin. She also knew that one day she *would* have his baby...as well as his heart. With this man she would have all the things she'd ever wanted but had been afraid to go after.

A life with Rory was all that really mattered to her. It was the only thing she wanted.

FIVE

"Hungry?"

Cat shifted positions on the black leather sofa, not remembering how and when she'd gotten there, and glanced over at Rory. He was on the floor naked, on his knees, placing more logs in the fireplace. He looked so completely male, so powerfully sexual, that all she could do was stare. Apparently he didn't know just what a tempting pose he was in. He had one of the finest butts she'd ever seen.

When she didn't answer, he glanced over his shoulder and saw just where her gaze had been. He smiled. "What are you doing?"

"Watching you."

"Is that a good thing or a bad thing?"

She laughed. "Considering how we've spent the first hour, I'd like to think it's a good thing."

"I'd like to think so, too. I miss being with you."

"In bed?"

He was glad she'd asked. "No, sex between us will always be good. But I missed your company, as well. I missed knowing you would be coming by on Friday nights and I would talk you into staying over. I miss taking you to the movies, dinner, and our talks. Hell, I missed spending time with you, period, Cat."

He watched a slow smile touch her lips. She liked knowing she'd been missed. "And do you know what the hardest day was of all?" he asked.

"No, what?"

"Your birthday. I know how special your birthday is to you, and I regretted not being there to make it even more exceptional."

She shifted, trying to get more comfortable on the sofa while remembering that day. Her parents never had a lot of money, but they always made sure each of their six children had birthdays they would remember. There had never been a birthday when she didn't get something, even if it was something inexpensive like a box of crayons and a coloring book.

She glanced back over at Rory. "Dad said you came by." Her parents and Rory had developed a close relationship that didn't end when the affair had. Although her mother and father never brought it up, she heard Rory had dropped by to check on them periodically.

"Yes, I decided to leave my gift to you with your father instead of dropping it off at your place."

Cat nodded, remembering the beautiful bracelet he'd given her. Considering they had broken up, at the time she'd thought it had been kind of him to get her anything. She had left a message on his answering machine thanking him. "You could have come over, Rory."

"No, I couldn't."

Startled, she blinked. And then she remembered. She had said a lot of things to him that night, and now she vividly recalled telling him not to show his face around her place again. She suddenly felt a thick knot in her throat. It was a wonder he was even speaking to her. She'd been in rare form that night and had gone off on him something terrible.

"Rory, I—"

"No, it doesn't matter," he said, crawling back over to the sofa. "We're back together, and that's all that matters." He reached out and slowly began caressing her arm. "We want the same things now, so there won't be a misunderstanding between us ever again. Neither of us want love and commitment. Now, I'm going to ask you again. Are you hungry?"

Hearing him state that false assumption hurt. "Yes, I'm hungry."

He stood, and then he took her hand and pulled her up with him. Neither had bothered to put their clothes back on. "Then I think we'd better get dressed so I can feed you. How do salmon patties and grits sound?"

"Mouthwatering."

"Like this?"

He pulled her closer to him, and the mouth that settled over hers was firm, and the taste and scent of him were renewing her senses. Cat practically melted against him, and she felt herself moaning deep in her throat. When he raised his head, the eyes looking down at her were dark, heated.

"Umm, no. Not even close. Mouthwatering salmon patties can't compete with your kiss," she said honestly. "And I think that's what I missed the most. Seeing you each day, and knowing that before you left at night you would give me a kiss to make my toes tingle, a kiss that would make it much easier to get through the next day. Then there were our talks, and the time we spent together doing things, like the time you showed me how to landscape my yard. There were so many things I missed not having you around, Rory."

Hearing her say that made him feel good. She'd never admitted that she liked having him around before, although he'd assumed she did. Her saying it definitely hit a positive chord. He bent his head and took her mouth gently. The warmth of his lips touching hers increased his pulse rate.

Cat reached out and cupped the back of Rory's head. She could tell from his expression that her words had surprised him. Had he not known she had enjoyed his company? If that was the case, then she would use time this weekend to make sure he understood that now she knew how special things had been between them, and he was wrong in thinking she didn't want love and commitment. But if a loveless affair was all he was interested in now, what was she going to do?

When he ended the kiss, she buried her face against his throat. "My overnight bag is still where I left it, by the door," she said, needing to concentrate on something other than his mouth.

"Need help unpacking?"

"I packed light, which means I didn't bring a lot of clothes."

"Oh, and why was that?" he asked, sliding his palm along her cheek.

Cat inwardly berated herself for almost giving something away. "I thought I was going to be here alone and didn't need a lot of clothes. I had planned to spend most of my time inside."

"Well, I'm here with you, and you'll be spending some time outside, starting in the morning. How would you like going fishing with me?"

"Fishing?"

"Yes."

She grinned. "Umm, that will depend."

"On what?"

"On how much sleep I get tonight."

Rory broke out in a hearty laugh. "In that case, you won't be going fishing with me in the morning. Just be prepared to help cook my catch when I get back."

Cat smiled. "Okay, you have a deal."

Rory smiled in undisguised delight as he watched Cat pull the items out of her overnight bag. "You weren't lying when you said you packed light, were you?"

Startled, Cat turned, and her eyes met his. She felt heat move into her cheeks. She didn't know he'd been standing in the doorway and wondered what he thought about ail the sexy lingerie she had brought. The only clothes she packed that were decent enough to wear outside was the outfit she'd arrived in and the one she had changed into after her shower: a pair of white capri pants and a green midriff top. "Ah well, the lighter, the better."

"Yeah, and I personally think less is best," he said, grinning mischievously.

Cat rolled her eyes. "Aren't you supposed to be preparing dinner?"

He chuckled. "Yes, in fact, I came to let you know that everything is ready." He crossed the room, stood next to her, and picked up a book she had unpacked. *Landscaping Made Simple*.

Rory raised a brow, smiling. "You're going after my job? I don't see you being the dirt-under-the-fingernails type."

Cat laughed. She couldn't see herself being one either. "No, I decided to learn something about what you do. After we broke up, it dawned on me just how little I knew. You would mention things; we mostly talked about my work."

She stood still for a moment, biting her lip, and knowing he would be too kind to say that the reason they had mostly talked about her work was that her work—and only her work—had been the focus of any of their discussions. She had enjoyed talking to him about her goals, her plans for the future, her various clients, and the different proposals she and Lisa had been working on. It wasn't until they had broken up that she realized just how little she knew about what his landscaping company was all about. She had an idea, and he had helped her put together her yard. But still, she hadn't realized how selfish she'd been in making it "all about her" and not dwelling on his needs.

"So what have you learned so far?"

She couldn't help giving him a flirty little smile. "One thing I learned is that landscaping is for the birds, literally. I didn't know until I read that book that bird lovers can actually landscape their yard to attract birds. Did you know that certain birds, like the brown thrashers, house wrens, and orioles eat a variety of insects and if you landscape your yard with flowers that draw certain types of insects, then you're in business."

Rory nodded. "Yes, I knew that." And he was impressed that now she did, and most important, that she had cared enough about what his job entailed to have taken the time to find out.

"What about mating?" he asked, placing the book aside.

"Mating?"

"Yes, since you learned something about birds, did you also read about how they mate?"

Cat's brow furrowed. "No, it wasn't in the book."

"Umm, how unfortunate," he said, smiling.

"Do you know something I don't know?" she asked, smiling back.

"Possibly. They don't mate like humans."

She laughed. "I didn't think so."

"Their courtship and mating rituals are among the most varied for all species. It's said that a bird without a mate is a bird without an offspring."

Cat chuckled. "Now that's definitely not true with humans."

"Definitely."

Cat enjoyed this sort of banter with Rory. Before, their conversations always tended to be more on the serious side. She was about to say something when her stomach rumbled.

"I think I'd better feed you now."

"Yes, I think you'd better."

After dinner they had cleaned up the kitchen together before going outside on the porch to sit in the swing. They were sitting close together, with Cat practically in Rory's lap, and for over an hour he questioned her on how much she knew about landscaping.

"How would you like to go with me when I fly out and give an estimate for my next project? We're about to bid on a shopping mall in Los Angeles."

She turned in his arms and glanced up at him. Lisa would take off and go on those sort of trips with Peyton all the time, but Cat had never traveled anywhere with Rory, mainly because he'd never asked her. But then she knew why. It would have been a waste of time on his part, since she never would have allowed herself any time off from her work.

"Um, sure. I'd like that. Thanks for the invite. Just let me know when."

Rory looked surprised. "Just like that?"

She frowned. "Just like what?"

"You would go out of town with me, just like that? What about your own work?"

"There shouldn't be any problems if it's during a time we don't have planned seminars. No big deal."

Rory remembered a time when it would have been a big deal. They had been alone at the cabin for little more than five hours, and already he could see changes in her. Changes he definitely liked. He stood and brought her up with him. He took hold of her hand. "Come on—let's go."

She lifted a brow. "Where are we going?"

"Inside. To make love."

SIX

Very early the next morning, Rory slipped out of bed. He glanced back over his shoulder at Cat while he slipped into his jeans. She was sleeping peacefully, dead to the world, an understandable state, since they had hardly slept at all last night.

They were lucky the cabin was out in the middle of nowhere, on private land. There hadn't been any neighbors around to hear the sound of the headboard hitting the walls and no reason to drown out the moans, cries, and, in some instances, the screams of pleasure that had been torn from both of them. A clear indication of how their night had gone. His Cat had also clawed up his back pretty good, which was another sign. But then no pain, no gain.

"Rory?"

He turned. She had opened her eyes just enough to look at him. She wasn't as dead to the world as he'd thought. "Yes, sweetheart?"

"Where are you going?"

"Fishing."

She switched her gaze from him to the window. "But it's still dark outside."

He grinned as he walked back over to the bed and sat down on the edge. He gently pulled her into his arms, sliding his arm in back of her so she could rest her head on his shoulder. "Yeah, and that's the best time."

extreme satisfaction

"Umm, who am I to argue, since you've proved countless times that you know a lot about perfect timing."

He glanced down at her. "You think so?"

"I know so."

"Thanks for that vote of confidence." He could tell she was still sleepy, and he was tempted to kiss her until she forgot all about sleeping, but doing so meant he would forget all about going fishing. He would take the time to taste her—all over—when he returned. Besides, he didn't intend to stay away long. The lake was within walking distance and could easily be seen through the trees. If things went as planned and the fish were biting as he hoped, he would be back before she woke up good.

Although he decided not to kiss her, he went ahead and indulged his pleasure by nibbling on her neck for a while, knowing full well he was placing a hickey there. Then he ran his tongue along the soft little lobe of her ear, enjoying the sound of his Cat purring.

Knowing he'd better stop before he changed his mind about going fishing, he placed her back in bed and stood. "Miss me."

When she didn't say anything, he smiled. She had drifted back off to sleep.

Cat slowly came awake thinking that if a person could die from having too many orgasms, then she would definitely be dead by now. The number of times he'd made her come had been relentless, extraordinary, mind-blowing madness. It had definitely been one of those record-setting nights. She gave a half-smile, thinking that she didn't have any complaints, even with the fact that her body was pretty sore.

Turning over, she glanced at the clock. It was ten in the morning already. She remembered waking up earlier, right before Rory left to go fishing and then drifting back off to sleep. She shifted again in bed, knowing it was time she got up and faced the world.

Five minutes later, and Cat was standing under the spray of water as it washed down over her back. Eyes closed, she threw her head back, enjoying the feel of the warm gush of liquid caressing her all over. Then suddenly she felt a nibble on the soft curve of her neck and quickly turned around. Rory was back and had stripped naked to join in her shower. She could read the look in the deep, dark eyes staring at her. He wanted to make love to her again.

Right now. Right here.

He gently took the soap out of her hand and began lathering her all over, making her body quiver beneath his touch. And then he got on his knees, to lather her stomach, which brought him right in front of the area between her legs, an area he had branded his two years ago in this very cabin, an area he had reclaimed numerous times since she had arrived yesterday.

She knew without a doubt that once again he was about to give her extreme satisfaction, almost to the point of delerium. Her assumptions proved true when he tossed the soap aside and pulled her forward, out from beneath the spray of water, and he leaned closer until her hot center was right in his face.

"Open."

Although he gave the command, he didn't wait for her to comply.

Rory needed this: the taste of her. He had gotten it last night, but it hadn't been enough. Not nearly enough. The heat of her made her scent that much more profound, erotic, intense, and the ache inside him grew that much more unbearable.

The fish had been biting, which was a good thing. As soon as he'd been satisfied that he'd caught enough, he turned his mind to another type of satisfaction. Only the kind that Cat could provide. When he had walked into the cabin and heard the shower going, he knew what he wanted to do. What he planned to do.

He leaned closer to her, reached out, and gently parted her womanly folds, still swollen from last night's workout. And then he kissed

extreme satisfaction

her there, letting his tongue taste the sweet nectar he sought. He heard her groan and widen her legs for him the same exact moment her fingers clutched his head firmly to hold it in place. Little did she know that he didn't intend to go anywhere until he'd gotten his fill.

He worked his tongue around inside her slowly, teasingly, until the stroking got harder, more intense, and greedier. In this case, less wasn't best. More was better, and he wanted more.

When he felt her on the verge of coming, he grabbed hold of her lips, locked his mouth tight on her, and worked his tongue like nobody's business, forcing her to come.

She did.

And he enjoyed every bit of her.

When it was almost impossible for her to stand on her own, he gathered her into his arms and held her. A part of him didn't want their weekend to end. They still had a lot to talk about. A lot to straighten out, and lots of assumptions to set right. But now at this moment, nothing was more profound to him than holding the woman he loved so close to his heart, where he knew she would always be.

"Who taught you to take care of fish?"

Startled, Cat turned around. This was the third time Rory had caught her unawares. After their shower, he had taken a nap. She, surprisingly, had had an exceptional burst of energy. After dressing, she had gone into the kitchen to find his cooler filled with the fish he'd caught. Deciding that since he had been the one to catch their meal, the least she could do was to cook it, she had immediately begun the task of cleaning the fish before getting the grease and frying pan ready. Even though the kitchen vents were on full blast and the windows open, there was no way the aroma of fried fish wouldn't make its way to their bedroom.

"My dad. He used to go fishing all the time, and once or twice he took me and my brothers and sisters with him. But I don't ever remember getting up as early as you did this morning."

He lifted a brow. "I didn't know that."

"What?"

"That you've gone fishing before."

She grinned. "Yes. You even brought me here once with you to fish."

He smiled. "I brought you here under the pretense of going fishing, but we both knew that fishing was the last thing on either of our minds. Getting it on for the first time was."

Cat laughed. "Yes, that's true. But still, you never invited me back."

"Yes, I did."

She blinked. "You did?"

"Yes. Several times. But you were always too busy to come back."

With his words, memories floated through her mind, forcing her to remember. He had asked her to spend weekends at the cabin with him fishing, but at the time she'd been too busy plotting and planning how to achieve her professional goals.

She sighed deeply, disgusted. It didn't seem to her that she'd been much of a girlfriend. In fact, she could go so far as to consider herself one selfish bitch. It was a wonder he wanted to have any dealings with her at all, let alone repair their relationship. At that moment, she fully understood why he was satisfied with them just having an affair. If she wasn't all that hot as girlfriend material, he probably assumed she definitely would not make a good wife . . . if he'd still been in the market for one.

"So what can I do to help?"

She glanced over at him, and he had that incredible smile on his face that had the dimples to die for right along with it. Any woman would be stupid not to want this loving, handsome, unselfish man in her life. "It depends on what you want to go along with it," she finally answered. "The fish is already done."

"Yeah, and it smells good, too."

"Thanks."

"How about if we include a salad and baked sweet potatoes?"

"Sounds good to me."

When they sat down to eat a half hour later, she told him she wanted him to talk about his work for a change. He told her that the business he and Peyton had started together right out of college was doing great, and now that they had expanded nationally, a lot of good contracts were coming in. It surprised her to see that she hadn't been the only one of them who'd had dreams and goals. But it seemed she was the only one who had gotten totally obsessed with them.

"You've been busy," she commented as they both cleared the table.

He smiled over at her. "And so have you. Peyton has kept me abreast on how well things are going for you and Lisa."

"I'm surprised you wanted to know."

"Why would I not?"

"My obsession with work is the reason we broke up."

"No it wasn't. Your obsession with not wanting to ever get married was."

She shrugged. "Same thing, since I considered a commitment of that sort as interfering with the long-range goals I'd established."

He nodded. "Well, you don't have to worry about that anymore, since I've told you my new philosophy. I understand why you felt the way you did, because I now find myself in the same predicament. Our company is expanding, so I'm a busy man these days. I've increased my traveling, and taking the company on a national level is the most important thing going on in my life right now. I don't have time for anything else remotely serious."

Cat placed the dishes in the sink and then leaned against the counter. "And your views changed just because of me?"

Rory came to stand beside her. "No, they didn't change just because of you. But what happened between us did make me question why I had made such a fuss. Things had been good between us, and if no strings attached and no expectations was what you wanted, then so be it. Although we weren't married, we spent a lot of time together, and got along better than some married people, so I asked myself, why did I even rock the boat."

Because at the time you thought you wanted more, she wanted to tell him. And now she was the one who wanted more, but he didn't. "So what would you like to do now?"

He shoved his hands into the pockets of his jeans. "How would you like to take a walk? I'd like very much to show you something."

Her curiosity piqued, she said, "All right. I'd love to go for a walk with you."

SEVEN

Cat wondered just where Rory was taking her as he led her past the lake where he'd gone fishing that morning, through several yards of dense woods, and over a small pond and narrow stream. Eventually they reached an area where another cabin sat in the clearing.

It was obvious the place was in need of repairs, but where it was positioned provided a panoramic view of the mountains that loomed in the distance. It was a breathtaking sight, a perfect spot.

"Well, what you do think?" Rory asked, smiling.

The expression on his face was one of joy, accomplishment, and satisfaction—those were emotions a high achiever like Cat could easily recognize. Therefore she knew the answer to the question she was about to ask but inquired anyway. "Who does it belong to?"

"It's mine. I bought it a couple of months ago. I've had my eye on it for a long time and thought it would never go on the market, but it finally did. The original owner, who was a friend of Peyton's parents, died last year, and it took his siblings a long time to decide what to do with it."

"Congratulations, Rory. That's wonderful, and the view is beautiful from here."

Rory placed his arms around her waist, bringing her closer, to him. "I think so, too. The time I spent in this area with Peyton made me want a place around here of my own. Come on and let me show you around."

They spent the next hour or so walking around his property. He gave her a tour of the inside of the cabin and pointed out things he planned to do, changes he intended to make in the future.

When they came to the stream, Cat looked around, and her mind went into daydream mode. An image of a small child wading in the stream suddenly filled her thoughts. Her and Rory's child. The image was so vivid and clear that it almost took her breath away.

"Cat, are you all right?" Rory asked, studying her.

She turned and looked at him. "I know this might sound crazy, but in my mind I envisioned a little boy playing in this stream. He was your child." She decided not to mention the fact that she'd imagined him as being her son, too.

His lips curved, and for one long moment he met her gaze and didn't say anything. Then he said, "That's a possibility if I'm not too old to enjoy a child, but right now marriage and children are the farthest things from my mind. My top priority is expanding my business and getting this place livable, which means this will take up a lot of my time. I'm glad you'll understand."

She blinked. She had clearly missed something. "I'll understand what?"

"The weekends when I'll be away, working out here. It would be too much to ask for you to be inconvenienced while I accomplish the goal I've set of getting this place right before the summer."

"When you're out here working, where do you sleep? Back at Peyton and Lisa's cabin?"

"No, it would be too time consuming and too much of a hassle coming back and forth through the woods with all the supplies that I have to bring with me. Usually I use one of the company trucks to haul my supplies and rent one of those pop-up campers to hook behind it. And I've gotten pretty good at putting up a tent."

extreme satisfaction

The thought of sleeping in a tent with him outdoors and under the stars sounded truly romantic, and there was no need to wonder why he assumed she wouldn't want to share such an adventure with him. He'd made such a suggestion in the past, and she had turned him down. She sighed deeply, thinking that this weekend with him had definitely been an eye-opener of just how much she had taken for granted ... as well as just how much she had lost.

"If you don't mind, I'd like to take an inventory of the things I'm going to need the next time I'm here to work on this place," he said.

"No, I don't mind." She watched as he took a small writing pad out of his back pocket and begin jotting stuff down. Although he had brought her here and had shown her what seemed to be something that was very important to him, for some reason she felt as if she was being excluded from this part of his life. Before their breakup, he had shared practically everything with her, but that was when he'd had marriage on his mind and thought what they'd shared was forever.

She thought of her earlier vision and smiled. At that moment, she decided on a new goal and intended to do whatever it took to make her vision come true.

It was late afternoon when they returned to the cabin.

"Do you want to sit on the back porch, watch the stars, and eat a bowl of popcorn?"

The back porch was screened in to keep out pesky mosquitoes, and it provided a perfect view of the mountains and the lake. Last night they had sat outside on the front porch when the weather had been fine, but tonight there was a distinct drop in the temperature. "Sitting outdoors in the cold doesn't exactly turn me on. How will I stay warm?"

He met her gaze. "I'll keep you warm." The look in his eyes promised more than just his warmth.

"Now, the thought of that *does* turn me on," she said as her lips curved into a smile.

"Good. Let's go inside and take care of that popcorn."

An hour or so later they lay curled up together on the daybed under several blankets, eating popcorn and watching the stars. It was a beautiful night, and good at his word, Rory was keeping her warm. His body was generating plenty of heat, in more ways than one. The rush of sensations that just being near him evoked was hot, and the only time she experienced such intensity was when she was with him.

"What time will you leave tomorrow?" he asked.

His question reminded her that tomorrow would be their last day at the cabin. "I'd like to leave as late as possible," she said honestly. "I love it here." She shifted positions and turned in his arms. "What time are you leaving?"

He leaned over and caressed her cheek. "Not until after you do. I want to spend every moment that I can with you."

"Oh, Rory," she whispered, touched by his words. She framed his face with her hands and at that moment, nothing could stop her from kissing him. Desire rose within her instantly, and she slipped her tongue into his mouth. He automatically took control, eagerly, hungrily making a need within her pound like a physical ache.

He pulled her to him, letting his hand caress her bottom, molding her to him, and then his hands moved to slip under her blouse and close over her breasts, stroking them lightly.

"Rory." His name was again whispered from her lips, and she shuddered from his touch.

"Come on, baby. Let's go inside and heat up the place."

The moment Rory closed the door behind them, he pulled her into his arms and began kissing her like tomorrow didn't exist.

And maybe it didn't.

She knew that the affair he had offered her that first night was totally unacceptable. There was no way that she could share a "no strings attached, no expectations" type of relationship with him. She wanted attachment; she wanted expectations. Point blank, she wanted him as a permanent fixture in her life, but he didn't want her in the same way, which was no one's fault but hers. The reality of that meant that this weekend would be all they had together. He might not know it yet, but he would before she left tomorrow.

Not wanting to dwell on what she would be losing, she turned her complete attention back to Rory and everything he was doing to her. She really had no choice. He was a master at creating desire within her, igniting emotions and pleasing her beyond her wildest dreams. He was her Mr. Satisfaction. Only he could drive her to the point of no return, and as always, she was a willing participant.

Rory felt his control slipping as he carried Cat into the bedroom. Tomorrow would be their last day at the cabin, and he should be telling her the truth instead of making love to her, but a part of him still wasn't sure just what Cat wanted. He knew he had said things to make her think, but had it been effective? Did she actually believe him when he'd said that he wanted only a "no strings attached and no expectations" relationship? And if so, would she fight for something more or accept whatever?

Dammit, he wanted her to fight, come out kicking and screaming that that wasn't what she wanted and he could take his offer and shove it. So far, she wasn't doing that, which made him think she was okay with his offer. He didn't like the thought.

He clenched his jaw in disappointment, knowing she would leave tomorrow, willingly accepting a noncommitted relationship between them.

"Rory, I want you."

She wanted him. Never had she said that she loved him. He'd just assumed, like a lot of people, that she had. But now he wasn't sure. He needed to hear it but doubted that he ever would. "And I want you, too," he whispered as he placed her on the bed.

He had told her he loved her that last night, and she'd told him she didn't want his love. But if she only knew just how much he wanted hers. For him, love, wanting, and desire were tied into one. Each time he made love to her, he was loving her. Each time he kissed her, he was loving her. For him, love extended to the physical as well as the emotional.

And tonight he wanted to take the physical as far as he could. He wanted to make her want him as much as he wanted her. He wanted to make her love him as much as he loved her.

He told himself to slow down when he began removing her clothes, but he didn't want to slow down. There was an urgency that was driving him, making him impatient, sexually aroused to the point where he had to be inside her. The hungry heat that was accumulating in his gut was almost driving him to the edge.

Once he had removed all her clothes, he tackled the chore of removing his own. In no time, he was standing by the bed totally naked. "Ready or not, baby, here I come," he said huskily, climbing back on the bed.

"How many times … will you come?" she asked softly, stretching back, shifting her hips and giving him a good view of the area between her legs.

"I'll come as many times as you want."

"Promise?

"Hell yeah." And then he leaned over and kissed her with wild abandon, a primitive need.

Cat kissed him back with the same urgency, desire, and exigency. It was as if something within her snapped, and with a strength she didn't know she had, she lifted her body, shifted, and pushed him down in the bed beneath her. She looked down at him, saw his surprised expression, and gave him a heated grin.

"That was some move."

"You haven't seen anything yet, Mr. Dawkins."

And then she leaned over and kissed him, in all the ways he had ever kissed her. She heard him moan. Or then again, it may have been a growl. Either one was acceptable, as her tongue continued to take charge of his. Deciding that her fingers weren't busy enough, she reached down and grabbed hold of him and felt his entire body tense when she did so. But she intended to keep his mind occupied with their kiss and move things up a notch and let her tongue wallow in the wet heat of his mouth. And when she heard him moan again, she knew she had succeeded.

Now for taking care of what was down south, her fingers gripped his hardness, his bare flesh, and gently squeezed, loving the feel of the thick width, texture, and length of him. He shuddered in her mouth, and the sensations that act evoked made the womanhood between her legs pulse. But she knew her satisfaction would come later. Right now she just wanted to concentrate on his.

She released his mouth, kissed the side of his neck, then went to his chest and licked the flat nipples until they hardened. She heard the growl in his chest as she moved her mouth lower, wanting to do something to him that she had never done before.

When he realized what she was about to do, he grabbed hold of her shoulders to stop her. She lifted her head and smiled. "No, I want to do this. I need to do this. Let me."

He held her gaze for a long moment, then leaned upward and gave her a gentle kiss on her lips, and the moment his lips touched hers, she knew he was giving her his consent. She tightened her hold on him and smiled at his sudden sharp intake of breath.

Unbearable pleasure rose inside Cat as she began placing kisses on the hard plane of Rory's stomach, slowly working her way lower. She felt his fingers tightly grip her shoulders when she moved closer and breathed on his rigid shaft. And when she took him into her mouth, she felt his body shift, his hips lift, and a low, primal sound escape his lips.

And then she let her mouth go to work, kissing him in a way she had never kissed another man, letting her mouth pleasure a part of him that had given her so much pleasure.

"You got to stop," he whispered huskily.

She shook her head.

A tortured cry was wrung from him. "You're killing me."

She didn't stop what she was doing. The erotic frisson of mouth and tongue had him moaning words she'd never heard out of him before.

"Why? Why are you doing this?" he forced out between choppy breaths.

She pulled back, licked her lips, and looked at him. Cat knew at that moment she had to tell him the truth. "Because I love you."

He stared at her; the intensity of his gaze made her tremble, and before she could blink, he had leaned forward, flipped her over, shifted her body beneath his, and spread open her legs. And before she could draw her next breath, he thrust inside her.

"Rory!"

Her body shattered into a climax the moment he entered her, but he kept thrusting in and out, extracting another orgasm out of her. And then another. Spasm after spasm racked her body, and all she could do was tremble as wave after wave of pleasure hit her, took her under.

"Cat!"

It seemed those same waves were carrying Rory under, and with one final thrust, he exploded deep within her. And the one thing that stood out in his mind as his body rode the sensation was that the woman he loved had told him she loved him.

Several moments passed before Rory felt air fill his lungs again. Shifting his body off Cat, he rolled over to the side then leaned down and gave her a slow smile. "Did you mean what you said?"

She knew exactly what he was asking. "Yes, I meant it."

He kissed her gently. "You don't know how much I needed to hear that. You've never said that before."

She reached up and wiped sweat off his forehead with her finger-tips and said, "Then maybe I should have. It would probably have saved me a lot of pain and heartache the past twelve months."

"There's something I need to say. Something you should know."

Something inside Cat panicked. If he was going to tell her that he was sorry but he didn't love her, she didn't want to hear it right now. "Please, let's not talk anymore. Could we just savor the moment? We can talk in the morning. I want tonight for action and not talking."

He stared at her, and a smile creased his lips. "Whatever you want, sweetheart."

"Okay," she said, pushing him back and crawling over him. "I want to be on top this time."

EIGHT

Cat forced herself awake the next morning, finding the spot beside her in bed empty. She smiled, remembering vividly what she and Rory had done through most of the night.

She turned over on her back and stared at the ceiling. Making love with Rory was always a unique experience, and she was transformed into a sex kitten in bed. No, last night she had been more of a tiger.

She remembered the exact moment she had confessed that she loved him, and even now, when she wasn't sure how he felt about her, she had no regrets in doing so. He had told her he loved her that night they broke up, but in anger she had told him where he should take his love and shove it. She had been a total fool.

Shifting in bed, she wondered where Rory had gone, and then she climbed out of bed and slipped into his oversize T-shirt that was thrown over a chair. Now that her confession of love was out of the way, she wanted to find him and tell him the rest of everything, including the fact that this weekend had been nothing but a setup, but one that had been well worth it.

She heard a sound outside and went to the window and glanced out. She saw Rory. He was sitting on the steps and staring into the distance. She sighed just from watching him. He was handsome, and the way the sun's rays slanted across his features made him even more striking. A shadow darkened his chin, denoting that he needed a shave, which made him look even sexier.

She turned when she heard her cell phone ringing and rushed across the room to pick it up. "Yes?"

"He knew."

Cat lifted her brow at hearing Lisa's voice. "Who knew?"

"Rory. He knew everything."

Cat took a deep breath, trying to grasp just what Lisa was telling her, hoping what her friend was claiming wasn't true. "What are you saying, Lisa?"

"I'm saying that Rory knew you were coming to the cabin. Peyton and Rory. They set us up like we set them up."

Cat shook her head. "But how could they have known?"

"That day in our office when you declared that you were placing Rory on your wish list, he heard you. He had come to the office to let me know Peyton was parked outside waiting on me. So Rory knew all about your plans to get him back … and he intended to teach you a lesson in the process."

"How do you know this?" Cat asked, slowly remembering that Rory hadn't really acted surprised to see her when she'd arrived at the cabin on Friday afternoon.

"Peyton let something slip out about you being at the cabin this weekend. I questioned him as to how he knew when no one had known of your plans but me and Mel. So I made him talk, which wasn't easy, and although he wouldn't tell me everything, he said that Rory knew about the wish list and your plan for the weekend and intended to teach you a lesson."

"Teach me a lesson?" she repeated. She closed her eyes. *Was this weekend about him teaching her a lesson and nothing more?*

Cat was silent as she walked back to the window and looked out. Rory was still sitting in that same spot. "Thanks, Lisa, for letting me know what's going on."

"What are you planning to do?"

"I'm leaving just as soon as I can pack my stuff, that's what I plan to do. There's no reason for me to stay any longer, since Rory has succeeded in getting out of me what he wanted."

"Which was?"

"A confession that I loved him so he could throw it back in my face, use it against me, and hurt me the same way that I hurt him."

"You don't know that for certain, Cat. It may not be that way at all."

"Yes, it is that way, Lisa. Otherwise, he would have told me the truth in the beginning." She wiped a tear from her eye. "Look, I'll talk to you later." Without giving Lisa a chance to say anything else, she disconnected the call.

NINE

"Where are you going?"

Cat didn't pause in what she was doing. She continued packing as she hissed angry words over her shoulder. "I'm leaving so I hope you had plenty of fun using me the way you did."

"What the hell are you talking about?"

Cat turned to glare at him, full of anger, fire, and humiliation. "I know everything, Rory. I know what you know. I also know that my showing up here wasn't a surprise to you and that you wanted to teach me a lesson for what I did last year. Do you deny it?"

He crossed his hands over his chest and returned her glare. "No, I don't deny it."

His words hit her like a blow. "You bastard. I hope you enjoyed getting your pound of flesh."

"I did. Every gorgeous inch of it. But what I really enjoyed was getting you to admit that you're in love with me."

"Why? So you can throw it in my face and use my love to hurt me the same way I hurt you last year?"

"No, I did it so I could be absolutely sure that my feelings for you were reciprocated and that you wanted me back for the right reason."

"What are you talking about?"

"I heard you that day, Cat. I heard you declare that you needed a man. Not me, but 'a man.' Then you proceeded to place me on this damn wish list. I didn't know whether you were doing so because you realized that you loved me or if you were just in need of a sexual fix."

Cat raised both eyebrows. "How could you not know that I loved you?"

"And how could I know it? You've never told me, and after the way we split, did you actually think I would assume any such thing?" he demanded.

She stared at him for a long moment, and then slowly shook her head. No, after all the things she'd said that night, there was no way he would have assumed that. "So you concocted this plan of revenge?"

"Revenge had nothing to do with this weekend, Cat. After Peyton and I figured what you and Lisa were up to, I decided to see how far you would go. I needed to know the truth before risking my heart to you again."

"But you claimed you only wanted a no strings attached, no expectations affair between us."

"Yes, and I said that to see what your reaction would be to my offer. If the only thing on your mind was sex, then you would have gone for it. But if you loved me, and I mean truly loved me, there was no way you would have been satisfied with sharing that kind of relationship with me."

He shoved his hands into the pockets of his jeans. "Last night when you admitted that you loved me, I was prepared to tell you the truth—and I started to, but you stopped me and said we would talk in the morning."

She remembered. At the time she had wanted him again and hadn't wanted to spend time talking. Beside, she hadn't been certain what he had wanted to say. "You could have made me listen."

"No, I could not."

She frowned. No, he could not. She had wanted him in a bad way last night, and once she had crawled on top of him, her mind had been on only one thing: riding him.

He took a few steps to stand in front of her. "I love you, Cat. I never stopped loving you. But I had to be sure that you loved me as well. What I told you the day you arrived was the truth. My life has been miserable this past year, but I couldn't settle back into the type of relationship that we had before. My love for you demanded more, something beyond that. I'd known the moment I laid eyes on you at Peyton and Lisa's wedding that I wanted a future with you—and that love, marriage, and babies would be part of the deal."

He reached out and took her hand in his. "I knew about your goals, your dreams, and at no time did I ever want to take them away from you. I only wanted to enhance them. I knew my timing was off that night and that you weren't ready and that I shouldn't have tried pushing you into anything. But I never thought you would send me away and end things between us like you did. Your rejection hurt. Surely you can understand my not wanting to rush into a situation for you to hurt me all over again."

She nodded. She had hurt him, which was something she hadn't meant to do, but the thought of giving up everything she'd worked for scared her. It had taken her twelve months to realize loving Rory didn't mean giving up anything, but was all about gaining everything.

"And something else you need to know," he said, interrupting her thoughts.

"What?"

"There was never a Shari. She was someone I made up to save my pride. I didn't want you to know that I couldn't get over you, that I was still pining for you, that I was still so deeply in love with you that some days I couldn't even think straight."

She sighed deeply before saying, "And neither could I. I had been so sure that once you saw things my way you would come back. And when you didn't, it forced me to realize just what I had lost, and just how much you meant to me."

"Was it so hard to love me?" he asked, his lips curving in a wry smile.

She shook her head. "No, in fact, it was too easy. You're wonderful, interesting, handsome, a perfect bed partner. I just didn't think I was ready for what you wanted at the time."

"And now?"

Her gaze remained steadfast on his when she answered by saying, "Being apart from you made me realize just how much you meant to me, Rory. It's always good having goals in life, but I had to find out the hard way that that's not the only thing a person should have in life. There is more to life than accomplishing major achievements, but I have to admit that when I added you to my wish list, I considered getting you to fall back in love with me again as my all-time major goal because my life would be nothing without you in it. And now if you were to ask me to share my life with you, you would definitely get a different answer from the one I gave you before."

He smiled. "Okay, let's just see about that."

With her hand still firmly clasped in his, he got down on a bended knee and looked up at her. Cat blinked when she realized just what he was doing. She watched as he pulled a small white box out of his jacket pocket.

"Cathleen Janelle McAlister, I love you, so very much. Will you make me a very happy man and marry me? Will you be my partner for life, the mother of my children, the joy of my life? Forever?"

Cat couldn't help the tears that began streaming down her face. "Oh, Rory."

He smiled up at her, his love shining in his eyes. "Sorry, but this is a yes-or-no question."

She chuckled through her tears. "Then my answer is definitely yes. I would be honored to marry you."

After placing the ring on her finger, he stood and pulled her into his arms. "I bought this ring for you eighteen months ago, but even

extreme satisfaction

after that night, I refused to believe that you wouldn't eventually wear it one day. I had refused to give up on you, Cat."

"But you never came around."

"No, I was giving you the distance I thought you needed. But things between us were far from over—trust me."

She smiled at her ring before taking a step forward and moving her hand up the back of his neck. "I do trust you. And I also love you."

"Say it again."

She met his intense stare. "I'll say it as often as you like. I love you, Rory."

"And I love you, Cat."

"And I love you double, triple, a thousand times over."

He swept her off her feet into his arms and quickly headed toward the bed, needing to have her close, as close as two people could get. And together they would get just what they most wanted and needed: extreme satisfaction.

EPILOGUE

Six Months Later

Four hours after being presented as man and wife at their wedding, Rory and Cat arrived at their honeymoon cabin. As a wedding gift, his parents had surprised them and had the cabin restored. Rory didn't care how the inside of the place looked, just so long as it had a bed.

Three months before the wedding, his Cat had declared her body off-limits. She wanted their wedding night to be like the first time for them, and no degree of persuasiveness on his part could change her mind. So here he was on his wedding day, horny as sin.

He carried her from the car and over the threshold into the house. When he kicked the door shut and proceeded to carry her straight to the bedroom, Cat looked over her shoulder and asked, "What about our luggage?"

He grinned down at her. "You won't be needing anything. For the next week or so, I'm going to like the look of you in bare skin."

She chuckled. "Is that a fact?"

"Yes, sweetheart, that's a fact."

He helped her remove her dress, bra, panties, and everything else that stood in the way of him getting what he wanted. He then quickly began removing his own clothes.

She watched him with interest as she stretched out on the bed. "Kind of in a hurry, aren't you?"

"If only you knew."

extreme satisfaction

"But I'm about to find out, right?"

He smiled at her. "Right."

And then he joined her on the bed, and with a small sigh, she went into his arms. He kissed her the way he had wanted to kiss her after the minister had proclaimed them man and wife, but had he kissed her this way then, there was no telling what it would have led to.

After he ended the kiss, she smiled up at him thoughtfully. "Did I ever tell you that I have this sinfully sexy man on my wish list?"

He skimmed his thumb over his wife's tight nipple. Then, lowering his head, he took his tongue and started licking it. "Do you?"

"Yes," she managed to say in a breathless whisper. "He's pretty high in my list of priorities."

"Is he worth it?"

When he placed his hands between her legs and began stroking her there, she purred. "Oh, I think so. In fact, I got a bad case of the hots for him."

"Does he know it?"

"He will before the night is over. And he did promise me that he was going to teach me all the ways to satisfy a man. He is Mr. Satisfaction, and from what I understand, his wife will become Mrs. Satisfaction," she said in a ragged breath when he stuck his finger inside her, stroking her deeper.

"Umm, sounds like the ultimate in gratification," he said, leaning up to kiss her lips.

"No holds barred, from what I understand."

"And I'm sure they were made for each other. The ideal couple," he said, easing his body over hers.

"They are and will always be. Forever."

And as Rory slid into his wife's body and felt her inner muscles clutch him tight, he stared down at her, knowing he was where he belonged. He then whispered huskily, "Yes, forever."

Read on for a preview of
Brenda Jackson's upcoming novel

TASTE OF PASSION

To be published by St. Martin's Press

Luke leaned against the bedpost and gritted his teeth against the sharp pain that tore up his leg. Taking a deep breath he eased down on the bed, appreciating the feel of the soft mattress beneath him.

He hated lying but when Mac had asked if he needed her help, he'd said he didn't, when actually he had. But his pride had kept him from telling the truth. Damn. And as a result, it had taken him a full hour to unpack the few things he'd brought with him. And moving around on his leg had irritated his knee somewhat. He needed to chill a bit, he thought, rubbing his thigh. Or else he'd run the risk of causing his body more harm than good and he'd have to kiss the Reno rodeo good-bye. And that was one thing that he refused to do.

"Just what do you think you're doing?"

"Sitting on the bed," he answered without bothering to look up. He knew who it was. Besides, at the moment there was an intense throb through most of his body and the last thing he needed was to increase that throb somewhere else.

She had taken a shower. He could tell. She had that fresh scent of soap, powder, and woman. The latter was what his mind latched on to and not for the first time. The nickname "Mac" didn't sound at all feminine and certainly didn't do justice to the woman it was applied to.

"And why aren't you in the bed?" she asked, coming into the

room and making a point of standing in front of him, right in his line of vision.

He couldn't pretend not to notice her so he looked up and instantly felt sweat bead his forehead and an increased throbbing in his body as his gaze met hers. He took a deep breath and stared back at her while thinking he'd probably made a grave mistake by asking to stay here while recuperating. She had changed out of her jeans and tank top and was wearing a printed top and matching skirt. Evidently she was staying inside for the rest of the day since he couldn't see her doing anything significant outside the way she was dressed.

Her body was what male dreams were made of, and her looks were as drop-dead gorgeous as any looks could get. She had a stunning face, a set of beautiful dark eyes, lips he knew were of the kissable kind—although at the moment they looked pouty and irritated—and silky black hair that hung past her shoulders. Her high cheekbones were evidence of her Native American ancestry and her creamy chocolate skin an attribute of her African-American side. He'd heard her mother's people had joined the Cherokee tribe as free men back in the eighteen hundreds. He also knew her mother had family living in the North and that when her parents and grandfather had died she had been sent to live with an aunt in Boston for a while.

"Luke?"

It was then that he realized he hadn't responded to her question. "The reason I'm sitting on the bed, Mac, is because I just finished putting my things away."

"It took you that long?"

He cocked his head. "Yeah, it took me that long."

She placed her hands on her hips and stared back at him, her expression one of annoyance. "Why didn't you call for me? I could have helped. I did offer my services."

"I know," he said. "And I appreciated it," he added. "But I preferred doing things myself," he pointed out.

"Fine. So look what you have to show for your stubbornness. You're in pain and don't try denying it because I can tell. Now I'm going to have to help you after all."

He frowned. "No, you don't."

"Yes, I do," she said, straightening her shoulders. "And if I were you, I wouldn't try giving me a hard time, especially not now."

He lifted a curious brow. "Why especially not now?"

"Trust me, you don't want to know."

"Trust me. I do."

A frustrated sigh escaped from Mackenzie's throat before she said, "Someone wrecked my mailbox."

He lifted a brow. "What do you mean someone wrecked it?" He remembered seeing her mailbox earlier when they'd arrived. It was a huge brick roadside structure that had been erected at the gate leading onto her property.

"Just what I said. From the time I got home until a few minutes ago when one of the ranch hands noticed the damage, someone must have hit it with their car and kept on going."

He shook his head. "That certainly wasn't a very nice thing to do."

"No, it wasn't. That mailbox had fond memories for me since my dad built it for my mom. I remember the day he did it. I was eleven at the time. They had visited some friends in Denver and had seen one and Dad knew how much she liked it and decided to build her one himself."

Luke reached out and cupped her cheek. He could hear the sadness in her voice. "I'm sorry about that, Mac."

He could tell from her expression that his touch surprised her. Without being obvious about it, she eased her face away from his hand and plastered a smile on her face. "No big deal."

He knew that it *had* been a big deal, although she was pretending otherwise, and it bothered him. "Before I leave I'll make it my business to replace it," he said.

taste of passion

"You don't have to do that. It's not your fault that someone was thoughtless and reckless."

"Doesn't matter. Besides, I'm pretty good when it comes to bricks and mortar. Whenever I came home and they were shorthanded, Blade and Slade were notorious for putting me to work at one of their construction sites." He then stood and wished he hadn't. A sharp pain shot up his leg and he gritted his teeth to keep from cursing.

"When was the last time you took your pain pills, Luke?"

The sharpness in her voice was as deep as the pain he'd just felt in his leg. He glanced over at her. "Not sure."

"Not sure?"

From the look on her face evidently that hadn't been a good answer. "Before I left the hospital," he decided to come clean and say.

Her eyes narrowed. "The doctor told you to take a couple more of them when you got here."

"Yeah, but I've been busy."

"Only because you were too stubborn to accept my help," she said, moving toward the bed to turn the covers back. "All men are bullheaded to a certain degree but cowboys are the worst."

He felt the need to lean against the bedpost again. "Why cowboys?"

"I don't know. You tell me since you're one of them."

Yes, he was one of them and proud of it. He got distracted for a moment when she leaned over and fluffed the pillow, presenting him with her profile, which looked as good as the rest of her. "You don't have to do that."

"Too late. I just did," she said, before walking away from the bed and back to him. "Now I need you to sit back down so I can help you."

He lifted a brow. "Help me to do what?"

"Take off your clothes."

I don't think so. He had never liked having a woman undress him, refusing to give a female even that much control. On the other hand, he'd never had a problem undressing a woman and hadn't yet met a woman who'd complained about him doing so. "I can undress my-self, Mac."

"I don't doubt that, but the quicker it's done the sooner you can get some rest."

Getting rest sounded good, he thought.

"And once you take a couple of pain pills you won't hurt for a while," she added.

And as far as he was concerned that sounded even better. But still. "Don't you have anything better to do?" he asked.

She blew out a frustrated breath as she looked up at him. "Yes, sev-eral things, but I won't be able to concentrate on them until I know you're okay."

Luke pressed his lips into a tight line and said, "I didn't mean to come here and cause you trouble."

"You're not. But I have to admit that I wish you had dropped the stubbornness at the door before you entered."

He frowned. "I'm not stubborn," he said defensively.

"Yes you are. You keep it up and I'm going to nickname you 'mule.'"

He lowered himself on the edge of the bed, amused by her words. "I'm not that bad."

"So you say."

When she reached for the front of his shirt he automatically grabbed her hand. "What do you think you're doing?"

She rolled her eyes. "Taking off your shirt. I need to check the bandage."

"Oh."

He tried remaining calm as her fingers went to work at his buttons and found it difficult to do so. He tried looking at the paintings on the walls, the various live plants in the room, and the toy box that sat in the corner. But none of those things could hold his attention like the woman standing in front of him. So he thought, *What the hell,* and he looked at her.

taste of passion

Thankfully, she wasn't looking back. Instead her full concentration was on working his buttons free, and it took everything he had not to groan out loud when her tongue darted out of her mouth to moisten her lips.

"There. All done." He watched as a slow, satisfied smile slid over those same lips when she eased the shirt off his shoulders and down his arms. His guts immediately clenched. He felt a shiver touch his body.

"You okay?" she asked with concern.

"Yeah. Sure. I'm fine." That was another lie. He wasn't fine. His body seemed to be on automatic throb around her. Ashton would probably do him in if he had any idea what thoughts were running through Luke's mind about everything he'd like to do to his cousin. And they weren't thoughts that had popped up suddenly. Hell, if he were completely honest then he would admit he'd been attracted to Mac from the first. But he'd been smart enough not to start anything he knew he couldn't finish. And his only goal in life, his main focus, was staying in good standing with the PRCA and doing everything possible to regain his title this year. One thing he knew for certain was that serious relationships and rodeos didn't mix. Women had this thing about men being gone away from home most of the time while competing. In the end they tended to see the rodeo as competing for their time and ultimately they became jealous. He didn't have time for such foolishness. He was not a forever kind of guy and was definitely not looking for a forever kind of woman. Rodeo was the only mistress he wanted. Granted, his injuries were a setback but he would not let them get the best of him.

"Your bandage looks fine but you're going to have to make sure it stays dry when you shower," Mac said, reeling his attention back in. "It won't get changed until tomorrow. Now for your pants."

My pants? Is she kidding? Does she really think I'm going to let her take them off me? He forced himself to lean forward to stare into her eyes and said in a tone that could not be misunderstood, "Trust me, Mac, taking off my pants is the last thing you'd want to do right now."

It wasn't difficult to hear the catch in her throat when she glanced down at his lap and took note of what he was kindly trying to say. Hell, what did she expect? He was a man. She was a woman. Some things a person couldn't hide. He had kissed her a couple of days ago so he was well aware of how she tasted. She was standing pretty close so he knew just how she smelled. In his book all those things equaled desire with a capital *D*. It then occurred to him that other than the day she had been with him in his hospital room while Camden had stepped out, this was the first time the two of them had ever truly been alone. At other times people had been around.

"All right, you can finish things up on your own," she said, easing back. And he could hear the forced steadiness of her voice. "But at least let me help you with your boots."

That seemed like a reasonable request, and considering the pain in his leg, it was one he could appreciate. "Okay. Thanks." He inhaled deeply, thinking the next six weeks here with her should be pretty interesting.

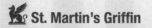

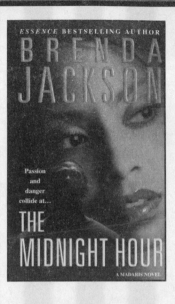
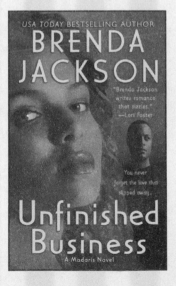